PRAISE FOR *BUMMER CAMP*

"Ann Garvin's *Bummer Camp* is for anyone who's ever spent any time in a cabin or making lanyards or being bitten by mosquitoes while walking in a piney woods. It's the funny, insightful story of two sisters who must band together to save their family's legacy, a summer camp in danger of being dismantled by the bad guys. Garvin's trademark humor and insight shine through every page, in all the quirky characters. Don't miss it. You'll laugh out loud."

—Maddie Dawson, *Washington Post* bestselling author of *Matchmaking for Beginners*

"After finishing *Bummer Camp*, I see why Ann Garvin is so beloved. Ann is a fabulous storyteller, a master writer, and just plain very funny."

—Bob Eckstein, *New York Times* bestselling author of *Footnotes from the Most Fascinating Museums*

"*Bummer Camp* is a perfectly balanced cocktail of family annoyance, sharky business foes, and just enough pot brownies to keep the whole thing afloat."

—Michelle Wildgen, author of *Wine People*

"You've got a friend in Ann Garvin, a writer with immense empathy, heart, and smarts. *Bummer Camp* is a hilarious, whip-smart, and wise valentine to the weirdo and outsider in all of us. A delightful novel."

—Nickolas Butler, author of *Shotgun Lovesongs* and *Godspeed*

PRAISE FOR *THERE'S NO COMING BACK FROM THIS*

"As a novelist, author Ann Garvin has an impressive and genuine flair for the kind of narrative-driven storytelling style that will keep readers with an interest in romantic comedy simply riveted from first page to last."

—*Midwest Book Review*

"Charming, witty, and real, *There's No Coming Back from This* will have you laughing, cheering, and looking at your own past through Poppy-colored glasses."

—Sara Goodman Confino, bestselling author of *She's Up to No Good*

"Brimming with wit and wisdom, *There's No Coming Back from This* is the story of one woman's attempt to find meaning in the middle of a mess she didn't create but has no choice but to clean up—which is to say, this is one relatable book. I laughed, teared up, and sped through the pages even as I attempted to savor them. Ann Garvin's latest just happens to be her absolute best."

—Camille Pagán, bestselling author of *Good for You*

"Readers will root so hard for Poppy Lively as she navigates the cutthroat world of Hollywood with a scruffy dog strapped to her body. Full of warmth and humor, Poppy and her motley crew of coworkers will worm their way into your heart and stick around for a very long time."

—Lyn Liao Butler, Amazon bestselling author of *Someone Else's Life* and *Red Thread of Fate*

"An Ann Garvin novel is like curling up beside your favorite, wittiest friend and laughing and crying all at once about the hilarity and heartbreak of life. In classic Ann Garvin style, *There's No Coming Back from This* is an engaging look at motherhood, friendship, and dating that will remind readers everywhere it's never too late to start over—or find out where we're truly meant to be. Don't pick this one up unless you're prepared to read it all the way through; it's impossible to put down! Five huge stars!"

—Kristy Woodson Harvey, *New York Times* bestselling author of *The Wedding Veil*

"Ann Garvin's genius lies in creating endearing, authentic women in the throes of midlife. *There's No Coming Back from This* is another gem. Just when Poppy Lively thinks her life has bottomed out, it throws her one more plot twist, and this fifty-year-old single mom digs deep in her own Midwest Nice way to finally become the hero of her own story. Readers will cheer for Poppy, and her little dog Kevin, too!"

—Mary Kay Andrews, *New York Times* bestselling author of *The Homewreckers*

"Ann Garvin has written my favorite kind of book—a hilarious yet suspenseful story starring a down-on-her-luck, sassy, midlife heroine who has to reinvent herself to avoid complete disaster. Throw in a new job working backstage in Hollywood and some surprising villains, and you've got a novel you can't put down. I raced through it, loving every page."

—Maddie Dawson, *Washington Post* bestselling author of *Matchmaking for Beginners* and *Snap Out of It*

PRAISE FOR *I THOUGHT YOU SAID THIS WOULD WORK*

"Despite dealing with some heavy topics—cancer, widowhood, and the impending birth of a first child—Garvin's book is laugh-out-loud funny."
—*Library Journal*

"Ann Garvin writes brilliantly about women."
—*Good Morning America*

"A charming exploration of female friendship and cancer's uncanny ability to put perceived slights into perspective . . . *I Thought You Said This Would Work* is a testament to the power of one's own voice and the mistruths in the stories we tell ourselves, and an introspective, heartwarming, and witty farce."
—*Booklist*

"Both humorous and incredibly heartfelt, *I Thought You Said This Would Work* is a feel-good story that will stay with you long after the final page."
—BookTrib

"Garvin does excellent work in balancing the heartbreaking realities of illness and the unfair hands we are often dealt with goofy, laugh-out-loud moments that leave readers wanting more."
—*Erie Reader*

"Equal parts hilarious and heartfelt, *I Thought You Said This Would Work* kept me reaching for tissues—from laughing so hard. This book is a pure delight."
—Colleen Oakley, *USA Today* bestselling author of *You Were There Too*

"Ann Garvin navigates the twists and turns of female friendship like few writers working today. *I Thought You Said This Would Work* is at once profound, hilarious, and ridiculously entertaining. Her best novel yet—I didn't want it to end!"

—Karen Karbo, *New York Times* bestselling author of *Yeah, No. Not Happening.*

"Laughter, tears, and an unforgettable cast of characters: *I Thought You Said This Would Work* has everything I love, so it's no surprise that I adored this novel. Ann Garvin's latest, about three unlikely allies on the road trip to end all road trips, is the sort of life-affirming story we all need right now. I can't recommend it highly enough."

—Camille Pagán, bestselling author of *This Won't End Well*

"Ann Garvin knows how to find the ooey-gooey center of your emotions to make you laugh, cry, and hoot in appreciation. *I Thought You Said This Would Work* celebrates female friendship in all its complicated glory. Read immediately, curled up with a furry friend and hot cup of coffee."

—Amy E. Reichert, author of *The Kindred Spirits Supper Club*

"Anyone who has ever known the healing power of love—from friends both two-footed and four—will fall hard for Garvin's latest book. Like the road trip at the heart of its story, *I Thought You Said This Would Work* surprises [and] thrills at every turn."

—Gretchen Anthony, bestselling author of *Evergreen Tidings from the Baumgartners* and *The Kids Are Gonna Ask*

"*I Thought You Said This Would Work* is a heartbreaking and hilarious story of how we rescue each other. It's a great, big, generous, warmhearted page-turner about best friends and love and loss and forgiveness and dogs, told with absolute honesty and humor. You couldn't ask for more from a novel."

—Lauren Fox, author of *Send for Me*

BUMMER CAMP

OTHER TITLES BY ANN GARVIN

There's No Coming Back from This

I Thought You Said This Would Work

BUMMER CAMP

CAMP

A NOVEL

Ann Garvin

LAKE UNION
PUBLISHING

Published by Lake Union Publishing, Seattle

www.apub.com

Amazon, the Amazon logo, and Lake Union Publishing are trademarks of Amazon.com, Inc., or its affiliates.

ISBN-13: 9781662518560 (paperback)
ISBN-13: 9781662518577 (digital)

Cover design and illustration by Liz Casal

Printed in the United States of America

To all the weirdos of the world, and when I say weirdos, I mean all of us.

"Am I really wonderful?" asked the Scarecrow.

"You are unusual," replied Glinda.

—*The Wonderful Wizard of Oz*

CHAPTER ONE

OLD MAID OF THE MIST

The first rescue-me text from her sinkhole of a sister, Ginger, came in the middle of the night. Cat had been mentally flipping through the roster of pretty-good colleagues, wondering who she could wake if her water broke somewhere other than in a hospital bed. Calling 911 should be reserved for heart attacks and burst spleens. Not a healthy pregnant lady who could sit on a towel and drive herself twenty-five minutes if push came to labor and delivery.

When the second text arrived with a cheery ping, Cat ignored it and used the bathroom for the third time. Pregnancy was like having Niagara Falls in her indoor plumbing, and Cat McCarthy was the *Old Maid of the Mist*.

Cat eased herself into her bed, yanked the covers to her chin, and looked at the clock. She was in the phase of her pregnancy where no amount of sleep was enough sleep. But Ginger's texts had a dark magnetism to them. They urged Cat to act impulsively, in the same way that a whirlpool at the bottom of a waterfall beckoned. The swirling void whispered, "You could jump. Do it. Why not?" But Cat knew why not—Ginger's calls had urgent requirements.

Emergencies needed total commitment, and the only person Cat was giving her all to was the baby growing inside her. She'd worked hard to avoid Ginger's pleas for assistance, wild conspiracy theories, and grandiose plans that usually swamped and sank like one of the ancient canoes at the sleepaway camp she'd grown up on.

She missed her sister, but Cat had cleaned up Ginger's tie-dye buckets, explained away bonfires left untended, and tried to help her sister's newborn to latch and nurse. At thirty-seven, Cat couldn't spare her energy for someone else's messes anymore; she would soon have her own baby to consider.

In her house, with only Lefty, her three-legged yellow Lab, Cat loved that she disturbed no one with her nighttime trips to the bathroom. And she also hated it a little bit; loneliness can be as insistent as a needy sister. After distancing herself from her demanding childhood home and family when she turned seventeen, she didn't think it seemed right to make new friends. Friends who might ask for help, people who she didn't want to let down.

A text pinged, and she felt the immediate prick of guilt like a phantom limb reminding Cat her DNA was calling. She turned her phone over so she wouldn't see the messages, and something about that motion set off the memory of her father's voice: "Your sister needs you, Cat." Her father, champion of the underdog, lover of treasure hunts, and the first to utter the phrase "cash is king" whenever the expansion of their family-owned theater camp was broached. "There is no growth if beholden to the banks," he'd say, and so the little-camp-that-could limped along, often due to Cat's work ethic and overdeveloped sense of duty.

Over a year ago, her parents had gone on the road to teach others how to run a successful camp for kids. Instead of hiring a director, Fred and Eleanor had unbelievably, shockingly, outrageously, left Ginger and Bard to run the place.

Her father's last words to Cat were, "Take care of Ginger."

To which she'd replied, "No, Dad."

"Bard then. Take care of him."

Cat knew that her dad loved both his daughters. He wanted them to be close, bound together so they'd have double the weight when the winds of life blew hard. But Summer Camp was one of those hard winds for Cat, whether her father acknowledged it or not. The camp was once a nonprofit for sight-impaired kids; her parents had converted the space to a theater camp for grade-schoolers and named it Summer Camp. A head-shakingly unoriginal name. But if her mother had it her way, she would name everything in her path Summer. "The name evokes everything good about the seasons. 'Shall I compare thee to a summer's day?'" she'd say and raise her eyebrows as if a Shakespeare quote could justify anything.

How could her parents teach others to run an organization when the place needed Cat's help to survive? She imagined her father, teaching with a PowerPoint. "Step One. Get a Cat. A responsible one."

Her phone pinged again, and she hit the side button to silence any more incoming messages. The closer she got to her delivery date, the harder it was to fight the hormone-bonding energy that encouraged her to respond.

"Go on," her glands whispered. "It costs you nothing to reply."

"Go to bed, brain, you're drunk," Cat said.

She'd saved for the down payment on her dream cottage, took out a mortgage big enough to update the house, and meticulously, frugally, created this home for her soon-to-be family of two. One step back into the stress-quagmire of her family would risk it all.

Cat stared at her newly painted ceiling, and her thoughts slid to Bard, Ginger's son. What if he needed her? Cat's nephew, with his eager-to-please smile, his soft voice calling her Aunt Kitty. Bard was a sixteen-and-a-half-year-old with shockingly clear blue eyes and the worst case of tactile defensiveness Cat had ever seen, and that was saying something—she worked at the Waldon Pond Elementary School and had seen bags and bags of kids who didn't like to be touched.

When he was fifteen, Cat had given him his nickname, "Shirtless." He'd aged enough to become a lifeguard, but wearing the staff shirt made him itchy and unhappy. "I can't do it, Aunt Kitty," he'd said, yanking at his neck and underarms.

"Tell Grandpa. You're a lifeguard. You must be ready at a moment's notice to save a life, unencumbered by confining clothing. Tell him that if he wants fast rescue, you shall remain shirtless."

"I henceforth will be known as Shirtless the Saver," he said, peeling off the restrictive mantle. He sighed in relief. "You get it," he'd said, and she'd heard clear as his eyes shone bright: *I love you.*

With the light of the moon and thoughts of her nephew, Cat turned her phone over and squinted at her sister's text.

Ginger: Something hinky is going on.

Hinky? She hit delete. A true emergency never started with the word *hinky.* Cat took Lefty's paw and renewed her vow to love dogs and only people she'd made herself. If someone else had made a person, those humans were on their own. If her father wanted the camp to survive, he could come home and investigate the *hinky* that seemed to be going down up north. She'd happily visit all of them after the emergency was over, during a calm period, the only times Cat did return to see her family.

A thousand years ago, her father had bought the camp, seeing it as an industrious way to keep Cat's mother immersed in her theater obsession and not playing the part of Blanche DuBois on hometown street corners. While Stevens Point, Wisconsin, was a college town, it was the kind of place where you could shoot a deer a block off Main Street but not shout *Stella!* in the Burger King, as her mother had done whenever the mood overtook her.

Too young to resist her parents, Cat was pulled from her adored public school at age seven to be homeschooled or, more accurately, camp-schooled. A camp was only a summer camp for the attendees. Running a camp was a year-round job of planning, hiring, promoting, licensing, inspection, and upkeep.

As the oldest child, Cat became Ginger's trickle-down tutor, nursemaid, and babysitter from birth on. Cat went to college as soon as she could and earned a teaching license; during graduation, her father's hound-dog eyes pierced her heart. Her mother, always the dramaturge, cut her graduation cake singing "How Ya Gonna Keep 'em Down on the Farm (After They've Seen Paree?)."

Her phone lit up.

Ginger: Cat. Cat. Cat.

Ginger: The camp is going under. Come get us.

Ginger: I hired the wrong person to help us. He didn't help us.

This last text could have meant she'd hired the right person, but he wasn't doing what she wanted.

She'd hired someone she couldn't manipulate. She'd hired the wrong person to help, full stop. The innocent use of the word *us* was a way to add Bard into the conversation. A little emotional *Yoo-hoo!*

Then she went all out.

Ginger: Even Bard thinks so.

Ginger: We're coming to your house. Literally, I'm calling an Uber.

Unlikely but not impossible. Cat scooted out of bed, shouldered her robe, and shuffled into the kitchen for one cup of decaf coffee. She was thirty-seven, cut her own hair, bought brown bananas on sale, and drove a MINI Cooper that was so old it had a cassette player with a Jackson Browne tape lodged inside it. "Running on Empty" played on a loop unless the volume was cranked down. She was sick of Jackson and his crummy implications of her running away, but she put up with him. Keeping that car had helped her save up for this house with locking doors and no kids singing Willy Wonka tunes at all hours. A home that was not a sleepaway camp with endless emergencies that were actual emergencies.

The phone vibrated in her pocket, and Cat resisted looking at it until the coffee had dripped into the pot. She poured the steaming liquid into her Codependent Is So 1990 mug and lifted it. With a hand on her belly, she sat and tried to casually eye her phone.

Shirtless. Despite his sensitivity, he was good at not sounding unneeded alarms.

Shirtless: We're bankrupt. The guy my mom hired is not great. You're still on the mortgage. Don't come.

Every hair on her neck stood at attention and shouted, *Nope. Nope. Nope.* One of the last times Cat had been at camp, she'd had to brave her mother's simultaneously laser-focused and airy-fairy-judgmental attentions. Her father's droopy, loving, accusing, *Et tu?* basset hound eyes pressed her to stay. Amid and despite it all, Cat signed the papers that assured her that Summer Camp and any debt or profit that occurred therewith were not hers.

Another phone vibration.

This time it was Steve. Cat's frown deepened. The father of her child, Steve. The man who knew nothing of Cat's pregnancy.

Was the moon full, or what?

Cat had met him on a dating app she'd downloaded in a weak moment after watching *Love Actually* for the fifteenth time. At dinner, before Cat had reconciled the man in front of her as older and shorter than his profile insisted, Steve said, "We can be friends. Sex between us would never work."

Cat thought *You wish* to the friend part and *Duh* to the sex part because obviously, but then, offended, wanted to say, *Wait, why not?* Not that she was burning to have sex with him, but nobody wanted to be sized up before the entrée as an immediate sexy-no.

The date proceeded in the same way others had before Steve—a night of show-and-tell for the man, displaying zero curiosity for who Cat was. While Steve called himself an entrepreneur whose time was nigh, Cat knew if asked, he wouldn't be able to come up with her job or the color of her eyes. He wasn't seeing *her*, and he certainly hadn't asked her questions about herself. That was fine; she didn't want him either.

Cat huffed a feeble laugh when he made a joke about wanting a sugar mama.

"You're fun," Steve said.

You don't have a clue what I am.

When Steve surprised her and called again, Cat agreed to have a drink, if only to inquire, in a Margaret Mead anthropologist way, about their unworkable sex potential. *The hubris—how does one get the hubris?* Cat wondered. In the end it became a moot point because Cat drank two sangrias, which was two more than she was used to, and slept with Steve.

Steve said at the perfect level of intoxication, "You know, Cat, your eyes are kind of pretty." And the no-sex became marginal sex, because why not? She'd never agree to see him again, he was looking for someone to make his life easier, and Cat had sworn off making anyone's life anything anymore.

After a semisober obligatory postcoital chat, Steve couldn't get out of her place fast enough, leaving behind a nylon man-bag she'd kicked under her bed, where it had sat for the last seven months. This explained today's somewhat cryptic text:

Steve: Left bag at your place. I'll use my key.

His key, that was a laugh.

That fateful and fertile night, there had been some combination of drunken *Let me help you get the door, blah, blah, blah* that had gone on, and her key had ended up in his pocket.

Steve: I have a question for you.

"Oh boy," Cat said to Lefty. He had no idea how many questions he'd have if he saw her. And there was no way that would happen today. While other homes sported LIVE, LAUGH, LOVE signage, Cat's cottage had a LIFE, LIBERTY, AND THE PURSUIT OF HAPPINESS sisal doormat inside. A shotgun reminder that Cat stepped on every day, something she needed because at her core, she was a softy. Still, Cat knew from experience that an innocent ask can be nothing or lead to leaving your childhood home to get out from under it all.

Her phone pinged another time, and Lefty reacted exactly like Cat did, with a head snap and a stare. She peered at it.

Shirtless: I think you better come. I'm worried about Mom.

CHAPTER TWO

UNLIKE ME AND YOU, PLANTS NEED CO_2

"It's go time, Lefty."

Cat threw on a stretchy black onesie and avoided the tall mirror in the bedroom. She grabbed the labor and delivery go bag, packed for a hospital stay or going on the lam for a night or two. When the dog saw Cat snatch her luggage, he knew they were about to hit the road and parked his butt by the door. As she threw dog food, Lefty's water dish, and treats in a paper bag, she considered staying and talking to Steve. But remembering their last night together had her moving again.

He'd gotten one arm out of his shirt and jogged to his car to get Viagra out of the glove compartment. The glove compartment, seriously? By the time he returned, Cat had lost the flicker of interest from that one compliment and almost said, *Ha ha, just kidding. Off you go.*

Instead, she told herself that physical touch was essential for humans and to try to enjoy the skin-to-skin of it all. In the short time that their bodies were in contact, Cat was reminded that not all touching was therapeutic. She didn't love it when a sticky kid at school grabbed her arm or a man in a restaurant caressed her lower back while moving past her; nor did she like to be touched by Steve.

Still, she soldiered on, thrilled when she heard, "Oh. Oh," and his body slumped after less than a minute. Cat should have listened to him; sex for them was a no-go that had gone on, and now there was no denying it. To make matters worse, he'd unexpectedly said after rolling onto his back, "I regret not having a crib lizard or two."

"Crib lizard?"

Steve went on to utter the phrases, "Lost legacy. End of the Jameson line." As if he were a pro athlete and not a fairly unsuccessful business-man with an oddly patchy hairline and an avoidant-avoidant nature regarding, as far as Cat could tell, all people. "Never liked kids. Not really. The trouble is you have to take care of it."

It? Cat would have said if her mind weren't calculating the best way to get rid of him. "When can I see you again?" she said, knowing a show of interest would be the kryptonite needed to repel him out the door and into his car. And she'd been right.

He hopped up and, while sorting out his fly, said, "Soon, babe."

Babe? Gross.

Then, probably wondering why on earth she'd want to see him again, he said, "Your biological clock must be deafening. Tick-tock."

When she gave him a look that clearly stated, *Are you out of your mind?* Steve clarified: "You know. Motherhood." Then he took a hard swing at impersonating a human and said, "I'd love that for you," with his left eyebrow arched, trying to get the emotion right. "Not for me, though, no thanks. I'm a lone wolf."

As if Cat was angling for something like a relationship from him, *double gross.*

Four weeks later and pregnant—yes, they'd used birth control, a 99 percent effective method that made Cat the one out of a hundred women who'd dodged the IUD goalie for the fertilization-win. Why? Had it been fate? The cosmos gifting her what she'd always wanted but without the big, obnoxious string of a man attached?

She hadn't pursued a child for the millions of reasons people don't get around to doing something they want: too many obstacles, too expensive, complex relationships, inertia.

The precise reasons she hadn't told Steve she was pregnant.

She was seven months gone, and there would be no newsy chat today about reproduction and delivery dates. No awkward door answering where Steve would surely notice her pregnant belly, do the math, squint at Cat, and hatch a plan for the future of his DNA that she wanted nothing to do with. What if seeing her pregnant sparked a desire for a succession plan or, worse, a beard? If he had a child, people might anthropomorphize him, bestow human qualities on him, and trust him to do business with.

Nope. For now, she'd do herself a favor and keep the news from Steve until the baby had her name on the birth certificate. She eased herself onto the floor by her bed, lay sideways, and tried to hook the cringey man-bag with a yardstick. It was frustratingly lodged between a rolled-up sock and an empty water bottle. Sneezing twice, she snagged the sack, held it like a dead animal, and hung it on the outside door handle.

"Time to go."

Without taking even one more sip, she threw the coffee in the sink, sloshing the warm, milky liquid onto her hand. With a quick wipe on her pants, she texted Shirtless.

Cat: I'll be right there, leaving in ten. Don't tell your mom.

"Up you go," Cat said to Lefty while pulling her long brown hair into a ponytail and slamming the door with her foot. She started the car, heard the tape player kick in at the chorus of Jackson Browne's "Running on Empty," and she hit the gas. She dialed her father's number, and it rang until his recorded voice answered, "Failure is the chance to begin again. Try later." And disconnected. He didn't know how to listen to voicemails, so she didn't yell in the phone, "What's happening, Dad??" Once she arrived at camp, the spotty service would make it near impossible to reach him. The only time cell phones worked at camp was in the wee early-morning hours with 100 percent humidity or during a winter ice storm. No one knew why. Cat tried three more times with no satisfaction and hung up.

Her MINI knew the way to camp, or at least it felt like it did. It was early in the day, so she could drive the four hours without pulling over for a nap. She'd get there, see what was going on, take a quick nap, and drive home.

In and out, she promised a sweet and fragile future in her belly. *We'll be in and out in a hot minute.* As she got closer, she dreaded how many times she'd have to say, "I'm not staying. Where's the mortgage? I don't want to know. I'm leaving before dark."

At one of the all too familiar highway junctions, Cat took her foot off the gas, the car slowed, and she was fourteen again, reliving the incident where she understood the importance of being her sister's keeper.

Typically, watching over Ginger had been a matter of supervising her on tasks in the laundry or when painting the sets, making sure the brushes were cleaned and the paint cans capped. After that night, Cat saw that growing up playing make-believe among the lightning bugs did not prepare anyone for living anywhere else. Specifically, Ginger.

The dress rehearsal for their *Much Ado About Nothing* production had gone reasonably well. It was the night before the parent pickup, when the adults would watch their children with braces trip and giggle over lines like *I love you with so much of my heart that none is left to protest.*

Cat pulled her MINI Cooper onto the shoulder, letting the engine idle, remembering. She could almost hear the snap and pop of the campfire, the groans of the campers when a marshmallow fell into the fire, the friendly jeering at the kid eating all the chocolate. Ginger had been particularly absent-minded that week, focused on one of the campers her age—the one with genetically gifted muscular abdominals that even their father noticed during free swimming.

"Strong kid," her father had said.

That week, Cat's mother and father were short-tempered and occupied with a broken sump pump in the theater building, and Cat was sick of Ginger making mushy eyes at Cory Schipper at the firepit, after one of their father's elaborate treasure hunts. Cat was in no mood for the Nature Center sing-along, starting with the photosynthesis song: *Unlike me and you, plants need CO_2 and they make oxygen that stops us turning blue.* The song had awkward syncopation; nobody could get it right, and it included forced enthusiasm about oxygenation. Cat wanted a cookie instead of singing about the miracle of chlorophyll, so she went to the Mess Hall.

After brushing crumbs from her shirt, she walked unhurriedly across the lawn and into the theater to make sure that Ginger had locked the prop closet. It was a damn good thing Cat was there because if she hadn't been, Ginger would have killed the boy she had a crush on.

Ginger often recruited younger kids or cute boys to help her do her end-of-day chores. Other times, she'd wander off and forget her duties altogether, so Cat had been in charge of quality control since she was ten. With the gooey-fingered, singing kids behind her, Cat was halfway across the gymnasium floor when she heard Ginger's unmistakable high-pitched panic-gasp from backstage. Cat didn't pick up her pace; in fact, she slowed down. And this was the moment that she knew the truth about herself.

Turning the corner, Cat found Ginger hovering over Cory Schipper, curled on his side, clutching his neck, eyes bulging and wheezing. Ginger smacked him on the back, shouting, "I'm so sorry. Breathe, Cory!"

Cat sprinted the last few feet to their side. "Cory, where's your inhaler?" Everyone at camp knew the boy had asthma; some of his activities were restricted, and minor injuries seemed to set it off, so he couldn't use the tire swing or the ropes course. Cat riffled through the pockets of his windbreaker, found the plastic contraption, flicked the cap off, and shoved it into his mouth. She discharged the medicine, but Cory hadn't created a tight enough seal with his lips, and the lifesaving medicine whispered out of his mouth. Cat said, "Block his nose, Ginger."

Her sister hesitated, and Cat shouted, "Ginger!" Then she used her fingers to hold his lips around the device and squeezed it again; this time Cory was able to inhale, and his eyes rolled back into his head for a second of relief.

"What happened?" Cat snapped at Ginger, who'd withdrawn a handful of steps, letting Cat, as usual, take over. Cory coughed twice and threw up, barely missing the toe of Cat's sneaker.

"You're cleaning that up, Ginger," Cat said, pointing to the sick. "How did he get like this?" Cat wanted answers and to scream so loudly at Ginger that the ropes course would shudder and shrink away.

"He grabbed at my shirt, Cat. I kicked him in the . . ." And instead of saying it, she pointed to her crotch. "It was an accident. I just wanted to get him off me." That's when Cat noticed a button hanging from a thread in the middle of Ginger's favorite shirt, which had a cherry appliqué on the pocket. "I forgot he had asthma."

Cat whirled on Cory and brought her leg back to kick him in the ribs; he flinched and clutched his inhaler. She stopped herself, not wanting another breathing attack.

"He helped me put the rest of the props away. But then . . ."

This was bigger than dried paint cans and an unlocked prop closet. This was . . . something that made Cat's fourteen-year-old self feel yucky.

"Dad. Go get Dad," Cat said.

Ginger wiped her face with the sleeve of her shirt and ferociously shook her head no, her eyes wide. The space smelled like sour acid. Cat knew why Ginger didn't want their father. There would be parental lectures condemning Ginger's irresponsible behavior. He'd ask what she'd had in mind by bringing a boy back into the dark stage. And *What did you think would happen?* Cat knew Ginger. Her sister was an innocent. She'd thought maybe the boy would say she was pretty; they'd hold hands. Ginger had helped write cue cards for *Romeo and Juliet*. What did any of them know about boys, other than peeking at some of the older counselors making out in the Rippling Ridge encampment?

Her parents' disciplinary coaching would include a sex discussion like Cat's mother had given Cat when she started her period. The foulest thing she'd ever gone through was when her mother used a boiled egg and a Swedish Fish to demonstrate the biology of it all. Her mother had, gratefully, left props out of the lesson on what she called "intimate, interpersonal intercourse." As if there weren't enough *i*'s already, her mother enunciated *vagina*, as if the *i* were the longest letter in the sex alphabet and needed extra beats when pronouncing.

The misery of her father's looks of reproach when he'd ask Cat with his eyes, *Where were you—you, your sister's keeper. How did you let it get that far?* Not just from her parents. Everyone knew Cat was in charge of Ginger, and had Cory died of a cock-blocked asthma attack, it would have been on Cat. The thought of all the conversations, everyone's attempts to turn Ginger into Cat and Cat into a more vigilant version of her fourteen-year-old self, was too much.

That night, Cat stood over Cory, who looked sweaty and sorry but was shaking his head no, trying to explain. "My compass caught on her button," he said, holding up an actual compass. "She jumped back when I tried to get it loose."

Cat swung her head to look at Ginger.

"A compass?" she said.

Cory's lip quivered.

Cat knew these dopes needed a script, or they'd go off on their own, saying who knew what? And kids were brutal.

"Cory. Clean that barf up, and if there is even a smudge left, I'll tell everyone you showed Ginger your dink."

Cory's eyes went as wide as they had when he'd gasped for air.

"You tell everyone you fell hard running up the stairs, and Ginger saved your life. I was never here. Come on, Ginger. I have to tell you something about boys."

The night ended with Cat drawing pictures in the sand of the swimming area, enough to warn her off being alone with boys.

Ginger had said, "Oh, Kitty. I'm so sorry." She had a mosquito bite on her forehead, a dusting of sun on her upturned nose.

"It's okay. It's okay." Cat noticed the dirt in her kid sister's nails.

When Cat explained the part where the sperm met the egg, Ginger had gagged, giggled, and acted like she wanted to dive headlong into the lake. "Mom and Dad?" she asked and heaved again.

They built a penis in the sand by the bigger canoe and stomped on it, laughing, then ran back to their family cabin, safe from the future realities of boys, sex, or dying from asphyxiation.

Cory returned to his cabin to recover, and in the morning, he told everyone Ginger was a hero.

For Cat's part, she went to her bunk and replayed the scenario with that stupid photosynthesis song stuck on repeat in her head. *Unlike me and you, plants need CO_2,* as if mocking her. Cory's dusky face. If Cat had not stepped up, Cory might have stopped breathing, which would have been her fault. How was she supposed to live with the fact that she'd almost turned around? And that was when Cat realized that if you were in charge of someone, you'd better not have any needs of your own.

The next morning, Cat, exhausted and bleary-eyed from growing up in one day, watched the kids slap Ginger on the back, Cory looking on, hoping his acting skills had gotten better that week. That's when she saw her mother examining Cat. Did she know Cat wasn't a good person? That she hadn't rushed to help her sister?

CHAPTER THREE

ONLY SOMETHINGS GET THE ADO

She was rushing now, wasn't she? Wasn't she?! Cat defended herself from her internal voice, the enemy of the good, that crouched in her mind, challenging her motives for everything. She'd read somewhere that not everyone had an internal monologue cheering, berating, explaining, and Cat, and her inside voice, gasped.

At this moment, as she eased her MINI back onto the highway, her voice said, *You know full well you are not rushing to—you are rushing away from—dealing with Steve.* If he ever asked why she wasn't home when he'd come to get his bag, she could blame the camp.

Cat hitched the steering wheel left, then right, dodging the bloody remains of deer, raccoons, and possums dotting the shoulders like brutal mile markers. Ignored by natives, the roadkill was only occasionally cleaned up by the Department of Natural Resources. *It's rural Wisconsin, y'all*—basically dodgeball for wild animals.

Lefty sat shotgun, and Cat needed something to do rather than cycle through self-recrimination and justification as she drove. If it hadn't been for Steve, she'd have thought to grab the legal papers she'd signed in front of her father.

Now she had to:

1. Find mortgage papers. Examine signatures. Assess camp solvency. Figure out her responsibility.
2. Find Ginger.
3. Talk to Gary, the longtime groundskeeper who, for some unknown reason, made himself scarce whenever she returned. Most likely he was trapping snapping turtles and keeping the tire swing safe.
4. Drive home.

She'd miss Steve and clear the runway of any camp responsibilities so when the baby came, she could be the single-focused mother she wanted to be. Cat rolled Lefty's window halfway down and the dog stuck his head out, ears fluttering in the slipstream. She tried not to catastrophize, not to believe that the only outcome after today would leave Cat penniless after bailing the camp out. Where she and her newborn would be forced to live in one of the two Birch cabins. Having to explain to her toddler as she grew up that they lived in Birch A, not Birch B, because no one had come up with another genus of tree when they'd named the second cabin back in the day.

Lefty pulled his head inside and gave her the side-eye.

"No. You're right," she said. She got ahold of herself.

If the new administrator was not a lunatic and the camp was flush, then Cat's to-do list would go back to before that morning call to action.

1. Grow baby.
2. Deliver baby.
3. Text Steve about the baby after she's signed the birth certificate with her daughter's legal name as McCarthy.
4. Raise baby to be an emotionally intelligent adult who makes good choices based on morals, ethics, desires, and kindness while teaching her boundaries and how to say no when she wants to say no, something she obviously hasn't quite gotten the hang of.

"No," she whispered, and Lefty didn't react; he knew she wasn't talking to him.

The familiar smell of pine flitted into the car and reminded her of . . . so much. She added a number 5 to her list. *Talk to Shirtless.* He was a kid amid this adult problem; she'd involve him only if she absolutely needed to. He wouldn't have texted her if he wasn't worried about losing his home.

Adorably touchy, Bard was naturally named after Shakespeare, as Ginger couldn't imagine having a child who wasn't as devoted to theater as the family was. Even Ginger found it ironic when it was crystal clear that Bard was terrifically introverted, shy, and stage averse.

Cat had seen it early, but the family finally capitulated when the six-year-old Bard was cast as Ferdinand the Bull. He had only to sit under a cardboard tree and sniff orange tissue paper flowers, but Bard froze like a mini towheaded elderly politician too long at the podium—mouth agape, hollow-eyed, and picking at a scab on his foot.

"It's okay, sweetie," Ginger had assured him as she eased him off the stage in his furry bull costume. "I promise you. Never again." It was not easy for a restrained, tender child to grow up among theater people, the touchiest, huggiest people known to man. Against all odds, her nephew thrived at the camp; it was his safe place as long as there were no performances to step up to. No lines to deliver, and he didn't have to take a tranquilizer.

Whenever Bard left the camp, he wore a T-shirt with instructions. Other kids his age had their pronouns printed on their shirts, but Bard's shirts said DON'T TOUCH ME. Which, of course, only egged people on to, indeed, touch him every chance they got.

Farmland turned wooded, and small towns arrived and departed as quickly as the speed limit allowed. Cat spotted the entrance to the grounds, touching off a mix of nostalgia, fragments of memories, kids laughing and splashing, and the dinner bell. The scent of the late days of August, the Midwest's last call for alcohol, shorts, and swimsuits, rode in on the breeze of her open window. The endless cleaning of her and

Ginger's workspaces, her father pulling her into conversations about modeling responsible behavior.

The WELCOME TO SUMMER CAMP sign looked freshly painted, arching high above her car. The beaver mascot in the center clutched a birch log, his crosshatched tail held high. Someone, Gary, had planted rows and rows of marigolds along the split-rail fence, which had no tumbledown or missing slats. The white gravel rocks that made up the parking lot were free of dandelions and the Queen Anne's lace that usually made the place look partially deserted. This all boded well for her *Get in and get out* promise.

Slowly, Cat steered the car into the parking lot, stones pinging under the tires. Cat never told the truth about that day with Cory Schipper, and Ginger would rather go blind than give up the moment she was credited as a hero. The sisters rarely spoke of it, almost never. Once after Bard was born, Ginger said something, a bit of hard-won wisdom many years later.

"You know, Cat. No one is ever praised for their weaknesses. There are no awards for hanging in there. Doing the best that you can. Not making it to the summit." They'd been sitting on a blanket, the sun and breeze creating the picture of a perfect day. A visit Cat had made because there appeared to be no emergency in sight.

Ginger plucked a piece of grass from the lawn and said, "I think that's what that play is about, you know?" She chewed on the blade. "Rarely is there much ado about nothing. And when there is, they created a whole play about it. Only the somethings get the ado. That's the way of the world."

Ginger dropped the grass and put her eyelashes close to Bard's tummy, already aware of his sensitivities. "You'll get so much ado, buddy, because you are different from me. You really are something."

Cat had wanted to comfort her sister. Deny the crap assessment of herself. "You're something! Different in a good way!" she'd said.

Ginger scoffed. "Differently abled," she said. "I wonder if the label makers knew how condescending that name is when they came up with it. Unless you were able in the ways everyone is 'able,' you are 'different.'

Who gets to pick the right kind of able?" she said, and Bard tried to grab her finger and shove it in his mouth. "I'd rather be called dumb," she said. "That's what people are thinking."

"I don't think that," Cat said. "I just think you're . . ."

"Yeah, different. I know."

Cat pulled Lefty into a hug, holding him to her until that moment's pain and love had crested and released its grip on her throat. It was her turn to have a child; would she be any better talking to her than she'd talked to her sister? Better lives, that's what everyone wanted for their children, that and for them to be better people.

No other cars were in the lot, just the camp's transport van. She saw no campers, no staff, no maintenance. It was eerily quiet, an unusually cool sunny day in late August, but inside Cat was the beginning of an anxious-avoidant storm.

So help me, Ginger, if the camp is fine and you put Shirtless up to texting me, I will block you for life and do a 180 out of here.

"Stay," she said to Lefty, and he whined. He did not like it when Cat wandered off, surely feeling her change in energy. Cat tiptoed across the open lot, listening hard, scanning the manicured grounds. You had to hand it to Gary: the place might be about to collapse, but he always did his job. To the left were the Craft Lodge and the Health Hut, with the Mess Hall in the center and the Canteen to the right—brown buildings, recently painted. Cat glanced at the lake in the distance down the green grassy hill that called to her, reminding her how homesick you could feel in a place that used to be home.

She knew where they might be. The Administration Building housed the stage and gymnasium, and toward the lake was a roofed gathering area with a stone fireplace and high rough-hewn ceiling. As she approached, she heard it. Applause? Yes, Cat heard clapping. Even and firm, not scattered and thready. Multiple participants. Grown-up and organized, not kid-like. Then a loud microphone squeal, followed by a man's voice saying, "Welcome to Summer Camp, ladies and gentlemen. Can I get a 'Hello, Bob'?"

CHAPTER FOUR

FEEL AMAZING, BE AWESOME

Cat automatically tiptoed past the office and the theater and slowed, approaching the covered outside space with the big stone fireplace. Odd, she thought, on this last Tuesday of camp, campers were typically gone, and the staff were off cleaning cabins for the next week. There was never an assembly—at least not in the olden days when Cat made the schedule.

The woodpile where, as a kid, she'd spied on camp counselors gossiping, or her parents' disagreements on theater stuff, covered Cat's approach. She nudged a damp log an inch, and there before her sat at least fifty adults in metal folding chairs. Each head faced a man in khakis and a green polo standing on a platform, holding a microphone.

This was her father's podium, and Cat watched as an outsider, curious and detached while at the same time comfortable that, if discovered, she had the right to be there, hiding.

The alert crowd waited for the man to give them another chance to crow. Cat watched him scan the crowd, and he paused when his gaze passed the woodpile. He couldn't see her, but she held her breath. After a beat, his gaze moved to a grouping of younger adults in camp counselor uniforms—T-shirts the same green as the man's polo and khaki shorts, no one looking the least bit clean or pressed. Cat released her breath and reached into her memory. Why did he look familiar?

"Speech. Speech. Speech," the crowd chanted, switching to "Bob, Bob, Bob," and Cat watched him fix his collar, run a hand through his hair, positively preening.

Bob, the wrongly hired man. This was he. The source of the trouble that had dragged her back to camp, when the last thing she wanted or needed was to be dragged anywhere for anyone. Should she step in, give herself away, or stay quiet? Collect data?

He patted the air: "Now, now. You don't have to work that hard to get me to talk about this camp." The crowd laughed good-naturedly. Whoever these people were, they loved this man, this Bob, no doubt about it. Cat tried to place him. Television? Politics? A blonde woman Ginger's age, her chair canted for the best possible view of the stage, studied Bob like he was a map of the world and she had her bags packed.

It was harder to tell how the younger staff felt about Bob. They had the collective air of a nervous grouping of birds, as if anything could happen at any minute and they needed to be ready to fly off in all directions. Against the wall, fidgeting with the others, stood Shirtless.

There was no way her nephew could be concentrating with the seams of his shirt right-side in. Cat knew there was an expiration date on the wearing of it, and Shirtless was counting the seconds to when he could tear it off. She considered trying to catch his eye, ease his worries; the boy must be in turmoil.

Ginger was nowhere in sight. It was surreal to see this stranger holding court in place of her father. Her impulse was to charge in, break up the party, demand information, but instead she wanted to see for herself what was happening without Ginger the unreliable narrator chirping in her ear.

Then Bob, with the yellow glow of the afternoon sun around his shoulders, pulled the mic close to his lips and, with no notes, began speaking.

"We've postponed the bonfire and final sing-along because of you"—he spread his hands out lavishly to indicate the roomful of adults, their smiles lifted, waiting—"our campers, the people who've most recently experienced the magic and have graciously agreed to let me practice my speech for the fundraising gala in three days' time."

Cat frowned. Gala? The word *gala* had never been used in relation to this rustic place, with its log cabins and frogs trilling from dusk till dawn.

Not your business, Cat. Who cares? she asked herself.

There was a smattering of respectful applause from the audience, followed by a collective quieting. Indulgent Bob, appearing the image of a hardworking, compelling, and earnest camp director, said, "Hit it, Camille."

The adoring blonde in the front row, older on second glance, flipped a switch by the fireplace. The overhead lights went out, and a sizable, yellowed movie screen was unrolled in fits and starts; the halting, squeaky unfurling added an air of suspense. A movie projector flickered on, and Bob centered his shoulders. "These hallowed grounds and I have a long history, as many of you know. I was one of those kids from the early days of Summer Camp."

Hallowed grounds? Cat moved a piece of bark that was poking her in the hip. They were kind of revered, honored. At least by her parents and all the kids who attended. It had felt like home for a lot of them.

Over Bob's head, the grassy expanse of the camp came to life on-screen. The footage was before the totem pole had been installed, before we'd understood the insensitivity of binding a commemoration of ancestry to a place where kids ate hot dogs morning, noon, and night. There was the Canteen when it was no more than a rolling cart near the Mess Hall.

Cat recognized the images of her childhood and, once again, felt the pull of belonging that often as not turned to obligation. She removed her hand from the logs as if the wood itself held the power to entrap. The projector flashed a picture of none other than a younger Bob, about eight years old, with enormous glasses, a massive overbite, and a bowl cut: Jerry Lewis with a catcher's mitt.

The crowd gasped and laughed. The astonishing juxtaposition between the boy on the screen and the groomed, handsome man before them affected the adults present. No doubt the men wished they had aged as well, and the women wanted to be both mother and lover to the past and present Bob.

Cat knew him then—he'd been a returning camper four, maybe five times, a terrible swimmer and even worse at ball sports. Sight impaired. Ginger's age.

"This camp changed my life," he said. "That's only partially true. Orthodontia, LASIK surgery, and training for a half-marathon helped as well." He laughed modestly. "Not just my life," he went on, and Cat could have sworn he winked at her, unless he was flirting with the damp pine logs that hid her. At this point she didn't care if he saw her—she was here for the explanation, even if she'd washed her hands of the place long ago.

Bob turned and eyed the old movie screen as if he'd worshipped its water stains and rough edges. "Ahhh, when the camp was young." He sighed. "The Mess Hall and the swimming pier, all in place, waiting for kids to come."

Summertime scenes shimmered and blinked while Bob narrated: "This was the place for the less-than-perfect to experience summer without able-bodied kids their age smirking at their uncoordinated efforts, missed soccer goals, or their head-hitting-tree moments."

Cat cringed at the man's insensitive language her father never used. It was as if this man were a relic of the old-timey camp, or that because he'd attended, he could label himself along with others. In truth, the camp was founded for those with vision impairment, and soon children with other disabilities were welcomed. Something her father continued when the place transitioned to doing theater.

Bob rubbed his forehead as if he fondly recalled his injuries—an underestimated kid who'd showed 'em all that he was a contender. Cat was annoyed, remembered he spent a lot of time trying to kiss the legally blind girls down by the latrines. Her father would grab him by the shirt collar and send him to the swim area to wash down canoes. Strange, that recollection, so crisp in her memory, something she hadn't thought of in fifteen years or more.

"When the McCarthys took over and created Summer Camp, central Wisconsin became a hub for theater arts."

Cat almost laughed out loud. If a bunch of little kids with lisps forgetting their lines as Oompa-Loompas, Munchkins, and Shakespearean wood sprites constituted a hub, then okay, they were a hub.

"A camp this size is expensive to maintain, and before long the grounds deteriorated. The spiders amassed in the Thunderbird One cabin. Mold grew in the swim area, and our beloved camp needed some tender loving care." Cat heard a woman sigh, and the group made tiny noises of disappointment. "Summer Camp started to die." Bob paused, letting the audience recall their recent time at the camp and allowing images on the big screen to underscore the magic of the place. Cat scoffed, feeling defensive of her family's efforts. It was fine for Cat to grumble about the place, but an outsider had no idea what this place took to run.

Bob dropped his eyes, and Cat wondered if he had eyelash extensions. He knew how to use silence; she'd give him that. Then he lifted his head and said, "You all know I was chosen to rejuvenate the camp because of my"—cough, cough—"success. And you will go home today with a copy of my *New York Times* bestseller *Feel Amazing, Be Awesome*."

Rejuvenate? I don't think it needed rejuvenation, Cat thought. That was definitely overstating what he was needed for. Not knowing, in fact, what Bob had been hired for.

The big screen showed photos of Bob holding his book next to Dwayne "The Rock" Johnson, one of the New Kids on the Block, and the lesser Wahlberg, his arm thrown casually around Bob's shoulders. Cat's eyes went wide; she was glad she'd stayed put, hadn't given up her advantage.

"For those who don't know, my book tells the story of two bunnies, Alistair and Raj, who went on a series of adventures, after which both bunnies felt amazing, but only one of them, Raj, indeed became awesome. Alistair's adventure started with multiple procreations, which led to a frantic search for greens and hollow logs for his various families. Exhausted, Alistair realized that being all things to all bunnies was not fulfilling. On the other hand, Raj had moved with moderation toward fatherhood, had found joy in his single child while eating local carrots and being mindful."

Mindful—Cat squinted at the man—*try being mindful while running this place. Try chaoticful,* she thought, defensive of everyone at the camp who'd never appeared mindful.

Cat eyed the men in the group. They appeared to be considering their own lives, evaluating whether they fell into the Alistair or Raj camp. The women were eager for Bob to continue, and Cat waited for him to reveal the link between the fall of the camp and the bunnies. Cat was an anthropologist in that moment, she told herself. This was information, not her problem to solve.

"It's like our friendly bunnies learned . . ." Bob hesitated, drawing out the lesson as if it were so weighty it needed its own runway to take flight. "There are lots of ways to feel amazing, but to truly be awesome, you must get off the American treadmill." Someone dashed past the back of the shelter and out of sight. It could have been Ginger, if she'd dyed her blonde hair pink.

"Thus"—he gestured broadly—"this camp! Anxious and depressed people need a place to go to get better. Away from the judgments of society, the onslaught of life." The green expanse of the camp returned to the big screen in tandem with the barely perceptible soundtrack of Judy Garland's "Somewhere Over the Rainbow."

"I believe that depressed people aren't sick. They don't need medication; they need the extended support and creativity only a camp atmosphere can provide."

Was he reconfiguring the camp? Changing it from a kids' camp to one for adults? Anxious and depressed adults in fact. Did he sincerely think a week in the Wisconsin woods could cure mental illness? If he did, he needed meds himself.

The music merged into the driving beat of a 2010 dance hit, Flo Rida's "Club Can't Handle Me." Maybe he thought the song of their youth symbolized confidence, spirit, and drive, the exact qualities Bob knew investors would open their wallets for—as if they could purchase them for themselves. The crowd clapped with the beat, some campers stood and shimmied, and one chubby-ish man put his fingers in his mouth, whistled loudly, and shouted, "Woo-woo!" in a falsetto the Bee Gees would have been envious of.

If Bob did this and ran this place into the ground, she would find a lawyer and hold him accountable. Then, remembering the promises she'd made to herself, Cat amended her thoughts. She'd find a lawyer for Ginger to hold him accountable. Better yet, she'd make Ginger find a lawyer. She'd suggest Ginger find a lawyer. Cat put a hand to her head; detachment was not for wussies.

Bob displayed a little white man's overbite, tried a shoulder pop, and for just a second Cat thought he might drop into his awkward eighth-grade dance moves. Instead, he exercised surprising judgment and refrained. "You know how long it takes to get a mental health appointment," Bob said. "And when you do get in, they hand you pills and send you on your way. What if," he said emphatically as the trumpet music in the background moved toward a crescendo, "you could get quality time away? If we put the drug companies out of business?"

This entire speech was so off base Cat started to feel giddy. If she were the old Cat, she'd interrupt this ridiculousness. Teach him a thing or two about what her parents had given up to create the theater camp, for him to waltz in here and propose a redo of these proportions. She scoffed loudly enough for a woman in the row closest to Cat to glance at the woodpile.

He paused, letting the music and the photographs of sunsets, camping gear, and bonfires manipulate their emotions. Bob shook his head theatrically. "If we get a handle on mental health, we can stop talking about gun control. Am I right? If we can save just one person, we can save a nation."

Oh boy, he's jumped the shark. Cat tried to control a bubble of laughter in her chest, but she couldn't, and it sounded like a sob. Bob shouted, "Amen!"

Camille added a reverent "Hallelujah," and the phrase *The cure for what ails (the) US* flashed across the screen. Bob lifted one fist in the air like a diminutive, not–Black Panther and said, "We call this place, this rehab for worriers, Summer Camp. And this place must go on." Then, at the speed of a television commercial listing the side effects of a drug, he said, "We take cash, credit cards, Venmo, Zelle, PayPal, Canteen funds, and anything from our Amazon gift wish list."

Before Cat could react to Bob going forward with this wild plan while hitting up the people he'd just promised to help, she heard her sister's voice in her ear: "What did I tell you? Hinky, am I right?"

And then Cat saw the adoring look on her sister's face.

CHAPTER FIVE

THE BUNNY TATTOO

Cat startled and clapped her left hand over her mouth, muffling a surprised gasp. "Dammit," she hissed, nearly grabbing Ginger's upper arm and squeezing it until she squirmed away like when they were six and eight years old.

Ginger nodded. "Was I right? I was right." She raised her eyebrows. "You heard him." Ginger's eyes darted to the spy hole in the stack of logs. "You saw him," she said quickly, as if she couldn't wait for Cat to confirm because what Ginger wanted to say was what came next: "I told you." She gestured toward the big screen as if all the information was on display, and Cat had better get on the Ginger train because it was leaving the station.

It had been a year since Cat had seen Ginger, but through her sister's flurry and fracas, she noticed the wispy ends of her pixie cut had been dyed fuchsia, and a tiny gold hoop sparkled in her eyebrow. The total effect was "woodland fairy on uppers."

When Ginger was on a tear, it was best to let her wind down rather than respond to her assertions. The result of Ginger's panicky stream of consciousness occasionally brought out the calm in Cat, if only to be in devilish opposition to her sister.

"He's completely restructured the camp," Ginger stage-whispered. "We don't do any theater. All the campers are nervy oldies. No kids anywhere. And it's all about *Feel Amazing, Be Awesome* and bunnies. He doesn't believe in meds! No meds, Cat." Beckoning Cat to follow her, Ginger moved and dropped her voice. "Shirtless and I have ours stashed because . . . well, you know why." She stopped, looked at Cat pointedly, grabbed her arm, and towed her from the logjam lookout. Cat knew, all right. She never wanted to see Ginger's listlessness after delivering Shirtless ever again. He was the result of Ginger taking a drug holiday seventeen years ago.

Bumping gracelessly behind her sister, Cat said, "Didn't you interview that guy before you hired him?" They moved up the path away from the crowd in the makeshift theater. They stopped in front of the window to the camp's main building that contained offices, the Auditorium slash theater. Cat caught their reflection in the glass, Ginger an inch shorter, leaning in, and Cat, dark, tilted away, a potato on skinny sticks for legs. An adult reflection of their childhood postures, if not physiques. "Did you ask him what his plans were? Did you write a job description? Make him sign a contract?"

Ginger dropped her eyes, and Cat knew that look. Nothing said *I didn't do any of those things* more than that semi-guilty, *You know me, those are not my skills* expression. Then, with her gaze downward, Ginger widened her eyes. "You're fat," she said.

Cat sensed delight.

"No! You're pregnant." Ginger put her hand over her eyes as if this was the last straw toward her undoing. It was as if Cat had strolled in for a visit when Ginger had a full day planned and could not possibly add an in utero child to the agenda. There should have been processing with the prospect of Ginger becoming an aunt. What if she was asked to babysit? She was not great with babies, etc. Everything was always about Ginger.

Cat had been dragging her feet about telling her family because once they knew, she'd no longer be able to keep her distance. What kind of monster would keep a grandchild separate from their family because the mother was afraid she'd be asked for more than she could offer? That she might fail to deliver?

"Yes, I'm pregnant."

Ginger took her sister's tight belly into her hands and teared up like a surprising flash flood in the tiniest of creek beds. Cat felt their sisterly connection, but only for a beat. Whether Ginger was sincerely touched or not, Cat's priority was assessing whether this call-to-camp might ruin her future. "The contract. Where's his contract? I can't be on the mortgage. Did the wrong papers get filed or something? Do I still own a portion of this camp? Have you been in touch with Dad?" The baby rolled like she always did when Cat spoke forcefully. As if to tell her to ease up and conserve energy. Life is a triathlon—Bedroom. Bathroom. Breakfast—not scuttle, scramble, sleep. Not capture the flag.

"I don't know. You know I don't know anything about a mortgage. Dad handled all of that. Bob told me you own a lot of the camp. I said, 'No, you're wrong, Bob. Cat is free and clear.'" Ginger puffed up like an actor impersonating someone in charge. "He said there's proof. He has proof." The certainty went out of Ginger, and she shrugged. "It's not unlike Dad to have a plan B. He probably knew I'd screw things up. Kept you on the mortgage to help when I did."

The matter-of-fact way Ginger accepted her father's lack of confidence . . . Cat could see the defeat in Ginger's rounded shoulders when she spoke. Cat wanted to comfort her, but wasn't that the old pattern, the slippery slope into a rescue mission?

Instead, Cat said, "There's no way Dad would leave me on the mortgage, have me sign fake papers or whatever. The man wouldn't hide an Easter basket without a map."

Her father would frown, watching little Bard zooming around the grounds with his hand-drawn directions. "It seems mean, Kitty. A map makes it a game." He was resourceful and protective, but he also knew what Cat knew: that his family needed camp—the bigger world was too much for that mother-son team.

She shook her head. "I refuse to believe that he did some kind of bait and switch with legal documents."

Cat could see Ginger wasn't convinced, and Cat didn't have time for this. Once again she felt caught between wanting to assure Ginger and slap her.

"You must know more than you're letting on. What's going on? What gala is he talking about? You don't get to shrug and say, 'I don't know.'"

"Don't you think I know that?"

"I don't know what you know. I'm here because you called me, and that's all the information I have," Cat said, hearing the frustration in her voice, her desperation to figure it all out without being a forensic accountant slash single-handed camp savior.

"Okay. Okay," Ginger said, dropping her eyes to Cat's belly. Remembering this other piece of new news. "You look beautiful," she said, using her genuine face, the one she made by accident when she wasn't overwhelmed and asking for help.

In that moment Cat wished she had told her sister earlier, and the thought softened her resolve to stay separated. She encircled Ginger's wrist with her hand with a wry expression.

That's when Cat saw the tattoo of a bunny. Whenever she slept with someone, she memorialized it with a symbolic tattoo. Ginger was like a WWII fighter pilot who etched victory markings on the chassis of her warplane. Sadly, it wasn't about conquests. She'd explained it to Cat when Shirtless was born, after Cat had spied a tiny drumstick in the crux of her sister's arm.

"When I'm old and in the nursing home, I want to be reminded of the people who touched me. There won't be that many. You're the pretty one."

And with that, another memory gurgled to the surface. Cat and Ginger, prepubescent teens. They'd been in the kitchen stealing cookies for a campfire picnic when their mom and a camper's parent had entered the Mess Hall. Ginger stuffed her cookie in her mouth, and they scrambled behind the supply room door. The other mother was discussing food allergies and the high-fat diet her child required. Said how lucky their mother was that her kids didn't have allergies. "Which daughter is which? Such charming creatures." As if Ginger and Cat were sprites found in the forest and so alike that she required assistance telling us apart.

"Cat's the fair one," their mother had said, as in beautiful, playing the role of a medieval lady. Cat yanked Ginger out the back door, not wanting to hear anything more. Young Ginger had a Rubenesque beauty that made her the perfect Shakespearean lady. Ginger let the cookie pieces drop from her mouth onto the floor. Later Cat heard her mother finish describing the sisters, something the two hadn't heard in their rush to leave the kitchen. "Cat's the fair one; Ginger is filled with grace." Cat could never convince Ginger that this was not said in apology or hindsight.

Years could pass, a thousand compliments delivered, but one off-hand, unkind comment thoughtlessly served could gnaw away at a person's confidence for the rest of their life. Ginger never could shake that assessment off.

Years later, Cat ran her thumb over a nickel-size rabbit in profile on her sister's wrist.

"His interview was sex." Cat said this in concert with how she felt: certain, sad for Ginger, and knowing that the problem that had brought her to camp was not just a missing signature on the mortgage. The usual family quicksand reached past terra firma and tugged down every limb.

"No! I interviewed him, I swear." Ginger crossed her fingers and put them to her lips, the sign they only ever used when telling the absolute truth. "I did sleep with him, but not until after I hired him." She swung away from Cat. "You weren't here. Dad wasn't here. I made a mistake."

Then, as if announcing to the trees, "Ginger made another mistake. I can't run this place. Surprise, surprise."

"You said you could, Ginger," Cat said, with heavy emphasis on the initial *G*. The way she said her sister's name when she was dead serious. "You said, and I quote, 'I can run this place,' and when Dad said he would help find someone, you said, 'No, Daddy. I've got this.'"

"I thought I did." She twisted the silver ring she wore on her middle finger, the one with BARD engraved on the inside. She was thinking of her son. Good, this affected him too. Cat thought like a parent might—a lesson here, a teachable moment.

"I tell you what I know," Ginger said. "In January, after Mom and Dad left, I thought I could manage. By February, camp enrollment was super low, and applications for staff were nonexistent. I guess being a camp counselor isn't cool anymore. Tech is cool. Working at an elephant rescue in Africa, very cool. Kids watching kids singing 'The Lonely Goatherd' song onstage, not cool."

"COVID killed the kids' camp," news at six, Cat remembered her mother saying during one of Cat's visits home.

"I didn't know how to recruit more people, so Bard and I decided to advertise for assistance. And PS, I didn't call you for help."

"How? If the camp is in so much financial trouble, where did that money come from?" Cat said, ignoring anything she might have to give Ginger credit for.

"We had money in the bank. We did! When Bob applied, we had the best talk about how the world has changed. That people need people and nature and play more than ever. You don't need as many staff when the campers are adults, so staffing was easier."

This was the one sentence that made sense, so Cat didn't shout *Keep talking!* like she wanted to.

"He had fans who enrolled in camp. We had a good year; he had great ideas for scaling. We talked for three hours about possibilities and potential." Ginger had the dreamy look she got when performing Juliet as a kid—fragile, hopeful, and lost in the sauce of unreality. She shook her head. "You saw him. He's so convincing."

Despite Ginger's loving gaze, her skin was pale, and she had lost weight, maybe too much. Cat could see their dad's angular chin and mother's hollows under her eyes. Her sister appeared healthier but also more fragile, if that was a thing. Cat wasn't indestructible; she was carrying a human. Wasn't there ANY dispensation for an active womb?

"Do you even know what the word 'scaling' means?"

"Making a good idea better, bringing in more people," Ginger said.

"It means level up. Spending money to make money. Pivot—take something small and make it bigger."

"That makes sense," Ginger said.

"No, it doesn't, Ginger. If he spent too much to make it into this haven he's proposing, we may be broke. And if I'm on the mortgage and own this place, they will come after me." It was Cat's turn to yank the infuriating, flawed, beloved Ginger around. She grabbed her sister right on the bunny tattoo.

"We're going to the office. Find the files."

Ginger resisted, put her finger to her lips, her eyes darting left to right. "Elaine is always listening."

"Who is Elaine?" Cat said. "Ginger, is Bob married? He has a wife." She said it like a statement. Like, *Of course he does. Why wouldn't he? That tracks, for sure.*

Ginger straightened, pointed to Cat's pregnancy, and, with the presence of the president of the United States' press secretary, said, "You want to get into this right now?"

Cat gave her sister a *That's fair* look.

Transforming seamlessly back into her sister, Ginger raised her voice, her eyes darting, and said, "Come on! I'll show you the new swimming dock."

"I don't want to see the dock," Cat said, pulling her arm free.

"Then we can see the new tire on the swing." Ginger widened her eyes as if to say *Play along* and marched in the direction of the water, then veered erratically toward the Administration Building. As if she were dodging sniper fire, she hunched into a jog, motioning for Cat to follow her.

CHAPTER SIX

DOGGIE PADDLE DEPRESSION SWIM

"That was sneaky," Cat said, because it wasn't the least bit sneaky and if anyone was watching, they had to be wondering what game the two women were playing.

"Elaine is everywhere and nowhere. She's like a ghost. Like, boo, she's there," Ginger said as they arrived at the Administration Building. The structure was built in the '60s, with a stage flush against the back wall and shiny wood floors. Her father had lacquered those old boards every winter, offsetting the dusty velvet curtains that hid the stage's wings.

Dust particles drifted in the light from the windows, and Cat tried to block out Ginger's nutty narration. This was the stage where Ginger and the camper kids had performed plays with enough cast members so that no awkward kid was left out: *Charlie and the Chocolate Factory*, *The King and I*, *The Sound of Music*, *The Wizard of Oz*, and *Annie*. Ginger always played Annie and would sing "It's the hard-nut life" in performances, just to bug their father. It made Cat howl with laughter, their own secret family joke amid a musical.

The main office sat connected to the theater slash gymnasium and looked out over the front lawn of the camp. Cat pushed past the flash of the voices and the tug of her playful memories and walked through the unlocked office door. Ginger allowed herself to be towed.

"I try to stay out of Elaine's way. She's terrifying."

"You slept with her husband; it's not like you are friends."

"You're not wrong there," Ginger said, getting distracted by the social dynamics of sleeping with a man who was married and how that might play out in interactions.

"I'm going to try and do the impossible and pull up my mortgage documents on my phone," Cat said. "Shoot. My battery is almost dead. Give me your phone."

"Bob has everybody's phones and cords locked up. I only get mine at night. It's part of our media detox program. He has this theory that the intermittent feedback of social media causes depression . . ."

"This is diabolical," Cat said. "There's no other word for it."

"Lots of places take phones. We're dopamine addicts," Ginger said as if she had any idea what a neurotransmitter was or did.

"Prisons take your phones. Cults take your phones," Cat said, trying to open a document while her battery went into the red zone.

"Coverage is terrible here. The roaming kills your battery," Ginger said, calmly watching Cat scroll. "Oh. There. Yup. Your phone died. Do you have your cord?"

"No. In fact I don't, Ginger."

"Did you bring a paper copy of your mortgage?" Ginger said.

"When there's an SOS, people don't usually stop and think, 'Where are my documents and cords?'" Cat said, trying not to lose her mind. She concentrated on her sister's face, younger and older at this place where everyone seemed ageless. Cat tried to soften her tone.

"After we search this office, you're going to get phones and cords from Bob; then we'll pull up my documents and compare what we have. Or, better yet, I'll go get the documents and my charger and come back tomorrow."

Ginger tried to keep her face steady at the mention of Cat leaving. "We'll find the files," she said. "We'll talk to Bob, charge phones."

Ginger was at her most helpful when someone else was in charge. Not just someone but her grown-up, hyper-responsible, and resourceful sister.

"Then I'll call Dad."

"They never pick up."

"Sometimes Mom does," Cat said to be obstinate.

"Okaaaaaay," Ginger said, drawing out the word like, *Suit yourself.*

In truth, when Cat reached out, their parents rarely picked up. Boomer parents were a hands-off generation, and chatty phone calls were an extravagance. Her father surely had his hands full with their mother, and it was his habit to focus on his wife's needs instead of the pretty-okay and somewhat-stable kids.

The office was uncharacteristically austere, with only a laptop computer, one file folder, and a small stack of Alistair and Raj books on a metal desk. When her parents occupied this space, it had been alive with theater memorabilia and *Playbills* from their past, newspaper clippings and script pages littering the walls. Photographs of the campers and performances covered every inch of the bulletin board—evidence of her parents' devotion to the people and the place. Today it was devoid of artifacts, personality, or place—as if the office had been neutered, the humanity stripped from it. Cat felt the absence of her parents, their things, in that moment.

The office smelled sweet and damp, like a friendly mold had been waiting to greet Cat and say, *You're back! Yay!* The welcome bolstered Cat's desire to get to the bottom of whatever was going on and get out. She was not back.

Cat tugged at the desk drawer, the old-fashioned steel file cabinet handles, one, two, three, four, but everything was locked tight. Massive difference from years gone by, when nothing was ever secured because no one could find their keys. She slammed the drawer, which upset an empty, coffee-stained mug with the two bunnies Cat now knew as Alistair and Raj. Someone had drawn a noose around Alistair and put two *X*'s over Raj's eyes. As Cat righted the disturbing mug, she read the words printed evenly on a manila folder: *Gala RSVPs and VIPs*.

"Tell me about this gala," Cat said. If Bob had a workable plan to get donations, that would solve the immediacy of sorting out who was and wasn't on the mortgage. But no money and Cat's name on the bottom line was an anchor that would drag her back in time as if she'd never left the camp behind.

"You heard his pitch. He wants people to become like patrons or investors. That's why there's going to be a gala. Bob's an idea guy," Ginger said with admiration and as if she and he were birds of a feather.

"We've never had a fundraiser before. Did you think to ask why now?"

"He said it would bring publicity, and people would see what a great idea this is," Ginger said.

"Changing this camp from a kids' theater camp to an adult camp is one thing. Maybe it's more profitable," Cat said. "I don't know. But you can't ask for money from people who've already paid. Especially if they are anxious and depressed people. It's not ethical."

"I mean, some of them are just grumpy."

"That's not the point, Ginger. A mailing list and a few gentle requests for small donations . . . Mom and Dad did this. Hitting up vulnerable people is not okay. Does Bob have a business plan? Or is he hoping people will just give him money because he used to wear glasses and got in shape?"

Cat had been an intimate observer of how the camp's financials worked, the shoestring budget, and her father's frugal ways. Keeping it simple on purpose. Never scaling, as so many businesses did, and then failing because of it.

"He said this year was his pilot—the camp as a haven for people who don't fit in the world," Ginger said. "You know, to help them fit in. He says that he can hire real professionals if there's real money. Like therapists with degrees and everything. He said anxiety and depression can be eradicated."

"Who did he hire for this year?" Cat said slowly, an unease settling in even deeper.

"We all pitched in. I did art therapy. Shirtless led all the water cures. We had a grad student who took a yoga elective at Stevens Point. We had a whole menu of therapies, Empathy Games, Affirmation Catchphrases, Therapy Taboo, and the Doggie Paddle Depression Swim, where you breathe through the discomfort." Cat held her hand like a stop sign, but Ginger kept talking. "Bob gave massages. He said he almost had the certification, and his wife did Reiki. She has crazy-strong hands. Mostly, I think she likes it when people cry."

"Nobody had a license for anything? And people touched each other? And you were sleeping with Bob."

"I didn't think you wanted to be in charge, Cat," Ginger said, meeting Cat's eyes with defiance.

"I don't. You called me. I'm just . . ." *Falling into old patterns,* she thought.

"Seriously, we have bigger fish to catch, Cat," Ginger said.

Cat didn't correct her sister's faulty phrasing because Ginger was possibly right in this case. It sounded like the "professional" staff were the same people who helped elementary school kids memorize their lines and dog-paddle at the swimming pier. College kids. Not professionals specializing in caring for mental illness. During Ginger's bout with depression after Bard's birth, if she hadn't gotten professional help, who knows what would have happened. Cat would never forget Ginger's sallow face, her protruding collarbones and weight loss. How she held on to Cat at the doctor's office, cried with relief after taking her first antidepressant.

"Bob thought he'd take a stab at what no health professional to date has been able to get a handle on? He thinks paying college students to teach angsty people how to swamp a canoe and get back in without dying is the trick researchers have missed for decades?"

"It's an important skill. Surviving a sinking ship. You know that better than anyone."

The reference to Cat's escape was an obvious hit, but this conversation was not about Cat leaving, saving herself. It was about Bob's delusions and what felt like betrayal and fraud.

"Do you hear yourself?" Cat pinched the bridge of her nose. Talking to Ginger was like climbing a tree. You thought you were reaching for a logical branch, but her sister would point to a skinny twig as if it were substantial enough to hold the weight of whatever the discussion was about. "No. Ginger. That's not the point."

"The point is that if the camp is in trouble, Shirtless and I will be living with you. And I know you don't want that," Ginger said.

"Okay. That actually *is* the point," Cat said, opening the folder and scanning the names. "Seriously, though, who could Bob have invited that would contribute enough to amount to anything? I doubt a professor at Stevens Point has enough disposable cash to buy one of our canoes."

In a calm, professional-caregiver way, Cat ran her index finger down the page of invitees for this hinky gala, considering that maybe none of the invited were real people. Was everything a sham? But no, there was the name of the mayor of Stevens Point, and she recognized the chancellor of the college, and Ira Glass, from *This American Life*? Terry Gross from NPR. The governor of Wisconsin, *Outside* magazine, and the list went on. "Is this a joke?"

Ginger lifted her eyebrows and shook her head *no*.

"There are huge names on this list. This can't be," Cat said, pointing. "Did CNN really RSVP? That's not possible, is it?"

"He knows people. From when his book went big, before it got canceled."

"If the camp is broke and I'm on the mortgage, Bob had better have something more compelling to pitch than a passionate story about his childhood and his weird little bunnies."

Cat had no sooner finished this sentence than she came upon the *J*'s and a name that was as jarring as anything she'd seen. Jameson, Steve J.

"No," she said.

There was an asterisk and hashtag by his name. Cat flipped to the back page, tore off the staple holding the packet together, and looked for a key to the symbols. On the bottom of the last page, an asterisk meant he had RSVP'd, yes, that Steve, her Steve, the one who didn't know she was pregnant with his baby Steve, had been invited to her camp.

CHAPTER SEVEN

THE UNDERDOGS

Cat dropped the invitation list. Seeing Steve's name on a piece of paper at her childhood home felt like the Joker showing up in a kiddie cartoon. He had no business slicing through the membrane that separated her past from her present. "What in the hell is he doing on this list?"

"Who?" Ginger bent her head to read, but Cat slipped the paper into the folder. This was not the time to have a conversation about who the father of this baby was. And it was on brand for Ginger not to have asked that question yet.

She tried to recall the one conversation she'd had with Steve about her childhood. Cat hadn't brought it up, that was certain.

"Your family owns that nerdy theater camp," he'd said on their second date.

"Yeah, how'd you know?"

"Everyone knows about that place. Perfect spot for a water park," he'd said.

Cat had blown past the water park comment and focused on the phrase *Everyone knows about that place*. "Everyone knows?" The camp was small and remote; she doubted it was on anyone's radar. They kept to themselves, caused no trouble in town.

"Big money, water parks," Steve said.

Cat had scoffed, surprised at the strength of her aversion to the idea. Aside from the truth that Wisconsin water parks were mini cities of plastic and *E. coli* built where stunning wildernesses had been, she hadn't taken the notion seriously. No one in their right mind would plow over the camp's pristine acreage and replace it with urine-filled pools that gave swimmers folliculitis.

Steven had filled her wineglass, and Cat hadn't thought another thing about it. Until now. Cat froze like she'd just heard the lock on a cage jangle into place. "Ginger, how much did you know about all of this? The gala idea? Who was invited?"

Her sister had opened her mouth to speak when a short, solid gargoyle of a woman moved silently and smoothly into the doorway as if on rollers. "What, may I ask, are you two doing here?" She sounded like a cross between Joan Crawford and the Wicked Witch of the West.

Cat felt unaccountably guilty and childlike, while Ginger recoiled, whispering "The wife" as she shrank from the woman's gaze.

"I'm Cat—"

But the woman interrupted her. "I know who you are. Why are you in my husband's office?"

A veteran of standing up to controlling parents and football coaches, Cat got ahold of herself, squared her shoulders, and said, "You're mistaken there. My name is on the mortgage. Thus, I own this camp, and ergo, this is my office." Cat cringed at her use of the words *ergo* and *thus*. A throwback from too much Shakespeare, evidently brought on by proximity to the old Auditorium.

Uncowed, the woman replied, "You are thrice in error, my dear. Have no fear. I am here to set you straight."

Cat had to give it to the old bat. She'd one-upped her using the word *thrice*. If Cat hadn't been so ill-informed, she would have taken another shot, maybe in a British accent, possibly used the word *fortnight*—two weeks' time, not the video game.

"My husband's contract clearly states that rejuvenation of the grounds and the successful completion of one pivotal year will result in the transfer of ownership of said property to the camp director in residence at the time."

"That's preposterous," Cat said, unable to stop the bluster and formal language while her brain tried to grasp this new information.

"Well, that may be, dear girl, but you have your sister to thank for this. Her awesome signature is on the document, and she felt amazing when she signed it."

There was no mistaking the satisfied leer in Bob's wife's tone—the knowing way she used *amazing* and *awesome* to drive her point home. That a contract had been drawn up and knowingly signed if not fully read by Ginger—because something less than legal and more sexual had been negotiated at the same time. Ginger confirmed this by taking another small step back, shrinking even more behind Cat's shoulder.

"I didn't catch your name," Cat said, stalling. Was it possible that Cat wouldn't have to do a thing to get out from under the camp? She could stand back and let whatever contract Ginger had signed relieve Cat from her responsibilities, potential ownership and all? Or was it one of those be-careful-what-you-wish-for situations? When you think you know exactly what you want but are faced with the fine print, the details of your sunny yellow dreams suddenly turning into gray areas and the specter of a plastic wilderness being built over a real one.

"Elaine," Ginger whispered, warm and moist in her ear.

"Ms. Durand," Elaine said. "It's a pleasure to finally meet you." Ironic because the woman's voice was the least pleasurable thing around.

Nobody smiled or offered a hand to shake. Cat stood, her feet firmly planted on the worn flooring, her hand resting possessively on the top of the metal desk, the cool surface where her parents planned theater production after production, carefully considering the needs of elementary school children, adapting scenes for kids with lisps and spotty memories. Instilling pride and mastery into a line typically recited by adults. *Out, damned spot!*

"If you're looking for your parents' tchotchkes"—Elaine said the word as if it were spoiled milk she wanted to spit out—"they're in a box somewhere."

"Artifacts of their life's work? Yes. I would like them."

"I understand you don't involve yourself much here." The reference to Cat's absence tweaked her poorly buried guilt at leaving their father to fend for himself. "Once Bob and I took control, well, we had priorities. The grounds, the programming, the future. You, of all people, knew what a dump this place was, or you would have stayed."

The word *dump* rang a defensive bell in Cat, who said, "You don't mow a lawn and take over a camp, Elaine. I don't care what piece of paper you guys think you signed. Green grass and a bunch of anxious people do not a successful camp make."

"'Do not a successful camp make,'" Ginger said, like an uncertain Greek chorus.

Despite Cat's irritation at Ginger's mousy, predictable, irresponsible behavior, she felt every ounce the protector at this moment. Not only because of their genetics and history but also because Ginger and, yes, Shirtless, were emblematic of humanity's Achilles' heel: the gentle soul often bringing out the worst in others. Woe to anyone who didn't have every single capitalist duck in a row because there was always someone ready and willing to take advantage of them.

Feeling boxed in by Elaine's bully energy, Cat stepped toward her. She had to get control of her desire to push this woman out of the camp, down the road, and into a drainage culvert. Because Elaine, despicable energy aside, could be Cat's first-class ticket out—forever washing her hands of this place. She could shrug her shoulders and report that Ginger had signed the place away. Nothing Cat could do.

Out of the cloudless summer sky, Ginger said, "Apparently I don't have full authority to sign over ownership of this camp, as Cat's name is still on the mortgage." And without taking a breath, she said, "You'd have known that if you'd done your due diligence."

Cat turned her head, made direct eye contact with her sister, and mouthed *Due diligence?* Ginger had said a lot of surprising things in their lives, but never had she used a legal phrase correctly before.

"I read, you know," Ginger hissed, returning to her teenage self.

"I mean. Do you?" Cat said, like a snotty kid, in front of the woman who wanted nothing else than to divide and conquer them. Cat collected herself and was about to say, *Examination of the complete documents will reveal* . . . but stopped herself. She didn't know where the documents were, what they said, or if she wanted (or more importantly needed) to be part of this land-grab conversation. She blinked with fatigue. Solving this puzzle of camp ownership, debt, and whether a lawn care requirement led to ownership had Cat feeling like she'd been shot with an Ambien.

"We'll take good care of the place," Elaine said softly, kindly.

Part of Cat's brain wanted to reach out for that silky-sweet come-hither voice and offer a no-fuss capitulation. But a memory dodged her exhaustion and rolled into place. In college, Cat asleep in her twin bed in her dorm room had been startled awake by banging on the door. A man's voice shouted like a storybook wolf, "Open up. Let me in." Cat had left the door unlocked for her roommate. All the man had to do was try the knob, and Cat knew he would soon. As silently as the old springs of the bed allowed, Cat crept toward the dead bolt, the floor creaked, and the man said, barely above a whisper, "Yes, that's right. Unlock the door. It'll be fine."

A fraction of a second after Cat had shakily flung the lock in place, the man grabbed the doorknob and shook it. Panting, hands clasped on her chest, Cat watched the brass knob rattle, knowing nothing would have been fine if it had opened. Nothing at all.

"We have no intention of conversing about this at this juncture without examination of the budget, legal documents, et cetera, et cetera, et cetera," Cat said like the King of Siam, a part she'd been the stand-in for decades before. *What the hell?*

Unfazed, Elaine said, "The camp is one big debt. If you wanted this place, you never would have let it get this bad. Never left it to that one." She gestured with her chin to Ginger as if Elaine wouldn't spare the breath to say her sister's name. "Or your weirdo nephew who can't put on a shirt without a breakdown."

"Hey," Ginger said, offended.

"Hey," Cat said, equally offended.

Shirtless didn't say a word as he stepped, that second, into the room. He didn't need to; the skin on his neck spoke for him. In Shirtless's flush of red splotches, Cat saw that he'd heard Elaine, and his response was shame and dermatitis. Something he'd developed as soon as he'd acquired a sense of self.

Shirtless. So tall, broad, and handsome, with their father's aquiline nose—his perfect profile for a romantic lead, if not for his aversion to leading, standing out, sticking out. Since Cat had spied him at the meeting, he'd pulled his camp shirt off and stuffed it into the back pocket of his shorts. Shirtless scratched his neck and noticed his mother giving him a head shake. He dropped his hand and stuffed it in his pocket.

A young woman appeared at his shoulder and said, "Shirtless. Are you coming to the Mess Hall?"

Cat saw the red in his neck fade slightly. The young woman, possibly Shirtless's age, took his forearm, and instead of flinching with sensitivity, he allowed it. Either her nephew had changed dramatically, or this woman was something special. He caught Cat's eye again and widened his in warning, before allowing the young woman to lead him out of the hall and away.

Elaine smirked. "Ahhhh, Shirtless. Poor thing. Yes, you'll have to find a place for him, won't you? Somewhere he can show off that physique, shall we say? Doubt he'll go far without his little friend. Someone with her own limitations. But he's used to that with his mother. No?"

Cat was a lot of things. Independent. Stubborn. Easily annoyed. But embedded in her core was the cold, hard, unmovable fact that she could not abide a predator. Playground hierarchy, multilevel-marketing-leggings-selling neighbor, fake mental health camp, or, for that matter, intolerant bank. If a hostile takeover was involved, win or lose, Cat couldn't help but fight for the underdog. For all their faults, her parents had created a space, a few weeks a year, for kids who loved make-believe to play without boundaries. Elaine was a bully and, in Cat's mind, what was wrong with the world.

Cat smoothed her hand over her belly protectively and sized Elaine up. The thought of single-handedly prying Elaine and Bob loose from Summer Camp swamped Cat's energy.

Ginger tugged her elbow, and Cat inhaled. "Look, Ellen. Can I call you Ellen?"

"Elaine," the woman said.

"Ellen, if you think that because we grew up at a theater camp, we have a loosey-goosey grasp on reality, you are sorely mistaken," Cat said.

"Is that right?" the woman said, unmoved. No question she didn't buy what Cat was selling.

"That's right," Ginger piped up. "My sister is a lawyer and will take you to court. Don't think for one minute she hasn't been keeping an eye on this camp."

Cat tried not to blink, frown, or gasp at the bald-faced lie and watched Elaine's expression. Was that a micro-moment of uncertainty that passed across her sourpuss face? That maybe she'd missed this important juris doctor detail?

Theater was what they were good at, Cat and Ginger, and Cat leaned into the falsity that she was equipped with a legal degree. Cat felt like this outsider had no business judging this place, finding she and her sister lacking. Even if she had left years ago, she had something to say.

"This camp is our family's home. Our legacy. And we're not handing it over to the likes of you." Cat pushed past the woman, trying for a theatrical exit, the kind that brought gasps as intermission curtains swung closed. But halfway out the door, Ginger stepped on the back of Cat's right shoe, then left, yanking both shoes off Cat's feet. When

Cat bent to pull her sneaker back into place, Ginger all but climbed onto her back.

"Jesus, Ginger," Cat said.

"Sorryeee, Cat. Maybe don't stop walking without warning me."

"Get off my shoe," Cat hissed.

"Maybe tie them a little tighter next time."

Cat felt Elaine's eyes on them, knowing with certainty that Bob's wife did not need to say a thing to win this argument. It was clear who were the underdogs in this situation, and it wasn't oddball Bob and his mean wife, Elaine.

CHAPTER EIGHT

NIRVANA

Outside and away from Elaine's piercing gaze, Cat hopped on each foot, snugging her shoes back on.

Her big belly pulled her balance right then left until she felt a hand on her elbow and a voice saying, "Whoa, mama." The chubby dancing man from Bob's speech.

"Yeah, 'Whoa, mama,'" Ginger said but in a teasing way. "I've got her, Norm."

Norm gave Ginger the thumbs-up and chuckled off.

"Did you mean it, Cat? You'll help?" Ginger's astonished expression set Cat's teeth on edge.

"I'm here, aren't I?" Cat stared at her sister. Wasn't she helping right this second? Didn't she drop everything and drive here to face the dizzying déjà vu of her family memories while she grew her own inside her?

"What was that woman talking about? Bob owns the place if he mows the lawn?" Cat added, trying to keep her frustration in check. "Where's his contract? What exactly does it say?"

"I left the job description and contract writing up to him. I don't know how to do that stuff. And before you explode, I may not know all his plans"—and she gestured to the space where Bob had given his speech—"but I promise you, he's a good guy."

Cat clenched her jaw to keep all the words, phrases, and long-form lectures that her brain was shoveling forward from flying out of her mouth. She took a slow breath and exhaled to calm herself.

Her sister was serious, and they were all going to get hurt because of it.

"I know what you're thinking, but you don't know him like I do. He helps me."

"I need to get Lefty out of the car," Cat said, wanting more than anything to feel his soft new-potato nose in her palm, his calming presence a reminder of her home. When Cat was in her life away from camp, her mind didn't buzz with thoughts of bullies, family, legacy, patterns, and potential failure. She'd created a life that worked, that she could manage. A quiet refuge of one, soon to be two. If she focused on getting home, she could stay detached from the chaos.

"You sit here. I'll get him." Ginger steered Cat to a small stone wall in front of the Administration Building. Cat closed her eyes, grateful to take a minute. A small truce. She touched a rough rock ledge, so much shorter than she recalled, and nodded at Ginger.

"Remember when that kid with the glass eye clotheslined himself on this thing, and his eye popped out?" Cat said.

"Do I? I still have nightmares about that. Then Dad wiped it with his red hankie and eased it back in." Ginger affected their father's voice: "'You can't play Othello with a hole in your head, buddy.'"

That soft red piece of cloth in his pocket, always ready for sweat, tears, or whatever human liquids needed wiping up. Cat hoped he'd left one of those behind somewhere. "I never could stand the juicy stuff. I could never go into the Nurses' Lodge."

"That fishhook in that kid's thumb laid you out," Ginger said.

"My blood. Their blood. Even the suggestion of it does me in."

Ginger gently tucked a strand of hair behind Cat's ear. "No blood here today. Hang tight, I'll be right back."

Cat had about twenty seconds of peace, then watched as a swarm of people moved from the meeting space onto the sidewalks and lawn.

Each hauled a combination of rolling bags, duffels, and backpacks. Some had cloth totes with Summer Camp branding—*The Cure for What Ails (the) US*—the tiny word *the* between *Ails* and *US* adding to the puzzling message.

People threw their arms around each other and made promises of phone calls and real-world meetings. Cat could hear individual conversations ricochet from the Administration Building to the lake and back. The camp was an acoustical drum—roaming campers historically had to be extra quiet if they didn't want their secrets heard. Her father used to police the camp's nighttime goings-on while seated on this very perch.

Like a swarm of starlings, the exiting campers moved as one, each dressed in the familiar postcamp fashion—flannel shirts tied around middles, bandannas knotted at throats, and woven bracelets on wrists. No one looked anxious or depressed. In the center of it all, Bob Durand set the pace. Like a short celebrity, he made eye contact, clasped hands, and wished the best. Cat squinted, tried to see what the campers saw. The Bob of her youth didn't have two popcorn kernels for brain cells rolling around in his head. Had he changed, or was he still the discombobulated, horny Bob, who aspired to be anything but the bigger boys' target?

She swatted at a mosquito, unable to look away. The women loved him, touching his arm, vying for attention, moving close to whisper something in his ear. The men smiled admiringly, and Cat could almost hear their thoughts—*That son of a bitch has a way with the ladies*, head shakes, *Gotta hand it to him*. If they'd only known Bob when Cat knew Bob, they'd never think such a thing.

The sound of air brakes, bus wheels, gravel grinding under tires, and Bob announced, "Ladies and gentlemen, your chariot home awaits." The crowd groaned, laughed, and slowed.

They did not want to leave.

Lefty bounded to Cat's side, his tongue lolling out of his doggie grin as if they'd been apart for a month, Ginger close behind.

"There's Bob," Ginger said simply, handing Cat a water bottle and granola bar she'd retrieved from Cat's car. "Take a drink, you look pale."

"He was an idiot back in the day," Cat said, sipping her water.

"He's not an idiot. He's . . . creative," Ginger said. "And smarter than you think."

Cat saw there was hurt there, the way her sister put her thumb over her tattoo.

"He doesn't love Elaine."

Cat could have said something frank about how numerous women before Ginger had probably said that, but instead she said, "He's handsome. In a short-king, less muscular Tom Cruise way."

"All those women around him are slipping their phone numbers into his hands. By the end of the day, his pockets will be lined with torn scraps of paper and digits. He has an old cigar box filled with them. He thinks it shows people have hope for the future, even if it's not a future with him."

"That's weird. And wrong. Gross."

Ginger shrugged. "Yeah, well. People are lonely."

Cat watched Ginger watch Bob and, for the first time, considered that even among an ever-changing stream of people arriving and departing, Ginger knew what she was talking about. People were lonely.

"See that man with the crazy-angry eyebrows? We call him the 'mad dad.' At least we did when he came two weeks ago. He bitched constantly about his kids, twin boys who sucked at sports. Apparently he was a high school wrestling hero. The first day here, he challenged all the other men to a grapple. I thought grapple was a kind of juice, y'know? Anyway, he got steadily more chill as the weeks went on and won the Zen beach-raking competition. His raking technique . . ." Ginger took a bite of Cat's granola bar and said, "Stunning."

Cat snatched what was left of her snack and scowled at her sister. An expression that Ginger didn't see, her eyes on Bob as he passed them.

"That woman, trailing behind Bob"—Ginger indicated with her chin—"she came with these huge lips that deflated when she took a sauna and then jumped into the mud pit. When she realized her lips were gone, she shouted, 'C'est la vie!' When she gets home, she's going to start a campaign against fillers called C'est La Lips. I guess she's fairly wealthy." Ginger reached for the granola bar, but Cat blocked her with her elbow and shoved the rest of the sticky, hot bits in her mouth.

"It's time to talk to Bob," Cat said, losing an oat as she spoke.

"Let the people get on the bus before you unload on Bob. If you confront him now, it could get messy. If investors are in that group, we don't want to tarnish the postcamp glow."

This reasonable advice from the sister who'd hired Bob stopped Cat from grabbing him by the back of the neck and hauling him into the office.

"Okay. I'll wait until the bus leaves. I'll talk to Bob, and then I need to get home. Get into my own computer. Look at the mortgage in my files. I need information."

If she got a cord from Bob, she could charge her phone, pull up her files, compare documents with her sister, but all Cat could think about was being home in her own space, without the camp and her sister breathing down her neck with their *What next?* energy that was screwing with her logical thinking.

"You're not staying the night?" Ginger said, sounding like the little sister who needed back scratches to fall asleep at night. Cat's fingertips tingled with the memory of her sister's tiny ribs, her soft skin. She heard Ginger's soft child's voice: "To the left, Kitty. Now to the right. Right there. Oops, it moved." Her sister's voice was so young. So needy.

Cat saw Ginger trying not to tug out a tuft of hair or two because she couldn't help herself. Her sister had made a lot of progress—Cat saw her clasp her hands together. The exiting campers were lined up at the rustic entrance to the parking lot. "What's happening over there?"

"Those two women manning the table are handing back any meds they checked in with, their craft projects, et cetera," said Ginger. "The blonde is Wynn, the cook. She gives everyone a treat for the road. The other one, June, works in the Health Hut. She's Bard's friend. They're all friends, really."

"None of them look old enough to do those jobs."

"That's what I'm telling you, Cat. Everyone was hired as an assistant to the chef, nurse, or yogi, but none of the people Elaine said she hired showed up. I know you think I'm a total conspiracy theorist, but nothing Elaine said would happen . . . happened. Elaine is the problem."

"I doubt Elaine is trying to overthrow a rustic theater getaway. Especially now that it's run by a generation of kids who couldn't make the rotary dial on our old-fashioned red emergency phones call 911 if they needed to," said Cat.

"Yes, they can. I showed them," Ginger said, missing the original point. "All the kids did a great job faking it as professionals. Honestly, Cat, Dad would be proud. We may not be doing classical theater, but everyone on staff is an amazing actor. And look." Ginger gestured to the still-congealed mass of people moving as one. "Everyone is happier than when they came, which Bob said would happen, and it did."

"Dad would not be proud. Bob swindled these people with fake treatments. And where's the money? They had to pay something. Why is the camp going broke? Is the camp going broke?"

"Obviously. That's why I called you. I think Elaine used all the money on the grounds and supplies for the gala. Bob wanted a small party to showcase the simple beauty of the place. But no, Elaine said it had to be fancy."

The exiting campers made a well-ordered line past the table where June and Wynn were, and Cat and Ginger moved closer. No one acknowledged them; it was as if they were ghosts from the past, eavesdropping on the present. Cat recognized the man who'd steadied her. He hefted an old army green duffel onto his shoulder, accepted his phone from June.

"So, June? What's life going to look like for you after camp?" said Norm.

"I'm trying not to think about it. Literally." Her pale skin flushed and connected the freckles that dusted her cheeks. This was Shirtless's friend, and her gentle nature was as obvious as her hazel eyes and thick, lush eyelashes. People who worked at a summer camp were a certain kind of person. They didn't have the aspirations of millionaires or internships as a finance bro. They were kids who wanted to sing songs about squirrels, play, and make damn sure everyone was having a good, safe time.

The other woman handing out tidily wrapped baked goods put her arm around her friend's shoulders. "You've got a whole summer of being a nurse behind you. And you're so good at it."

June shot a guilty gaze at her friend, clearly uncomfortable with the title, hanging on for the final moments when she could return to being whatever she was when she wasn't playing nurse with people who possibly needed a nurse. "I just want to keep working here."

"I sure as shit don't want to go home. I can tell you that," the man said, looking over his shoulder like he might make a break for it, hiding out in one of the cabins. "Everyone needs a place like this. To get out in the fresh air. Swim, play hard, get in shape."

Wynn reached into her cardboard box of goodies and said, "Here, Norm. I made you this." He took the package and gazed at the Chex Mix within, his caterpillar eyebrows tenting, making him look like he might cry. "We all have a bit of returnaphobia. It's hard to think about real life when you're in nirvana. That used to be a band name, did you know that?"

Norm smiled. "I did know that."

The two women looked at him with interest. Straight backs, eyes wide, they resembled two meerkats: one dark-haired, one fair. Interested, sweet, and untroubled women stopping in the march toward life and loss to listen to the mad-sad man. Someone possibly knowledgeable about a band where the lead singer committed suicide, leaving behind a whole generation of fans who believed in the moniker.

"Yes, Nirvana was very popular," he added kindly.

"Hang on. I have another treat for you," Wynn said. In the bottom of her box sat a lone baggie of cookies tied with a ribbon, a card stapled to it like a flag. "I used red and blue for your decoration because I know how much you like the Patriots. Plus, I gave you extra because of how hard you worked this week."

He didn't reach for it right away. Cat saw he wanted to say something to this sunny girl with her Meg Ryan smile, the one from Meg's early career, not the oddly crafted one of her later years.

"Thank you," he said with real appreciation.

Wynn seemed to ooze lemon custard happiness from her pores. "Bye-bye, Grumpus. Helloooo, Happy," she said in a thoroughly engaging way. "Now, don't gobble them up all at once."

"One per night as needed," June added, sounding like a nurse giving a prescription.

Norm tried to give them back. "I gained weight from your cooking. I don't need going-away fat too."

As if Cat had suddenly materialized, Norm blinked and offered her the cookie bag, "Here, you're eating for two."

Wynn put her hand out like a basketball player blocking a shot and said "Nope" abruptly, then softened her tone, adding, "No tag backs. They're yours."

June, quick like a bunny, tossed a baggie of a white powder-covered mix at Cat, who caught it with one hand. "It's Chex Mix with sugar and peanut butter. It's got a little protein."

"Ohhhh, fast hands," said Norm. "You girls are something special." And he hitched his duffel an inch higher and walked in the wrong direction for the bus.

Cat caught a traded glance between the two women; they were in on something, and Cat looked for confirmation from Ginger. Her sister was hauling ass into the Craft Lodge, yanking Cat's go bag behind her, the traitor Lefty hop-running along behind. She returned to examining June and Wynn, but Cat found them sweet and sunny as the next camper approached.

Alone and seemingly beneath notice, Cat watched the adults boarding the bus, just as she had seen children and their parents do for years. Instead of her mother and father in the parking lot, handing out printed participation diplomas and requoting lines from the play they'd all performed, there stood Bob. An unhurried Elaine joined him, a clipboard tucked under her arm.

It was an odd feeling to be here but not involved in the mechanisms of campers leaving. Watching Bob and Elaine, who were not her parents, on the site of her home that, until she had proof, wasn't hers anymore. The detached feeling she'd previously cultivated clicked toward maternal as she watched a camper stumble on the bus step. It was as if she were on one side of a soap bubble, and if she wasn't careful, it would pop and she'd be inside it all again.

Like a lone spirit of campers past, Cat slipped away, intending to return to Bob's office, where she could search every nook and cranny. She'd wipe fingerprints away with a camp T-shirt and leave it behind, so there'd be no trace of her after she'd left.

CHAPTER NINE

HAPPY RATS

With Bob in the parking lot, no longer funneling people toward the exit, stray campers boomeranged back onto the grounds for one last wistful glance at the serene lake, the pine-scented grounds, the memories.

Cat dodged a woman who, now rearmed with her camera, stopped to take a selfie while flashing a peace sign. Cat might not want to give her childhood, her future, to the camp, but she understood the appeal of the place. The uncomplicated, playful life, the lure of group culture where everyone present was on the same page. A page they'd never considered turning before they arrived at camp. A hike in the mud? Hell yeah. So many s'mores that your eyelids are sticky, absolutely. Hanging from a harness with a barely qualified college student with ADHD, you bet!

She listed sideways with the weight of her stomach while trying to inconspicuously hustle around the mournful leftovers. A woman in a jumbo-size tie-dyed T-shirt stepped out of Cat's blind spot and into her path. "Do you know where Bob is?"

"In the parking lot," said Cat, trying to move past her.

"I'm going to give this to Bob," said the woman instead of sprinting off.

Cat eyed a dream catcher with purple-and-green-variegated yarn crisscrossing several purple-stained Popsicle sticks. Before Cat could reply with *Good for you?* or another vague phrase to head off a conversation, another woman joined the first and said, "If we hang back, we might get to talk to him without the entire camp of drippy idiots butting in."

Drippy idiots? Cat thought that was a bold insult from a woman clutching a pair of irregularly sewn moccasins and wearing a name tag with the words I'M JOLLY JANICE written in purple Sharpie.

A ginger-haired man with shorty-cargo shorts and thick socks, looking every bit older-leprechaun-goes-hiking, said, "Bob?"

The two women nodded toward the parking lot and watched the man trudge off. It was like a middle-aged Easter egg hunt where Bob was the egg, and everyone wanted him for their basket.

Cat backed away from the women and ungracefully jog-walked the last few feet into the Administration Building. A couple sprang apart at the sound of the opening doors with a hot, guilty, and disheveled look—the man's arm at an awkward angle down the woman's green camp shirt.

"Bob's in the parking lot," Cat said, knowing they'd want to know for the same reasons she did: How long did they have to do whatever deed they had in mind before the bus left? After turning the tight corner, she grabbed the doorknob. Locked now. No worries. Cat retrieved a gray folding chair, startling the couple again. "You guys. Find another spot."

The pair darted away, and Cat dragged a chair outside the office door. She heaved herself up and slid a light square ceiling tile back from a metal support. Her father hid things. Keys, maps, shiny things. Easter was his favorite holiday, as long as no one cried while looking for a basket. He'd hate to see her searching anxiously for the camp's finances or mortgage papers, as Cat was doing this minute.

Voices: "Bob and Elaine?" A door opened and closed. Someone shouted "Amanda," like the woman might be drowning. Cat blinked, dust dropping from the space, her fingers blindly reaching. There it was. She grasped a key attached to a strap. She returned the panel, stepped off the chair, and slid the key into the lock.

Inside the office, Cat closed the door firmly behind her and examined the small leather bracelet that functioned as a key ring. Cat ran her fingers over the etched words: FAILURE IS A CHANCE TO BEGIN AGAIN. Her father had made them for kids' prizes or as souvenirs to purchase from the Canteen.

After one of Ginger's screwups while under Cat's supervision, her father had made the first bracelet of its kind. Now, she realized he'd done it as a motivator; then, Cat had recoiled at the word *failure* attached to her wrist. Later that day, Cat unsnapped the leather band while swimming and let it sink to the bottom of the lake.

He'd tried, her father, and without him the place would have gone under long ago. He held the answers, and if Cat could charge her damn phone or get ahold of one that actually connected to a tower somewhere, she'd call him until he picked up.

A sharp noise outside moved Cat to action, and then she saw that the *Gala RSVPs and VIPs* folder was gone. "Dammit, Janet," she said, a phrase from her mother, one Cat hadn't used in ten years.

She tried several drawers again, then eased herself to the floor, looking for a magnetic key holder attached to the metal desk, another safeguard her father loved. Several clots of petrified gum clung to the bottom of the desk, and Cat yanked her hand back. "Gross, Ginger." When her sister was grounded to office duty for missing curfew or sleeping through the morning meeting, she'd attach her gum as a gluey protest against their parents' punishments.

The thin center drawer slid open easily, and a pen and pencil rattled next to a cluster of rubber bands, a pink old-school slab eraser, and two dusty jelly beans. Some joker hit the horn on the bus, making Cat jump as if she were trespassing and weren't part owner. She was sitting back on her heels, ready to lean into the catastrophe of getting herself off the floor, when she spotted a small, squat safe near the copy machine.

On her hands and knees, she grasped the safe handle, and the door swung open. Empty. "Ugh. Why is everything so hard." She looked at the acoustic tile above her head—a yellow pencil stuck out of one of the holes.

This day had not been on her to-do list, and a wave of fatigue slid over her again. She considered curling up and napping, letting everyone find her tired breaking-and-entering self. This could be her pregnancy exhaustion, but Cat suspected it was the beginning of how she often felt when overwhelmed by asks. Her therapist had suggested that Cat adopt it later in life as a passive way of saying no to bids for help. A no could be cajoled, argued with; a nap had to be tiptoed around. Either way it was a reminder for Cat to watch her boundaries.

When the office door creaked open an inch, Cat had the impulse to hide, press herself against the copy machine. Instead, bold as you please, she stood there, belly out, ready for a rumble.

Bob slid quietly into the office looking like a kid hiding from a seeker. Once the door had clicked shut, Bob pressed his back against it and said, "Think. Think. Think." He closed his eyes, rolled toward the paneling, and knocked his head against the woody knots shaped like owls and ghost faces. Bump, bump, bump, his head hit the wall as if a head injury brought genius.

"Bob. What the hell?" Cat said.

He stopped, and without looking at Cat, he grasped the doorknob as if to escape.

"Durand," Cat said, in her father's tone that held the message *Halt or I'll shoot.*

He sighed, pulled his charming-boy-Bob mask over his features, and said, "Cat McCarthy. I've been looking all over for you."

"Is that right?" Cat said.

"It surely is. I came in here to do a little reset." He made his eyes go wide with relatability and said, "Being in charge can be taxing. But you know that, Cat McCarthy, the most practical of the McCarthy girls."

"Women."

"Of course," he said, nodding rapidly. "Women. All grown-up women." He shook himself like a wet dog, right down to his fingertips. "I'm thrilled you're here. Big plans for this place. You'll be so proud of what we've achieved. Ginger and Shirtless. Amazing people. Just amazing."

"What's this about the camp being bankrupt?"

"That's a powerful word." Bob's gaze skittered around as if he was looking for listening ears.

"Is it true? Is there enough money to keep the camp solvent?"

Cat knew if there wasn't enough money to pay the bills, and if her name was on legal papers associated with a bankruptcy, no matter what her father intended or was cosmically fair, her nest egg would be dissolved, the creditors paid. Her no-muss, no-fuss dreams of being a mother would become epically fussy.

"We don't have quite as much as we'd hoped now," Bob said.

"Do you and Elaine have enough to buy this place from us? Because if you want it, we're not going to just give it to you."

Cat shoved the image of her father's deflated face, his sad understanding eyes when she delivered the news that they'd sold the place to cover debts, to keep her house and finances intact. Would he see it as a betrayal, or would he blame himself? Cat swallowed the hard, guilty lump the thought created in her throat.

"Oh no. Nope. We sure can't. That's why—" he started, but Cat had had enough.

"I need you to hand over all financial forms, the mortgage files, my father's original documents, the title, and whatever ridiculous contract"—Cat used air quotes when she said *contract*—"you and Ginger signed when you came on board. I need to see the budget, property tax bill, bank balances, and exactly where the money is coming from and going. If my sister and her son are correct, I'm still legally on the paperwork, and withholding that from me is a felony." Cat had no earthly idea if that was true or not, but if she didn't know, she suspected Bob didn't either.

"Of course," he said as if all was fine, as if she hadn't just seen him knocking his head against the wall. Then his smile widened, and he dropped his arms and clasped his hands as if he was about to take a bow. "My goodness, it's terrific to see you, Cat. Cat McCarthy." He tsked three times, shaking his head. "And may I say, don't you look beautiful. Substantial."

"I'm pregnant, Bob."

"Well, of course you are," he said, but it was clear he hadn't put her tight round belly together with a pregnancy even for a second. "And a lawyer, I hear. Just tremendous."

"Where do you keep the files, Bob? I'm tired," she said, knowing she should come clean about having never gone to law school. Could she get in trouble for impersonating someone who knew something useful? These thoughts made her realize how sapped of energy she was. There were times during the pregnancy when she felt energetic, alert, and ready to clean the junk drawer and organize every single baby accoutrement she'd purchased at Target and lugged into her living room. Then there were the other days where she felt as if she'd been roofied by the baby. These were the days she eyed an empty grocery cart at the Metro Market and sized it for space and sturdiness as a napping location.

Recently, after a trip to the post office, Cat had sat on a park bench with her eyes closed, needing a microsleep to take the edge off her drug-like fatigue, until a policeman said, "No sleeping," as if she'd put up a tent and built a campfire. Cat tried to explain that she needed a minute before she got behind the wheel. He'd interrupted her. "Move it along," he'd said as if he were a copper in a black-and-white movie. Noticing her pregnancy, he'd added, "Ma'am," stopping short of a hat tilt.

"I need a cord to charge my phone. I need Ginger's phone," Cat said.

"Walk with me," Bob said, and because Cat knew there was nothing in the office and was too tired to argue, she followed Bob out of the office. "Did you see the flower bed by the Mess Hall?" he said with pride. "People really like those little touches."

"Not if the place goes under while you're adding flowers, Bob."

He nodded reasonably, as if she'd made a good point.

He steered her down the main path, and Cat saw they were heading toward the Director's Cabin, her family's old residence, which sat behind the Administration Building and across the road.

"When my book skyrocketed onto the bestseller lists, it was a whirlwind of excitement and opportunity. I plowed my business forward, headstrong and naive. That's when I saw the folly of not hiring a PR team. That interview with Gayle, Oprah's best friend, started the trouble."

Cat knew some of this. She'd seen the news, but listening took less energy than talking or demanding. As long as they were on their way to retrieving the files, he could yak it up, for all she cared.

"When that right-wing watchdog group touted my book as part of a pro-choice, anti–Catholic Church agenda, I had no idea how to cope. I had to google the Catholic Church's stand on procreation and bunnies to understand the review. I didn't have an agenda, indeed not a religious or political one. I said to Elaine, 'Am I running for office? Like, did I agree to that accidentally?'"

You could see Bob had not gotten over being so misunderstood.

"Alistair and Raj were different but friendly. How is that a bad thing?" Bob said, and Cat wondered how often Elaine had to listen to Bob explain that he was in fact a simpleton and not the big thinker people were giving him credit for. "That's why this opportunity is so important to me. I want to show everyone I understand people. People can feel better if they can just get away."

Ironically, publishing his Alistair and Raj story made it clear to Cat how deeply he did not understand the sheer complexity of people. Nor did he understand that there was more to a successful concept than a good idea. There was, among other things, accounting.

They were halfway across the parking lot, the bus and campers had gone, and her car sat where she'd left it. Bob stopped and turned to Cat. "If all goes as planned this time, I will make a human Rat Park."

Cat had to ask. "Rat Park?"

"Rat Park! That Canadian researcher's theory is that rats only get addicted to heroin when you isolate them, but if you create a community where they can eat and play, they refuse opiates. I mean, not all opiates, of course. Not the naturally occurring ones that come from mating. But rats and playtime equal happy rats. No meds needed."

"You're saying the happy rats just say no?"

"Exactly," Bob said, shaking his head agreeably. "You've always been so smart."

"Those people that just left. Were they addicts?"

"No, nothing like that. Just run-of-the-mill sad people. You know, people that have run aground, so to speak. Or maybe they don't fit in anymore." He bent his head, cupped his mouth, lowered his voice: "I call them Unusuals. Not to their face, mind you. Nobody wants to be unusual."

If she hadn't been so tired, so focused on getting all the documents, Cat might have asked Bob if this idea had come from his own life, he being the original *unusual* she recalled from camp. He'd come wearing a necktie at seven years old and couldn't be persuaded to remove it until he'd gotten soaked in a balloon fight, if Cat remembered correctly.

"Or," Bob continued, scratching his forehead, "they've gotten themselves into an anxious and depressed frame of mind."

"You mean they've been diagnosed with a mood disorder?"

"Well, I don't know anything about a diagnosis. But you know those nervy people who sleep a lot. We get them out of bed into a canoe. And boom, happiness ensues."

"'Boom, happiness ensues?'" Cat said, trying for a sardonic tone, but Bob nodded rapidly, as if he were a British cartoon: *By Jove, she's got it!*

An older-model transport van clunked up beside them, Elaine in the driver's seat, and before Cat realized what was happening, Bob said, "Go get some of that canoe happiness for yourself while we're at the bank getting the papers." Then he grasped one of her hands, stood between Cat and her view of Elaine, and said convincingly, "You can trust me, Cat."

Cat had a flash of what Ginger probably felt, that Bob was a sincere person and they were in good hands. In a quick movement, the passenger-side door swung open, and Bob got in. "We keep everything in a safety-deposit box for security reasons. You understand." He glanced at his watch and said, "We want to get there before they close."

The door slammed shut, the van lurched forward several feet, and then it stopped with a jerk. Bob stuck his head out the window.

"By the way. The gala will help with any budget shortcomings, and thanks for sending Steve our way. You know, the water park guy? He took all the mystery out of our banking needs. I'd never even heard of a balloon loan."

Elaine hit the gas, Bob groped for the dashboard, and Cat's fatigue slid into alarm at hearing *gala, Steve, banking,* and *balloon loan* stuffed together and tossed out of a moving vehicle's window.

As if her voice were a parachute and she was tumbling from a great height, Cat shouted, "Where are the phones, Bob?" with such force she felt her tonsils vibrate with the effort. And Bob casually waved goodbye, without a care in the world.

CHAPTER TEN

A CUDDLE WITH AL

Cat tasted gravel dust from Elaine's speedy exit. Sending Steve their way? A balloon loan? Her stomach lurched with the sour implications of each of those undigestible variables. She pointed herself to the Craft Lodge to corner Ginger. Her sister had to know more than she had confessed.

Panting after speed walking across the lawn, Cat worked to catch her breath at the bottom of the cabin's stairs. It felt like the baby's fist had ahold of a lung, as if to say, *Hold on, lady, take it easy.* As Cat straightened, Ginger opened the door, and Lefty bounded out.

"Ginger," Cat said, letting her voice climb the front steps instead of her hardworking body. "Do you know anything about a balloon loan?"

"Did Bob order one of those big balloons for the camp?" Ginger said, and she waved Cat up the stairs.

"No. Ginger." Cat exhaled, and the words came out harsher than she wanted. "A balloon loan is a huge payment when a loan becomes due. It would be a disaster for this place. Did someone take out a loan?" Cat considered asking Ginger if she'd ever heard of Steve. Had he been to the camp? Why did he seem to be showing up on lists and lips connected to the camp and its finances?

Ginger blinked at the word *disaster* and took a step toward her sister. "I put you in the guest room across from my room. Is that okay, or did you want to sleep in the same room with me?" It was a nod to their olden days, when they'd cuddled together in one twin bed because Ginger was afraid of the dark.

"I want to know how much debt we're in. That's what I want to know. Can you please keep up?"

Ginger gave her head an impatient shake as if it were Cat who was missing the point of this conversation. "Just because my thoughts don't mirror yours with exactly the same intensity doesn't mean I'm not keeping up. I called you for help, didn't I? I know we're in trouble."

Lefty licked Cat's hand, then flopped onto his back and shimmied. He was no doubt rolling in something foul, as if to punish Cat for not bringing him to this field of dreams sooner.

She'd have to bathe him, or she'd be gagging all night.

"Shirtless can bathe him," Ginger said, reading her mind. "I tried not to call, and that was wrong. So I called, okay? I don't have answers."

Cat's breathing slowed. Ginger was right, of course; calling Cat, not calling her, it was a lose-lose for Ginger. But whose fault was that? Not Cat's. She was tired of being Ginger's garbageman, her closer, like George Clooney when he tried to play a bad guy but never truly managed it because he was so profoundly decent.

Ginger shielded her eyes from the sun. Her faraway gaze said she was well aware of their pattern and didn't like it any more than Cat did.

"I'm just . . . I'm just trying to understand," Cat said, reaching for Ginger's hand to stop her from stripping her thumb's cuticle off with her middle finger. She was a cuticle peeler from way back. It was one of a collection of nerve-shredding habits. Anything that flaked or had a grippable edge, Ginger would tug until it came loose in times of stress.

Ginger shook her hand free and shoved it in her shorts pocket. "You should have seen some of the people that applied, Cat. There was this ancient hobbity-looking man. An off-off-Broadway veteran, he called himself. He'd reimagined *Death of a Salesman*, but without the death and with less of an emphasis on capitalism and toxic masculinity. He needed a place to put his two-act play up. Two acts? Even I know you have to have three acts for a play."

If Ginger hadn't quit smoking for Shirtless all those years ago, she'd have paused to take a long drag. Given the circumstances, she had made a terrific decision not to hire a hobbit.

"I didn't even call him back. Then, there was a lady who made dream catchers by the ton. Apparently, she'd been sober for a year and made two a day for every day she went without cooking sherry. She wanted to be an artist in residence and be the camp director." Ginger laughed a genuine laugh. "I almost said, 'You won't stay sober running this camp, no matter how much cultural appropriation of the Native American heritage you wind around a stick.'"

That made Cat laugh. Ginger had always been a mix of things. One moment, a fully functional person who knew things and could make Cat laugh harder than any person she knew.

But then there was the other Ginger, who could talk about Star Trek and UFOs for hours. Once, fully sober, Ginger had explained the hollow moon hypothesis and that the moon was actually a spaceship. You never knew which Ginger was running the place. Even Ginger didn't know.

"I'm sure it was hard to hire help. I should give you more credit for knowing you needed a hand," Cat said.

Ginger gave her a withering look. "Don't patronize me, Cat. It's not like there are a thousand people lining up to direct a theater camp in Wisconsin. We did the best we could."

Cat wasn't sure who the *we* in that sentence was, but she needed real answers. "I'm going to drive to the next town, buy a charger, and call Dad. He'll have access to the bank information. Can read it to me. At least I'll know what we're dealing with."

"No. Cat, don't. Give me a day. I can't bear to have him know I screwed this up. Like I always do. He'll be so . . . unsurprised." She slipped her hand out of her pocket and started in on her cuticle again.

Cat tugged Ginger off the wooden steps of the Craft Lodge and onto the grass. "Dad wouldn't have left you in charge if he didn't think you could do it."

"Um. No. Mom insisted they get on the road. There wasn't time for anyone else." She met Cat's eyes and said, "What is the matter with me? Why can't I be you?"

The comment split Cat's brain right down the middle, and if she could have spoken, one side of her mouth would have said with frustration, *I wish*, and the other side would have said, *Nobody wants that*. Her sister Ginger was everything Cat wasn't. Artistic, easily content, creative, and loved nothing more than a group hug. Cat needed solitude, clean lines, no gray areas, no sloppy relationships that might bleed into her space. Require something Cat couldn't give. Ginger still had energy to be heroic, and Cat wanted to manage and answer only to herself.

Today she'd do the minimal right thing and get in her car after getting a look at whatever version of papers Bob had at the bank. Without those documents, her papers might or might not be useful. If she left before Bob returned, she wouldn't have enough information when the bankers came for her savings, her newly renovated house. Then where would she and her tiny family of two live? If she didn't want the silken rope of her dream to slip through her fingers, she was stuck. At least until Bob returned from the bank.

"Hey, Britt, I hear Alistair and Raj are pregnant," Ginger called over Cat's head.

A woman in green cargo shorts, holding a bunny the size of a large toaster, moved quickly to their side, looking alarmed. "Who told you? Do you think everyone knows?"

"Is it a secret?" Ginger looked toward the Mess Hall, immediately on board for a caper.

Brittany looked suspiciously at Cat.

"This is my sister," said Ginger. "She's pregnant too."

"I shouldn't have put Alistair and Raj in the same cage. I got Alistair's gender wrong. Bunnies are hard to sex."

"Brittany is our animal therapy counselor. She runs our petting zoo and is saving money for veterinarian school," said Ginger. "We have the two star bunnies from Bob's book. People love them. Very comforting to hold."

"I like animals," said Brittany, and there was an awkward moment where Cat considered what to say after this obvious number one qualification for vet school. She almost said *That's good* but was rescued from the uninspired dialogue situation when Brittany said, "Can you not tell people until the staff evals are over? I don't want any negatives when I ask Bob if I can come back next year. I put everything toward paying off my undergrad."

"I promise not to say a thing," Ginger said, and she mimed pulling a zipper over her lips.

Brittany turned her attention to Cat, evidently expecting an oath of silence. Cat mimicked Ginger's move and invisi-zipped her lips.

"I don't usually like secrets," Brittany whispered into Alistair's ear. "That's why I like animals. Their only secret is that they love you, and they give that one up every day."

Cat was in no mood to make small talk and glanced at Ginger to get them out of this conversation.

"Alistair is the boy," Brittany went on. "I didn't press hard enough around his thingy to make it stick out." She lifted the bunny as if she was going to demonstrate but, to Cat's relief, only repositioned the animal in her arms.

Brittany reminded Cat of when Ginger was a kid and carried her artistic obsessions everywhere. Instead of animals, Ginger loved drawing. She had paintbrushes in her pockets or oily pastel crayons she used to draw on flat rocks or a swatch of curly birch bark. She'd make a map for Cat that led to a bit of treasure—a broken robin's egg. A perfect acorn. Cat glanced between Ginger and Brittany and thought those two would make great sisters.

"I need to work here next year," said Brittany. "I'm trying to get in-state residency, and then I can afford to go to the U. It's my dream school. Otherwise, I have to quit altogether and make money for a while."

Cat felt sorry for Brittany, she did, but life was hard for everyone. There had to be other camps she could work at next year. Camps for people like Brittany and Ginger. In other states, in the mountains, maybe with an ocean view, a place where people would value their odd talents.

"This camp is close to my parents' house. My dad had a stroke. I can get there fast if I need to help my mom. She's kind of old and needs help too."

The longer she listened, the harder it was to compartmentalize this camp as only Cat's problem. That it was her finances at risk, her family who would need to relocate. The longer she stayed and met the others, the more Cat saw how much damage would be done if the place went under.

"Do you guys still fill our cookie jar with sugar cookies? My blood sugar could use a little shoring up." Cat wanted to change the subject, escort her brain away from worst-case scenarios and appease it with a cookie.

"Yes," Ginger said with the most enthusiasm Cat had detected in her voice so far.

"You do look pale," Brittany said. The girl handed Alistair to Cat as if the bunny were a floppy-eared overstuffed toy with posable limbs and not a live thirteen-pound bunny and said, "Here. Hold him. He's magical. Everyone feels better after a cuddle with Al."

CHAPTER ELEVEN

THE YIN AND THE YANG

Alistair didn't seem to mind being handed over to Cat without consent despite her juggling the bunny's limbs to keep him organized. She found that his bum and tail fit neatly in the triangle-shaped indentation on top of her belly, between her breasts, and his air-soft ears stroked her jaw. Like so much of this camp, he smelled of cedar, and a wave of nostalgia swooped around her like a bat echolocating Cat's weaknesses.

"See? Al is a charmer," Brittany said. "Let's go get that cookie."

Alistair's nose snuffled Cat's jaw, and his whiskers read her like a retired man devouring a newspaper in a coffee shop. She hoped Alistair knew she meant well and was doing her best, but she also needed to bounce. "Bounce," she whispered into his ear; "is that what all the bunny kids say?"

"Are you talking to Alistair?" Ginger said, teasing her.

Cat considered saying yes, but she shouldn't be here talking to bunnies, getting a cookie, thinking about a good ol' avoidant nap. She should be home packing, reading about babies, and practicing cooking with one arm while holding a smoked ham mimicking the weight of a newborn. She fantasized about touching the changing table for one comforting second. Lefty bumped her leg, reminding her he was here to help.

Ginger pulled the door of the Mess Hall open and stopped. "You sure you want to go in? Bob always delivers a postweek pep talk, and everyone is in here waiting for him."

"Are you going to tell them he's gone to the bank?" Cat said.

A series of minute expressions scrolled across Ginger's face—if you knew her, you could read her thought process. *No. Why would I?* Moving to realization—*Oh wait. Bob's gone. I'm in charge.* To: *Uh-oh.* And circling right back to where she'd started. *No. Do I have to?*

"Well, I'm not going to say anything. I don't work here," Cat said. "I'm just visiting against my will."

Brittany herded Ginger, Cat, and Alistair through the door and into the fray of the crowded dining room, an uncomplicated space with concrete floors and rows of picnic tables. The honeyed walls of natural wood and forest-green beams overhead warmed the place, and it smelled like bacon and pancakes—a longtime staple of Cat's life at camp. She could almost taste the maple syrup.

For the first time, Cat saw all the people who depended on this camp crammed into one place. There had to be twenty-five tanned, ungroomed, and impossibly young staff. Back when she was a kid, the hired counselors seemed worldly, experienced, and sophisticated. This bunch had freckles on their noses and grass stains everywhere, and each competed with the others to be heard, be the funniest, and have the best story. So young and yet most likely the same age as the counselors when Cat had lived on the grounds.

And like the staff from back in the day, they'd done their jobs well and were waiting for a rah-rah speech from their boss. Unlike Bob, her father had wanted a young and playful staff. They were meant to play along with the campers and watch over them. Not be their therapists, their meditation guides, their cure for what ails us. These poor kids, reality awaited them, and she was a really tough master.

It had been different for Cat; she'd had a dose of reality all too often. There were poison ivy, ticks, a deep lake, dense woods, and adult-size hazards that forced Cat to grow up quickly by watching over her sister. She rubbed her cheek against Alistair's downy head and tried to hang on to observing the group as an outsider—one who was not responsible for everyone.

Conversation in the room built to a feverish pitch, supported by the August heat and post-workweek gaiety. Shirtless had the appearance of a tired hat looking for a high shelf to rest on. When he spotted Cat, he smiled with heartbreaking relief and moved through the crowd.

"Hi, Aunt Kitty."

Cat lifted as high as she could on her tiptoes, and they touched foreheads. The best kind of hug for the tactilely defensive. Something they'd devised when Shirtless was a kindergartner and then repeated every single time they got together.

"Thanks for coming. We tried to keep you out of it." He glanced at Ginger, then bent to snuggle Lefty, giving him a hearty ruffle under his neck.

"I know. It's okay." Because what else could she possibly say to her beloved nephew? He lived and worked with people who embraced his nickname, made him feel accepted. Of course it was okay that she was here. At least for today.

"Mom, where's Bob?" Shirtless straightened, and Cat saw his nostrils flare. One of his ways to self-soothe was to inhale and hold it for the count of four, sometimes giving his next sentence extra force if he wasn't careful.

"Hey, losers." A gratingly loud voice pierced the steady rumble of conversation in the room. A sinewy man with a Kennedy jawline walked through the front doors with the woman, Camille, who ran the projector screen.

Shirtless exhaled—"Hello, douche"—loud enough for everyone in their circle to hear. Cat heard Brittany laugh. "That's Matt, the quote unquote thalamus yoga teacher," said Shirtless.

"Thalamus yoga? What kind of yoga is that?" Cat asked, knowing that the thalamus was a part of the brain, not primarily concerned with relaxation.

"It's not a thing. He made it up. Bob thinks Matt studied under some famous hypothalamus yogi. Mostly during class he lies down, and everyone falls asleep."

June and Wynn, the two women Cat saw returning belongings to the campers, strolled into their circle. Wynn handed Shirtless a butter-scotch candy and said, "I can't believe summer's over."

"Stop. I don't want to talk about it," said June.

"Neither do I. But I won't miss those two," said Wynn.

"I can't stand how Camille talks about spiritual wellness and God like she has inside information," Brittany said.

"You know she wasn't qualified to do anything at camp, but she sang in the chorus of the university's production of *Joseph and the Amazing Technicolor Dreamcoat*. She told Bob it gave her spiritual experience," said Shirtless.

Cat squinted at the blonde woman as she made her way through the crowd, head held high with the surety of God's BFF.

"She told me she wants to change her name to Spirit. Wants a Bible-study week all her own," Wynn said, then sipped from a water bottle with a marijuana leaf sticker on the side. "She wants people to know at 'hello' what she's all about."

"You guys. This is my sister. She's . . ." Ginger hesitated, unsure of how to explain Cat's sudden presence. "She's visiting."

Practically in unison, the three smiled and said "Hello" and "Welcome," honestly delighted to meet Cat. It was a sweet welcome for the woman who, an hour ago, had considered letting Bob and Elaine take over because they'd trimmed a bush or two.

This was a mistake. Cat had to get out of this room, couldn't bear to see all the hopeful, expectant faces, kids who trusted the adults who made them promises.

The slamming of doors, chatter, laughter, and frantic attempts to end the week on a high note amplified as each second ticked by without Bob's leadership presence. Cat noticed June put one finger in her ear while fixing her earring, as if she were grooming instead of reducing the raucous intensity of the crowded space. Cat suspected June was a bit like Shirtless, a battle against stimulation ever raging inside her.

Wynn touched June's back and said, "Check out the ropes course guy. He's tying knots to impress Jan in boating."

June said in a practiced voice, "I still can't tell if the boating girl is interested."

"Oh, she's interested, all right."

Cat saw this was how their friendship worked. Wynn kept things light and fun, while June's tendency was to move inward and away, not unlike Ginger and Cat's childhood dynamic.

The yin and the yang, their father had called Cat and Ginger.

June sighed. "Oh, Wynnie, I'm going to miss you."

Cat shifted her gaze to Shirtless, who had a calm affection on his face.

"Nope. You won't," Wynn said, "because once we get our phones back, I will be texting you constantly, so you won't forget me."

Interrupting this lovely exchange, the yoga teacher pushed his way over, stood before their group, and said, "Namaste, ladies."

"Beat it, Matt," Wynn said without taking her eyes off the room.

"Chill, girl. I'm trying to bring some Zen to this gathering. Where's King Bob?" he asked.

"Don't call him that. He hates that," June said.

"You'd know," Matt said with good-natured teasing.

"Stick to fake yoga, Matt." Blood rushed into Shirtless's face, turning his skin from tan to torch.

"Summer's over, girls. It's time to take the gloves off." Matt feigned a lazy boxing stance and thumbed his nose.

The double doors of the Mess Hall opened, and in walked Gary, wearing his own version of a uniform: khaki pants, a forest-green T-shirt with a pocket, a leather tool belt, and a pair of gloves tucked into his waistband.

Cat hadn't seen him in literal years. Her recall of the groundskeeper appeared to be the most inaccurate of all her camp memories. She'd remembered him as much older than she, with an unkempt beard and dirt under his nails. Today, though, she couldn't help but stare at this obviously gorgeous man.

"How old is Gary?" she said to Ginger, handing Alistair over her shoulder to Brittany.

"He turned forty-one last week. Wynn made a cake."

"I thought he was Dad's age," Cat said, trying to reconcile her incredibly faulty memory where Gary was concerned.

"When you're seventeen, a college grad is kind of old," said Ginger. "Plus, he always had that full beard compensating for being bald so young. It went gray, so he shaved it. Still barely speaks, though." She shrugged as if he were long-owned furniture she barely noticed.

"Without that beard, he looks like a young Paul Newman," Cat said.

Wynn said, "Who?"

"Who?" said June.

Cat didn't bother clarifying. She was too busy gaping at the man who had her seriously questioning her ability to recall anything.

Gary surveyed the room and located Cat, who closed her open mouth. Then he met Ginger's eyes, and she gave him a nod. He cleared his throat and spoke. "No meeting. Bob and Elaine are off-site. Clean your cabins." He looked like he would say more but stopped and walked out the way he'd come in.

"That's the most I've ever heard him say," Matt said. "What's going on? Something's going on."

The effect of Gary's announcement was neither calming nor organizing. It was as if everyone held a heavy bag of fragile dishes and needed a stable place to put it down, but the ground had just shifted. There was silence, then a buzz of questions.

"Wait, what?"

"No meeting?"

"What about the gala?"

"Seriously?"

June took a step backward toward the door, knowing that when uncertainty prevailed, people often turned in the direction of the medical person. June didn't want to provide leadership. That was clear.

"I'm getting out of here," she said.

"I'm with you," Cat said, but before she got to the door, Camille's sandpaper voice scraped through space.

"Everyone," Camille said and then clapped her hands like Cat imagined she did when she led sing-alongs. "Yoo-hoo! Everyone!"

Cat felt more than saw Ginger stiffen, and the energy in the Mess Hall snapped like an untethered live wire.

Some of the staff turned toward her voice. "You guys," she said, sounding annoyed that she didn't have everyone's attention. "I'm sure Bob and Elaine are busily making sure everything is on point for tomorrow, and they trust us to carry on. Business as per usual."

"Isn't it weird how her southern accent comes and goes? Her Long Island is showing today," Wynn said. She untwisted a bread tie from a plastic bag and broke off a piece of a muffin.

"I'd like to say a few words, if you would indulge me," Camille said.

There was a loud yawn from the center of the crowd.

"This being the last day of camp is sad for all of us." Camille made an exaggerated pouty face and paused for effect.

Matt brushed between Ginger and Bard toward the exit. He yanked the door open and slammed it shut twice.

The muscles in Camille's jaw tightened. She exhaled and said, "I think I speak for all of us in administration when I say this has been a wonderful summer, and the relationships we've built are not the false intimacy of inhabiting this camp together. You are my family."

A muscle flexed in Ginger's jaw. Cat waited for her sister to take back the reins, but it wasn't necessary. The staff turned away from Camille and toward Ginger.

"Off you go. Do what Gary said," Ginger said, her chin high.

Somebody in the back shouted, "Wynn, is dinner ready?"

Wynn lifted her muffin in the air. "Leftovers at five!" she shouted. "Camp karaoke later. June's starting with 'Proud Mary'!"

June shook her head *no* so vigorously that the pencil behind her ear flew out and landed at Shirtless's feet.

Equally alarmed, Camille sputtered, "Oh no! Wait. I have more!"

The shuffling, talking, and noise of the exiting crowd made it clear that in uncertain times, people didn't want to be Camille's family. They wanted leftovers and badly sung hits from the '70s.

Ginger broke from their group and moved through the cluster of staff to Camille's side. Cat followed as if attached by a string and heard her sister say in a manufactured offhand voice, "Bob is on his way to the bank to grab files for my sister."

Camille shot Ginger a distinctly haughty look. "No. He's not doing that," Camille said. "He doesn't keep important papers at the bank. Doesn't trust 'em. You know that, right?"

Cat could see Ginger rooting around in her knowledge of Bob and coming up blank. Cat might have been frustrated with her sister, as one sibling always is at the failings of the other, but she wasn't going to let someone else take a shot at her. If this was a bar fight, Cat would take off her earrings.

"We spoke to Bob and Elaine, his wife. You know her, right?" Cat said, holding a neutral expression, letting her words do the work. "They were on the way to the bank."

"Together?" Camille said a little too quickly, definitely caught off guard.

Cat ignored the question and said, "Nice glasses." The glasses looked new. The woman had two red spots where the bridge pads hit her nose, as if she rarely wore them. Cat had a hunch.

Camille straightened the brown horn-rimmed spectacles. "I ran out of contacts. I have to wear these during the day, but I won't wear them at the gala." She took them off, winked at Cat, tried to focus, and took a step back.

"Oh, you should wear them more often. They make your eyes look less close together." The words came out in a tone that said, *Stand back, rookie. Whatever is happening, leave my sister out of this.*

"Close together?" Camille said.

Cat grabbed her sister by the shoulder, not waiting to see if Camille bumped her way out of the Mess Hall to find herself a mirror. "Are you two competing for Bob or something?"

CHAPTER TWELVE

HOT AND BOTHERED

"Cat, you bisch," Ginger said, pressing her lips together, suppressing a laugh. "You don't even know her."

"I know when I see someone pushing my sister around."

Ginger made a tiny sound, like the release of a tight, emo violin string, which should have made Cat want to hug her. Instead, the sound goosed the gas pedal on Cat's desire to get home. If she didn't leave soon, all the stories, the hopes and dreams of the campers would paralyze Cat with empathy.

"If anyone is going to torture you, it's me," Cat said. Making a joke as she tried to ignore the unmarked signposts of her youth that begged for attention. The Big Rock that doubled as home base when playing tag. The Canteen, where they bought gobs of penny candy on weekends and ate all of it on the ropes course platform before the new campers arrived. The divot near the stone wall their mother called a "fairy circle," where she convinced everyone that pixies had dance parties with lightning bugs on nights when the moon was full. Taking care of everything was the tax of all this beauty, and Cat wasn't willing to pay that physical or psychological bill anymore.

"Look, Ginger, I gotta go."

Lefty bounded ahead, circled and tumbled in the plush grass as if this was the best day of his life. So much freedom, so many petting hands!

Traitor, thought Cat, but gently. She understood. Not a single person since they'd arrived had remarked on his three-leggedness. There had been no laughter, no condescending remarks on Lefty's hop-gallop, no morbid questions about what had happened to him. Cat barely registered his leggy triad unless some idiot at the dog park would ask, "Is it fair to keep a dog alive when so obviously impaired?" To which Cat would reply, "In our opinion, only an impaired person would ask that question."

"Attaboy," Cat said while thinking, *Get your fill; we're heading home soon.*

"Kitty, I—" started Ginger, sounding like an apology might be on the way.

Cat interrupted her. "I'm heading over to our house. I mean the Director's Cabin, Bob and Elaine's," she said, correcting herself. "I need to see what I can discover while they're gone."

"Good idea!" Ginger said. "Let's go."

Cat braked, Lefty banged into her leg, and she faced Ginger.

"Is that true about banks? What Camille said. Does Bob not trust banks?"

"I don't know. I never heard him say that."

"How did he pay everyone? Checks? Bank transfers? Where did he keep admission fees, the emergency fund?"

Ginger blinked and tilted her head like the question was an odd one. "Oh, he didn't pay us. We were a co-op. We signed papers where we all agreed to bank our paychecks. At the end of the summer, Elaine said we'd be paid a lump sum that would be larger because of the interest it had accrued."

"What? No. You're kidding me." Cat grabbed her sister's arm.

"Amazing, right? Everybody except Gary." Ginger looked in the distance, toward the lake, as if this was the first time she'd wondered about that. "Bob paid him cash. That I do remember."

Cat stared at her sister. Blinked once. Twice. "No one has been paid. The camp has money troubles. Bob is hitting campers up for money and planning a fundraiser." She heard her voice rising with each sentence, so that when she got to "Why am I only hearing this now?" it came out as a frustrated squawk.

Right here. This was why Cat had left all those years ago. As many fanciful memories Cat had of this camp, there were just as many where Cat had been called to fix something Ginger had broken. Bleach in washing machines filled with colored laundry, forgotten garden hoses on for hours after filling water balloons. A set build for a play, without factoring in how long it would take to paint a backdrop. A peanut butter cookie shared with kids without checking for allergies.

Camp was a blast for some people, if you weren't in charge of it.

The heartburn that plagued Cat at night, lying down, was suddenly off schedule and bubbling up. She burped, pressed where her belly met her sternum. If she weren't so pregnant, with hormones softening her heart, she would have dug her fingernails into her sister's arm until she screeched. But Ginger's hopeful face, a tiny glow of sun lazily reclining on her cheekbones—it was too much to fight.

Ginger was confident Bob wouldn't forsake them. Why wouldn't she be? She had lived in a storybook forest without villains, playing dress-up and trusting people to memorize their lines, someone always present holding cue cards when help was needed. The only times the emergency sirens were used were during a tornado warning or when someone had spotted the geriatric snapping turtle in the lake.

It wasn't until after Cat had gone to college that she realized how sheltered their lives had been. A topic in orientation had been innocuously labeled Safety, where students were reminded to never leave a drink unattended, learn the signs of alcohol poisoning, and sign up for text messages in case of a pop-up pep rally or active shooter.

Cat had trouble sleeping the entire first semester and realized Summer Camp had been a liability for understanding a world full of dangers. A happy childhood did not prepare a person for the real world.

It took Cat a year to reliably recognize a falseness, crocodile tears, a user. Once pegged, though, she hung close. At least you knew where you stood with a snake. Cat knew Steve was as fake as a beauty queen's tan. You didn't have to feel bad not helping a fake, and they wouldn't hurt you when they left.

"Bob knows these kids have tuition to pay. June wants to finish nursing school and come back here," Ginger said. "And Bard"—she smiled—"Shirtless, I've never seen him so accepted. So upbeat. He talks about expanding the waterfront to include sailing classes and water therapy for other tactically defensive people. Is considering physical therapy school, not all at once, you know, but slowly. Bob knows this. He'd never put their future at risk."

This soliloquy only cemented Cat's belief that Ginger was not meant for the world. She'd been insulated; would she even know what a Ponzi or pyramid scheme was? Not that Bob was smart enough to pull off a multilevel anything, but Ginger would be the perfect target for an organized scammer.

Everything Cat had learned since arriving was a champion Ping-Pong battle of frustration and a foreshadowing of sorrow. "Let's not get too far ahead of ourselves." Cat needed information before she could extricate herself to get on the road with her bank account and plans intact. "I'll go see what I can find in the cabin. You locate Shirtless, and talk to Gary to see what he knows."

"Oh. Okay," Ginger said with metered enthusiasm. Cat knew Ginger wanted to stay glued to her side. Cat could not think straight with Ginger near.

"I'll find you," Cat said when Ginger hesitated, finally turning toward the lake. Cat and Lefty tried to waddle-jog the short distance through the parking lot and across the county road where their old family cabin stood. "Lefty, stay," said Cat, and the dog sneezed once and sat. She climbed the concrete steps to the front door and swung it wide, the hinges groaning in complaint. She'd returned enough times that she was grateful that entering her old home didn't paralyze her with confusing emotions. She was, however, startled to see Gary halfway up a stepladder near the fireplace, changing a light bulb in a ceiling fan. Her first thought (*That's a nice ass*) thankfully did not come out of her mouth. Instead, she said, "What are you doing in here?"

If asked why she sounded so hostile toward a man she barely knew—the only person on-site qualified to do his job and who was actively doing it—she'd have to admit something painful. That Gary had stayed to do all the things that made the outside of the camp stay campy. He didn't bitch about it, feel overwhelmed, want his own life. No, he'd taken root without question and helped her parents when Cat had chosen not to. His presence felt like a rebuke, and his barely concealed scorn highlighted it.

Cat took a second and allowed herself to watch his forearm muscles flex as he twisted the bulb into the socket. He fished a camp bandanna out of his back pocket while she waited for a response.

"My job," Gary said as he wiped the fixture, sending dust particles into the air over Cat's head.

"What?" Cat said. She'd lost track of their conversation while watching him work.

"I'm doing my job."

"Oh. Right," Cat said.

Despite her faulty recollections of Gary being an old man, she did remember correctly that he spoke only when he absolutely had to. Interpreting silences was tricky for the guilty, defensive, snappish Cat. Was he judging her? Criticizing? Was she beneath his notice?

Did he know who she was?

Gary descended the ladder. In seconds, they'd be face-to-face, and she'd be searching for something to say, and he'd still be silent, and then what? *Pull yourself together, Cat.*

"Did Bob go to the bank?" Cat said more loudly than she intended.

"Bob. Not my job."

"Well, he's not my job either," she said. "I'm going . . ." Cat stopped herself. She was not going to explain her actions. She owed him nothing.

Turning toward her parents' bedroom, she remembered these floorboards, the nights she walked them sick with the stomach flu, a bad dream, or an episode of nonspecific dread. Her mother would sometimes pull her in bed with them, and Cat would snuggle into her neck and feel safe.

In the doorway, Cat spied the empty closet, hangers on the floor, and a green camp shirt wadded up on the unmade bed. The room looked ransacked. *No,* she thought. *Abandoned.* Drawers gaped open, empty. A sock crumpled in the corner of the room without a partner. No personal effects.

"They left!" she yelled over her shoulder. "Son of a bitch, they packed up and left. I watched them leave!"

Gary shifted his position, and the ladder groaned.

"Gary," she said with her last ounce of guileless hope. "Do you think Bob went to the bank?" Cat turned and moved down the hall. "Is he coming back?"

"Are you back?"

Startled by the question, she hesitated. "I mean . . . I am for a minute."

"What do you care?"

"My sister and nephew live here."

He looked at her, took a beat, and then said, "They've always lived here."

"I just found out I'm still on the mortgage. That Bob . . ." And she left the name hanging between them.

"Oh . . . I see." He shook his head. "Bummer," Gary said in a low, deep voice that sounded like he might've been having a good time.

She wanted to say, *I don't like your tone.* Instead, she said, "What. What do you see?" Cat folded her arms across her chest defensively, her belly providing a shelf.

"You came for your half. Makes sense."

Cat pulled her head back, offended. "No, I'm not. I didn't know I was on the mortgage. I'd signed it over. Or so I thought. This is all news to me. Bob. The changes. Everything."

"Well, yeah. You haven't been around."

Gary had a way of pacing his words, rushing some, slowing others, for maximum disdain.

"No. Right. I haven't been around," she said, wishing she'd said it first. That way, she wouldn't feel so accused. Blamed. "I'm not supposed to be here right now. I'm supposed to be . . ." She paused, wanting to finish the sentence with *living my life*. Or *taking care of myself instead of everyone else in the world*.

Gary turned his head and, for the first time, looked her in the eye. He lifted an eyebrow.

He was waiting for her to finish the sentence.

"Not here," she said.

He folded his bottom lip a fraction of an inch, making him look like a parent sure the child in front of him was lying. Gary tipped the stepladder toward his body and let gravity close the ladder. The sound of the aluminum legs coming together signaled the end of this interaction.

He turned toward Cat, who stood between Gary and the door.

Cat tried to put her fists on her hips, but her pregnant belly was having none of her postural outrage. "Look, I just need to know. Is there any hope Bob and Elaine went to the bank?"

"Unsure," Gary said.

Like an average conversational person, Cat waited for Gary to say more.

In one admittedly graceful movement, Gary flipped the ladder sideways and carried the unwieldly thing like a briefcase. He adjusted his tool belt and waited for her to move out of his way. The rudeness of the moment did it for Cat.

"Oh, give me a break, Gary. Why do I need to work this hard for a complete sentence from you?"

"Cat." He said her name with a familiarity that zinged right through her. "I do not know where Bob is."

Maybe if she stood here, in his slow way he'd sigh and release her from her obligations. Tell her to go home. There was nothing she could do. Or he'd tell her not to worry; the camp had seen trouble before and made it through. She could leave it all to him. But no. He gestured for Cat to let him by. She stepped away from the door and watched him move without touching her and head out the door in his nice-fitting, forest-green, slightly faded pants.

"I need information," she said. Her voice was smaller than she'd heard it for some time. "I went into the office. Nothing is in the drawers or the safe."

Gary shrugged. Lefty stood up and trotted alongside the man, and Cat wiped her hand over her forehead, finding it warm and dry. A surprise, considering she felt hot and bothered. Very hot and bothered indeed.

CHAPTER THIRTEEN
SEQUENCES OF FRAGRANCES

Suddenly, the urge to find a bathroom was upon Cat, shoving aside any thoughts other than *I hope there's toilet paper*. The impulse was both the first and final warning. She suspected it was because she'd ignored her pelvic floor most of her life. The body was so demanding. Eat fruit. Get enough sleep. Floss.

Who had time for contracting muscles you couldn't even see?

Cat slid aside the pocket door to the half bath outside her parents' bedroom. She wriggled out of her onesie, advertised on the Target website as an "elegant maternity jumpsuit." Pretty sure Gary didn't spot Cat and think, *Oh, so elegant*. More likely he saw her, and a beanbag chair popped into his thoughts.

Cat exhaled, noticing the speckled flooring had held up heroically, probably toxically, and wondered if she should be wearing a mask. Of course the toilet paper spool was empty. Why wouldn't it be? Cat checked under the sink cabinet. There was a scrub brush, a plunger, and an empty mousetrap, but no paper.

"Don't even start with me," she said, opening a drawer in the old vanity. There sat her father's old camera, a relic even he'd stopped using, and one roll of grayish-looking industrial toilet paper was sitting on top of a manila file folder.

She took both out, used the toilet paper, redressed, washed her hands, shut the toilet bowl lid, and sat on it. Cat's lower back ached, and her tennis shoes squeezed her widening feet. The words *Bob. Do Not Lose This Folder* were penciled on the cover of the folder. Whether this was Bob's reminder to himself or Elaine's edict, it appeared that, in fact, Bob had lost it. Either way, it was Cat's now. She pressed her back against the toilet tank and opened the folder.

The first page was the guest list she'd already seen, the names too famous to fathom why they'd come to her childhood sleepaway camp for nerds. Even if they were invited. Cat flipped to the next page. A research study. Someone had highlighted in yellow the first paragraph and the title, "The Effects of Acute Exercise on Mood," by A. L. Wertz. "Compared to a control group, anxious and depressed individuals who attended a cycling class experienced increased levels of well-being and vigor and reduced levels of anger, depression, fatigue, and confusion, as measured by Spielberg's Profile of Mood States (POMS). Statistically significant at $p < 0.05$ confidence interval. $N = 1,000$. Double-blinded and placebo-controlled."

Maybe this was Bob's attempt to find some data to support mood and exercise, even though the camp didn't have bikes, and for sure Bob wouldn't know what a control group was.

The following page was slightly more interesting. It was a rough pencil sketch of the campgrounds. Lake, Auditorium, cabins, Mess Hall, parking . . . the basics. There were miniature sticky notes stuck near each area. Meet & Greet, Food Tent, Presentation, Book Signing, Auction.

Behind the map were pages from a website: *How to Plan a Gala. Linda Zinda's guide for anyone's budget.* It was a straightforward series of to-do lists underneath timeline headers.

Twelve months in advance: Choose a date, decide on the number of guests, and so on. Linda Zinda had benchmarks for nine, five, and one month, down to the night of the gala, where the only box to check was *Enjoy!*

Cat riffled through the seven pages of double-spaced items, from creating a budget to recruiting sponsors to organizing auction items. The only box checked on the entire document was at the *Six to eight weeks before the event* section. Someone had placed a check mark in *Personalize and mail printed invitations.* On the bottom of one of the pages, someone had drawn a box and placed a big proud check mark in it with the words *Supplies ordered.* The next page was a list of the supplies, from tablecloths to cutlery, hanging lanterns and fairy lights. Cat had wanted more of the story, what was actually happening or going to happen, and now with each piece of paper, her anxiety ratcheted up a notch.

Underneath Linda Zinda's underutilized planning packet was a thick, buff-colored piece of card stock embossed with the words OVER THE RAINBOW and the Summer Camp logo: A beaver with a stick in his mouth, his flat tail over his head, his eyes wide and incredulous. It was as if even the beaver knew the branding was off on this invite. The camp was rustic, and this invitation advertised glamour, luxury, and money if a recipient didn't connect the song title to *The Wizard of Oz,* possibly Gay Pride?

Cat held her breath. Did she want to see what was stuffed inside the cottony envelope?

Too late: a card slipped out and fluttered to her feet. Cat squinted at the piece of paper as she picked it up. A pie chart and graph titled *Success data* were printed in gold Times New Roman, and three sentences were underneath.

> Compared to a control group, anxious and depressed individuals who attended Summer Camp experienced increased levels of well-being and vigor and reduced levels of anger, depression, fatigue, and confusion, as measured by Spielberg's Profile of Mood States (POMS). Statistically significant at $p < 0.05$ confidence interval. N = 1,000. Double-blinded and placebo-controlled.

Cat flipped to the first page of the research paper. Someone—Bob? Elaine?—had copied the summary word for word, substituting *Summer Camp* for *a cycling class*. A square of vellum separated the RSVP card that held the words *Join us for the cure for what ails (the) US*. Cat ran a shaky finger over a Post-it Note with the words *Fifty-five invitations sent* and a date. Exactly three days from today.

As if that wasn't enough, there was a Chicago newspaper article titled "The Little Camp That Could," with an aerial photograph of Summer Camp. Cat skimmed the words, unable to fathom how this might have happened. *Abandoned theater camp. Bestselling author Bob Durand. The happiest people take a break,* and there was the so-called data.

Cat stood, the papers dropping from her lap onto the floor. Fraud. If Bob and Elaine sent invitations and press releases out with falsified data indicating that this camp, ostensibly for anxious and depressed adults, successfully created less anxious and depressed adults? It was fraud, and her name would be attached to it.

Movers and shakers had been invited under false pretenses. What if they showed up at the same time as the bankers came to evict them from the bankrupt camp? How did foreclosure even happen? She'd seen *It's a Wonderful Life*, where the townspeople mobbed the bank asking for their money. And what of the kids all waiting for their summer paychecks?

Were they all sitting ducks, floating on the property until the powers that be motored over them—forcing out the good-faith kids who'd put their trust in Bob because Cat had left and Ginger was in charge, and everyone knew she wasn't up to the task? Did Gary know all of this? If he did, he wasn't letting on. And Shirtless, with his rash and sad eyes. How could he not blame Cat?

He couldn't blame his grandparents. They'd tried their best.

Any way she sliced it, she needed to find out what signatures were on the mortgage. Cat moved all the papers into a pile and bent around her stomach to pick them up. Sweating, she knew what to do. She'd go home and read the signed mortgage papers that relieved her from responsibility. Calm her emotions with the long drive. With contracts in hand, she'd get a solid night's sleep and make an omelet with two eggs. Not just the whites. She'd drive back to camp armed with information in a day or so. They'd figure out how to call off the gala. They could sell the supplies on Facebook Marketplace.

Cat stepped out of the bathroom. She needed to get to her car without running into any more disasters. Like in a heist movie, she visualized the layout of the building. Walk through the wooded path out the back door and enter the parking lot unseen. Cat touched her car keys, deep in her stretchy pocket. She'd text when she got home, Went for files. Be back soon. If her sister threw her luggage in the lake, so be it. Her spare onesie, Revlon ColorStay lipstick, and old underwear could be replaced.

At the threshold to the outside, Cat held the overly tight spring-loaded screen so it wouldn't bang shut like when they were kids. She almost heard her mother shouting, "Don't slam the door!" See her father's laughing eyes. Watch as Ginger, her mind occupied, banged through the exit without looking back.

On the path, Cat touched the old stump where they'd left gifts for the crows they'd tried to befriend. She ducked under the long, thin needles of a white pine branch and dodged a rock in the path, the one that had cut Ginger's shin while she was playing hide-and-seek when she was eight. Cat had seen the aged, shiny scar that very day.

A wildly swinging branch at the edge of the parking lot caught her eye. That man, Norm, furtive, like a squirrel protecting a nut. He stopped, lifted his chin as if to search the air for predators, then cut across the grass and disappeared behind a cabin.

The coast was clear. Cat entered the path near rural County Road A, her car ten yards away. She hit the unlock button on her keys, and the lights blinked on and off. As if she were a spy running for her life from the Russians, she performed a squat jog that 007 wished he could do as well with a cauldron for a belly. At the passenger side of the car, the handle warm from the sun, she glanced around, opened the door, and slid inside.

The keys found their home with a satisfying snap into the ignition, and she looked through the windshield. At the camp entrance, under the rustic sign that said WELCOME TO SUMMER CAMP, stood Shirtless, with Lefty offering support with his tripod of strong doggie legs. Both dog and boy had the sweetest, most hopeful, yet confused expressions as they spotted Cat. She continued to hold her breath. Her mind rushed through options. Drive over, explain she'd be right back. She'd call tomorrow. Come back in a couple of days. The gala date rang in her memory. She'd be back tomorrow. Stay tomorrow night. Sort things out.

Shirtless raised his hand and waved. It had a forlorn quality to it, a hopeless little *There she goes again* wave. An *I get it, Aunt Kitty. I understand. You've gotta go.* Cat released her breath. She had the magical thought that maybe she could rewind the tape so he never felt the way he must be feeling right now, and Cat hadn't seen it. And then she saw her miserable and obvious plan to save herself skitter like cockroaches at sunrise. Cat was who she was, and there was no denying it. There was no way she'd leave that boy to manage what was next.

Cat removed the keys, grabbed the pair of Birkenstocks on the passenger-side floor mat, pushed the door open, and clutched the manila folder. "Getting a blister. Had to change shoes," she called out.

Shirtless's face opened to a sunny grin, but Lefty knew what was up. No doubt he could hear her elevated heartbeat a mile away, smell her nervous perspiration, taste the salt in the air before her tears hit her cheek. He knew what she smelled like when she felt trapped, had sensed it on the drive to camp. He'd felt her joy when she learned of the baby, something he had to have known the night it happened. He'd felt her certainty when she decided that a child she made would be different. That she could take care of a being she'd made from scratch. Bring into the world another being Lefty would protect. At least, that's what Cat suspected, dogs being the superior, empathetic beings they were.

It was the same sequence of fragrances he sensed today. And that's why his tail never ceased to wag. He wasn't worried about Cat driving off and leaving them.

CHAPTER FOURTEEN

FORTUNE FAVORS THE BOLD

Lefty had the same wide-mouthed grin, and Cat dropped her Birkenstock sandals onto the asphalt, tugged her wet tennis shoes off, and pitched them onto the front seat. Nobody would trust her if they knew how close she'd come to leaving, and she needed people to trust her if she was going to help them.

With the gala information file tucked under her arm absorbing her nervous sweat, Cat slipped her feet into her clogs, a loving, auntlike smile pasted on her face. "Hi, you two," she said as she scuffed through the camp entrance. Her hand dropped to Lefty's head as she touched her forehead to Shirtless's shoulder. "I like that they call you 'Shirtless,'" she said.

"Yeah. You know . . ." He shrugged and smiled. "They get me."

"If the shirt fits, take it off," Cat said, joking, and her nephew smiled indulgently, too young to know the old-timey mashed-up phrases his family often used.

"You've changed," he said, eyeing her pregnant belly.

"I sure have. A couple of months to go. And look at you! You're a man!"

Shirtless flushed and tossed a tennis ball and watched as Lefty bolted to retrieve it. He didn't want to comment on his newish manness. "I'm sorry I texted you. Mom made me."

"She did? Well, that tracks. I was ignoring her. I needed to know about the mortgage. You did me a solid."

If Shirtless had been a typical kid, Cat would have thrown her arm around his shoulders or ruffled his strawberry-blond hair, which looked like it needed conditioning. Touch was not his love language, so Cat had to rely on words and actions to communicate her devotion. Like staying put when she was needed, even if it was just for the night.

It was good training for being a mom, she told herself as she stood in the pea gravel of the parking lot. She'd had a lot of practice with Shirtless over the years. Birthday parties, eighth-grade graduation, watching him get through lifeguard training when he didn't like to be touched. She'd had a shirt made that said DON'T TOUCH UNLESS DYING, and they'd laughed together.

"Mom wasn't doing that badly, you know. Everybody chipped in. We were getting it done. But then she got overwhelmed. Bob helped, but Elaine makes everything complicated."

There wasn't much runway between being overwhelmed and falling apart with her sister. One day she'd seem fine, and the next she'd be talking about how people had it out for her. It wasn't fun to watch and was hard to get on top of once the obsessing started.

"She thought hiring someone was the right thing. We all did. I sat in on his interview. Bob never said he wanted to stop doing theater for kids and bring in nervy adults. That came later, when it seemed like our attendance was going to be low. People forgot how to be together during COVID. It's been hard to find staff too."

Cat wished she could soothe Bard with a hug or say the right, generous thing. That's what she would have wanted. But loving someone wasn't always about doing unto others as you'd have done unto you. Maybe love was as simple as showing up and doing what you don't want to do.

"I was confused when Bob said you were on the mortgage and said we had money problems. Grandpa was so good with finances. He used to talk to me about putting money away for rainy days. I wish I'd paid more attention."

"You're the kid, Shirtless. It's not your job to keep the grown-ups in line."

Shirtless had been monitoring his mother's moods and actions since before kindergarten. Cat remembered little Shirtless grabbing Cat by the thumb when she'd returned to the camp for a visit. The five-year-old led her to the Boathouse, where Ginger was crying over one of a hundred things that plagued her. Shirtless was sure Cat had the verbal wrench to stop his mother's tears. And she had.

Now, he was taller than Cat and still hoped for a thumb to hold.

"Mom's better. She's really stepped up. I learned a lot about the business from her. It's like an internship. Most people don't get this kind of experience until college."

Cat eyed him. He didn't seem to be protecting Ginger. He wasn't overemphasizing words to be believed. He was grateful, Cat could see it.

"I can tell she's nervous you're here, though. She wants you to see that she's"—he paused to pick the right word—"different from when you were kids."

Cat examined the boy's face for changes; puberty had stolen the softness of his jaw. She nodded. "I can understand why I make her nervous. You can be a CEO running a company, and your parent walks into a room, and you realize you forgot to make your bed, you know?"

He laughed, like he could see it, and Cat was certain he understood what she was saying. "So tell me about this girl you're sweet on." He snapped his head in her direction and quickly looked away. "I saw her touch your arm, and you didn't crawl out of your skin. If you're hiding something, you'll have to work harder when I'm around."

A blush spread across his face, connecting his freckles one by one. She could see he wanted to talk about June, but maybe not with a woman who, moments ago, was in her car looking like she might bolt.

"Is that the mortgage papers?" he asked, indicating the folder under her arm.

"Oh. No. I wish."

Loud voices rang from the Mess Hall, and the two headed for the building. "What's happening in there?" Cat said.

As they got closer, what began as cheering turned to a chant. "Fight. Fight. Fight." Someone rang the dinner bell, keeping time with the crowd.

Cat marched into the Mess Hall like she owned the camp because, dammit, maybe she did. She elbowed through at least a dozen kids smelling like dirt, perspiration, and hair that needed a good scrubbing. In the center of a circle stood Camille, brandishing a cafeteria tray. Matt, the yoga douche from earlier, stood, hands in his pockets, chin out, saying, "I dare you."

"Take it back. Bob wouldn't leave."

"Wake up, you little Jesus freak, he already did."

Cat swept her gaze over the crowd, looking for someone in charge, and sure as shit, Gary stood in the corner, watching with a half smile on his face. That was enough for Cat to launch herself belly and all into the ring. She snatched the tray from Camille, overestimating the strength it would take, and clobbered Matt's arm with it.

"Owww," he said as if he'd been shot.

"Give me a break, you big bendy baby. You sure you want to cry about the mommy who hit you? I'm seven months pregnant." Cat made a note to add that tagline to everything she did going forward. It was a fantastic OB-GYN exclamation point that she could use for another couple of months. "Bob's gone. Deal with it."

"Why do you care?" Camille said, examining her nails as if Cat had broken one.

"She is part owner of Summer Camp!" said Ginger, swinging her arm around Cat. *Oh no!* The Cat was literally out of the bag, and she wriggled away, wanting to denounce ownership.

"Maybe," she said. Cat raised her hand, like a reluctant politician. She'd been waddling around the grounds as if she were queen of camp. When, in fact, she didn't want to be part of any reigning sovereignty.

The room filled with the sounds of mixed reactions. Some noticing Cat for the first time, others caring little, and still others remarking, "Ohhhhh," as if to say, *It's all clear now*, even though what could possibly have been made clear?

The camp was so familiar to Cat that she'd waltzed onto the grounds as if everyone else were a stranger, a transient, and this was her home. There hadn't been a single second since she'd parked her car that Cat had felt she needed to explain who she was. She'd felt nostalgic, a little invisible, even experienced déjà vu, but never as if she didn't have every right to be here and assert herself. This must be what it felt like to be a middle-aged white man entering basically every building in the US, except maybe Planned Parenthood.

"Well, then, maybe you can tell us where Bob went. Why hasn't he given his usual speech, and when are we getting paid?" Matt said, off his heels and ready to spar.

Their mother used to say to a kid who'd forgotten a line onstage, "When in doubt, distract!"

"Behave like you're not seven years old, teasing the girl you have a crush on," Cat said, glancing at Camille. Matt huffed off to sit in the corner. "Stop baiting him, Camille," she added, and Camille's smug grin flatlined.

"Everybody, if you've cleaned your posts, sit down and wait for dinner," Ginger said. Then, like a referee in a ring with two fighters, she lifted arms with Cat and announced, "The McCarthy girls. Together again!" Hoping for applause. But no one knew there'd been a split or that a team might be needed.

"Where's Bob?" Matt asked, saving the sisters from an awkward silence where cheers could have been.

"Oh, shut up," Cat said, and miraculously he did.

The dinner bell clanged, and like Pavlov's dogs, the entire group lined up and chattered excitedly about a rounded scoop of mac 'n' cheese and a slice of Texas toast. With the staff occupied, Cat moved to Gary's side.

"Were you going to stand there silently and let them fight it out?"

Gary gestured to the folder Cat clutched to her chest and said, "What difference does it make?"

He knew what was in this folder, knew what was coming and was doing nothing but grumping around and changing light bulbs. Cat felt like clobbering Gary with the cafeteria tray she still had in her hand, but then she heard a timid voice in her ear.

"Thank goodness you're here." It was June, with a smile that looked like taped-together heartbreak and hope that only the darlingest of people can manage.

Taking Cat's cafeteria tray, June moved in line behind Shirtless. The two kids shared a relieved look, having handed the camp over to the responsible sister. Cat's mouth went dry with the feeling of having something foisted on her without her consent.

"I need to talk to you," Cat said to Ginger and bolted toward the door.

CHAPTER FIFTEEN

MISTAKE MAKERS

Cat shuffled out the double screen doors, letting them slap shut behind her. Outside the Mess Hall, the clattering of utensils, dishes, and chatter pushed her across the lawn. Ginger caught up to Cat and said, "What is wrong with you?"

"Why did you tell them I'm part owner? We don't know that. We don't know anything."

"It's probably true. Anyway, most people are proud of what their family has achieved. I thought you'd like to be introduced so they knew you weren't a stranger. As somewhat in charge."

Cat shook her head hard. "No. You don't get it. I don't want to be held accountable for these kids' futures."

"You're not alone, Cat. I'm here too. Together, we can make sure they're well cared for."

Cat was not comforted by that fact in the least. She knew how the two sisters as a team worked: Cat ordered Ginger around, and her sister did tasks or didn't; you never knew. Then, if something didn't get done, Cat felt responsible. Their father might not come right out and say it, but he would pull Cat aside, give her advice about coaching an employee. Motivating people to do their best, and she'd want to rebel, and shout, *I didn't hire her!*

Her outrage came from the unfairness of it all. She'd disappointed her father by not being able to control Ginger. The only way to make sure it wouldn't happen again was to leave her childhood home.

Ginger eyed her sister. "Oh. I see. You don't want to be associated with me. You don't want to work with me."

"Ginger, not everything is about you."

"Not everything is about *you*," Ginger said even louder.

"Gah. Maybe some things are. If I'm on the mortgage and this place goes under, they will take all my savings. Where will I live? I'll have a baby."

"I have a son," Ginger said, standing her ground. "You don't think I get it?"

"I'm going to call Dad on the landline in the office," said Cat.

"No surprise there. Always the tattletale. Perfect Cat," Ginger sneered.

Cat lost a sandal trying to pivot and head for the Administration Building. She jammed her foot into her shoe and kept going.

"I've waited long enough."

Ginger caught up to Cat at the door, angry but polite. She let her sister go through, then said, "What are you going to tell him. That I suck again?"

Cat dropped the sweaty folder on the desk beside the almond-colored rotary phone. She grimaced at the grime on the headset and held it a good inch from her face. Who knew what antibiotic-resistant grunge could be clinging to that Typhoid Mary of a telephone.

"Tell them I did everything he said to do. I asked for help. I googled things," Ginger said.

"You can tell him yourself, as soon as I get him on the line." She listened for a dial tone. When none came, she pressed the hang-up buttons on the cradle multiple times.

Paused. Listened. No dial tone.

"Did you forget his number, Kitty Cat?"

Cat stepped back, moved her belly aside, and saw, there on the floor, a pair of scissors and the cut cord of the phone. She tilted her head, staring, and the gears went chunk, chunk, chunk in her brain, pushing and pulling together her thoughts. "The phone lines have been cut."

"No way," Ginger said as she pushed past Cat to see. "What the . . ."

Cat whipped around to the small alcove, where the copier sat, under two wooden shelves that held several reams of printer paper. Someone had hung a sign that read KEEP CALM AND PRINT ON next to a Wi-Fi router, the word LINKSYS printed on the side. No lights glittered. Cat stepped forward as if sneaking up on a critter that might pounce and saw that someone had snapped the little antenna in two. There were no electrical cords anywhere.

"They sabotaged the system," Ginger said.

"Your boyfriend, Bob. First, they ransacked Mom and Dad's cabin; then he vandalized this," Cat said, pointing all over the office.

"He'd never do this. I don't believe it."

"Believe it."

Their father had prided himself on the one phone line to the world. Had brokered a scattering of red emergency phones throughout the camp that went straight to 911. But she didn't need firefighters; she needed an accountant, a party planner, a bankruptcy expert. More than anything, she needed that crook Bob and his slimy wife to come back.

"Fifty people are coming in three days. We can't cancel the gala. We don't have their emails or phone numbers. They'll come expecting a party." Cat counted off on her fingers: "Food. Drinks. A show. A reason to be here. Rich people. Bankers. People who don't like their time wasted. Do not take kindly to being lured anywhere with false promises."

"No way. Bob would be here if he could. He would not leave."

"The only way to call off the party would be to sling a sign over the highway saying 'Keep calm and turn around' and hope they take it seriously." Cat was panting, staring at Ginger, who looked stricken.

Cut phone lines turned the camp into an island with no options for assistance. Cat couldn't help but picture the grounds as the future site of a bacteria-filled water park with plastic slides the size of a five-story building. No place for her sister and nephew—Shirtless would crawl out of his skin, let alone his shirt. Was that what this was all about? Had she brought this on with her one lonely night with Steve? That couldn't be, could it?

Cat snatched up the file folder, the only concrete thing she had, and pushed out of the office and back to the grass. Ginger followed her sister, looking for answers, comfort, and forgiveness.

The late afternoon soon turned to what poets called the *gloaming*. It was the quietest and loveliest time of day if you weren't in an apocalyptic-style panic. Cat stopped. "Ginger. I need a minute. I know this isn't your fault. I think it might be mine."

"It's not your fault," Ginger said, defending her sister as if Cat hadn't just had a tirade.

"Please, Ginger. I'm going to the water. I'll find you. Don't do anything. Don't tell anyone about the lines. Okay?"

Ginger nodded, and Cat felt her sister's eyes on her as she walked toward the water. She located the concrete bench shaped like an old log in the swimming area. It had been in that spot for as long as Cat could remember.

She wiped the sweat on her upper lip using the neck of her T-shirt. "Okay," she whispered, "what do you know? For sure." She unclipped the cheap green plastic mechanical pencil from the folder and wrote a *P*, the pencil lead breaking off from the pressure. She clicked the eraser, eased her approach, and wrote *People are coming*.

Thanks for sending Steve our way, Bob had said before vanishing with Elaine. Had Steve been playing inside baseball this whole time? The camp was one of the only things he'd asked her about. Except that night they'd had sex. "Birth control?" he'd said, rushing to unzip his jeans, as if that were her job.

"Obviously," she'd said because, in her experience, it *was* her job. But the assumption annoyed her, and her desire flagged. Cat had read an article in *Forbes*, no less, stating that humans needed four hugs a day to survive, eight to maintain, whatever that was, and twelve to thrive. Sex, even the mediocre kind, had to count for at least half the hugs needed to not die. So she'd gone along with it, desire be damned.

Her IUD, though underutilized, was in place because she did not leave things to chance. She wouldn't be in this predicament if he'd answered the birth control question for himself. That was where her feminist outrage wobbled. She loved this tiny measuring cup of their comingled genetics, even though she pictured her cells as the dominant players, their pointy elbows crowding his obnoxious double helices out.

She shook her head. Tried to focus on the bobbing swimming pier and listened to the water hit the old stained tanks that kept it afloat. She fixed her eye on an orange buoy that indicated where the sandy lake floor slanted to a deeper spot. If the camp was bankrupt, what choices did she have? How could she preserve her savings, her life?

Picking up the pencil, she wrote:
Options.

1. Sell camp.
2. Pay off debt.
3. Pay staff.

She clicked to refresh the lead and wrote :

4. Steve???

His name, entangled with the camp and her child. How was she going to sort it all out? What was he doing, advising Elaine and Bob? What if he made a bid for the camp? Cat wanted the baby inside her named and in her arms before she had to consider the legalities related to Steve. If he'd manipulated her from the start . . . the thought made her sick. She hesitated before she wrote the number 5.

Her fingers itched to type a Google search, but there were no general answers to the questions she wanted to ask: What was her responsibility? Why keep the camp going? What happened to the boundary work she'd done with a therapist? Where was her resolve? Her eyes settled on number 1.

Sell camp. She searched her gut feeling on this, and there was no peaceful relief to be found.

Goldfinches chirped nearby, and the water lapped the shore in the light breeze that moved the smallest leaves in the trees. All of this gone, bulldozed, paved. Where would that leave Ginger and Shirtless? The staff. The bunnies? Gary, even though he was categorically not her concern.

There was another route before calling a Realtor, placing bids, giving over to—and here she cringed—the vultures. Cat clicked the eraser and prepared her pencil lead for the stress and pressure of adding a number 5 to the list. Footsteps stopped her when Wynn approached, her expression closed.

"Hi," Cat said, making her presence known.

"Oh. Hey," she said. "I take a dip after dinner every night. Feels so good. Shirtless and June are cleaning up the kitchen."

"Oh, that's so nice of them."

"It's their turn. Everybody rotates through cleanup. We all pitch in."

Wynn wore a long, plain, navy T-shirt over her turquoise swimsuit and a lemon-colored towel around her neck. She kicked off a pair of tie-dyed Crocs and put her toe in the water and shivered. "It's cooling off quick tonight. It'll feel good, though," she said, coaxing herself in. "Feel free to join me."

Cat was touched by the invite. She couldn't have said why. "Can I ask you a question?" Cat said.

Wynn nodded, flicking the water with her toe.

"Have you cooked at other camps?" Cat shook her head. "I mean, you don't look much older than Shirtless. How did you know how to prepare food for such a big group?"

"I'm a little older than most of the kids here. I look young." Wynn stepped closer. "I learned on this job. I'm a quick study," she said, but not like she was complimenting herself, more like it was a joke. That she was possibly the opposite.

"How did you find out about the job?" Cat said.

Wynn eyed her as if mentally flipping through a folder of stories ranked most to least revealing of herself and settled somewhere in between. "I ran into Bob at the college. He . . ." And here she hesitated. Wynn was editing as she spoke, trying to decide how much to say.

"He was recruiting for staffing positions. I ran into him after a class. I was a mess. I am a business major with a women's studies minor. We had to design the perfect listing for products on Amazon, to sell. I wrote the description for a glitter silicone sex toy." She raised her eyebrows, letting Cat picture precisely what that might be. "I did the whole assignment, but I messed up something kind of big. The product was phthalate-free silicone, but I wrote 'phallic-free.'"

Cat cringed to show Wynn that she saw the humor in that error. If you're making a glitter phallus, it can't be phallic-free.

"Funny, right? But the professor ripped me apart in front of everyone in the class. Said, 'Do you know how much money the company would lose with that kind of error? Companies have gone under because of simple proofreading carelessness.'"

"Is that true?" Cat asked.

"Maybe. I don't know. I hadn't taken my ADHD meds in a couple days. Couldn't afford to renew them. I do a lot better on the time-release ones, but they're expensive." Then, as if conceding a point: "Either way, I'm a born mistake maker. I should change majors, but another year of loans. I didn't see how I could do it."

Cat could see that telling this story was stressing Wynn out. The girl fidgeted, bit the inside of her cheek. "Bob handed me a flyer for the camp. Said he knew what it's like to screw up. Said he needed a cook for the summer. I ran it by my parents, because . . ." Wynn was definitely leaving out key details, which was good. Cat knew too much already about the staff and their needs. "My dad wanted me to take golf lessons this summer. Said it would help me make business deals." She kicked a rock. "He's . . . traditional." She dropped her voice, mimicking her father: "'Failure's not an option, Wynnie.'"

"You're here, though. Your parents okayed it?"

"Ha! No. He wanted me to move home, save money. Work in his office. He's super mad at me. Cut me off financially."

"So do you think this camp is 'the cure for what ails us'?" Cat wanted to hear what this camp meant to this young woman. Was it just a job, a way to torture her parents, or did she subscribe to the cult of Bob, his cheerful belief in his childhood camp?

"Maybe. Sometimes. Yes. Do you?"

"Actually, I might be more like your dad. Or maybe I've spent too much time here to see the magic anymore," Cat said, and she saw a tic of disappointment in the girl's face. "You're young, though. Go ahead and believe in whatever magic you need. There's no harm in that."

"Okay, old lady," Wynn said, making fun of Cat. She dropped her towel, crossed her arms at the hem of her shirt, and pulled her T-shirt off, exposing a small back crisscrossed with tan lines from multiple suits and tank tops. A map of a summer of sunning, swimming, and changing. "My dad won't be so mad once we get paid. He'll see we aren't a bunch of losers." She flashed a brief no-offense shrug, then turned her eyes to the horizon.

Cat followed Wynn's gaze across the clear, spring-fed waters of their family's lake, ostensibly her lake if the rumors were right.

So that's how it was then. It was either Cat's savings or this girl's savings that were on the line. Sure, it depended on the debt, the selling price of the camp, etc., but bankruptcy typically paid pennies on the dollar. And neither of them, Cat nor Wynn, could make a life on pennies.

"This place," Wynn said. "Everybody here is a big mistake maker."

"Bob and Elaine. They're not coming back, are they?"

"Bob probably would. Elaine is the boss of him, and she is the devil."

Wynn took two big steps and did a shallow dive into the water, and she was gone. When she resurfaced, Wynn swam out to about the center of the lake; then she flipped onto her back and floated.

Cat returned to her Options list. Read each numerical entry, returning to the number 5. She wrote *Gala*, circling the word until the pencil lead broke again.

Mistake makers. Wynn pushed against the swimming dock and executed a pretty good flip turn.

There was no way to cancel the gala, at least not one Cat could see. So they do it. They throw the party. They could clear up the fraudulent data sent out with the invitations—call it enthusiasm, or a sample of the research they would do if they had the money. Hint, hint. Maybe the guests would take pity on the place, and they'd collect enough cash to pay the staff so that the camp didn't get sued by the parents. Cat would lay all the facts out to the staff: That Bob wasn't coming back, but the gala must go on. She wouldn't take charge; she would run support—a gala consultant, if you will—then, when all was said and done, she could go home, knowing she'd kept her promises to herself, come rain or shine.

CHAPTER SIXTEEN

THE SECRET GARDEN

Cat left Wynn swimming, the girl's curls, like a spray of baby's breath, marking her place in the lake. Supporting her belly, Cat trudged up the path toward the white eagle perched on top of the totem pole, his oddly human eyes following her as if to say, *I can't leave. I'm sunk in concrete.*

What's your excuse?

Lefty bolted from the Craft Lodge and sprinted toward Cat, wearing a green staff shirt tied like a toga around his middle. Cat stopped to catch her breath and absorb Lefty's exuberant love as he licked her palm. The day had taken a soft turn into evening, the time of day Cat called the *lonely hour.* As Cat stepped over the threshold, Ginger held the cabin door.

"Did you get something to eat?"

Cat would have answered, but she stared, stunned into silence. The tan and dull Craft Lodge, where she'd spent many rainy days making lanyards, was an art installation.

Ginger had done what she'd always talked about doing. She'd painted faux bricks on the walls, adorning them with ivy and flowers. A bumpy beach ball–size papier-mâché sun hung from a corner of the ceiling; heads of sunflowers turned toward the light. Giant tissue paper flowers were everywhere, topiary trees in the shapes of squirrels and bunnies. Ginger had taken everything she'd learned about set building and created a magical space.

"Oh my gosh, you did it," Cat said. "It's the Secret Garden."

Ginger nodded, patting the top of one of the topiary bunnies as if it were her beloved pet. It was breathtakingly creative, more impressionist than realist, and Cat wished she could give her sister her due. But she pictured Ginger, flecked in paint, brushing, mixing, forming clouds with cotton and glue, building trees out of chicken wire. All while the camp with its real trees and flowers went glug, glug, glug into a real lake of debt—hauling everyone along with it.

"Well, it's beautiful," Cat said, wishing she could be one of those people who hid her feelings better. Ginger's fingers left the bunny's head, plucked a flower off the wall, smelled it, smiled, and crumpled it in her palm. Lefty stopped panting and sat.

To make up for the hundreds of hours it must have taken to paint the Craft Lodge, Ginger lifted a tray from the counter and placed it next to Cat. "I thought you had to be hungry," she said. Lefty stared at Cat, waiting to see if she'd take the offering of a sandwich wrapped in wax paper, the edges folded crisply at the corners. A carton of milk with a bendy straw sat next to an assortment of carrots, sliced red peppers, and possibly jicama next to a teacup filled with a creamy substance.

"Is that hummus?" Cat asked.

"I told Wynn you liked it," Ginger said.

Cat had enough generosity to keep to herself the fact that pregnancy multiplied the gassy elements of chickpeas. She reached for a carrot. "Thanks. I do like it." Cat peeled the wax paper off the sandwich, peeked inside the slices of whole-grain bread, and said, "Egg salad."

"Your favorite."

When you've created a life of being beholden to no one, no one knows your favorite sandwich, let alone hands you one, particularly not after a fight and a stingy assessment of the haven they'd created with their mind and a few campy supplies.

Cat took a bite even though her throat felt thick, and swallowing without crying might've been difficult. Ginger handed Cat her drink, knowing her sister well. Lefty relaxed onto his side as she ate, his three legs extended but ever ready to man a rampart. Ginger tugged at her eyebrow ring and gazed out one of the high windows toward the parking lot.

"He's gone," Cat said.

"He'd never miss the gala," said Ginger, stalwart in the face of the facts.

Cat chewed a carrot so she wouldn't say what she was thinking: that Ginger, while great at fantasy, wasn't the person to turn to when reality was needed. "You're going to have to put on the gala without him."

Ginger clasped her hands under her chin, and her shoulders dropped with relief. "I can . . . ," she started, and Cat knew what was coming. Artistic suggestions, grandiose ideas, and the hopeful energy of someone who, for example, couldn't sew but would make a parachute and jump from a plane. She interrupted her sister by clearing her throat and standing. Lefty scrambled awake, ready to follow Cat to bed.

"Just wait," Cat said. Maybe in the beginning of the day, she would have said something sharp, but the food in her belly sang her a lullaby.

Staying in their old family cabin was too close for comfort, so Cat moved toward the back bedrooms of the Craft Lodge. One room for Ginger and the other for a sick person or a guest, depending.

"I have ideas," said Ginger as she opened a drawer.

Before disappearing down the short hall to find her luggage, her bed, and a quiet spot where no more information might be offered, Cat said, "I have conditions."

Ginger nodded. Closed the drawer, this a dance they'd engaged in for years. Cat the admired authority. Ginger the number two.

"I'll be behind the scenes. I will remain invisible during the gala." Ginger gave Cat an uncertain look but didn't dare ask, at the risk of appearing contrary. Cat would wait to explain Steve, the guest list, and the baby who'd just elbowed her ribs; it would only muddy up this conversation. "The people have been invited, and there's no way to call it off. Maybe someone will donate something. Miracles do happen," Cat said, touching her tight belly at the same time she wondered how many divine interventions one person gets.

Cat ran her fingers over the trellis painted on the wall, stroked a butterscotch-colored tissue paper flower the size of a large KitchenAid mixing bowl. A memory of her mother bubbled up, sitting between the sisters and folding the fragile paper into blooms. Her mother admonished Cat's imperfect efforts while Ginger concentrated, adding depth without even trying.

The Secret Garden book was a bedtime story. A healthy child playing with a sick one, hidden away where the world couldn't find them. Cat knew if she saved the camp once, she'd have to save it a hundred more times. It was time to end this safety net for Ginger and Bard. It was time for the two to enter the world and get their heads out of the clouds. "If we raise money, we'll pay the staff; then maybe we can sell the camp to get out of whatever debt there is. If Dad wanted it, he should have stayed." The energy in the room sparked as if Cat's words had scuffed across a carpet, charging the space between them.

"No, Cat. We won't have to sell. Bob had a plan, and I know you don't believe me but—"

"I can't, Ginger. I can't deal with some Bob-mystery. The facts are this. If I'm partial owner and the place goes under, I go under with it. If I'm not an actual owner and the place goes down, well, it's not like I can turn my back on you and Bard. Or Mom and Dad, for that matter. Eventually they'll come home, and where will all of you live? In either scenario, we all end up living together in my house, if I still have one to live in."

Ginger shook her head, as if Cat wasn't getting it. The trust she had in Bob, that he wouldn't let her down. What would that be like to have in life? *Blind Faith, a Comfort and a Cross: The Ginger McCarthy Story.* Ginger would be quoted in interviews: *I thought Bob was my soulmate, but instead our whole family had to move into my sister's basement.*

"Look, if Bob comes back, no one will be happier than me. But until then, the gala is the next step."

Lefty bumped her leg like a debate coach. *You've made your point; now move on.* "I have to go lie down for a minute," Cat said, and Lefty followed.

Ginger nodded. "We've got this, Kitty."

Hearing her nickname, only ever used at this camp, was like a sleepy little kiss on her heart. "I know you do," Cat said as she moved into her room. Ginger had turned the chenille bedspread down and placed a vase of flowers on the bedside table.

Marigolds. Her favorite.

———

Cat opened her eyes to absolute darkness and disorientation until the room's smell had grounded her. She rolled on her side, suspecting it was 1:58 a.m. Her sleep schedule was set by her bladder, and it was more reliable than FedEx. The cabin, gorgeously quiet, without gurgling plumbing or errant car alarms going off near the high school, was the perfect temperature. Cat obediently went to the bathroom as Lefty sighed to let her know he was nearby. She tiptoed through the Secret Garden, down the hall, and out of the Craft Lodge.

August nights in the Wisconsin woods held no harbinger of the cool weather. The warmth and humidity in the air held Cat like a water blanket, making friends with dry skin that had gotten too much sun the day before. She'd been a night stroller her whole life, less so after leaving behind the safety of the camp. The streets of any given city held risks the crickets at the camp knew nothing of.

With the cool grass feeling like clean, damp hair between her toes, she walked and recalled her soundless treks to sit in a canoe and write in her diary—something that amounted to many Dear Diary beginnings but minimal plot. There was precious little for a teenage girl to write about—the counselors were too old to crush on, the theater kids too young. The night was the only time she wasn't responsible for Ginger, though, and there were times she did write about this.

Cat had moved off the path to the soft sand when she heard a splash, then another, not far from shore. She tucked behind a tree and watched as a head emerged, then a neck and broad shoulders—a torso then abruptly moved into her sight line. A swimmer with a trim waist and forearms. Gary.

Covered by darkness and behind a straight, thick trunk, Cat did not look away. Gary stopped, dropped his head back, and ran his hands over his face and hair. In the moonlight, Gary was the cover of a romance novel. Droplets of water made their way down his fat-free glistening skin. Should she call out? Let him know she was there?

He took a step, hip turning toward land. Cat saw that Gary had what lean, muscular athletes have: a gorgeous display of the anterior muscles of the pelvic girdle. She'd been a health teacher too long; it was sad that, even when Cat ogled a man, she thought in physiological terms. To be fair, it had been a while, seven months to be exact, since she'd seen a man naked. And Steve was not Gary, not by a long, apple-shaped-risk-of-heart-disease shot.

She should call out. Stop him. Gary took another step, and Cat followed that lean joint down, past his lower abdominals to, yup, there it was. The money shot. Yikes. Cat exhaled, suddenly needing to pee again.

Cat wished Ginger were here so she could see this. Under Gary's work clothes, he was all Michelangelo sculpture–like. Did she know? Did everyone know this spectacular physique was in charge of mowing? Mesmerized by the view, she watched as he took the last few steps onto the pebbled beach, displaying his only imperfection. He had small calf muscles. So small in fact, they hardly looked up to the task of keeping Adonis upright. She and Ginger would laugh and give themselves away if her sister had been standing by her.

As she assessed his thin legs and the imbalanced structural load of his body, Cat lifted her eyes up, up, up to his face, where she found his eyes. Staring at her for one, two, three seconds. She froze, every nerve on edge.

Then he bent gloriously to pick up his towel and began drying off. Had he seen her? It wasn't possible unless this grumpy Adonis could see through a tree. Then her Kegels, like his calves—not ready for prime-time action—sent up a warning flare.

She closed her eyes and concentrated on not peeing in her onesie. She heard Gary start up the hill. When he passed the spot where Cat hid, she got an excellent look at the hollows of his hip and butt. When he was entirely out of sight, she tore off the shoulders of her stretchy suit, squatted, and whispered "Holy gluteus maximus" while relieving herself. She used a crumpled tissue in her pocket and dropped it in her hiding place, promising she would pick it up and throw it away later.

With eyes as big as a deer's, she moved to the top of the hill, Gary gone, the Craft Lodge in sight. The damp grass cooled her body up to the back of her neck. By morning, her path in the grass would disappear, replaced with early-morning dew, and Cat would wonder if she'd been dreaming or if one more unpredictable obstacle to her old life had been placed in her path.

CHAPTER SEVENTEEN

ESCAPE ROOM

"Cat. Wake up, honey"—and she did because if Ginger was calling her *honey*, something wasn't right.

"Is Bob back?" Cat said, before she'd even opened her eyes. It was as if her mind had been awake all night, itching to get the show on the road. She turned toward Ginger's voice into a patch of sunlight and felt a scrubbing of sand between her sheets—the memory of Gary's skinny-dip returned. As if Ginger could view her thoughts, Cat sat up, her eyes wide, the sheet falling from her shoulders.

"No. He's not back," Ginger said. "Why are you naked?"

"Why do you care?" she snapped. Cat had stripped down for a lot of reasons last night, but she wasn't about to explain any of them to Ginger. One of the problems of pregnancy was there were a lot of sexy hormones playing around in her body and no place for them to go after growing the baby was done for the day. Her body was in overdrive, in the home stretch, rounding third, or however you wanted to put it, and it needed some action. The only happy ending that could happen this week would be when Cat and Lefty got on the road home.

"Sheesh, you're crabby."

"I slept like crap, I'm not in my own bed, and we're running out of time. Who would be overjoyed in this situation?"

"Some people," Ginger said. "Shirtless, for example. He was chipper this morning. I had him take Lefty for a run."

Ginger touched Cat, and the movement felt very *Brace yourself.*

"What's going on," Cat said, sliding her wrist out of her sister's cold-fingered grasp.

"Don't be mad," Ginger said.

Instantly furious at the implication that she was a mad person twice this morning, Cat blinked and oof'ed herself out of bed. In Cat's teaching life, she was hard to rattle. A kid once barfed all over study hall and passed out. Cat didn't panic or retch even once while evacuating the classroom, mopping the kid up, and getting a trash bin for the rest of his stomach contents before he came to. His parents wrote her a thank-you note for maintaining their son's dignity and privacy under pressure. It came with a coupon for Buffalo Wild Wings that had expired before she could use it.

"Tell me what's going on," Cat said in the barely concealed urgent tone she used when supervising first graders and one had a bead stuffed up her nose.

"There are no supplies for the gala," Ginger said.

"Okay. Well, that can't be. I have the inventory." In a series of brisk moves, Cat dropped her sheet, grabbed a different but identical onesie from her luggage, and found the folder.

"Your boobs are huge," Ginger said.

"Yours were huge too. Where did you look for the supplies?"

"Where else? The only big supply closet we have."

"Did you look anywhere else?" Cat said, pulling on her maternity bra, then a T-shirt, and finally yanking the one-size-fits-all suit over her shoulder like suspenders.

"Where else would I look, Cat?"

"Nothing is as it's supposed to be here," Cat said, objectively sounding mad. "The supplies could be anywhere. Right?"

"Your straps are messed up."

In her haste to redress, Cat had pulled her head through the wrong armhole, leaving her in a Tarzan cross-body situation. Her left T-shirt-covered breast stuck out like the swollen gland that it was. Exasperated, Cat yanked at a strap and tried to pull it over her head. Ginger got involved, making it worse, and Cat said, "Don't. Ughhhh. Why are you helping me?"

Ginger stepped back and said, "Suit yourself," which sounded like their mother.

"Give me the key."

Ginger dangled a key with a silver-circled tag attached by a bent piece of black-coated electrical wire. The words *Supply closet* were penned in their mother's cramped handwriting. Strange how her mother's presence whispered between the lines of her father's louder voice here at camp.

"Get me a half cup of coffee. Not decaf. Do they have eggs? I'll meet you in the Mess Hall." Cat pushed her feet into her sandals, thinking the last thing she needed was her baby sister tagging along, asking questions no one but Bob could answer. Cat would race over to the supply closet and see what was actually going on.

"You can really move," Ginger said with appreciation. "When I was pregnant, I put my head between my legs every time I stood up. Mom gave me that crystallized ginger she loves until I barfed on Hamlet's skull. That's how I got started with papier-mâché. Mom made me make a new one before opening night. You know how she was. I scrubbed it with bleach, but no, not good enough for the germophobe."

"We don't have time for memory lane," Cat snapped, startling herself at how sharply the words came out of her mouth. "I've got to focus," she said as a nonapology. "Go on. I'll be right there."

Ginger huffed and stubbornly moved out of the cabin slower than Cat would have liked, just to be contrary. After a trip to the bathroom, Cat arrived at the Admin Building, the floors slippery with humidity. She slid an inch, caught herself, and said, "Bob," as if it was the best curse she could come up with.

Everything about Bob's disappearance didn't fit the Bob she'd seen in front of the crowd, passionately discussing his vision for the camp. Sure, he was a poor man's Tony Robbins, but he didn't know that. Even as a kid, he was a shitty little show-off. He'd stand on the diving pier, all skinny legs in too-big plaid swimming trunks, promising a swan dive. Then he'd spring off the board, execute a weeny cannonball, and splash the two sight-impaired girls who'd turned toward the noise. He obviously didn't care about the outcome. He cared about the attention, the possibility of adoration. One look at the audience made it clear that the adult campers were just as enamored with Bob, and he'd positively preened with their admiration.

In the storage closet, a narrow room, one of the few that didn't leak during heavy rain, Cat fit the silver key into the lock. With the ease of hinges oiled carefully by the fastidious and fat-free Gary, the door swung open without a sound.

The shelves meant to hold supplies for the gala—tablecloths, decorations, centerpieces—were filled with nothing that made a gala gala-o-rific. Cat's breath caught, and she would have doubled over with the gut-punching reality of the empty shelves, but her midriff allowed none of that. Instead, she clenched her fists.

Up against the wall were two larger-than-life-size cardboard cutouts of Alistair and Raj wearing barbershop quartet–style red-and-white-striped vests with straw hats. Alistair looked forever contrite in contrast to Raj, with his smugly superior grin. Cat pulled her arm back and punched Raj in the face hard, visualizing Bob. The cardboard bunny jutted back and bounced forward as if angling for a fight.

Cat pulled the long string that hung from a bare bulb in the ceiling and blinked at the contents. Was there anything usable? Anything at all? The room was packed to the ceiling with costumes and props from decades' worth of plays. There was the gigantic lollipop from a production of *Willy Wonka*, licorice whips made from foam pool noodles, and cardboard chocolate bars.

Hanging from a rod above her head were costumes from *The Wizard of Oz*. A springy monkey tail covered in faux fur curled around a painted paper towel roll spear. Pink tulle and black-and-yellow satin were slung like garland along the upper shelf and wound their way around a refrigerator-box-turned Shakespearean-esque turret chipping green paint onto the dusty floor.

Bob had sent out invitations and collected RSVPs, and the grounds looked undeniably prepared for visitors. Why go to all the trouble and toss aside a chance to raise real money while grandstanding to become a petty party supply thief?

Suddenly, Cat felt swamped with the same overwhelmed feeling she got whenever she tried to picture delivering a baby the shape of a sizable skinless turkey breast out of her petite lady parts. It was too big. She hated pain; no matter how she figured it, the baby would be too big, and there would be pain.

In the past, she'd reminded herself that women worldwide delivered their turkey breasts every damn day, all day. In fields, leaky blow-up swimming pools, and highly equipped birthing centers. She could do it if they could do it, and that was enough to calm her down. In this case, there were no legions of women throwing a gala in two days without supplies to a bunch of VIPs who were being lured to the backwoods to experience fraud and be asked to fund it.

Cat braced herself against Raj's corrugated elbow and tried to slow her breathing.

She pictured a stream of expensive cars winding through the country roads. Each Lexus, BMW, and the occasional millionaire-next-door Honda would turn the corner and see a plain old kids' camp. No expansive white tent, no chocolate fountain, no tartare anything. Media vans with satellite dishes and microphones would park, and Ira Glass, with his nasal, oddly pausing cadences filled with question marks, would ask the tricky question: *Is this place a fake? Listen on* This American Life.

Each person, more famous than the last, would step out of their cars in their shiny Tory Burch sandals and tangerine-colored Versace loafers: a benefactor's idea of camp chic. They'd walk through the arbor and what? Meet Camille in her Birkenstocks, leading a Christian rock sing-along. Or Gary, who would eke out a "Bob's gone" and then wander off?

The light bulb in the storage closet flickered, and Cat recalled her father calling the kids at camp the Littles. He did it to prompt himself that they were all little people who needed a helping hand and a beautiful location. Her child twitched, reminding Cat that all too soon, her own little child would leave her perfect, protected nest and join the rest of the people fighting to enjoy a tree and the simplicity of stars in the sky.

"No. Nope," Cat said, feeling the old outrage of someone else's plans taking precedence over her own. Cat snatched a cardboard spear leaning in the folds of a glittery green curtain, the corrugated rod made stiff with silver paint. She twirled the spear like a drum major in front of a marching band and hit a fake fur tail, sending the monkeys over her head into a spiral.

Ginger appeared with a wary expression, holding a thick ceramic cup of coffee. Cat stood firm, a soldier preparing to storm a grassy field during a Civil War reenactment.

"Don't tell anyone there's no supplies yet. I'm going to the Piggly Wiggly and buying them out of whatever I can find on the list."

"It closed."

"No, it didn't."

Ginger gave Cat a look that said, *You've been gone, and are we really going to fight about this again?*

"Is there a Costco or something?" Cat said.

"Three hours away. You drive a MINI, and Bob and Elaine took the van. The other one is getting new brakes."

Cat had to get out of the storage closet; it had the feeling of an escape room with no drawers or ledges where a key could be hidden.

"Follow me," Cat said, taking a firm step forward.

Ginger, her eyes wide, stepped aside and followed her older sister into the office. Cat shoved aside the family's old record player and vinyl copies of musicals that sat near the decades-old intercom. She selected one of the two nested walkie-talkies and clipped it to her onesie, pulling the stretchy neckline down until the device rested on her belly. She handed the other to Ginger. "Keep it on."

Ginger nodded seriously.

Holding the spear upright with her left hand, Cat steadied herself, took a breath, and flipped on the intercom. A blast of feedback echoed throughout the camp, then silenced. She lifted the microphone, squeezed the trigger, and said in a forceful voice, "Shirtless and Gary, please report to the Mess Hall."

The words echoed through the camp just as announcements had when she was a kid, announcing rainy-day activities or an open field to play capture the flag. Cat steadied herself as she felt a shift in the space-time continuum that might've been a rattle of low blood sugar. The silence that followed felt like a moment where every living being—every piece of grass, veiny leaf, and pointy pine needle—seemed to lean in to view what might happen next.

CHAPTER EIGHTEEN

THE GREAT BAMBOOZLER

Cat charged out of the Administration Building just as Gary was rounding the Rippling Ridge encampment. He rode straight-backed in the golf cart seat like General Custer on his faithful steed, but with much less *Let's go to war* and a lot of *What do you want?* energy in his stance.

"Come on, Gary," Cat said as if he were a slow-moving child.

Shirtless met the two sisters at the Mess Hall and held the door for them. Cat motioned for Ginger to go ahead and saw Gary had a *You're not the boss of me* look on his face. With less than a foot between them, Cat yanked the walkie-talkie on her chest to her mouth, staring straight at him, and shouted into the speaker, "Come! On! Gary!"

The device at Gary's hip surged to life with Cat's staticky command. When he didn't move, Cat said into the gadget, without breaking eye contact, "Do you read me? Tiny Dancer? Come in."

Shirtless gasped, and Ginger ran for cover inside the building.

With his large, capable hands and uncommonly slender fingers, Gary coolly twisted the volume off.

She lowered the walkie-talkie, held the door, and gestured for him to go ahead.

Gary dismounted, stepped to the door, and said, "No. After you."

Shirtless whistled through his teeth and said, "He mad."

"Well. I'm mad too," Cat said with less conviction after playing dueling eyeballs with Gary. This simmering chemistry she felt for this epically annoying, self-important, hot AF smug groundskeeper had her rattled. What was her deal, and for that matter, what was his deal? She wasn't the problem here at Summer Camp. He should be thrilled that someone was wrangling the Littles. "Thrilled," she said aloud, and promised she'd go to therapy until she'd dislodged Gary's . . . everything from her mind.

Inside the Mess Hall, Shirtless went to stand next to June, their forearms close but not touching. Ginger appeared ready for anything, and Cat didn't dare let her eyes roam in Gary's direction. Wynn moved into view with a bowl and a whisk dripping something creamy. Cat nodded, grateful for her attendance.

"Okay, everybody, this is how it is," Cat said, feeling like a seven-months-pregnant Joan of Arc with her sword. "There's a gala happening in two days."

The group looked puzzled. *Like yeah, was that ever in question?*

Gary coughed. Raised his eyebrows. Expecting Cat to announce that she was leaving. Again.

"There's no party supplies. Bob's gone. You can't cancel. You need money," Cat said, purposefully using the word *you* instead of *we*, and while no one probably noticed, she congratulated herself on her distancing language. She let the information sink in as Brittany joined the group.

"How are we going to throw a party without anything?" Brittany said.

"Yeah. It's a problem. But you have to. I'm not a party planner, but I know there's no fiesta without food. Wynn, has there been any food delivered that could be used to feed a bunch of rich people?"

Wynn glanced up at the clock. "They were supposed to come yesterday, early morning. Sometimes the truck is late, but not this late." She put the aluminum bowl on the counter with a ting.

"Is it safe to say nothing has been ordered for the gala?" Cat said.

The Mess Hall screen door whined open, and all heads turned with one last glorious display of hope for Bob. Bob, with his affable apologies, his warm, overly confident demeanor. Bob, Christ the King. Savior of misfits.

Instead, it was Camille, followed closely by an irritated Matt.

"Nothing has been ordered for the gala?" Camille said, meaning, *You are wrong about this.*

"Yeah, come on in. You may as well hear this too," Cat said.

"There's no supplies, Camille. The camp is in deep trouble," Ginger said, delighted to have information the annoying woman wasn't privy to.

In a quick pivot, as if Camille had been asked to summarize the situation, she said, "It appears that Bob and Elaine have been delayed in going into town for supplies. I'm certain they'll return soon and help us prepare for the gala." Her words brushed through the air like there was some invisible rug under which she could sweep everyone's questioning looks. "In the meantime, let's get everybody together. We can have a sing-along. I've got the music for a VeggieTales medley. Maybe we can all nap."

"Oh no," Cat said, slapping the spear on the top of one of the wooden picnic tables. "No, that is not what is happening." She gestured like Camille's words had left a stink in the room. "We . . . *you* have nothing! There's no internet. We . . . you, can't order stuff, we're broke, and we can't cancel the party. On top of that, you might remember pledging your salaries to help this camp get through August? Well, that money is gone too. As far as I can tell, nobody is getting paid."

"No paychecks?" Brittany said, suddenly the speediest mind in the room.

Cat pointed to her as if to say, *Yes, finally. A genius among you.*

Camille, in her faded T-shirt printed with the saying *Got Happy?* a smiling sun made out of the *O*, stepped forward. "I don't believe you."

"I don't care," Cat said.

"We should call the police," June said, then sat on one of the benches and flushed pink. Shirtless moved to her side and whispered something, and she said, "This can't be happening."

"Bob would not leave us," Camille said with conviction. "I know it. He had big plans for the camp after this summer. Concrete plans."

Cat noticed that Ginger did not argue, and this ignited her ire anew.

"Have you met Bob? I talked to him for five minutes, and it's clear he's nothing but plans," said Cat.

"I should have listened to my dad," June said, "but he's biased. He hates him. He said Bob couldn't go the distance." June dropped her chin and imitated her father's voice. "'Bobby can't go the distance, Junie.'" Then, restoring her usual helium-filled voice, she continued, "He told me that before I came to camp."

"That's slander," Camille said with such legal fortitude that Cat considered the implications.

"Not if it's true," countered Wynn, surprising everyone with her certainty.

"My dad was way older, but he always said"—June dropped her voice again—"'My little brother never disappoints in his disappointing.'"

Everyone looked at June like a team of rustic synchronized swimmers. "Bob's your uncle?" said Cat.

"Yup. Uncle Bob. The Great Bamboozler, my dad called him. Bamboozler Bob. But I always liked Uncle Bob. He's always so nice. Positive. I thought our family needed positivity."

Neither Ginger nor Shirtless seemed surprised at this information.

"You are Bob's niece?" Cat said.

"I don't believe any of this." Camille crossed her arms and shook her head.

Gary broke his silence. "Have you checked Bob's cabin?" Cat glowered at Gary. He knew she'd been there. What was he on about?

Camille lit up like a flashbulb. "I will. I'll go right now!" She strode directly to the large double doors of the Mess Hall, happy to be the one to solve this mystery, find Bob, and put all things right. "Cat," Camille said, pointing as she walked, "get everybody together. Bob is going to have orders. Wynn, you get ready for the menu. June, pull yourself together. You don't want Bob to see you having lost faith in the family, and Shirtless, put your shirt on. A clean one. With the camp logo." With that, the bossy evangelist banged out the door into the afternoon.

Matt turned an imaginary crank on his fist to raise his middle finger and flip off Camille like a fourteen-year-old middle-school boy, then followed her out the door.

"He's obsessed with her," said June. "It makes no sense, but he is."

Gary leaned into Cat, and she felt his warm breath brush her ear. "Finish what you have to say," he whispered, more a challenge than a support. Cat knew Gary expected her to give up.

"No more college for me," Wynn said, dropping the whisk into the bowl.

"I'm screwed too," Brittany said.

A collective grumble rose from the group, and it wouldn't be long before the staff realized how bad off they were. Cat caught Ginger's gaze, motioned for her to chime in.

At that second, Norm, the man Cat had seen moving around the camp and accepting treats at the exit, held open the double screen doors of the Mess Hall like Moses entering the hall of thieves. "I finished my cookies!" He half staggered, half swaggered into the room in cargo shorts and bare feet. "I love this place. I am on your side." He leaned against one of the picnic tables. "I'm dizzy, tired, hungry, and want to shower without everyone watching me, though." His energy was seven-year-old about to have a tantrum. "But I know what you're up to, and I want in."

Norm's speech was so random the staff had a variety of baffled looks on their faces.

"Norm," Wynn said evenly, "we had a deal. What are you doing here, and how many cookies did you eat?"

He looked at Wynn with bloodshot, half-moon eyes and smiled. "You are a delightful child," he said. "And naughty. I ate all of them." He sighed and said in a confessional tone, "All of them. I'm a stress eater. It's my fatal flaw."

"I wish I had known that, Norm," Wynn began.

"Okay. What's happening. Where did you come from? You shouldn't be here," Cat interrupted.

Norm walked like a big-footed baby into the kitchen, where Wynn held a sugar cookie. The man took it, and Wynn mimed the universal sign for smoking dope—pinched fingers to her lips—then pointed to him.

"I cannot leave this camp without my money. I have tuition due. This is not an option," said June. This display of boundaries from the girl who quietly handed out Band-Aids and comfort felt almost heroic.

"Okay, everyone," Ginger said.

"My dad was against me coming here," said June. "He's always so sure what's good for me. I can't go home without doing everything humanly possible to get paid."

"Yes!" Cat said.

"We'll put on a party, collect the money, pay ourselves," Shirtless said.

"Exactly." Cat pointed to her nephew. This is what she'd wanted: If they saw what was at stake, they'd take charge.

"In nursing school, they tell you that when things get disorganized, to fall back on this nursing process thing. I liked it. I like organizing."

June walked over to the giant old chalkboard used for scheduling hanging on the wall.

"I mean, not sure we have time for that," Cat said, feeling the pace sag. She suspected nothing said *dull* like the Nursing Process.

June grabbed the chamois cloth that hung by a red cord and, with purpose, wiped out the schedule of Empathy Games, Affirmation Catchphrases, and Doggie Paddle Depression Swim until she had a large, clean slate. Shirtless moved to her side and handed her a piece of chalk.

"Okay. 'Assessment' is the first part," June said and wrote *Money gone. People coming.*

No supplies. On the board.

"We have supplies. Just not party supplies," Wynn said, and June erased *No supplies* with the heel of her hand.

Cat itched to chime in, take over. She tried to get Ginger's attention to get her sister to lead, but she was comforting Brittany. The Littles needed to get moving. The gala wasn't a flowchart and a campfire with marshmallows.

From the back of the kitchen, sounding like his head was in the refrigerator, Norm's voice floated into the room: "Guys, guys." He moved behind the counter, where Wynn pulled the cellophane off a bowl. "I'm a spy." Using his bare hands, he scooped a tangle of noodles into his mouth, sucking the last few strands in with a wet slurp.

Wynn mimed smoking weed again, adding a silent cough and waving away imaginary smoke, and then wobbled with a goofy expression to confirm that Norm was high and out of his mind.

"This jackass Steve hired me to appraise the value of this place. Wants to buy it, turn it into a water park," Norm said.

Cat's mouth dropped open.

"Water park," June said as if on an inner tube with a slow, hissing leak.

Norm pulled a noodle from the bowl and sucked it into his pursed lips with a slurpy pop.

"He said it's run by a moron. Owned by a family of idiots. Sitting ducks."

"Moron?" Cat said, seeing Steve in her bedroom lo seven months ago. Watched him reach for his pants, his soft banker's belly like unbaked bread dough contracting as he tried to right the wrong of placing both legs into one pant leg. The perplexing concentration on his face. The man had to sit on the bed and start over. Idiots? The words a cymbal crash, waking her John Philip Sousa / "The Stars and Stripes Forever" patriotism for her family and this camp once again.

Gary moved to Ginger's side, put his hand on her shoulder, and sent a murderous look at Norm, who said quickly, "But Steve's a dick, and I love you guys. And this place is amazing. These noodles are the best thing I've ever tasted in my whole entire life." He took another handful, looked at the group, and said with wet eyes, "What you do here is magic. I hate banks. I'm with you guys." He lifted his arm in a raised pasta-fisted show of solidarity. He said this with such spiritual reverence that everyone sat slightly stunned by his noodle love.

Everyone but Cat, who, with the words *moron* and *idiots* ringing in her ears, walked over to the chalkboard, selected the longest piece of chalk in the tray, and on her tiptoes, her belly skimming the slate, wrote *Take Back the Camp*.

Cat cleared her throat and addressed the group. "We'll give them idiots. Idiots right between the eyes," she said, pointing to the Littles with her piece of chalk. Cat swept the room with a scathing glare and forgot her detachment pronouns. "We are not morons and idiots. We are amazing. We are warriors." Shirtless itched his bare chest, a hive starting at his collarbone. Brittany shouldered one of the bunnies as if to protect her from Cat, who'd taken on the tone of an army general. "We are going to throw a party that will show everyone that we are not to be messed with. This is war!"

Ginger flushed with pleasure; her arm around Brittany's shoulders, she scratched the bunny behind its ears. June took Shirtless's fingers away from his scratchy spot and gazed at Cat with anticipation.

"Huzzah," Cat said like a pregnant Prussian soldier with a full supply closet and a band of trained party planners at her side.

CHAPTER NINETEEN

THERE'S NO "I" IN "ME"

The Mess Hall went quiet, each person taking in Cat's sudden, some-what inexplicable spur to action and the abrupt, vengeful look in her eye. June cleared her throat and said, "The next steps to the process are . . ." In her perfect penmanship, June wrote the categories *Diagnosis*, *Plan*, *Implement*, and *Evaluation* next to where Cat with her own piece of chalk wrote MURDER in block letters.

"Are we killing someone?" Matt walked through the door like someone who had been waiting for homicide the entire summer, and now, finally, it was on the activity board.

Cat ignored him and said, "We need a plan if we're not going to leave here victims of slick Uncle Bob, his shitty wife, and a rich, impo-tent bastard who thinks he's in charge of the world."

Norm perked up. "Is Steve really impotent? Because that would be awesome."

"Mostly," Cat said. "Not entirely."

Ginger gave Cat a questioning look while June erased the word MURDER.

"Brittany, we've got a gala to plan. Go get anyone you think would be an asset. And PS, everyone, you're going to get paid."

"We have a whole plan in the Craft Lodge," said Ginger. "I worked on it when Bob first had the idea for a gala. Before Elaine took it over."

"Why didn't you say something?"

Ginger narrowed her eyes, and Cat recalled that her sister had mentioned something, but what had she been waiting for? "Go get it."

Ginger turned and literally ran out of the Mess Hall, passing the front windows with rare speed. Lefty, excited for some action, followed close at her heels.

"Nice. It's a coup. I love a coup," Matt said, neatly pivoting away from bloodletting to overthrowing.

Norm, elbow-deep in crunching his way through a box of Rice Krispies, swallowed and said, "Hear, hear."

"Okay," Cat said. "We don't have unlimited time. Camille will eventually get tired of going through every drawer in Bob and Elaine's cabin and come back. I'm not going to arm wrestle her for control. If we're going to do this, we can't split ranks. Either we're all in, or we go our separate ways."

The group muttered an assent except for Norm, who said, "Hip, hip, hooray!" Gary walked over and took the cereal box, put his hand on Norm's shoulder, and guided him to sit on one of the picnic table benches. He offered nothing in his expression, but Cat read disapproval. She wanted to say, *What? What, Gary? What is your problem? What do you suggest we do, you with your swimming body and strong jaw? Why don't you go prune a tree?* Thank goodness she didn't say that lame directive. He'd have rolled his eyes.

"While we wait for Ginger, let's brainstorm," Cat said.

The group blinked.

Cat clapped her hands. "Ideas, people. What should we do with the rich people? We need to impress them." And Cat knew that if the campers all bumbled together, at least they couldn't blame Cat when it all went south. "Okay," Cat said. "How will we persuade them to donate and write nice things about the camp in their news outlets and social media?"

The group blinked again.

"Just throw out some ideas. There are no bad ideas."

June said, "Maybe when they get here, we give them a tour, and then we can all talk about what this place means to us."

"Sincerity? Nobody will donate big bucks for that," said Matt, fixing his topknot. "I can do a master class on yoga."

"The richies do real yoga all day long, and you're not a master yogi," said Wynn.

"Hey," Matt said, outraged.

"No real yoga instructor says 'Downward dawg' and 'Namaste, bitches' every single time they teach a class," said Shirtless, his neck flushing pink.

June cut them off. "A tour with a theme like happiness is a journey, not a destination. Bob invited people to show them that a place like this is needed. We have to show them in one night that what we do over a week makes people feel better."

"Does it work, though?" Cat said too quickly, thinking of the fake data and fraudulent claims. Information that would have to be finessed during the presentation part of the gala.

"It worked for me," Wynn said, and Cat saw a memory of sadness around her cheery halo.

"Wynn, what about food? What do we have to work with?"

"I'm way ahead of you," Wynn said. "Elaine was supposed to order prime rib, and we were going to have it with twice-baked potatoes and cheesecake. I thought that was all very stuck-up. I mean, we're a camp, after all. If she had asked me, I would have told her we should do food stations all over camp."

"Elegant stations, right?" Cat interjected.

"Make portable stuff on sticks and in foil bags—like we do for campouts. Why be something we're not?" Wynn said.

"That's a great way to waste time, because it'll take forever for the ladies to walk around all dressed up," said June.

Shirtless said, "Like that wouldn't be hard. We have tons of Christmas lights left over from Christmas in July. Which I didn't get at all. But we could light the paths."

Brittany said, "I think we should all be wearing something that shows we're staff and unified. Not just our stupid uniforms—something more, you know. Happy."

June took notes on the chalkboard, and Matt said, "Where are we going to lead them to?"

"Something at the Auditorium, a presentation. Ginger can speak. Ask for checks," Cat said, thinking again about how to confess that everyone had been invited under false pretenses.

"Checks? Oh yeah, I saw Grandpa do that a bunch," said Shirtless, looking at Cat.

This was not the time for Cat to say what she was thinking. That the more she listened to the staff ideas, she realized the less they understood the kind of party that garnered the kind of money to save a business, her finances, her house. These thoughts were like a revving motor she couldn't shut off without action. What could she do that would direct without doing too much?

"Here's what's going to happen." Cat tapped her foot, thinking. "I'm going to pair everybody up and give you a job. You can't argue with me about your jobs, and I won't argue with you about what you do with them. You just have to stick with this journey idea. Deal?"

Everyone nodded, and she said, "Matt, you're with Camille. You have to keep her occupied."

Matt scoffed, "What? Why me?"

"You know full well why you," Wynn said. "You've been trying to bag her since day one. Now's your chance to put your Kuma Satra, yoga BS to the test."

"Kama Sutra," Cat corrected.

"I'll be with Camille!" Norm said, a Rice Krispie stuck on his chin.

A makeup-less, pale young woman crept in the side door, and Brittany said, "Hey! Good. We need you."

"I'm sorry, what is your name?" Cat said.

The woman looked like her name might be Beige but instead said, "Penelope."

"Okay, Penny, you and Brittany . . ."

"Penelope," she said.

"Pardon me. Penelope, you are paired with Brittany. She'll fill you in. You will work on staff appearance. If it's just the staff uniform, they must be clean and in good shape."

Brittany whispered to Penelope, who turned and left the Mess Hall. "Where's she going?" Cat said.

"Oh, that's just how she is. Give her a job, and she just starts it. She helps me clean all the pet cages and never complains. She gets to it."

"That's the spirit! Shirtless and June, you two are theme and decor, mapping where food should be. Wynn, everyone will help you with the food. Gary will send his guys." Cat didn't look at Gary for an affirmation. Why should she?

"Norm, you're with Gary."

"Gary, my man," Norm said with his eyes closed. He lifted his hand for a fist bump, but when the bro move went unanswered, he said, "I can be helpful, I'm a lawyer." Then he shrugged, put his head on the counter, and promptly fell asleep.

"Gary, you need to pick a couple of people to help you."

"Do I?" Gary said with mock amusement.

"Give me something to do with Camille," said Matt. "I can't just chase her around, running interference."

"We're going to need music," June said.

Cat snapped her fingers. "Perfect. Get her to pick a song to sing. Tell her it will be our centerpiece. Nothing from Joseph and that musical about his coat."

A loud banging at the Mess Hall door broke through the conversation as Penelope tried to open the door and wrestle a large, maybe six-foot panel into the room. Shirtless ran to her and grabbed the door. Inside, Penelope stood the panel on end and turned it toward the group.

It was a large piece of wood with the colors of the rainbow painted on it with glitter running its six-foot length.

June smiled, recognizing it. Penelope said, "It's part of a theater set. Not a good one, but we can use the props from it; it's all in the back of the Trading Post because we used them recently. There are like five of these. When it was a kids' camp, it was hard to find plays with enough parts for little kids. *The Wizard of Oz* has a ton of Munchkins."

Penelope didn't know who Cat was. It set off a strange impulse for Cat to say something like, *I know. I was there. This was my camp.* To defend the shabby rainbow. The kids helped as much as possible. They made everything.

"That is awesome, Penelope," said Shirtless.

Cat had to agree, it fit the Over the Rainbow on the invitations. It would be a good theme for a gala in the woods that hadn't seen a black tie or white tablecloth since its inception. There was a fanciful, jokey, hopeful campiness to *The Wizard of Oz*, and there was nothing more jokey and campy than this camp.

Cat snapped her fingers. "Matt, get Camille to sing 'Somewhere Over the Rainbow.' Get her to practice it like a thousand times."

Matt muttered, "I have the worst job ever." He pushed out the door to find Camille.

"The rest of the staff has to be brought up to date. Get the ropes course guy and that nature girl, whatever her name is. Get everybody involved. If someone balks, send them to Gary. There is no 'me' in 'team.'" Hoping everyone got the message that they were in this together; this wasn't on Cat.

Shirtless said, "Wait, that isn't right."

June said, "I."

Cat waited for her to continue, and when she didn't, she said, "You what?"

June said, "'I.' There is no 'I.'"

Cat said, "Oh yeah. 'I' then. There is no 'I' in 'me.'"

CHAPTER TWENTY

UNSPOOL YOUR BOBBIN

Cat stood back from the group, their heads down over one of the rustic Mess Hall tables, transformed into a gala-planning command center. She listened to the conversation. June's breathy, organized voice lay underneath Wynn's popping soprano. The two women: peanut butter and jelly, sweet and salty, friends for life.

Penelope clutched the rainbow panel and nodded emphatically whenever Brittany said, "You know?" about every third word. Penelope, so plain and agreeable. Shirtless had suggested horseshoes, a game nobody played or liked anymore, and June thought a CPR demonstration might be fun.

There they all sat, humming with optimism after being massively let down. A gush of warmth for the group flooded her chest, and she allowed it for one, two, three seconds before crowding it out with reason.

This gala was going to be absurd. Their only hope was that, once the guests entered the grounds, they'd get caught up in their campy ways. Like in theater, when the lights go out and all eyes are trained on the stage, there's a suspension of disbelief. The audience isn't looking for seams in the painted scenery; they're in on the joke, the understanding that a play is a performance that has a budget, and the hope is that ticket holders will go along for the ride. Her father had built this place on that notion.

Gary strolled over to stand next to Cat but didn't immediately speak. It felt manipulative, his few words delivered at a snail's pace. A device that forced people to match his speed and await his pearls of wisdom or look rude and impatient by comparison.

"What, Gary?"

"No partner, Queen Cat?"

"Don't call me that," Cat said.

It was a nickname from a skit she'd done a few months before leaving for college. Sometimes, their father would have kids perform short, well-known fairy tales. Improv exercises with a familiar storyline to help with stage fright before lines had to be memorized. They'd done "Snow White," and Cat had been the evil queen. She'd performed a bloodthirsty laugh, and it caught on. Before long, everyone was mimicking the evil cackle of Queen Cat, which had been funny until it got obnoxious and followed her everywhere.

"Fair-weather leader of the people?" His face was blank and hard to read, but his tone and words were filled with challenge.

"I didn't see you stepping up to take charge. You've been here all along while Bob took this camp and throttled it."

"Yup," he said with a nod. "Every day." He turned. This was the last word, and he'd delivered it like a sharp knife thrown at a target.

"You want me to go?" Cat hissed, eyeing the staff to keep her wrath from poisoning the room. "I'll go home. I'd love more than anything to go home. At least there . . ." She stopped herself before she brought up her vibrator or something equally mortifying. She turned, and Shirtless had his head down as he wrote something and wasn't looking at Cat, while everyone else in the room looked stunned. "At least there I can sleep through the night," she said unconvincingly. Cat turned and followed Gary out the door and watched as he stepped onto his golf cart. "Gary!"

Lefty came bounding over, with Ginger close behind, her sister panting and holding three tall rolls of white paper and a basket of multicolored markers. "What's going on? I just saw Matt. People have jobs?"

With Cat's eyes on Gary, motoring away, Cat said, "Yeah. I paired everyone up. They're in the Mess Hall, planning. What is wrong with Gary?"

Ginger went still. "You couldn't wait for me to get back? Or maybe you didn't even notice I left. Is that it? 'Stupid Ginger, the screwup. What could she possibly have to offer? What's the use anyway? She'll mess it up. So whatever.'"

"What? No. It's not like that at all."

"Oh, I'm sure it's not, Cat. It never is like anything."

"You called me to come help. I said I'd help. This is me, helping."

"Yes. I did. I called you to help. To assist," Ginger said. "You know what that word means, right? I can tell you what it doesn't mean. It doesn't mean take over."

"I'm not taking over!" Cat shouted. "They're all in there doing their own thing. Believe me, if I was taking over, there wouldn't be a round-robin horseshoes tournament."

One of the paper tubes slid out of Ginger's arms, and the happiness on her sister's face when Cat arrived shifted to stale defeat. "I'll get Shirtless to fill me in. C'mon, Lefty, let's get you some water."

"You have a job, Ginger."

"Do I, Cat? Did you give me a job? Did you find a job for your sister who's been running this camp? Did you give her something to do?" The sarcasm in her voice was needling. "I hope it's an easy job, because you know I might make a mess of it." Ginger pushed into the Mess Hall, Lefty following her, and Cat heard the welcoming voices of those within.

Cat nudged the white paper tube with her foot, picked it up, and turned away from the Mess Hall. Inside the Craft Lodge, she grabbed an orange-fringed throw pillow and eyed it for its effectiveness at muffling a scream. The idea exhausted her. What did people want?

She dropped the pillow and moved to her bedroom. Her luggage sat waiting at the end of the bed like a loyal pet. It seemed to look up at her with expectation as if to say, *Zip us up. We're ready to go.* Her car keys sat on the bedside table, and the baby in her belly made a slight movement.

It was always the same for her with Ginger. Nothing Cat ever did was wholly right. She tried to be the good girl, the helper, doing what was asked of her, but if the outcome wasn't exactly right, everyone let you know it. There were always notes, suggestions, and frowns if everyone wasn't happy, and yet nobody seemed to care if Cat was happy.

That was not a thing.

Damned if you do and damned if you don't—that is the helper's credo. That is the T-shirt, the coffee mug slogan for the helpers. Do your best, but if the best doesn't cut it? The helpers are blamed. It was what mothers talked about all the time, and she'd always understood it.

"No. Not this time."

With both hands supporting her baby belly, Cat slammed out the side door of the Craft Lodge and charged into the almost empty Mess Hall.

"Where's Ginger?"

Wynn started like a cartoon character, letting out a tiny "Oh," and she threw a dish towel onto the counter.

"Where's my sister?"

"Not here. By the lake? Not sure, but not here," Wynn said too quickly. Like she was hiding Ginger in the walk-in fridge.

Cat moved into the kitchen area, her head pivoting slowly like a child playing hide-and-seek. "Wynn. Is she here?"

"No." Wynn's eyes shifted to the muffins on the counter.

Cat's stomach growled, and she pointed to a fat brown muffin and said, "Can I have this?"

"Help yourself."

Cat took a bite and peeled the paper back, and food feel-good flooded her brain. "This is delicious," she said, losing a crumb, retrieving it, and finishing the muffin in two bites. "Why are you acting so weird?" Cat narrowed her eyes and, with her free hand, tugged the white cotton dish towel off a cookie sheet, uncovering a tray filled with drug paraphernalia. Marijuana grinders, a food scale, a baggie of dried greens, and recipe cards. Next to the contraband was a bowl of batter.

Wynn shrugged, turned, and smiled her huge Disneyland grin. Then, like a magician resetting a magic trick, tugged the dish towel back over her druggy loot. "People need medicine to get better. Everybody knows that."

"What people, honey?" Cat said, ramping her inquisition energy down so as not to scare away what Wynn might be saying.

"Everybody." Wynn dragged the step stool under the ceiling fan and pulled the cord to stop it.

"Who's everybody?" Cat asked, thinking of noodle-eating Norm. Hoping like hell *everybody* was only Norm. She stilled.

Wynn balanced one foot on the stool, the other on the counter, and hefted a metal box off the uppermost shelf on the wall. She grunted, and Cat held Wynn's ankle to steady her.

"Not everybody. A couple of people, though. Bob and Elaine don't like medicine, but they never said anything about weed." Wynn stepped down, placed the metal box on the counter, and opened it with the key around her neck. Inside was a jumble of twist-off bottles, a mortar and pestle, and a stack of index cards. "I found these blank cards here and recorded everything I made this summer. I thought I might write a cookbook sometime. You know, once everything is legal everywhere."

The cards were the old recipe cards that thousands of grandmothers used to record their best pie secrets and prize-winning brownie ingredients. Three cartoon lemons decorated the corners of the lined cards. Cat read the names of Wynn's unique recipes out loud: "Feel Better Sweet Rolls. Sunny Kale Smoothie. Good Morning Overnight Oats." She looked closer, reading to herself the words—*steel-cut oatmeal, chia seeds, almond milk*, and *sativa*—with slow understanding, followed by instant horror. "Wynn, did you just drug me?"

"No! I'd never do that! You're pregnant. Not that you couldn't use something to unspool your bobbin, if you know what I mean."

Cat erroneously felt relief because the answer to her next question could be catastrophic.

"Did you put weed in everybody's oatmeal?"

"No, silly." She took the card from Cat's hand and flipped it over. "Just in these people's."

Cat read the names; there were six in all. "You drugged six people."

"With oatmeal, yes. Other people got smoothies, rolls, and sometimes the clichéd classic brownie. That lady there," Wynn said, pointing to the name Mia Obenbrenner, "she came during the second session. Super droopy and nervous at the same time. She sulked and scowled, and I kind of admired her screw-you attitude."

"Please tell me that this is just an idea. That you didn't really do this."

Wynn smiled and spoke like a cartoon version of herself. "Oh, I did it, all right. I don't put a ton into the food. It's microdosing," she said, like that made it 100 percent A-okay. "After Mia's morning oatmeal dose, she learned to bead a belt in the Craft Lodge. People are a lot less picky at mealtimes too—they forget all about their gluten allergies, and they'll eat anything."

"Oh, sweetie, marijuana is not legal in Wisconsin," Cat said kindly, like Wynn was a child and it was nap time. Internally, Cat wanted to hold her head and shout, *How many laws are we going to break this month?* Labor laws, fraud, and drugging someone without their knowledge. That had to be assault. If someone, anyone sounded the alarm about any of this at the gala, Cat was going to have to hire a lawyer. Despite the ping-ponging of emotions popping off inside her, Cat modulated her tone and said, "What were you thinking?"

Wynn shrugged again. "People need medicine to get better. If you had pneumonia, you wouldn't sit around and sing a song. You would go to the doctor and get medicine."

Cat looked directly into her eyes. "But you aren't a doctor, Wynn. And these people didn't come to you."

"Well, they kind of did. They came to camp to feel better, and I made them feel better. Look." Wynn pointed at a name on the card. "Take Mr. Timmons."

Cat felt like a priest hearing details of a secret she might be asked to confess in a courtroom under oath. Shaking her head *no*, Cat couldn't stop her fingers from trembling as she read the muffin recipe for a Mr. Ray Timmons.

"He was so mean," said Wynn, looking over Cat's shoulder. "He came to camp because his wife kicked him out. Apparently he watched a ton of porn." Wynn giggled. "He ate a blueberry muffin with indica, and it calmed him down. When his wife came to pick him up, they sat by the mudhole and talked forever. It was nice."

"It's against the law. Like, on a lot of levels, Wynn. You know that, right?" Cat dropped the recipe card, the evidence into the tin box.

"It's usually fine. Norm wasn't supposed to eat all of them at once. He's a lawyer but works as a private detective, something about not passing the bar. Super stressed out. But, like, he loves us now."

"Drugging someone without their knowledge . . . ," said Cat. "We, you, could get in huge trouble if people find out."

"Oh, I should have told you. I tell everyone eventually."

"You do?" A wash of relief splashed over Cat. "Did you get them to sign something? Tell me they signed a waiver. Anything!"

"Ha. No, I'm not a lawyer. I send them home with their recipe card and a travel-size snack of the stuff they've been eating. The cards all have the cannabis strain and dosage on them."

Cat clapped her hand to her mouth as she felt the muffin she'd eaten ride the roundabout in her stomach, looking for a way out.

CHAPTER TWENTY-ONE
WRONG WITH CONVICTION

"You send them home with evidence, in your handwriting, that they've been drugged at this camp?"

Wynn looked like her pig had won the blue ribbon at 4-H camp. "Yup! Sometimes I get a thank-you note. They tell me how much my bakery helped them. That their life is different now. Better." She added, "Mr. Timmons gave up porn, by the way. He collects stamps now, and he and his wife are going to DC to the first post office museum to renew their vows. I got a letter last week."

"Are you medicating the staff?" Cat looked at the glass cookie jar, always filled with her favorite oatmeal raisin cookies.

"I thought about it. Camille could really use some Indica Kush. She's so uptight."

One by one, Cat placed the drug paraphernalia into the cashbox as if backing out of a hungry lion's cage. No wild movements. She was confiscating the evidence and . . . she didn't know what. Burn it in the firepit by the lake on a night when the breeze would blow it away from the Administration Building?

This new felony information would have put her over the edge if Ginger hadn't been her sister for years and years. Even after all their time apart, Cat was used to outrageous behaviors that had to be explained or hidden. There was the time Ginger dyed the hair of every Oompa-Loompa with a permanent purple dye just before Parents' Night. Another time when Ginger replaced all the frosting in a bag of Oreo cookies with toothpaste on the day the health inspector came to recertify the camp's kitchen. Drugs were worse, for sure, but Cat had been cramming for this particular exam for possibly her whole life.

When the last recipe card was safely stowed, Cat took Wynn's hands and bent her head to make eye contact. "Sweetie. I'm taking the box with me. We are not going to drug people anymore." Cat swung her head back and forth. "No more drugs."

Wynn mirrored Cat's head shake.

"Say it with me. 'No more drugging people,'" Cat said.

"No more drugging people," Wynn said, but on the last word, she broke eye contact. Cat let her have that moment of independence. Then, touching her forehead to Wynn's, she said, "I don't want this camp to be a case study for the federal Drug Enforcement Agency where we all go to prison because of a spicy blueberry muffin."

"We're not going to get in trouble. They love it. Ask Norm."

Cat nodded. "I will. I'll ask him," she said, needing to talk to a grown-up. "Look, you keep working," she said as she moved to the door. "I'll be back." Once outside, Cat whisper-talked through the screen. "Stop drugging people, Wynn. No more drugging people." When Wynn didn't say anything, Cat said, "Wynn!"

And she heard the girl's voice reluctantly say, "Okay, sure. I couldn't if I wanted to. You have my box."

Cat remembered where Gary liked to hide. She knew these paths well and hurried in the opposite direction of the lakefront, past the ropes course and through a crop of needled trees into a sunny patch of land called the Clearing, one of the only level spots for nighttime games, her father's scavenger hunts, and Gary's garden.

"Gary," she called. "Gary!" The metal container clattered on her hip as she hiked across the lawn.

Gary plucked a tomato from a vine and bit into the juicy fruit.

"Adorable Wynn is drugging people with pot-spiked food. You've got to babysit while I go . . ." Cat faltered. She didn't want to admit to this supercilious turd that she wanted to save herself. To get a look at the mortgage papers to find out if she was liable for . . . she searched for the term. *Drug running?* Was she a mule? No, she'd never transported anything. She glanced at the box in her hands. Thought, *Oh no.* Then *fingerprints.* She hoisted the box onto the top of her bump and stretched her onesie over, wiping at the sides where she'd held it with her bare hands.

"They don't need a babysitter."

Polishing more aggressively, she said, "I beg to differ. You saw Norm. He's probably sleeping it off and will go straight to Steve when he wakes up."

"Steve?"

Cat darted a guilty glance at Gary. "The guy he works for, the water park guy," she said, flustered. Avoiding any hint of her connection to the man who wanted to pave paradise and put up a water slide. Someone she'd possibly brought to the camp, like a Typhoid Mary.

Gary stopped examining a handsome green pepper and stepped toward her. He put his hands on the metal box and said, "Go."

Cat let him take the box, grateful to hand it over while at the same time wondering if she'd made herself a druggy middleman. That nervous thought went *poof* when his thumb brushed hers as his hands covered the box easily. Then he did that thing that men do in movies. He held her eyes and dropped them to her mouth. Her lips tingled. Gary moved an inch, and Cat tilted her head and opened her mouth like a baby bird. The air temperature changed, heated, then cooled as he moved half a foot to the side and walked past her.

"Whew," she said, accidentally, her brain drunk from a shot of desire brought on by one clear-eyed, two-second stare.

"You don't work here," he said.

Cat sat heavily on a three-legged stool at the end of the pepper row and watched Gary stride away. She wasn't employed at the camp, and she didn't want to be either. So why did she want to shout, like a bratty kid, *I do so!* He crested the hill and was almost out of sight when she shouted, "I'm not going!" An alarmed mallard took off in a flurry of paddling feet, flapping wings, and a squawk. "Look what you did. You scared the wildlife," Cat shouted. "Gary!" On the second syllable of Gary's name, another duck hightailed it out of cattails, its legs wheeling like a cartoon.

"I'm not going anywhere," she said to a half-eaten tomato by her toe. "That was ridiculous." Cat trudged out of the clearing and up the hill, pumping her arms and trying to clear her thoughts and find the Cat who didn't swoon over men, who kept complicated attachments to a pathological minimum. The Cat who loved lists, facts, plans, always finding her footing in a solid spreadsheet. The one who wouldn't be going anywhere because she wouldn't give him the satisfaction.

She returned to the Mess Hall door and headed to the chalkboard. With a piece of chalk, she wrote GALA in a big bubble font with shading, denoting a 3-D party plan below. The words GALA COUNTDOWN followed, and on her tiptoes, her belly pressed against the chalk tray, Cat wrote as if channeling Winston Churchill in his war room. Or, the sharpest mind in the Junior League. With chalk dust flying, she laid out an extensive tactical schedule complete with fifteen-minute breaks every two hours that led up to the moment when the guests would arrive. Cat took a step back to survey her work, fingers and much of her belly smudged and white.

Wynn strolled from behind the counter and stood next to Cat, stirring a bowl of something with a wooden spoon. "Impressive," she said. "I especially like the timing flowchart that shows how each job moves toward a common goal denoted by your disco ball and toasting champagne flutes."

"Thank you." Cat rubbed her hands together. "I think if everyone follows this schedule, we might be able to pull this off. It's going to be tight. Have you written up a food plan?"

"What's this say under my name? Wynn Apol?"

Cat removed the mixing bowl from Wynn's hands and took the girl's shoulders. "The woman you drugged will be here, and you have to apologize to her."

Wynn pulled free and frowned. "No. I'm not going to do that. I did her a favor. She thanked me for it."

"That's great. She'll understand, then. But you need to tell her you're sorry. We have to make sure that if she is interviewed as an alum, she won't mention you slipping drugs into her food."

A shadow passed over Wynn's sunshine, and she picked up the mixing bowl. "My twin was like you."

Cat tilted her head, unsure what words she should pay attention to. A sister? Like Cat?

Was? "What do you mean?"

"Wrong with conviction," Wynn said with a quiet look. "It killed her."

The golden girl Wynn, the Shirley Temple of camp, had a twin sister who'd died. Ginger's face sparked before Cat, like a flame, still alive, burning brightly.

"Simone thought food made her less perfect and broke her heart and, figuratively, everyone else's because of it. They prescribed antidepressants, which she refused to take. She didn't want to get better. She had a prescription for medical marijuana to stimulate her appetite, and she wanted nothing to do with it. It piled up while she wasted away."

Cat had made the mistake of thinking the girl's life had been as clear and bright as her complexion. She tried to touch her shoulder, but Wynn moved an inch away. Now she saw that some of her cheer was a mask for the pain.

"Knowing that my sister could have survived if she'd taken meds and food, but she was too sick to see it—it was too much for me. I should have crushed them into her Ensure, slid them into her feeding tube without telling her. I should have done it. But I didn't."

"So you do it now," Cat said, realizing that what she'd thought was irresponsible camp high jinks was Wynn's last-ditch effort to save someone because she couldn't save Simone. "You aren't responsible for your sister's death," Cat said in the kindest tone she could muster. The voice she'd use for her own child, maybe a daughter like Wynn or June.

"I don't think you're an expert on who's responsible for what, Kitty," Wynn said with a mischievous glint in her eye.

Cat might have challenged Wynn had she not been so taken aback by the woman's clear-eyed assessment of her and the use of the family nickname. She wanted to explain how the camp had taught her everything she needed to know about duty and obligation. How now, as possible partial owner of a camp that claimed to be a drug-free antidote for hardness and struggle, she would be the first in line when the handcuffs came off belts. When the police arrived and took them into custody, cautioned Cat to watch her head as she ducked into the police car.

She didn't say any of this because if Cat lost Ginger . . . her throat constricted at the unspoken notion of it. Cat swallowed so she could defend herself, but why? If Cat lost Ginger, she, too, might drug everyone. She'd do anything to save the home where she could ease her guilt and grief by providing nourishment to others, as Wynn was doing. Because if the place disappeared, she'd have to return to a world that was missing her other half.

"You know what, Wynn. You are right. I'm not an expert on who should do what. Having said that, do you think you could hold off on breaking any more laws until Friday night?"

Wynn nodded, smiling just enough to let Cat know she understood.

"After the gala, I'll give you the names of a couple of people that I think we should drug the heck out of."

CHAPTER
TWENTY-TWO

ARRESTING

After talking to Wynn, Cat needed to see her sister's face, but she knew from experience that it was too soon after their spat. When Cat apologized, she wanted Ginger to have cooled off enough to hear it.

She spotted Gary and Norm entering the Auditorium, two actual adults. One a hot, royal pain in the rump, the other a dumpy turncoat who might know some things about Steve that Cat probably needed to hear.

Shirtless sat outside the door of the Auditorium, his long fingers untangling strings of outside lights. It would be an excellent Zen exercise in prison. She wondered if they'd give her oat milk with her breakfast.

"This is going to take all day," said Shirtless.

"Maybe not all day. Okay? Maybe an hour," Cat said, feeling the clock ticking and the hours falling away. Especially if the police were barreling toward them.

Eager to escape the hot sun, Cat stepped inside the cool Auditorium listening for voices. In the theater, Norm stood amid wood and canvas backdrops meant for a children's theater production, not glitzy decorations for an adult gala. Norm held a panel while Gary steadied it and, with a nail gun, secured it in place.

The men hadn't seen Cat yet, and she watched them in the space her mother used to command kids to *Enunciate!* and her father shouted, *Break a leg!* "Once we get these secured, we can build the rainbow," said Norm. "Do you have another tool belt?"

Gary pointed with the handle of a hammer to the corner of the room. Norm retrieved a smaller belt, tried to clip it around his middle, and laughed. "I'm tubbier than you." He fixed the buckle. "Hey, man," Norm said, "I want you to know. I'm in this to win it. I'm not going to report anything. Bob's disappearing act, the flimsy staff, the drugs."

Cat's ears perked up, and still in the shadow, she moved closer to the stage.

Gary yanked a ladder over to the side of the stage and said, "The flats are numbered. I need seven."

Norm put a finger up. "I know where that one is." He slowly jogged over to the corner of the stage and hefted a green board to where Gary pointed the nail gun. "Gotcha," Norm said, adding, "I'm pretty good with one of those. I did a stint for Habitat for Humanity."

Gary ignored him, and Norm said, "Look, buddy. I know I came here under false pretenses. You know. Hired by the enemy and all. But I didn't know. I didn't know this place was . . . not as advertised, but also incredible in its own way."

Hearing Steve labeled as the enemy set Cat's teeth on edge in the way only a hard truth can. The father of her child wasn't the harmless, tone-deaf man she'd slept with. After one quick conversation, the kind everyone had on a first or second date—*Where did you grow up? Do you have any siblings?*—she'd been a patsy, a trusting, lonely person ripe for a takedown. Before a burst of outrage could emerge, a wash of purple shame butted in and took its familiar place in the center of her chest.

Steve must have realized their one night together hadn't been a total waste of time. She had something he might want. A bit of failing property that was ripe for the taking. A place to build a palace of plastic tubes and pools that would hold its structure long after the human race had gone. A system of drains and concrete that would be labeled as a complicated irrigation system for a dying planet by the aliens who were sure to misunderstand the structure.

Was this why Gary was treating her like a blight on the land? He knew she'd brought a parasite that could take down this place.

Gary pulled the trigger and secured the panel with three loud pops. Norm flinched.

"Dude. I get it. This is your place. I'm an interloper." Norm grabbed another panel, but Gary shifted the board before he could situate it and nailed it near Norm's ear.

Cat watched and listened, fascinated and a little turned on. Her inner feminist closed her eyes in disgust and said, *Remember Steve from seconds ago? Don't you ever learn?* She gave herself a shake.

"Seriously, man. How was I to know? This guy called. Offered me an outlandish amount of money." He rubbed his hand over his face from forehead to chin. "So much money, I'm telling you."

Gary shot another nail near Norm's finger.

"Dude. I'm giving the money back. I want this place to keep going. I don't want anyone to lose their job. I mean, that Brittany with her bunnies. She'll break your heart. You know?"

Gary stepped around Norm and lifted a green board. Norm said, "Oh shit, I should have gotten that for you. Sorry." Gary kicked it straight and raised the gun.

"Message received. I'll get out of your way." Norm put his hands up as if he were under arrest. "But level with me. It's just us in here. Two guys. You in love with her?"

Cat had been thinking about shooting Steve's tires out with the nail gun, but when she heard this question, she straightened and tuned in.

"With Cat. I mean, I get it, man, I do. She's"—he paused—"arresting."

Love? Gary hated her. Norm would be no help if this was an example of his expert analysis of things. Cat steeled herself for Gary's inevitable scoff, but he hit the nail gun two times in a way that felt like a period. End of conversation.

What had Norm seen that would possess him to say this to Gary? Was there something? Did Gary consider Cat more than an annoying fruit fly hovering over his cherished domain? She could almost feel her pupils dilate with the possibility.

"You don't want to talk about it. Fine. But you should stop looking at her like you do if it's supposed to be a secret."

Gary dragged a pallet and kicked it into place, forcing Norm to hop out of the way.

Cat suppressed a loud, *HA! Well there, that's settled it.* How could Norm possibly think Gary's look held anything but irritation and dislike? Cat knew exactly how he saw her. Men, such simple creatures.

Gary straightened his expression, the same grimness as always. Yet there was something coiled in his energy. An air of danger that Norm didn't seem to notice.

How strong was that weed, Cat wondered, that Norm would miss this?

Norm lifted his shirt to wipe his brow, exposing a soft, round, hairy tummy. "A word of advice. You can't love a girl like her too much. One whiff of need, and poof, she's gone."

Gary's jaw clenched.

Someone had to save that idiot Norm before he took a nail in his stomach. Cat hit the door handle hard, and the sound rattled through the Auditorium. "Gary. Norm. Are you finished here? Shirtless needs help with the lights, and someone has to chaperone Wynn."

The men, startled, shot each other comically guilty looks.

"I can go . . . ," Norm said like a child caught dicking around instead of working. Gary stopped him with the handle of the hammer. He pulled a pack of gum out of his pocket and offered a piece to Norm, who looked between them, unsure.

"I've outlined everything we need to do on the chalkboard. Can you finish strutting your man stuff in here and go help?"

"Are you strutting your man stuff, Gary?" said Norm. "Because I thought we talked about that. Keep your man stuff under wraps."

Gary might have smiled. He gestured. "Almost done. Auction tables next."

"Auction. What auction?"

"Ask your sister."

"Don't think I won't," Cat said ridiculously.

Gary turned away from Cat, another conversation ending because his nonverbals said so.

Infuriating.

"Norm!" Cat shouted. "Get the panel." Cat stormed out the door, but she heard Norm's voice before letting it slam into place.

"Arresting."

And the nail gun went off.

CHAPTER TWENTY-THREE

AMPHIBIANS?

Cat stepped into the sunlight, the truths clearer than ever. The only source of legal information was high and incredibly, epically unskilled at assessing situations. Gary and Ginger were pissed at her. Wynn and Bob had broken the law, probably multiple times, and the only thing that looked like an escape net was selling the camp to a barracuda. And yet, on they marched to put on a gala that was basically growing into an ungainly mess.

Cat stepped over two straightened strings of lights next to several clumps of tangled wires and light bulbs in need of sorting. She walked past the storm doors of the Mess Hall and into the dining room, which was packed with people.

Someone had erased much of Cat's plan and written a kitchen inventory over what was left of her words. Flour, sugar, butter, eggs, hamburger, honey, Fritos, hot dogs, chocolate, marshmallows, graham crackers, onions, baking soda, baking powder, milk, lemonade, maple syrup, and tahini. Before Cat could react, Wynn swooped around the corner from the kitchen with a tall purple cake in the center of a pizza pan and sang "Happy Birthday to You" on cue, as everyone else joined in.

It was her birthday. This had to be her sister's work. Always play-time for Ginger.

Cat had turned thirty-eight without realizing it. She recalled how her ob-gyn labeled her pregnancy as a geriatric one. The MD's nurse practitioner had corrected the white-haired man by saying "advanced maternal age," but the damage had been done. Time had marched forward without her permission, and these Littles wanted to celebrate.

She wanted to say, *Who has time for a birthday—our house is on fire?* Underneath her superficial timing worries was a simple fact. She didn't deserve a party thrown by these people. Who was she but someone trying to escape the place they were trying to preserve? She was as much a fraud as Bob. A seemingly nice person with ulterior motives.

The staff, their eyes fixed on Cat's wobbly smile, sang "Happy birthday, dear Caaattttt," with faltering confidence. Behind her, Matt said, "You look like you're passing a kidney stone."

Being Ginger's sister was like biting into a SweeTART; you couldn't help but make a sweet-and-sour expression.

Matt launched into the second verse: "How old are you now? How old are you now . . ."

Cat executed a slow turn, Clint Eastwood–style, and shot him an *I'll shiv you with a sharpened spoon* look. He stepped back, changed his mind, and put her in a playful headlock, ruffling her hair.

"You're one of us now," he said.

Cat reached around, grabbed Matt's topknot, and yanked it forward. He released her, laughing, and fixed his hair while he did a little boxer shuffle, punching the air.

Cat addressed the smiling group. "This is so nice. Why would you do this for me? Our deadline is so tight." She felt like the worst kind of parent, mentioning homework in the middle of lessons on how to fly.

June handed Cat a white fluted paper plate, the flimsy kind that bowed in the middle with the weight of confection and a plastic fork.

"We like to make time to celebrate birthdays." It was apparent why Shirtless let June touch his peevish skin: June's energy had a favorite blanket feel to it.

Cat took the plate. It had been a long time since anyone had celebrated her birthday. She glanced around the room. This was why the gala would fail. The Littles didn't realize the kind of single-minded focus a business needed when money was an issue. You couldn't take a detour to smell the roses. The rich invited guests knew that better than anyone.

The rest of the staff rushed the cake line, having recently been made aware of how quickly life could change at the camp: *Eat dessert first!* The cake smelled like raspberries, melted on Cat's taste buds, and lit her brain like a sparkler. Sugar, the good girl's party drug, the sleepy girl's fiesta before the siesta. She'd eat this and in thirty minutes feel the kind of fatigue that would hobble a decathlete. Cat reasoned that there wouldn't be cake in prison and took another bite.

Shirtless moved to her side and said, "This is the magic of camp. Making people the center of the universe is more important to us than anything."

Cat coughed at the thick buttery frosting coating her throat. Stopping her from saying anything negative like, *If the camp was magic, I wouldn't be here.*

Shirtless offered a sip from his cup of water.

Camille strolled in late, probably pissed she hadn't been called to bring her pitch pipe and sing "Happy Birthday."

"I can't eat that if there's wheat, dairy, or eggs in it." A collective eye roll rippled through the group like the wave at a college football game.

Wynn, the kindest of them all, lifted a smaller cake from behind the toaster oven and said, "And for you, I made this. I'm calling it my Free-Spirit Cake."

Everything about Camille galled Cat. She wasn't even sure why. It would have been a kick to needle her. Gush over Wynn's benevolence while highlighting Camille's sensitive gut. But there wasn't time. She scanned the room for Ginger, who must have been behind this cake, but she was nowhere in sight. Cat considered sounding the bell, their secret eight syncopated beats pulled from "Careless Whisper." Some eight-year-old kid had sung it for an audition, and Cat and Ginger found it so hilarious they'd peed their pants laughing and then made it their emergency call.

Dropping her frosting-smeared paper plate into the trash, Cat left the Mess Hall without notice. She found Ginger cross-legged on the floor in front of an open cupboard in the Craft Lodge amid piles of pot holders, lanyards, half-finished wallets, dream catchers, and several wooden birdhouses. Ginger's stiffened shoulders told Cat they were still fighting.

"Is my wallet in there?" Cat said, making a joke. Lefty's tail thumped when he heard Cat's voice. On rainy days, Cat had often tried to construct a beaded leather billfold. She hated crafts, so she always abandoned everything she'd started. She touched a tissue paper flower on the wall. "Norm and Gary are almost done in the theater. Remember when Dad used to coach the kids during dramatic scenes? 'Use your lost ambitions to fuel this scene.'"

"Amphibians?" Ginger said. The punch line of a toad joke between siblings.

"Are you still mad?" Cat asked.

Ginger slid out a collection of multicolored leaf prints made with ink from wild blueberries. "Would it matter?" she said.

"It would. Yes," Cat said.

"Happy birthday."

"You never forget," Cat said, then cleared her throat. "Can you come out of there? I'm sorry I was so bossy. I thought . . . well, you know what I thought." Cat needed to talk with Ginger about the fraudulent claims sent with each invitation. About getting in front of the fake data during the speech. There was Wynn and her weed muffins to address, but the beginning of her sugar high was wearing off, throttling Cat's skills of diplomacy and pacing.

"What is all this stuff?"

"The campers were supposed to take their crafts home. No one wanted the therapy art that reminded them of their divorces, dead-end careers, family problems."

"What's the plan now?" Cat said, hoping her sister would see Cat including her, that she was trying not to do what she always did: move too quickly, take over too much, discount her sister outright.

Ginger stood and lifted a cluster of seed-covered pine cones, a wrapping paper–covered tube turned kaleidoscope.

"My idea of art is making toast." When Ginger didn't nod knowingly, Cat added, "I am sorry. Calling me in to help and expecting me to be . . . calm is like trying to get you to put down a paintbrush." Cat lifted a sizable white wreath from the counter and said, "Is this made out of plastic spoons?"

"Yeah, a lady came who was massively into Christmas. She was working through some yuletide trauma but fell in love with the climbing wall and never returned to finish the wreath. It is ugly, right? All of this is."

Cat poked a yellow wool sock with red felt lips, blonde hair, and beaded earrings hand sewn where its sock puppet ears should be. Someone had stitched a cross on the neck. "Did the campers make Camille dolls?"

"There are five of them. We make them sing a lot of ABBA." Ginger gave Cat a half smile.

Cat slid her hand into the puppet and made it say, "Why am I so annoying?"

"We could sell the crafts. I read about what two writers did to pay for their master of fine arts degrees. They went to thrift stores and bought junk for a dollar or two."

"No one is going to buy this stuff."

"Jesus, Cat, can you just?"

"I'm sorry! I'm sorry, okay!"

"They wrote stories for the objects. It increased their value. They made thousands," said Ginger.

"No kidding. That's cool," Cat said, trying to think of a segue to fake data and drugs.

"We could have a silent auction. Each craft gets a story. We put out bidding sheets. We collect the money after." Ginger had the expression she wore when looking up at their father, hoping for a pat on the head. "You think this is dumb, don't you?"

"No, it's not that. We need good ideas." Cat shivered. "I ate the birthday cake. Thank you, by the way." When Cat was really tired, her temperature dropped a degree, which always helped propel her to a bed or couch with blankets.

"Cake is like anesthesia for you," Ginger said, lifting a hoodie from a nearby chair. Ginger helped Cat into the sweatshirt.

"Was that your plan?" Cat laughed and Ginger smiled. They knew each other so well. "I'm going to lie down. It's only five; don't let me sleep too long."

Ginger nodded.

"Wake me up. We have to get lights hung, set up tables, execute!" Cat said, pointing at her sister, her arm straight and intense, before she shuffled to her room. Cat eased herself into bed and rested her head on the sun-warmed pillow. Lefty galloped in and spooned her with his three good legs as she closed her eyes.

CHAPTER TWENTY-FOUR

FLIPPER

Cat woke with a start when Lefty booted her in the dog's dream effort to catch a squirrel. The bedside clock read 2:00 a.m. She hadn't taken an after-dessert nap; she'd gone to bed. Now wide awake, her mind raced as it returned to unfinished business: What would Ira Glass say when he arrived and discovered the camp was a sham? *Summer Camp. The cure for no one, on a two-part podcast.*

If she woke Ginger and started in on everything—the fake data, the speech, the legalities associated with misrepresentation, cancel culture, drugs, bankruptcy, her mortgage—she'd be accused of taking over, nudging her out.

It was nights like this that Cat longed to be a smoker. How amazing would it be to light a cigarette, stand outside, and say to hell with everything? Screw the fresh air, the toxin-free land, her pristine lungs. She could blow smoke rings like a boss babe, someone who kicked ass and took names later. But she swore her baby would have the pinkest cells when she entered the world. Peony-pretty lungs, an organic free-range crib in a storybook house with a loving mother who never made her grow up too fast, and wasn't doing time in prison on a drug charge.

She shut her eyes, feeling her rapid pulse behind her lids, in her neck. "You are not in charge," she said to herself and then went to the bathroom to relieve the pressure in her bladder. If she could fall back to sleep, she could stop thinking about how she should have let her sister fail more. That maybe that was what their father was trying to say all along with his bracelets, etc. *Failure isn't the end; it's a beginning.* It never felt like that to Cat, though. Failure felt like blame.

The baby rolled, reminding her that all this middle-of-the-night quarterbacking was tough on them. She had to find a way to calm down, go back to sleep.

When she was a kid and needed peace and quiet, she'd go to the lake. Cat would lie back, tilt her head, and submerge her ears so she could hear only the muffled sounds of frogs, lapping water, and her heartbeat.

"C'mon, boy," Cat said. "Time for a soothing dead man's float in our own personal pond." Barefoot, the two made a beeline across the grounds toward the water, and she didn't stop to take off her clothes. She strode right in, the sweatshirt tenting momentarily, then filling with water, and dove under. Lefty waded in knee deep, turned, lapped at the water, and lay down on the sand.

Cat surfaced and tried to take a stroke, but the waterlogged hoodie dragged her arm down. She attempted a roll to her back, but the thick fabric and doorstop of a belly hindered her movement, and she flopped around, ineffectually gulping water.

Immediate panic made her cough, buck, and reach, her clothing twisted and suffocating. She kicked down and banged her toe on a rock that was closer than expected. She stood, still coughing, and dragged herself upright. A bright light swung up from the beach and hit her in the eyes, illuminating that she was fighting water not deep enough to threaten a kitten.

Cat shielded her eyes and heard Gary's voice. "Cat."

His flat delivery of her name made her feel absurd in a way only Gary could do.

"Will you shut that off, Gary?"

He didn't. He dropped the beam, creating a path to the beach. She tried to thrash out more quietly than she'd gone in, but her clothing made grace impossible. She slopped to where Gary stood on the shore, his golf cart close, with Lefty riding shotgun.

"Hi, Tiny Dancer," she said, trying for a lighthearted power play practically drowned out by the thunderstorm of water rolling off her clothing. The clothing, she noted, clung to the bulbous curves of her elderly pregnant body.

"Want a lift?"

"Yes. If you would, please," she said, trying to daintily push a lily pad off her forehead.

"Flop up here, Flipper. We're going to SeaWorld."

Cat barked a laugh. "Gary made a joke. With so many words."

"Gary made a joke," he said, offering a hand towel.

She wiped her face and slid onto the plastic seat, Lefty between them, licking her neck lovingly. The golf cart lurched. She grabbed the metal handrail and tried not to give Gary more evidence that she was a wreck by rolling out of the vehicle.

Gary braked, and Cat inelegantly but victoriously, on her own volition, slid off the seat, Lefty following her lead.

She wriggled her arms out of the sleeves and tried to get the sweatshirt over her head. "Help me, will you, Gary?" He gave the fabric a good yank. He dropped the hoodie with a heavy thwack onto the front steps.

"Thanks," she said.

"Thank Lefty."

He stared at her, and Cat considered taking his hand and leading him to the bedroom . . . as if he would go willingly. What was her deal? Did she only want men who held her in disdain? Great. What a wonderful model for a child.

Gary didn't move.

"What?" Cat said.

"Don't swim at night," he said. "We don't allow it."

"We don't?" she asked, instantly annoyed. Sarcastically she said, "Don't we?"

She took the straps of her onesie and yanked them off her shoulders. "What about nudity—do we allow that?" she asked.

Gary shook his head, climbed into the cart, and started it. "Go to bed. Big day," he said. He motored away, and Cat did strip down. She walked inside in only her massive cotton bra and colossal underwear, grabbed a cotton blanket from the couch, and wrapped it around her. "I wouldn't want to see myself naked either, Lefty. Gross."

Half a peanut butter sandwich was on the counter, and she ate it, a banana, and a snack bag of sour cream and chive potato chips. Then she examined the crafts. In a flash, she saw the VIPs sneering at the camp merch. Saw through Steve's eyes the staff's failure to understand the world in which they were trying to impress: the rich who lived in cashmere bubbles, the press that wrote about wars, epic scandals, space launches. People had been invited to experience a mental health innovation and would find instead a catastrophe of Littles and two disorganized den mothers selling the wares of anxious and depressed adults who may or may not have been drugged.

Once again, Cat felt the downward tow of the lake, the sinking darkness of failure, the thing she had tried to avoid her whole life. Lefty licked her palm, herding her to the bathroom. She wriggled out of her wet bra, cranked the window open, placed her forehead on the screen, and listened. These woods, they'd seen it all before, and she could swear the trees whispered, *Cat, failure is the chance to begin again.*

She let the shower stream chase the pungent lake water from head to toe until the faucet ran cold. Stepping out, Cat saw a figure of a man just beyond the great tree, near the parking lot. She recognized Gary's stance. His eyes were trained on her building. She moved closer to the window and turned on the bathroom light.

When their eyes met, she thought about waving, flipping him off, or shouting *Hey, Tiny Dancer, get a load of these*, and grabbing her breasts. She did none of those things, but she didn't cover herself either. They stood looking at each other until Cat turned away.

CHAPTER TWENTY-FIVE

LOST THE THREAD

Cat woke and peered at the clock at the bedside table. Ten thirty-four? If not for the sun streaming into her room, her first thought would have been, *I have the whole night to sleep.* But it was 10:34 a.m. She'd overslept the day before the big day and didn't feel the least bit rested.

She should have sprinted from the bed, but her limbs had a heaviness that she would have associated with the flu. But she didn't feel achy or congestion, just fatigue on the cellular level. Sometime in the night, her brain must have decided that the future was going to be gloomy, and her emotions had gotten right on board. If not for her bladder, she would have had to pep-talk herself out of bed.

"Lefty?" she called from the bathroom. There was no sign of him. He was off having the time of his life and wasn't around to cheer her up with a nuzzle and a lick.

She felt foggy headed and hungover from binge drinking conflict the day before. "Grow up," she said, eye to eye in the mirror on the medicine cabinet. "This disaster is not only about you." With that kind and careful encouragement, Cat walked the short distance to the Mess

Hall, which was noisier than ever, and here she saw, in fact, that this was a disaster and it was for everyone.

No one noticed as she walked inside and stood next to Norm, who looked like a suburban dad watching a kids' soccer game that had been lost long ago. One hand holding a cup of coffee, the other in the pocket of his cargo shorts.

Wynn's voice sounded from somewhere out of sight. "The bag dinners need to be packaged, labeled, stored in the walk-in refrigerator, and ready to deliver to each campfire."

"They went with the bag dinners? Nothing elegant was ever served in a bag," Cat said, and Norm gave a little *You're right* head nod.

"Gary and I wound dough around skewers to bake at the campfires. There's more to do in the walk-in," Wynn said, still out of sight.

"But, like, there's no bark on the sticks. Right? Tell me they stripped the sticks and aren't going to tell everybody that bark is edible."

Norm gave her the side-eye and took a sip of his coffee.

"What about these?" Shirtless gestured to an enormous chafing dish of potatoes that looked singed on one side and raw on the other.

"Shirtless," Cat hissed. "There's a leaf in there."

"The rest of the spuds are in the back," said Wynn. "They need slicing, buttering, and roasting. Then it'll all go into the packages, along with sweet onion and peppers."

"Grab that leaf," Cat said, pointing to an oak or maybe maple leaf stuck to the only potato that appeared entirely cooked.

Norm reached across the picnic table and plucked the greenery out of the pan, and Cat knew that where there was one there were others.

"And the vegetarian tacos?" Brittany said, carrying a huge cardboard box labeled *Snack Pack Fritos.*

"The veg taco ingredients for the Walking Tacos are done and only need warming up. They're in the fridge. Someone will have to serve them during the gala."

"Shirtless," Cat said. "Are they actually going to put the taco filling into the Frito bag, hand it to the millionaires with a plastic fork, and say 'Bon appétit'?"

Shirtless gave Cat an odd look and an affirmative nod, and Norm said, "You're yelling, Cat."

"I'll serve the tacos," said June, eyeballing Cat.

"I've written instructions, labeled items and containers, and attached a map so people know where to put them. I need some helping hands now." Wynn walked past June with Bob Fosse jazz hands but didn't stop moving. She motioned June and Shirtless to a side counter near the large mixer and didn't seem to see Cat and Norm.

"Here is my list of cakes. Some are in progress, and others still have to be started." Wynn read off the list: "Blueberry Vanilla Bean Cake made with real, frozen blueberries, Brown Butter Cake, Kentucky Butter Cake, Peanut Butter Cake, and Caramelized Spice Cake. I already made piles of chocolate chip cookies that must be placed into waxed paper envelopes and sealed with twine. The buttercream frosting for most cakes is in this industrial mixer. I'm making a cake shaped like a hollow log. I'm going to decorate it with purple frosting mushrooms crawling up the side like a spiral staircase. I think a 'Summer Camp' sign should be on the top, but I can't find my tiny fairy lights with the battery pack. People can bid on it at the auction."

"Why are there so many cakes?" Cat said. "I never should have slept so long. I should have been here shutting down production. Fancy people only need one fancy cake." Her heart rate ratcheted up with the chaos. "Norm, these kids have planned a great six-year-old's birthday party, not a fundraising party for VIPs."

Norm took a wide step away from Cat. Wynn's eyes were bright, her cheeks flushed, and the thick humidity of the day had curled her hair into a wild mane. Cat looked at Shirtless, who was trying to hide his anxiety but was peeling flakes of skin off his lips with his teeth.

"If we stay on schedule, we can get all the cakes baked, frosted, and displayed before the gala starts tomorrow. If a cake goes flat, we make another cake," Wynn said, reading a clipboard.

"No more cake," Cat said so loudly that for one inhale the place went silent. The media were going to have a field day, the rich would keep their money, and if Steve wanted to buy the place and put up a water park, there was nothing to stop him. These kids would get tossed to the curb all because boo-hoo, Cat was kind of sleepy.

A soprano voice blasted through the PA system, followed by a needle scratch on a record. Volume was adjusted, and a squawk of feedback made everyone cringe. An instrumental version of "Somewhere Over the Rainbow" started and then stopped.

"Matt. Quit it" came through the speakers loud and clear. Camille trilled a vocal exercise, adding more chaos to the room.

Wynn held a fistful of chopsticks and said, "Shirtless, grab a string of dough from that dish and wind it around like this. Doing them all will take a while, but when you're done, I'll give you another job."

Cat cleared her throat. "Wynn. Can I talk to you?"

Shirtless lifted a corner of a white cotton cloth covering a stainless steel bin the size of a bathtub for a toy poodle. "All of these need to be wound around these sticks?"

"Every last one," Wynn said.

"Wynn," Cat said.

"June. If you put cookies into these individual envelopes, we can sell them as kiddie treats for parents to bring home."

June stood before a mountain of cookies and said, "How many people are coming to the gala?"

"Fifty," Cat volunteered, holding up five fingers and an O. Hoping to break in with useful information.

"There are enough cookies here for two times that," said June, and she sneaked over to stand by Cat. "I think she might have taken something."

"Like a drug?" Cat said dully. As if this wasn't in the realm of possibility for the girl who literally drugged people. "I should have stayed up."

Camille's voice again. The sound system cranked up—*Where trouble melts like chocolate spots*—but she spoke the words instead of singing them.

"Those aren't the words," Cat said.

"Wynn seemed fine a bit ago," said Shirtless, "but now she's kinda hyper."

Wynn counted the baked and sliced potatoes while tasting the frosting as it blended in the massive mixing machine.

"Wynn?" Cat said, but not loud enough to pull the girl's attention. "Where's my sister?" Cat said to June.

"She was here a minute ago. I'll find her," June said and rushed out the side door.

Wynn had moved on to count the cookies by twos. Wrote the number on her board. "I love a busy kitchen and a party to plan."

June returned with Ginger, looking alarmed.

"Wynnie?" Ginger said. "I think it's good to be ambitious but not wear yourself out."

"Maybe one of the benefactors owns a restaurant, right?" Wynn said. "They aren't going to hire me after eating our Walking Tacos, but they might after seeing one of my cakes. Cover the picnic tables with the butcher paper. We need eight stations. Two for dinner foods, two for the cakes, and two for takeaway treats."

"I'll do it!" Cat shouted.

Cat moved to the picnic tables and unrolled a sheet of glossy white paper, giving herself a nasty paper cut in the process. She stuffed her thumb into her mouth so she wouldn't see the blood ooze out in a thin line. Instead, she tasted iron, and she went instantly woozy.

"Heads up," Wynn called and tossed a roll of masking tape. "Get the edges taped down."

Like the ball-averse nonathlete she was, instead of trying to catch it, Cat ducked. Already off-kilter, one thumb in her mouth, one hand straight out nowhere near the tape, she lost her balance. Cat's vision sparked and clouded at the edges, and she lost the thread of the moment.

CHAPTER TWENTY-SIX

HOT GARY

Cat didn't hit the ground like a felled tree. It was more like a trust fall, but June was not substantial enough to do the *trust* part and only provided a soft body for Cat to land on. "Oof," breathed June at the same time Cat said, "Oaf."

"Are the tables covered?" Wynn called while counting Frito bags.

Cat's vision cleared, and she was with it enough to be grateful she hadn't seen her ungainly self go down.

Shirtless bolted from his station like a stringy, panicked praying mantis, his limbs going in sharp directions. He was used to hauling people out of the lake; it must have been odd to deploy those arms and legs without the resistance of water.

Cat felt hands on her shoulders and heard June's voice in her ear: "I've got you." Which of course, she didn't.

Standing was going to be a challenge, so Cat tried to roll over June's leg and get onto her knees. Which worked. On all fours, Cat saw three sets of shins, felt hands under her armpits, and someone part dragged, part walked Cat to a picnic bench inches away. There was a short stab of pain in her groin. She'd been to the doctor, who said more activity than usual could bring on round ligament pain. If she mentioned it, Ginger would put her ass in bed, and it was clear Cat needed to be reining in the mayhem, so she winced soundlessly.

Ginger squatted in front of Cat. "You okay, Kitty?"

"Yeah. Fine. Just lightheaded for a second. Let me take a look at what we have here."

"Shirtless, get water," Ginger said.

"It's fine," Cat said. "I'll get some."

Someone handed Cat ice water, and she drank it like a little kid, then gasped for air when finished.

"Frost the cakes, team!" Wynn said, sounding like she was in the back of the walk-in freezer.

June dusted herself off, hurried into the kitchen, and dipped a spatula into the sweet mixture. She placed a dollop of frosting onto a cake and tried to spread it. When the top crumbled, she panicked and lifted the spatula, and a chunk of the cake came out of the center.

Cat slid her eyes to Wynn, who was energetically winding dough around sticks, wholly absorbed in the spiral of the task. Watching the two women was like watching a tennis match slash cooking show with amateurs. "June," Wynn said, "did you finish covering the tables?"

"Not yet. I . . ." June tried to replace the top of the cake before Wynn moved to her side, but the frosting clung, the cake crumbled, and the color ran out of June's face.

Cat closed her eyes as a wave of wooziness swept over her again. When she opened them, Shirtless stood before her, holding a tuna sandwich wrapped in cellophane. Cat suppressed a gag. She could not do low blood sugar, falling, and fish in under five minutes.

"You have blood on your shorts," said Ginger.

Cat moved too quickly, lifting her thumb to show Ginger her paper cut, and buried her finger to the knuckle in Ginger's left nostril.

Ginger, shockingly, took the invasion in stride, brushed Cat's thumb aside, and pulled Cat off the bench seat to her feet. "Shirtless, give June a hand. I'm taking Cat back to the Craft Lodge. Keep an eye on them."

"No!" Cat said.

Wynn clanged pots and pans together and turned the water on and off. "I need a cake status."

"Roger that!" June shouted, the spatula dripping frosting and cake onto the counter.

Shirtless scratched his neck, and Ginger said, "Don't be stupid, Cat. I'll be right back. Call Gary if you need him."

"I'm not being stupid," Cat said, and even to her own ears she sounded stupid.

Ginger had her arm around Cat, semi-supporting her weight as the two walked between buildings. Free of the frenetic activity in the Mess Hall, Cat felt her head clearing a bit, and she found her footing.

"I'm fine now. I cut my thumb and felt kind of dizzy for a minute."

"You fell over," said Ginger. "You can't fall over when you are pregnant." She stopped walking. "Exactly how far away is your due date?"

"Two months. I'm fine."

"Pretty sure you don't know how you are. When I was pregnant, I was like a tippy teacup."

"Not a tippy teacup," Cat said, joking and embarrassed that she was being pulled from the assembly line.

"I'm just saying. I was always on the verge of going over. Mom said it was the same with her. Orthotics, or something to do with our feet."

"It's orthostatic blood pressure. And I don't have that," Cat said.

"I don't think that was the name," Ginger said.

"I have the fatigue," Cat said, trying to make a tiny joke. "I've had it since the beginning. I'm a little low on iron, that's all. I nap a lot and I'm fine."

"After around the eighth month, I was dizzy and exhausted until the week before I delivered. I was a superhero for that week, and then it was ol' dreamy Ginger back screwing off and annoying everyone."

"You made Shirtless. He's the best," Cat said, wanting more than anything for her sister to see what she'd done all by herself. "You did that."

"Okay," Ginger said, unused to straight-up compliments from her sister. Ginger held the side door to the Craft Lodge. "Lie down for a bit."

"Your nose is bleeding."

"Well, after you went down on top of our camp nurse, you jammed your thumb up to my eye socket." She wiped her nostrils, and somehow that made it worse. Ginger grabbed a tissue and clamped it to her face.

"I'm hungry," Cat said, hoping to use her hunger as an excuse and go back into that Mess Hall and explain what a real gala should look like.

Her sister lifted her arm, and a sandwich dropped from her armpit onto Cat's bed with a thunk.

"I'll eat this and go help. Look, I'm fine."

"Your body is not your own. And you don't know what's best for it. So you stay in here—do not go out in this humidity."

"I know my own body," Cat said in her snotty big sister voice.

"Do you? Have you ever made a human being before? Have you ever had a cocktail of hormones take over your body like a hacker takes over a computer? No. You haven't. So, Miss Go-Go-Go, you've got to take a break. Let someone help you for a change. We've got it under control."

"Do you? Because Wynn is in turbo mode, and it could go wrong in a lot of ways. And I need to talk to you about what you're going to say at the welcoming presentation."

Ginger mopped at her nose. "Oh, shut up, Cat. Just shut up. You left. I made a mistake. Now can you let me redeem myself and not make me look like a loser to everyone, including my son? You can stop acting like you're the only human who has planned a party without adequate notice. You can be exquisitely insufferable for a basically nice person."

Cat swallowed a clump of sandwich. She took another bite and watched her sister stanch the blood dribbling from her nose. Cat wanted to defend herself and tell Ginger how hard it was to be back at home and not belong anymore. To be relieved that she didn't fit in while wanting badly to be . . . acknowledged? Respected? No, that wasn't it. She wanted to be included without being wretched when things went badly. With all the garbage between them, there wasn't enough subtlety in the English language to get that right.

Instead, like the brat she was when in her sister's company, she said, "You called me, and I came."

After grabbing another tissue, Ginger said, "Stay here and don't give birth in the tub," and then slammed out the front door.

"I might," Cat said. Once her sister was out of earshot, she added, "But I'd need someone like me to help me."

Cat moved to her room, chewing and intending to grab a change of clothes and take a shower. Instead she lay back down in her bed and fell asleep.

———

Cat woke, her thoughts immediately abuzz. It was as if she'd fallen asleep mid to-do list, and her brain had been waiting for her to pick up where they'd left off. If no one donated anything, what were their options? What if one of the invitees had a soft spot for the wilderness? Maybe that someone, that outdoorsman-someone, would buy the camp and not tear it all down. Was this even an option? Was the camp up to code? What if outsiders waltzed in here and found a toxic moss or something? Then no matter what happened financially, this place would be history.

She recalled her father's words when insurance adjusters came to evaluate hail damage after a storm. "The suits can only see the decay and age of the place. They don't even see the thrilling splendor of nature." The men would frown at the dated swimming pier, the older-model canoes, nothing unsafe, but they wanted new everything and guaranteed safety.

"Safety isn't a thing in nature," he'd say. "They are fixated on the fact that the two safest buildings are the Mess Hall and the Craft Lodge, both located a hard sprint from the waterfront." Then he would chuckle. "And what an intoxicating dash it is."

After they'd left, her father said, "When people think that natural needs lipstick and seat belts, that's when you know they've taken a wrong turn in life."

But seat belts, airbags, and parachutes are necessities, she thought now, knowing she was catastrophizing because she wasn't doing anything concrete.

She turned and noticed a dinner tray by her bedside, pushed it aside, and got up. Cat would go to the kitchen, decorate a few of those naked cakes. She'd see if she could make a bunch of plain foil envelopes so they wouldn't have to use the gaudy red-and-yellow Frito sacks as feed bags. Maybe there was a way to tastefully bedazzle the white paper table covers.

She walked past Ginger's empty room. The night air smelled like rain, and sure enough, she could hear the steady pit-a-pat on the Craft Lodge's roof. "Nooooo," she said to the ceiling. Rain would bring the glistening fat earthworms to the surface, turn every path into shoe-sucking mud, and threaten any showcasing of the camp's canopy of stars. There was no checking the weather forecast, so Cat would have to remind everyone they needed a plan B for rain.

On the low counter that separated the sink and cupboards from the Secret Garden room sat the pile of unclaimed lanyards, moccasins, and multicolored pot holders that Ginger had hauled out of storage. She lifted a paper towel kaleidoscope to her eye, and when the outer door opened, startling her, she dropped it. Gary was equally surprised and emitted a high-pitched, girlish "Oh!" when he spotted Cat.

Cat almost razzed him about the soprano who lived in his throat, but she was catching her own breath. Then she recalled the night before, when she'd stood naked in front of the window, daring Gary to do what? Look away? Look closer and see her? See who she really was: a nice person with nothing to hide who was trying her best to help.

"Why are you up?"

"Well, Dad, I wanted to see what the grown-ups were up to."

"You fell."

Cat waved him off. "It was a topple at best. I was tired. But I've slept enough for two." She laughed at her accidental joke and pointed to her stomach. "Get it?"

"You can't give birth in the tub."

"So I hear," she said, then added, "You'd love that, wouldn't you?" Why would she say that? Nobody, least of all Gary, would love that. The gloop alone would have him mowing crop circles in the back acres for days to block it out. Gary's expression said *That was a weird thing to say*, so Cat agreed. "That was a weird thing to say. Sorry. This place brings out twelve-year-old-boy comebacks in me."

He walked toward her, sweeping his hands forward like he was herding a grouping of chickens. "Go on now. Back to bed."

It was Cat's turn to give him a look, and that's when she noticed he was wet from the rain. She grabbed a hand towel, tossed it, and said, "That's what we need now. Rain."

Like a hot guy from a romance novel, he caught the towel and wiped his head and neck with it.

"We're going to need a plan. Who's going to get rid of the worms?" she said, watching him dry his throat while maintaining eye contact with Cat. "When did you get so hot?" Cat said, thinking, *Why not say it? Who cares?* She was large with child, which was like being a hundred-year-old lady in terms of anti-hotness.

He fumbled the towel and kicked his leg, and the towel fell to the floor. Cat lifted her eyebrow, just the one, a move she'd perfected in high school to communicate her wry, wise, and weary ways.

"Did I embarrass you? Do you not know how hot you are?" She licked her middle fingertip, touched her hip, and made the sound of water hitting a griddle, *ssssssst*. "Smokin' hot," she said and then giggled.

Gary nodded like an indulgent babysitter and said, "All right. That's enough."

"There is never enough when teasing a grumpy person."

"You've had your fun," he said.

"Seven months ago, I did for about three minutes. But everything since then has been all pelvic exams and 'Come save the camp.'"

"How's that going?" He stepped toward the counter.

"My doctor said that at my age, a baggy bladder is a real possibility postpregnancy. And you know this camp is going under. So, not great." In a shocking moment of vulnerability, Cat's voice cracked. She kept talking as if nothing had happened and gestured to her middle and said, "I'm not who I used to be. In fact, I'm not sure who I am anymore. Or who we are, or will be, or whatever." Cat cleared her throat. "I'm awake because I'm going to go work in the kitchen. It's crazy town in there."

"Wynn will kill you," Gary said simply, instead of pouncing on her moment of softness with a scathing look. He touched the roof of a birdhouse. Lifted a ceramic something.

Cat suspected he was right. Wynn was very much like Cat in that way, certain and territorial. A low rumble outside rolled in the distance, two clouds knocking together, her mother used to say. Cat picked up a birdhouse and played with the hinged roof.

"What's this stuff?" Gary said.

"Ginger said people will pay for junk with an origin story attached. That's what these blank cards and ribbons are for. To write stories about the people who made the crafts and sell them"—Cat widened her eyes for effect—"for big money."

Skeptical was the only way to describe the look on Gary's face.

Maybe it was the ruinous rain on the roof, the moonless night, and the woods that insulated the people in the center like a thermos, but Cat gave in to the thing everyone else at this godforsaken camp seemed okay with: the idea that she knew almost nothing about much of anything.

"You think you know what you're doing when you decide to have a baby. It's all so abstract until your body grows like a time-lapse photo, fast and dramatic. You start thinking about how the baby will get to the outside of you. The horror stories." Cat grabbed a paper towel, blew her nose. "You realize your plans of going without an epidural are basically a child's daydream. Then there's being the only parent and all the ways you wreck them by loving them." Cat flicked her gaze at Gary. "And not wreck them a little bit, I mean like wreck them, wreck them."

If she couldn't save the camp, how in God's name would she keep a child alive? This was like one of her father's scavenger hunts, but timed. Solve the puzzle of throwing a successful gala quickly and win the prize of being a good mother, but if the buzzer sounds and the gala flops, so, too, will your child.

"I need a win here, Gary."

Gary had been standing, arms at his sides, as he watched her. He picked up the towel and tossed it into the sink, confident that it would go right in, taking nothing on the counter with it. Straight and true.

Cat put the birdhouse down. "Who am I to say Ginger's junk stories won't work? I guess at this point anything is worth a try."

She sat heavily, her mind too aware of the ticking clock, the lopsided, rickety crafts. She selected a thick, unevenly woven plastic lanyard and said, "'Artist: Anonymous.' Or better yet, I'll give the artist a pseudonym. I'll say all names were changed for confidentiality reasons." Cat dangled the plastic key chain in front of her and said, "'This item was created by Jason, who came to camp after losing his partner to cancer—Emilio, the love of his life, who went to the hospital to have a small lump examined in the base of his ear.'"

Cat tugged on the fringe at the bottom, wishing she had even one caffeinated coffee bean to chew on to spark her creativity—something her sister had overflowing tanks of.

"Um . . . 'What Emilio thought was adolescent acne revisiting him on his thirty-fifth birthday during their destination wedding in Hawaii, they came to find out was inoperable brain cancer.'" Cat twirled the lanyard key chain by the silver ring, picking up speed and confidence.

Gary pulled out one of the metal folding chairs and sat with a scrape of the legs against the floor.

"'They traveled the islands together, hiking the mountains of Kauai until Emilio couldn't do it anymore. Then Jason put him on his back to finish their hike to the peak, where Emilio took his last breath.'" Cat opened her eyes as wide as they would go and said with a big finish, "'This objet d'art was created here and helped Jason grieve. He donated this object in loving remembrance of Emilio.'" Cat stopped the spinning lanyard and held it in her fist.

Gary blinked and said, "Is that true?"

"No! I just made it up!"

"Gimme," Gary said and then held out his hand.

"Why, Hot Gary. You're on."

CHAPTER TWENTY-SEVEN

UNTIL THE SUN COMES UP AGAIN

Gary picked up a birdhouse and said, "'Artist Jill. Hit by a car. Husband at camp. Sad. He has a kid.'" He searched for more words, almost had them, shrugged, and shook his head.

"That's dark, Gary. What a surprise from cheerful you."

Cat took the birdhouse, careful not to touch his skin for fear of losing her mind with desire. "'Jill was running on the county road on a gorgeous summer morning a mile from her simple saltbox house, high on a hill overlooking her family farm.'" Cat took a breath, watching Gary's interest in the house in her hand. "'Jill's thoughts were on feeding her baby when she returned, when a drunk driver, intoxicated from a party, rounded the corner and hit her, tossing her into a shoulder.'"

Gary blinked, invested, worried.

"'When her husband checked the clock, his wife was five minutes late—he loved her so much every minute counted—and he rushed to find her. At the end of the driveway, he saw her running shoe and found her foggy, dusty, and in the drainage ditch. She was breathing, but her big toe was missing.'"

"Her toe?" Gary frowned.

"I've come to love imaginary Jill. I don't want anything too bad to happen to her, but she was a dancer, and a dancer can't pirouette without their toe."

"Really?"

"I'm thinking . . . yeah. You probably need your toe. 'Jill came to Summer Camp to mourn her toe and get a bird's-eye view of life, thus the bird feeder. PS. The baby was fine and is a favorite at daycare.'"

Gary blinked.

"How about I dictate, and you write," said Cat.

Gary foraged for a pencil, shook his writing hand, and said, "Okay."

As the night went on, Cat narrated while Gary concentrated on getting each moneymaking word recorded with his bafflingly feminine cursive. He gave his full concentration to each word, the tip of his tongue between his teeth, the nail of his thumb and forefinger pale with the pressure of getting it right.

"What brought you to this camp?" Cat said for the first time, wondering what Gary's origin story was.

After a long moment, Gary said, "I like working outside."

Cat cut a length of ribbon to attach a card to a clay sculpture that was either a mug, a shoe, or an elephant, depending on how you placed it on the counter. "And . . . ," Cat said.

"It's quiet."

It wasn't the first time Cat had seen a hot man and tried to attribute a depth that didn't exist to him. Just because Cat didn't want a relationship didn't mean she didn't have regular old lust in her heart. It ran hot and cold, depending on the person.

There'd been Dave, in a ballroom dance elective, whose natural rhythm mesmerized all the women in the class. She'd been paired up with him, and he scoffed loudly at Rob, who couldn't get the cha-cha beat right. Poof, Cat's attraction evaporated. Later, possibly no longer feeling her energy directed at him, Dave asked her to a practice dance. Cat declined, saying Rob was the jealous type, and she didn't want to put Dave in danger. "He isn't known for his kindness either," she said, which she'd thought was a scathing comeback at the time.

"Jeez, Gary, we don't have a lot of time. Can you write faster?" She'd attempted writing a story, but her handwriting was unreadable, even when she tried.

Gary ignored her. Okay, so he was just a good-looking guy who liked to mow grass, and Cat could settle down and stop thinking about his hands, which she was watching at that moment.

"What should we call this collection?" Cat said while stacking and restacking the empty cards.

Gary held up a finger.

"We need something catchy," she said. She lined up the crafts that they would work on next. Ordered and reordered them for something to do. "We want people to think that when they buy these projects, they're supporting the individual artist by funding the camp's future. As if a story attached to a wonky wreath would save us. Maybe if we called it 'Write-Off Art.' That way, we hint at a tax break while playing on the word *write*."

"Shh . . . concentrating."

"'Artful Angst'? 'DIY Desperation'? How about we call it 'We Made This Up.'"

"Cat," Gary said, putting his pen down.

Her name in his mouth stopped her. She wanted to hear him repeat it. But if she heard the hard *C*, the *A* finishing with a crisp *T* sound, she might have to touch him.

He'd say, *You've got to be kidding me,* and she would reply, *Yup, just kidding, LOL.*

"Fine. Go your own speed," she said, knowing she wouldn't slide her hand in his, not in a million years.

If you don't ask for anything from anyone, there are fewer noes in life. When you are alone, you can say yes to yourself. Yes, you can stop taking care of everyone. Yes, you can have a child. Yes, you can cook for yourself, be grateful, and let no one, least of all yourself, down.

Cat fiddled with a blank card next, the kaleidoscope from earlier in the night. She'd read somewhere that stories are usually about the author discovering their core wound. She peered through the tube; someone had sloppily glued tissue paper on the end, but Cat could still make out the corner of one of Gary's eyes.

At Cat's center, she feared pain. Not physical pain—while labor wouldn't be fun, that intense hurt would be short-lived. No, it was the long enduring pain of being let down, or letting someone she loved down, that sustained her avoidant dread. In her experience, that kind of torment was like herpes, a prickly evergreen-take that kept on taking.

"Fine," she said, threading a piece of twine into a single hole punch in the corner of one of the cards. She matched the stories to the crafts while she waited for Gary to catch up.

Cat twisted on the radio next to her; the antenna, a piece of tinfoil, snagged a bluegrass tune she'd never heard. The lilting melody drifted between the raindrops into one window and out the other. Cat gazed outside past the campgrounds into the pines that circled the property. The music made her feel like a romantic heroine waiting for her man to return from the war so she could get some help with the farm.

"What are you thinking about?" Gary asked in his slow, deliberate way that had her thinking that a simple hot guy maybe wasn't that attractive after all.

She wasn't about to confess her romantic notions of a lonely woman, home, and a man, so she blurted out, "Herpes," cringed, and followed up with, "You know, the gift that keeps on giving, and how glad I am that I don't have it."

"Right," he said in his cold tone.

He knew she was holding back, hiding, so she sighed and said, "I'm homesick, I guess."

Cat studied his tidy hands, short nails, the fine muscles in his forearms, and felt the chill. What if she said his name? Just *Gary*, with its hard start and soft finish. Would that delicious desire return, or was it gone? Good riddance. Cat opened her mouth. One word. His name.

"What are you looking at?" His expression was a twin to the one when he'd first seen her on the camp premises. Impatient, parental, and tired.

"Nothing," she said.

Minutes later, Shirtless and June crept in the front door and seemed startled to see Cat awake. "What are you doing here?" Cat said, checking the wall clock. "It's so late. You should be getting your rest."

"We came to relieve Gary."

Cat glanced at Gary, who was trying to suppress a yawn. June wore a purple bathrobe cinched at the waist and appeared to have been pulled from her bed. "As the nurse, I put you on an overnight watch."

That's what Gary's visit was about. Duty to the camp, to Shirtless and Ginger, and embarrassment bloomed within her. He wasn't here to say hello. To chat and see how she was feeling after her fall. Someone had given him the job to babysit her. Cat, the girl who'd left, the pregnant woman knocked up by an unscrupulous character. A bad actor. A liability who needed to be observed, not a part of the team who might be helpful. An annoying, bossy do-gooder who was too tired to be of any help.

"You guys should go. I feel great." She switched the radio off and said, "Tomorrow is the big day. I'm fine. We have a thousand things better to do than to watch me. I'm not a problem to solve. I'm here to make this whole thing less 'rustic hoedown' and more 'professional fundraiser.' None of this can happen if we're all exhausted."

Shirtless looked briefly offended, then relieved. "You think it's okay?" Shirtless said, taking June's hand.

June shrugged and nodded yes.

"Everyone needs their sleep." She snatched the pen out of Gary's grip and said, "You too. Off you go. I'm not going to give birth or fall and break a hip. Go on and find something to mow if you can't sleep."

Gary, stiff-backed and fully himself, walked out the door without looking back.

"Are you mad?" Shirtless said, after opening the door, the smell of rain floating in.

"Oh no, sweetie. I'm not mad at you. I'm angry at myself, and sorry I made everyone worry."

"It's okay. G'night, Aunt Kitty."

The door creaked to a close as the two Littles shuffled out and headed back to their bunks.

Cat shut the side window with a little extra push.

On her way to the bathroom, having to go, the one consistent thing she could count on, Cat brushed by the worktable and knocked a card to the floor. She retrieved it, turned on the light, and read what Gary had written.

This artist, at a young age, enlisted in the army. He learned how to shoot, crawl, huddle, and storm but never to talk to people. His buddy died, and he developed a stutter. He manages it with slow word choices. Home moved too fast. He needed peace and quiet and made this sand candle to light when the darkness came. To remind himself to stay with the people who understand him until the sun comes up again.

Gary had pressed hard with the pencil, and Cat felt the braille of his effort to communicate against her fingertips on the back side of the card. A stutter. His slow, deliberate, economic speech was more impediment than irritation. More intolerance of self than others.

They were alike, she and Gary, and Cat tried to swallow past a sudden sorrowful tightness in her throat.

CHAPTER TWENTY-EIGHT

WE DON'T HAVE TIME FOR THIS

Cat raked through her luggage. There was nothing inside her bag suitable for a night of mingling with the masters of the universe. While that didn't matter in her case—she'd stay hidden—it was the staff she worried about. Why had she left dressing the staff to Brittany, the girl who lived her life covered in animal fur? If they were serving cakes that looked like a series of swollen glands, the workers couldn't look like they'd been dragged off a desert island.

The first thing Cat would do this morning was collect one green Summer Camp polo from everyone, label them, scrub out the ketchup and pit stains, and run them on high in the dryer. Then, just before the guests arrived, she'd line everyone up and dress them.

"Good. That's a good plan. What else?" she said to herself. While they dried, Cat could spruce up the food stations with evergreens and put pine cones and sprigs of greenery on the auction tables for the craft stories. "Yes, there is still time to level up," she said, giving herself a pep talk.

She strode into the front of the Craft Lodge, and with one look at the piles of lumpy crafts, her spindly hopes dove into reality. She whirled around and rummaged through the cupboards for a basket to carry and display the crafts. Something log cabin–y that would underscore the down-home feel of the place and not highlight its shortcomings like a silver platter would. She'd line the basket with birch bark for a Mark Twain motif. How could she have believed that she should sit back and not take charge when she recalled the time her father had tried to trot out his beloved theater camp to outsiders?

Her father had invited the world-class American Players Theatre troupe to camp for a special performance of *The Two Gentlemen of Verona*. In Act 1, Scene 2, Ginger, playing Julia, said to a tiny Lucetta, "'They do not love that do not show their love.'" At which point, the celebrated actor watching from the audience whispered to her father, "Isn't she precious, trying so hard to act the part?" in the most condescending voice ever. Her idealistic, proud father, who thought his players ready for prime time, had been crushed. His sweet paternal filter had been forever lifted. Cat was in the audience watching her father's shoulders drop and his rose-colored glasses fog. She'd wanted to fix it all for him but understood something, even then. You had to be inside the camp to get it. You had to see it evolve to really understand how much work they'd all done. Otherwise, sure, Summer Theater Camp was just another kiddie show batting way out of their league.

The guests at the gala wouldn't get it either. The camp was an inside joke without the punch line. The night was not going to be successful without a miracle, and Cat knew she could still be that miracle.

Another thing that had to happen was some full-disclosure time with her sister. It was time to tell Ginger about Steve—who he was and how he'd found out about the camp. To show her the invitations with the false data so she could address it in her speech, if only to prime the pump for a possible conversation about selling the whole place to someone who wasn't Steve.

Just as she'd hauled an old pink-and-green Easter basket from under the sink, the Craft Lodge door swung open and Norm appeared, winded and sweating. "Where's Gary and Ginger? Camille is out of control. A lot is happening in the Auditorium."

Cat half jogged, half walked behind Norm, thinking she'd see Gary soon and had to be ready to apologize. What could she say? *I'm sorry I was mean about your speech impediment?* Did people use that term anymore? *Your speech differently abledness? I try hard to be a good person, but I can be . . . differently abled also?*

At the double doors of the Auditorium, Norm grabbed the handles and swung them wide. Cat saw June and Shirtless staring at the stage, where Camille stood throttling a microphone attached to a square brown speaker circa 1960. The Emerald City, in all its childish glory, sparkled in the background, and Camille opened her mouth and sang the opening line from "The Sound of Music" with great confidence and only partially on key.

Behind her, Matt straddled one snare drum, dreary in his yoga pants and hippie hairdo.

Camille said over her shoulder, "Matt, use the brush here. Mimic the wind. I'll do my own echo."

Shirtless's eyelid fluttered with a tiny muscle spasm, one of the boy's late-stage responses to stress. June looked worried.

Matt slid the brush around on the snare drum and gave Norm a look like a prisoner of war might give a hero at the gate of a war camp.

"Next one, Matty," Camille said, as she closed her eyes and launched into "Climb Ev'ry Mountain" in a commanding, spiritual voice.

Cat clapped her hands and said, "That's enough, you two," as if Matt and Camille were two naughty schnauzers who were misbehaving and doing their business. Then she turned to the group and, trying to be heard over Camille's warbling voice, said, "Everyone bring me one of your staff shirts please. ASAP." There were a lot of eyes darting around, possibly assessing which inappropriate woman to focus their actions on.

Ginger appeared unhurriedly from the office and walked to the stage, her face even with Camille's shins. "Camille," she said, her voice sounding raspy like it did when she didn't get a good night's sleep.

Camille held the note on the second syllable of *mountain* longer than needed, ignoring Ginger, who grabbed the base of the microphone and slid it as far as the electrical cord allowed.

Camille opened her eyes when her voice lost volume in the room. Cat watched Shirtless's eyes go into full blink mode, and she moved to his side. "I need your staff shirt," she whispered.

"Your song is 'Somewhere Over the Rainbow,'" said Ginger in a tone that sounded like when their mother said, *Don't start with me.*

"Oh, hello, Ginger. Nice to see you. Re: 'Somewhere,' I've been performing since I was eight. Bob knew that when he hired me. I'm capable of singing many songs." Meanwhile, Norm pushed folding chairs into even rows, and Camille said, "No, thank you. Put them back. We moved those for acoustic optimization."

Norm looked between Ginger and Camille, then moved to Cat's side.

"Do you have a staff polo?" Cat asked him.

"No. But listen. Wynn fed Camille a gluten-free cookie"—he looked at his wristwatch—"oh, forty minutes ago." Then he winked at Cat.

"The kind of cookies you ate too many of?"

"Yup. Spiked with only the best."

"That little shit," Cat said in awe but also thinking, *Drugs are not okay.* "We need to get you a staff shirt for tonight. Are you an extra large?"

"Hey," Norm said. "I resemble that remark."

Ginger took the side stairs. "You're not doing a medley, Camille. One song. 'Rainbow.' Then out of the way for our programming."

"Yes, get her sorted, Ginger. I'll take care of the rest," Cat said.

Ginger flashed an annoyed glance at Cat.

"Matt and I decided a few songs with a spiritual theme would match the night's divine motif. Bob will love it."

"There's no divine motif. We're doing '*The Wizard of Oz* goes to camp.' Bob isn't here."

That must have hurt to admit, but the sooner Ginger got on board, the sooner she could help Cat get this party started.

Camille lifted a superior eyebrow and said to Matt, "See, Matt, this is why I took charge of the entertainment. We need vision tonight." She strode to him and added, "Matt found this drum in storage. Did you know he used to play in middle school? We've been having a hoot." When she dropped her arm across his shoulders, it was clear their hoot was physical, not musical.

Ginger folded her arms across her chest. "Hitting some high notes with Camille, are you, Matt?"

Matt mouthed, *Get me out of here.*

Camille tugged Matt's topknot, wound her fingers through his hair, and said, "So soft." This went on for too long, with everyone shooting glances at each other. Cat realized that the cookie had just kicked in, and Norm chuckled under his breath.

Ginger coughed once, twice, and gagged, and Cat caught the scent of disaster. "What's that horrible smell?" Cat elbowed Norm.

"It's not me," he said, and gagged himself.

Ginger coughed hard, moving quickly away from the stage. "It's the plumbing. Get Gary." And she disappeared behind the stage.

"It does this sometimes when it rains," Shirtless said, holding his nose so his words had a swollen-adenoid quality. "Grandpa had to get the tree roots cut the last time. They plug up the system, and it backs up."

Cat might be able to clean a handful of shirts and break off some tree boughs, but she couldn't fumigate the entire auditorium before sundown. "Oh. Good God," she whispered and heard her own panic in the words, not a prayer. She reached for the walkie-talkie so she could shout Gary's name into the small device, but her mouth went dry and her stomach turned a full revolution with acidy sickness. "This can't be," she said at full volume.

The Auditorium doors slammed, and Gary said, "Everybody out."

Immediately on board, Norm said, "We're going to have to set up somewhere else. Matt, get Camille out of here, then come back."

Gary had Cat by the elbow and escorted her out of the gymnasium. "Out," he said.

Cat yanked her arm free. "We don't have time for this. I have to set up in here. Make it look nice."

"No. You're homesick. Go there." The slap of his words, as if slamming a door behind her.

"I am home. This is my home. It's more mine than yours," she said like a child stamping her foot, and she instantly felt sorry for the hurt that must have caused him.

He shook his head like Cat didn't get it. It was as if once a person left a place, they couldn't return. Maybe that's why Gary stayed. He thought he belonged where he stood, that belonging was a place for the body, not the heart. At that moment, she saw Hot Gary differently. Cat saw him as hot and sad. And not moving quickly enough.

"Gary," she said in a kinder tone, "I'm sorry. But also, we've got to get this smell out of here."

Gary didn't reply, which Cat felt was a win, even though he looked utterly annoyed.

The smell, getting stronger by the minute, chased Cat out and over to the Canteen. If she could get the laundry started, she could round up fans to set up and blow the rank odor out the back door of the Auditorium.

She found Brittany in the laundry room in the back of the Canteen holding a live chicken.

"Oh good. What are you doing right now?"

"This is Connie, our therapy chicken."

"Cluck, cluck, cluck, Connie," Cat said, and she moved to the corner of the Canteen and grabbed a light, plastic standing fan.

"You don't have to use baby talk. She understands. Connie. Go get your mirror." Connie necked it over to her nest, plucked a white plastic child's hand mirror out of its straw-like folds, and dropped it in Brittany's outstretched hand.

"Beautiful and smart," Cat said, and Connie stretched her neck for a pet. "No time, Connie. Can you run this over to the Auditorium?"

"You mean for the smell?" Brittany said.

Cat gave her a look. "Yes," she said evenly. "Then I'm going to round up staff shirts for a quick launder."

"Can't do laundry. The system is attached to the plumbing drains in the theater."

"You're kidding. What is everybody going to wear?"

"Pen and I have been working on something amazing." She plopped Connie into the bunny pen next to Alistair and Raj. "And don't worry about the smell. Gary took care of it last time. He took care of all the big things after your dad started to lose it."

"What?" Cat had been looking in cupboards and the one closet for more fans.

"You know, started to forget stuff. Found him that one time he wandered off. He'd get so angry when he couldn't find something. Gary could always calm him down."

Almost before Brittany said the last word, Cat was on the move.

CHAPTER TWENTY-NINE

A FERTILE CHIP

Cat jogged gracelessly by the beach, past the Thunderbird Cabins' path, toward the larger guest lodges, scanning the paths for Ginger. Her father. Forgetting things? Wandering off? To where? Brittany had to have it wrong. Cat swerved behind the Admin Building, the sewer smell thick in some spots, barely perceptible in others. When she got to the county road, she looked both ways and headed for the family cabin.

Their dad was the backbone of the camp, while their mother was the changeable thespian. If anyone was going to lose it, Cat would have put money on her nut of a mother. She'd spoken to them before they'd left the camp. And on the phone intermittently over the last year. Sure, the chats were short, but her parents despised the phone, always had. Where were they now? What else hadn't Ginger told her?

She pushed inside the building, and her round ligaments sent off a warning flare of pain. She dug the palms of her hands into her hip flexors and massaged. She'd stay hidden for the gala, but she couldn't be incapacitated, another weight around the neck of the camp.

The pocket door of the small bathroom slid aside, and Ginger walked out with a pencil twisted into her hair, holding a yellow notepad.

"Jeesh, you startled me," Ginger said, her voice worsening.

"You don't sound great," Cat said.

"The sulfur smell. It always gets into my throat," said Ginger.

"I've been looking for you," Cat said, trying to suppress any annoyance in her tone.

"I'm hiding. Trying to write the welcome speech. I want to get it down so that I can read the whole thing. Not get off track." Ginger looked at Cat like she knew what she was thinking, *Oh boy*, but not in a good way. Their father had a gentle, folksy way about him in front of a crowd. He was Tom Hanks, with a sincere hound-dog face that said, *I'll take good care of your kids, parents, don't you worry.*

"Your voice sounds terrible," Cat said. "Does it hurt?"

Ginger pinched her fingers together and mouthed *A little*. "Why did the squirrel bury his lottery tickets under a bush?" Ginger croaked.

"He was hedging his bets. Dad's favorite open," Cat said. "Was Dad forgetting things?"

Ginger lifted one shoulder but didn't meet Cat's eyes, then gestured again with her fingers. *A bit.*

"Like what bits?"

"A bunch of stuff." Ginger's voice sounded more painful with each word. She swallowed and gestured to her throat.

"A bunch of stuff?" Cat shook her head, wanting to deny this information.

Their father had been terrified of forgetfulness. His mother had had dementia, and he'd watched her deteriorate and had cared for her himself. Planted blueberry bushes around the camp for breakfast and brain health. He was in the habit of memorizing entire scripts. "Keeps the mind supple," he'd say.

"How bad was it?" Cat said, wanting to close her eyes, shield herself from what she was about to hear.

Ginger shook her head like Gary had. As if Cat were a stranger who wouldn't understand, didn't need to know, that it wasn't her business.

"How bad was it? Like his mom?" Cat pressed.

Ginger bobbled her head like, *Yes, maybe.*

"Where are they? You left Mom in charge of our father when she barely manages herself. Why didn't you call me? I would have come. You know I would have." Her voice had a pleading quality to it, as if she was trying to convince her sister that she loved her father, would do anything for him. That she hadn't been so disconnected to have missed something so massive as her father's mind slipping away.

Ginger pointed to her throat and shook her head *no.*

"Sign it," Cat said.

There were weeks when a group of hearing-impaired kids would come to camp, and every year, all the staff had a refresher for the most commonly used ASL signs to learn. Words like *sick, medicine, help, throw-up, dinnertime,* and *good night,* but other cute sign words like *bonfire, turtle, swim,* and *canoe*—language that mimicked the gestures.

Ginger and Cat had gotten so good at it that sometimes parents assumed the sisters had grown up signing. They used it as a secret language for mischief and gossip. The fact that Ginger had forgotten who she was dealing with galled Cat. *Sign it,* Cat signed. *Why didn't you tell me?*

We don't have time for this, Ginger signed with little energy.

We do have time for this. Cat put her hand to the side of her head, her fingers in the letter *Y* position. *Why didn't you call me?* Her anger flared. Something so important. Her father's health. And no one called? *Too distracted with Bob?* Cat signed, knowing it was a low blow. Not caring. They certainly hadn't cared about her.

Cat could see she was getting to Ginger. A flush had crept up her neck and colored her jaw.

Cat pointed to her sister. *You and Gary had the place handled?* she signed, exaggerating the crabby look, gesturing toward the Auditorium, then holding her nose at the odor. Cat leaned into the theater of the hearing-impaired communication, the artful emphasis they placed on words with their facial expressions and body language. It felt good to show her anger with her whole body. *Not handled!*

Stop, Ginger signed again. Then she placed the tip of her thumb, her five fingers open, fanning from her forehead—the sign for *Dad.* Then quickly, her anger showing in the force of her sign, her fingers flew, *Don't call Cat.* Following up with a letter *L* striking the opposite open hand. *Forbid.*

"Forbade you to call me? I don't believe it." Even as she said it, she knew that whatever Ginger was, she wasn't a cruel liar. Cat felt like a mouse trapped in a cage she'd made for herself. She'd wanted to get out; well, this was out, all right. She'd pushed for black and white, and she'd gotten it, and it felt like the dark-purple bruise of failure.

Cat examined her toes, the chipped red nail polish, old because it was uncomfortable to paint them with her belly in the way. Her father, of all people, had misunderstood. She didn't want out of the family; she just didn't want to be responsible for everything. Should she have made a list for them? No to ownership, staffing, camp problems. Yes to the family's needs that had nothing to do with the camp. No to the payroll. Yes to dementia. Yes to Bard's future. Yes to Ginger because without her in the world, Cat was only half of herself.

Ginger flapped her hands to get Cat to look at her.

He knew, Ginger signed. *He knew you would come and take over. He knew you didn't want that. He told me not to call.* Then she signed the saddest sign of all, both hands pressing on the right shoulder as if a heavy weight were attached: *Burden.*

"He would never be a burden to me," Cat said, wanting to show Ginger the list she'd just thrown together in her mind. *See, here! It's all right here!*

With her shoulders squared, Ginger signed, *But your sister is a burden. Your nephew?* Ginger wasn't angry or accusing. It was a fact that Ginger lived with, and she wanted Cat to know the people at this camp could handle reality.

No, Cat snapped with her fingers. Then, she gestured widely. "This camp is the burden. It was a burden to both of us. You and Bard are not the burden. It's this place."

Ginger calmly signed the sign they used for homesick kids who didn't want to go home or wanted to learn a handful of signs to impress their parents: fingers and thumb together at the side of the mouth, then moving the hand across the face toward the ear and back. *Home. Our home.*

No burden.

One person's trash is another person's treasure. Ginger had said this about the left-behind art, but it was true of everything, everywhere, all the time.

Selling the camp, or losing it to Steve. Insult to injury, that's what both of those options were. It had been pure folly, as her mother would say in her Agatha Christie accent. *What were you thinking, girls?*

Selling a house is a financial decision. Selling a home is an emotional one. In an effort to distance herself from having too much responsibility, she'd tried to separate the real estate from the people who owned it.

Selfish, Cat signed, and Ginger gave her an offended look.

"Not you," Cat said. "Me. Dad needed me. Not for the camp but for himself, and I was too selfish to see that."

Cat dropped her head, the universal sign of shame. Now, here she was, pregnant and alone, and no one had even asked who the father was—this moment was a glaring sign of her overcorrection in life. Her insistent solo-ness that she'd thought of as uber-capable independence.

She'd put herself on an island so that she wouldn't be responsible for anyone she loved, so she wouldn't let them down. She hadn't realized that the tension of being asked for something could be a string tied with a bow of love.

Ginger had an understanding expression as she watched her older sister grow into an adult right before her eyes.

"Dad got older. I never thought he would. He always seemed ageless. I guess I thought if he didn't age, I wouldn't have to either." Cat rubbed her stomach, her worry stone, her comfort globe.

Who's the father? Her sister signed her fingers carefully, asking kindly.

Ginger had waited for the right moment to ask this critical question. It hadn't been her sister's disinterest or self-involvement, as Cat had thought. It had been a question that couldn't be asked without love and understanding in the room between them, and Ginger, wisely, had waited. Ginger had grown up, too, possibly years before Cat.

"Oh, Ginger. I'm so sorry. I'm sorry I wasn't here. I'm so sorry you were alone to see Dad change."

With a quiet, motherly gaze, Ginger signed, *I wasn't alone.*

And of all the things Ginger had raspy-whispered, this was truest. It was only Cat who had been alone. Cat shook her head and dropped her hand from her security-tummy.

"How are we going to pull this night off?"

"We can," Ginger rasped. "This speech," she said, and she finished the sentence by signing. *I'll kick it off.*

"We can't smell like zombies and have a camp director that sounds like a two-packs-a-day smoker. Of all things, this place needs the message of health."

Ginger cleared her throat. Took a sip of water. "You give it." The words barely there.

"No. You don't understand. The father of this baby is the guy Norm worked for, the one who wants this place to go bankrupt so he can turn it into a water park. He's going to be here tonight. He doesn't know I'm pregnant. But he knew about the camp."

Cat saw Ginger trying to process so many bombshells simultaneously, the biggest one being the secret baby's relationship to the camp's problems.

"I don't know exactly how it all happened. All I remember is he mentioned the camp to me in passing. Maybe he did some googling? Connected the dots. Maybe he made a deal with Bob? I don't know."

"No," Ginger said with an adamant head shake.

Cat was impatient with her sister's hero worship of the man at the center of every crisis since she'd arrived. She almost fell back into trying to get her sister to see something Cat thought was obvious—Bob and

Steve had used them all. Focusing on her sister's faults as if she herself had nothing to do with the chaos was not the way to move forward.

Cat drew a circle around her stomach with her pointer finger. "This was a onetime thing with that guy. It was . . ." Cat mouthed the words *A mistake*, not wanting her baby to hear. "I'm afraid he'll try to leverage the baby. He's that kind of guy. He can't know about this baby. Not when the camp is so vulnerable. I can't do the speech."

Cat was a teacher; she taught, spoke, organized for a living. It was a skill she had that she'd inherited from her father and honed in classrooms, meetings, and with parents. It was something Cat could do to help that wouldn't step on her sister's toes, yet if she gave the speech, Steve would see a fertile chip to bargain with.

CHAPTER THIRTY

A MAIN CHARACTER

Everything about Ginger's demeanor said she understood that Steve, the pregnancy, and Cat were one more crap variable they'd all have to contend with. Someone, not Cat, would welcome the guests, champion the great outdoors, tout the institution, and explain why it should be preserved. A sincere person who knew this place better than anyone— and that individual pushed open the screen door as if on cue.

"Mom? Aunt Cat? The smell. It's not going to get better. We're moving everything to the Mess Hall and onto the trails. Wynn needs some help with the cakes."

"Bard," Ginger croaked, using his name so he knew she was serious. "My voice."

"You have to do the welcome speech," Cat said too abruptly.

Ginger glanced at Cat as if to coach her. *Slow down. Don't make it a big deal. Easy breezy.*

Bard stepped back and put his hands out as if he had encountered a wild boar in the living room of his grandparents' house. "No. No way."

"You have to," Ginger said, more hissing air than words.

"You promised," Bard said.

That promise was made when you were six, Ginger signed.

Shirtless shifted his gaze between the two women, looking for a way out.

"I have to stay hidden. I'm sorry, buddy," Cat said.

Blood rushed to his face; he shook his head with a forceful *no* and backed toward the door.

"It's not too much to ask. And you might regret it if you don't do it," Cat said, knowing she had no business saying these things to her nephew.

The muscles of Shirtless's jaw tensed, making him look more man than boy.

Unaware of the drama, Penelope arrived, put one hand on the center of his back, and pushed Shirtless back into the cabin. She looked the most put-together of anyone Cat had seen at the camp thus far. Her clothes weren't stained or wrinkled, and her springlike red curls looked conditioned. She had a clipboard in her hand and said, "Shirtless. It's your turn to get your outfit for tonight. Cat, I have you down for 3:20 p.m., which is in fifteen minutes." Penelope looked at her arm as if a watch were strapped to her wrist. "Ginger, you are at thirty-five minutes. Don't come together. Stay in your time slot. We can get it done faster then."

"What are you putting people in? What did you decide on?" Cat said.

"It was Ginger's brainstorm; I'm just executing," said Penelope.

"Oh, well, if you're short, you can give someone mine. I won't be in front of people."

"Here's what I told everybody," Penelope said. "You wear what's assigned. Nobody argues. No swapping or trading. If you make a stink, you don't get to eat. If you hate what you have to wear, nobody cares."

"Seriously, though. Is the laundry working? Are they wearing a uniform? Is it on brand? Just tell me if it's on brand."

Ginger dropped her head to the side, like *This again?*

"It's on brand," Ginger said.

Penelope flicked her pen toward the door. "Let's go, Shirtless."

"Make the words your own," Ginger whispered, handing Shirtless her speech.

Shirtless didn't move. Instead, he said to Cat, "If I have to speak, you have to show up. You get that, don't you, Aunt Cat?"

"We can talk about this, but my presence will only hurt us."

He shook his head, the same way Gary did, a disappointed, irritated move that cut deeper when her beloved nephew made it. A boy who'd gone through life masking his sensitivities was about to lose the place that made him feel most at home.

Cat nodded. "If the time is right, I promise to do what is needed."

"Will you, though?" Shirtless said, and he rolled the speech into a tube. "She knows it's too late."

"Bard. There are things you don't understand." Ginger had the expression of a mother confident she was doing the correct thing while questioning if she did anything right, ever.

"No. He's right to say . . . all of it." As Cat watched Shirtless slouch out of their childhood home, it was easy to see the entire situation through her nephew's eyes.

Cat had come to camp entirely certain that detachment and even disposal of this place was what she'd wanted—no, needed. Now, after just a few days, she was wholly invested in the people and the place, like a superfan for a failing football team. But even though it had taken only a few days to get her there, Cat *was* too late. She'd spent too much time on the sidelines; now, with her heart full of wanting, at the end of the night the buzzer would sound and it would be Capitalism 1, Summer Camp 0. Winner takes all.

I'm sorry, Cat signed.

For what?

Maybe everything.

Stop. Get your outfit. I'll meet you in the kitchen. Don't fight anybody, Ginger signed quickly, impatiently.

Cat didn't feel like fighting anyone anymore. Her eyes filled, and she signed the first sign they learned from their mother. *I love you.*

I know, Ginger signed with a sigh.

When Cat turned to go, she almost jetted into Gary, standing in the doorway watching them. He held a clothes hanger covered by a black bag and a soft look on his face, and Cat knew Norm had gotten everything wrong. Gary might've been sweet on her sister. It was an old, romantic term, but the look in his typically crabby eyes was all sugar.

"I love her too," Cat said, moving out the door. If nothing about Gary was clear, at least they agreed on this.

———

As she crossed the lawn for the umpteenth time in the last few days, Cat saw that the rain had done the place some good, aside from the misery of the smelly auditorium. The lush grass looked a shade greener, the trees succulent with moisture, and the flowers Gary had planted at the edges of the property bloomed as if rooting for the dingbats who had planned them.

The grounds staff had set up tables for Wynn's food stations, and all the string lights had been hung along the paths and, when switched on, were sure to give the place ambiance.

Someone—Gary and Norm?—had placed the Emerald City backdrop up against the Mess Hall doors; the stage rainbow looked nailed in place as the entrance to the outside gathering area. Yes, it looked like sixth-grade dance decor, but when the sun set and the small spotlights anchored at the shafts of the rainbow were switched on, maybe it would elevate to "high school prom on a plucky budget."

At the Canteen, Cat pushed against the rustic front door and into a store with shelves for the items campers might want. Swim goggles, caps, floaties, toothbrushes, sunscreen, and candy, so much candy. Cat fingered a pair of goggles like she was saying a tearful goodbye to an old friend, *I should have tried harder, I'm sorry.* Penelope, apparently the most organized of all the Littles, had prime locations for Bob's Summer

Camp merch: FAILURE IS THE CHANCE TO BEGIN AGAIN tote bags and embroidered terry cloth sweatbands hung from hooks on the walls. Two mannequins were dressed in white T-shirts with the words SUMMER CAMP above the beaver logo, the beaver sitting cross-legged meditating. There were even small baggies of sand with a tiny rake attached and a handwritten sign next to them: BRING HOME YOUR OWN ZEN GARDEN! Bob's book *Feel Amazing, Be Awesome* was front and center.

When the door smacked shut behind Cat, Penelope emerged from behind the counter with Brittany and Lefty.

"This is where you've been?" Cat said. The dog bumped his head against Cat's leg and gave her leg a lick.

"What's happening here?" Cat pointed to a burlap vest around Lefty's torso and a blue ribbon attached to an oddly shaped headpiece.

Expressionless, Penelope handed a garment bag to Cat, pulled a pencil from behind her ear, made a notation on a clipboard, and returned to the back room. Brittany placed a basket on the counter, and Cat unzipped the bag.

"What is this?" Cat said to Brittany, who glanced at Penelope as she returned with three pairs of ruby slippers.

"Which ones fit?" asked Penelope. "For some reason, they had three pairs in the back. I think sometimes they had a grown-up Dorothy and a kid Dorothy when they did productions. Maybe you know."

"Is everybody wearing *Wizard of Oz* costumes?" Cat said, trading her melancholy for impending dread.

Brittany wheezed a nervous giggle.

Penelope's name should have been Marlene or Enid, because she had the bearing of a spinster aunt who did not cotton to naysayers or questioners. "Uh, yeah."

"When was this decided?"

"You said it was a *Wizard of Oz* theme. Your sister came up with the idea of what to wear."

One look at Penelope's expression and Cat could see she wasn't fooling around. "I can't wear this," Cat said.

"You can and you are."

"I'll go talk to my sister."

"Don't you think she's got enough to do? You are Dorothy. Try on the shoes."

Brittany, trying to improve things by adding an animal to the situation, said, "This is your basket for Toto. We are putting Connie the chicken in it because Lefty won't fit, and his basket costume isn't that great. Connie isn't likely to run off. She'll sit where ya put her."

Cat pictured herself and the staff in costumes mostly made for children's theater, stretched, altered, bursting at the seams. "Look, Penelope." She considered saying *Tonight's event is not a costume party*, but what good would that do?

Instead she said, "I don't think you understand. Dorothy is the main character, and I will only be at the party in case of a major emergency. If they do need me, I have to appear . . . imposing. I can't be wearing . . ." Cat fanned her hands across the blue gingham pinafore dress. "This. Is my sister trying to get back at me?"

Brittany piped up again. "You can call Connie 'Toto.' She won't care. We might put her in like a gray sweater, but she hates wing impingement."

Cat waited for Penelope to respond.

Unsmiling and unsympathetic, Penelope looked at her for a long moment and finally said, "You have been wanting to go home since the day you got here. Put this on. Shut up about it, and you can finally go home."

Puuhhh was the sound that came out of Cat's mouth. As if she'd been hit in the stomach with a softball. One that delivered the truth that everyone saw her as she was. Someone who just wanted to get out of Dodge. "It won't fit," Cat said as a concession.

"I let it out," Penelope said, then spun on her heel and left.

Cat held up the garment bag and was about to make another sound of audible disgust, but Brittany said, "Which shoes fit? And don't yell at me. You gave Pen the job."

"Fine," she said. No one would see her anyway. Cat kicked off her Birkenstocks and tried on three pairs of red sequined shoes that pinched her little toes, each in different ways.

CHAPTER
THIRTY-ONE

THE CAKE FACTORY

After shoving the shoes into the bottom of her garment bag, Cat ran into Norm on his way to the Mess Hall. He nodded to Cat's hand. "What did you get?"

"Never mind."

"It can't be worse than mine."

Cat held her belly. "Do you remember anyone being seven months pregnant in *The Wizard of Oz*? I'll be the one in red heels and a pinafore, shaped like a washtub."

"Gotcha," he said. "Yeah, mine is more on brand. I'm the Mayor of the Munchkin City in the country of the Land of Oz."

"Oh man!"

"I'm all in now. One look at me in that green jacket and plaid vest, and I'll never work in this town again."

"That's not great for you because I don't see how there will be a camp after this fiasco." Suddenly, an image of her father giving all the welcoming speeches of her childhood. Straight backed and warm, clear in word and deed. His face, saying goodbye as she left for college, resigned, already missing her. "You should have what you want, Kitty."

"Why so negative?" Norm said.

"I've said it before, and I'll say it again: I'm not a . . ." But she stopped, knowing she was a good person, and this insistence that she wasn't was a lie that had kept her away from her family. She'd gone too far with a boundary and had gotten lost trying to figure out a way back.

When Norm saw she wouldn't finish, he said, "This place has a way of cutting through the garbage, doesn't it?"

"Drugs help." Cat gave a wry smile, and then because she didn't know him, and sometimes a stranger can take a confession better than family, she added, "I should have helped way before this, Norm. I really should have."

"Hey." He lifted his wrist and pointed to a leather bracelet. "Haven't you heard? 'Failure is a chance to begin again.'"

"Did Wynn give you this?"

"No, there was one hanging on a hook backstage. I didn't think anyone would mind. I won't show it off, or all the cool kids will want one."

As he said this, they pushed into the Mess Hall. One step over the threshold, and the frenetic energy slowed long enough for everyone to see that Norm and Cat were not Bob. They were still hoping. After everything, they believed, and they got to work.

Every picnic table had a handful of staff working feverishly on something. Nervous June placed multiple colored construction paper bidding sheets written in Sharpie marker under the camp art. The guy Cat knew only as Ropes Course Guy tied yarn and paper napkins around plastic cutlery, while Nature Center Girl gamely retied the yarn knots into small bows. Shirtless whittled points on a pile of branches for s'mores, the speech papers open on the table. He peered at Cat and returned to mouthing the words written on the page.

She had to hand it to the Littles: the event was going to be weird as Comic Con on Halloween, but there was going to be an event. Despite her hesitation to begin, her hot-and-cold guidance, her last-ditch effort to lend a hand, Cat saw that the campers hadn't needed her. She could take no credit or blame for the night. She waited for the relief to come, but instead she felt like a kid waiting to be picked for a dodgeball team. She gave herself an impatient shake. *This is what you wanted; you can't boo-hoo about it.*

"Norm!" Wynn called. "Go relieve Gary. He's setting up the tables outside. I need him."

"Roger that." He handed off his bracelet to Cat on his way out. "You look like you need this."

Cat hung her garment bag on a spike by the door and clipped the leather to her wrist, saying, "Hi, Dad," as if her father had just given her a loving squeeze.

"Britt, we need help with the Bear Poop." Wynn gestured to rows of Dixie cups filled with clumps of brown something on large aluminum cookie trays. "Spike the scat bags with the toothpick sign," Wynn said, pointing to a little printed toothpick flag that said *Bear Poop.* "It's chocolate-covered peanuts. Is it fancy enough for a gala? Of course not. There's no hiding that we're a camp in the woods. At this point, it's better to highlight than hide."

Cat's father used to say, *We're ragtag. We're summer stock. We're not Broadway. We know it. The parents know it. We're not trying to be something we're not. Highlight, not hide. People respect the truth.*

"Where did you hear that? 'Highlight, not hide'?" said Cat.

"Oh, hey, Cat," Wynn said as if she hadn't been standing in the group. "It's a Gingerism. She's got a bunch of 'em." To Britt again, Wynn said, "When you're done, put those treats in the walk-in. Nobody wants runny bear scat."

Gary pushed his way into the Mess Hall, and for a second, Cat was reminded of him as the young man, the lawn mower guy. Their eyes met, and she tried a smile, a prelude to the apology she'd give him if he ever let her get close enough to him to speak.

Ginger entered seconds later, found Shirtless's side, and spoke in his ear.

"Okay, everybody!" Wynn pushed a pencil into her lemon-yellow curls and read from a tiny paper pad in her hand. "About fifty people will arrive in under four hours."

There were murmurs, the staff shifted in their seats, and someone laughed nervously. Cat fidgeted with part *Let's get this over with* anticipation, part genuine curiosity and excitement.

"You guys. It's not that many people," Wynn said. "When my sister and I catered parties, we had double that. If you keep people moving and entertained, they don't eat as much. It'll be fine." Wynn wiped her hands on her apron and said, "Listen up. Here's the story we're telling with this food. Food makes us happy. Food reminds us of home. Home makes us happy. Home is over the rainbow. Summer Camp is a home away from home."

These people 100 percent believed that this gala would save the camp. Maybe they were right. Maybe they had a chance. Cat scanned the faces, saw unembarrassed pride, excitement, and complete buy-in. This was a community worth fighting for. This was a cause she could get behind, besides saving herself.

She hadn't been able to do things her way, and hadn't taken over, but Cat could still lend a hand. But she had the feeling like she was trying to dive into a game of double Dutch when she only knew how to skip a single rope.

Wynn scribbled something onto the paper. "Gary and his guys set up the campfires for cooking the bread and s'more stations. They will light them when people arrive. The Walking Tacos will be halfway through the camp. June will spoon the veggie meat into the Frito bags, and Shirtless is adding the salsa." Head nods all around, everyone on board. "They'll walk on the lighted path to the water. The potato boat station will be on the sand. Last, I found Elaine's alcohol stash by her gluten-free English muffins. Thank you, Elaine. So the golf carts will be moving bars; Gary's guys are drivers and bartenders, except we only have vodka lemonade. Penelope, you're up."

"Here's the timeline," said Penelope. "We welcome people. They walk and eat, and we herd them to the outside theater for Shirtless's speech."

There was a smattering of applause. Someone said, "You got this!"

Penelope continued, "We let them peruse the auction items and merch, push for donations, and cut the cake."

"Get to work," Wynn said. June handed her a glass of water, and Wynn took a sip. "Be careful with those cookies. They have to stay out of the humidity," she called to one of Gary's guys.

Cat could already see the girl's future. The owner of a diner, an older Wynn, her blonde curls streaked with gray, calling everyone *hon* and *sweetie* and giving away free coffee and weed after ten visits. Despite this hopeful vision, Cat saw dark rings under Wynn's eyes and followed the girl into the back of the kitchen with her tray of Bear Poop.

"Wynn. Give me a job. Please. I can help," Cat said and then came face-to-face with Wynn's unfinished cake factory, in the center of the Mess Hall, the plan B place where the guests might end up if it rained.

CHAPTER THIRTY-TWO

I TRIED TO BE YOU

Wynn stood over a cake the size of a large watermelon but shaped like a log. The girl had spent a lot of time frosting the cake to look like brown bark and decorating it with purple and lavender flowers. A mushroom sat near a frosted knot on the side, and Wynn busily mixed small cups of colored frosting with a toothpick. Next to the log cake were others— flats, tiered, and one yellow-frosted ball of a cake that could have been a grapefruit or maybe the moon.

Trying to minimize the disaster of all the unfinished confection on every surface, Cat said playfully, "This is a lot of cakes, girlfriend." If the night went under, if the place took her life as she knew it, at least she'd tried a damn Hail Mary pass along with the rest of the characters.

"I love cake," Wynn said. "We can do a cakewalk, or an auction. People will see that I can do more than make pancakes. That cooking is a viable career. My dad will see."

Cat had misjudged Wynn. She'd seen her only as a young person playing at being a professional at a summer camp job. Cat hadn't seen her as a kid driven by a fear of failure. One who needed success to convince herself and her parents that she was a serious person. A person with a neurodiverse brain that didn't fit into her father's plans to get her into a business world that made deals on the golf course. Cat knew what it was like to grow up with someone who had their future planned.

"Can I help get some of these closer to the finish line?"

Wynn stopped, wiped her forehead, smearing purple frosting across her face, and, as if for the first time, noticed the cakes like soldiers waiting to be addressed. "Um," she said, her voice faltering. The person who'd rallied the staff minutes ago seemed to evaporate, like a spirit leaving a medium's body. "What time is it?" Wynn said, the toothpick coated with purple frosting vibrating in her hand.

Cat heard something in the girl's voice, like a last nerve giving way.

"Never mind that. Lots of time. I'll decorate. You can trust me. Okay if I start on this one?" Cat moved to a sheet cake that looked easy and could serve a bunch of people. She dipped the spatula into a large bowl of frosting and glanced at Wynn. The humidity of the back room had turned the girl's curls into a wild crown, giving Wynn a delicate, unhinged look. Cat wanted to say something grounding, but suddenly her mouth was dry with the anxiety of frosting all the unfinished cakes.

"I'm really tired," Wynn said in a small voice.

"I bet you are. Look at all you've done."

"So many cakes," she said quietly.

Cat dropped the spatula into the tub of frosting and took the frosting-coated toothpick from Wynn's fingers. "Let's call this cake done. How about a catnap while I work on some of the others. Get them ready to decorate."

"You can sleep when you're dead," Wynn said without enthusiasm.

Cat suspected Wynn had said this many times in her young life.

"How about this. I'll wake you in twenty minutes. Okay? Then we can finish the cakes together."

"Twenty minutes?"

"Yes."

"Then we can finish the cakes?"

"Then we can finish the cakes. You can get dressed, and we'll see all your hard work through the eyes of the guests. Okay?"

"When Bob sees what we've done, he will be so proud. My dad, everybody can stop worrying about me."

Cat had the sense not to say *Bob won't see all this.* Instead, she said, "Your parents will be so excited."

Wynn rubbed her eye with her fist, and Cat thought about taking the corner of a wet washcloth, running it gently over the girl's face, maybe stopping to scrub the purple at her temple off. She didn't, but she did accompany the girl to her bedroom in the back of the kitchen. Wynn crawled into her twin bed with the rumpled quilted bedspread.

The girl snuggled next to a Beatrix Potter Peter Rabbit stuffie badly in need of a bath, a carrot in his paw hanging by a thread. Cat unlaced the girl's tennis shoes, speckled with food coloring and stained with grease, and placed them on the floor.

"Will you stay until I fall asleep?" Wynn said.

"If you want me to." The request filled Cat's throat, and she nodded, though Wynn's eyes were already shut.

"Twenty minutes," Wynn said and then went still, her breathing lengthening, deepening, her eyelids twitching. Cat's eyes wandered to the only thing of note in the room: a frilly pink gown with yards of sparkly tulle hanging on a wire hanger from a closet door. A plastic wand and tiara lay on a small desk. Glinda the Good Witch.

Wynn's infectious positivity and willow-wisp of curls would make Glinda proud. Cat covered the girl's narrow shoulders with a mustard-colored afghan, closed the café drapes, and left the room.

Then Cat, a woman who purchased baked treats at grocery stores, a fake helper as it were, started on the cakes. When Gary arrived an hour later, Cat put her finger to her lips and said, "Shh. Wynn's sleeping." He made her nervous standing in the room, everything odd and off between them.

Gary raised his eyebrows at the roomful of messily frosted cakes.

"I know what they look like," said Cat. The cakes were lumpy from craters filled with either cake pieces or gobs of frosting. Each time she attempted to smooth a ragged pothole, another clump would come loose, stick to whatever knife, spoon, or fingers Cat tried to smooth things over with. If she could have YouTubed the issue, maybe she could have frosted one of the cakes well enough for public presentation. Cursing Bob had been the only thing that kept her from panicking.

Gary picked up a spatula, and Cat said, "Don't touch the log or that flat sheet cake. Those are our only hope. In fact, if you want to do something, finish the Bear Poop." Cat made the mistake of looking at Gary, who looked irritated. "I know. I know it's too little, too late." She lifted her chin. "I get it, Gary. You're everything my father wanted. A devoted son who was in lockstep with his own dreams of continuing on despite . . ." She shook her head. Swallowed. "Despite his daughters who tried, screwed up, and then gave up their childhood to keep this camp limping along year after year." The foreign words attached to this unexamined thought had flown from her mouth like a caged bird suddenly free.

"And now my dad's out there with our mother, who also isn't you. Forgetting all this, the life he'd built, Ginger, and you." She coughed to hide the catch in her throat. "Me. So stand there and judge me all you want, but I've got to get these done because a little girl in the back thinks this camp will survive if we give out enough cake."

The sound of a slamming door startled Cat, and she dropped the spatula. She opened the bedroom door to find Wynn's bed empty and the Glinda costume no longer hanging from the closet door.

"Wynn," Cat called, seeing a flash of pink by Alistair and Raj's cage.

Gary charged past Cat, about to launch himself to the rescue, but stopped to say, "Finish a cake. Forget the rest." She should have been annoyed at this man telling her what to do. But she found that being told what to do felt like a cool, welcome breeze on a ferociously hot day.

After a clumsy swoop of the frosting knife, she finished with the cake. Then washed up and moved into the empty dining room to set it up as a happy little hoedown. The room's tables had been pushed to the periphery and were covered in red-checked paper tablecloths. There were colossal aluminum soup pots filled with ice and water bottles.

Someone had drawn a map of the camp on the long, slate chalkboard. Little chalky cartoon pine trees lined a yellow brick path leading to the lake. Summer Lake and the Swimming Pier were labeled, in what Cat saw now was Ginger's tidy script. Food stations were numbered as 1. Hors d'oeuvres, 2. Amuse-bouches, 3. Appetizers, 4. Main course, 5. Palate cleanser, 6. Dessert, and 7. Mignardise, with an arrow pointed to the little chalk drawing of the Mess Hall. Cat admired her sister's handiwork and hoped their visitors would see the LOL of labeling Bear Poop as mignardise.

Cat grabbed her garment bag and pushed outside through the door of the Emerald City backdrop. The late-afternoon sky, dark and cloudy, gave the camp a lavender cast. Norm directed drivers of the golf carts, and June fussed with a hazard-orange bow that tied the Auditorium doors shut, making it clear that the building was off-limits. Shirtless stood on the stage to the left of the doors in the outside theater Cat had seen Bob speaking from that first day of camp.

"Testing, testing, one, two, three," he said into Camille's microphone.

Ginger tapped Cat on the shoulder and signed, *I know you want to stay hidden. Please put your costume on. Show the staff we're in this together.*

Cat wanted to argue with her sister about the Dorothy costume. To protest. Pitch a fit. But Ginger was still massively annoyed at Cat; she could see it in the way her sister turned away from her. Instead of a fight, Cat said, "I'll go put it on."

Ginger nodded.

"Do you think Dad wished Gary was his son?"

Ginger gave Cat a tired expression and signed, *No.*

"Okay, well, I just gave him a big speech saying that." Cat looked at the sky. "It's a gift to know who you are. What you're good at. You've only been nothing but yourself, Ginger."

"I tried to be you. You're a really hard person to be," Ginger said as firmly as her voice allowed.

"Oh, believe me, I know," Cat said. "I'm no good at being me either."

They'd been trying to rid themselves of twin thorns in their sides urging them to be something they weren't for decades. If she'd had time, Cat would have held her sister's hand and tried to explain how wrong she'd been all these years. That Ginger was as she should have been all along.

CHAPTER THIRTY-THREE

EVEN IF NO ONE CAN SEE

Cat did what Ginger wanted and put her costume on. It was the least she could do for being such a pain this entire week—bossy, unhelpful, and indignant. She examined herself in the mirror over the Craft Lodge bathroom sink. Kids who came to theater camp were all ages and stages of puberty, so from Juliet to Veruca Salt, items had to be engineered with flexibility and hormones in mind. Presumably, they'd never had to contain the ripe body of a pregnant theater nerd, but the apron structure accommodated her shape well enough. There was no hiding her condition unless she stayed hidden, which was the plan. No one would notice when she stepped out of sight; the night would be a catastrophe with or without her.

She completed the ensemble by stuffing her feet into the red shoes and clicking her heels twice. June entered the Craft Lodge wearing a tight, slinky green gown and holding a black witch hat like a bucket.

"You look like Elphaba."

"That's me," June said, and she posed as if being introduced onstage, chin up, arm held high, wrist turning in a flourish. Then she broke character and returned to the self-conscious June who did not typically wear a skintight snake suit of a costume that made her look sexy and imperious at the same time.

"You look cute," June said, adding, "Your pigtails are lopsided. I can fix that."

Cat considered saying it didn't matter, that no one was going to see her, but she didn't. The campers were going to see her, and they didn't know that she was the misfit cog in the Jenga tower of the night.

June pulled a hairbrush from the pointed hat and sat Cat in a chair before her. "Okay if I start over?"

"Have at it," Cat said.

June eased the elastic ribbons that matched the Dorothy pinafore out of her hair and began a quick, confident brushing. When she hit the knot at the base of Cat's neck, a function of Cat's lazy grooming and fine, easily tangled strands, Cat let out an "Ouch!"

"It's a mess back here."

"Yeah. Do you have scissors in that hat?"

"Nope." Cat felt the girl tug her hair apart. "Penelope has me checking on everyone. I have safety pins, fabric tape, hair clips, green face paint, and character summaries. I'll show you yours when we're done here."

With each stroke, Cat tried to hold her head still. Her mother had a stiff brush she'd use on Cat's hair while Ginger taunted her sister. Eventually, their mom would give Cat's head a swat with the comb. The memory made her smile.

"Will the people coming think we're demented?"

"Oh, for sure," Cat said, but when she felt June's brush stroke falter, she added, "They know they're coming to the woods. They have to expect something different. Have you seen Wynn?" she added lightly.

June used the side of the brush to pull Cat's hair high and tight to the side of her head, where she threaded strands into a braid. "You know she was valedictorian in high school? Got a scholarship to that culinary school in Vermont. That really famous one. She's working here, everywhere, really, to pay for room and board there sometime in the future. Her dad isn't helping because he doesn't want her to go. Bob understood."

"She's such a contradiction. Smart and capable but so childlike," Cat said as June finished one side and started on the other.

"Her secret weapon is that people underestimate her."

"I wonder what my secret weapon is."

"Oh, I can tell you. Your secret weapon is you can be bossy, but people still like you. You're like what they say about dogs: all bark and no bite. You're a know-it-all, no offense, but everybody knows that's insecurity."

Cat felt the sting of tables turning, the older, wiser adult getting schooled by the kid.

"It must be hard for you to return here after being gone for so long." June swept Cat's hair forward.

This young woman's touch and the frank kindness in her words were like a pinprick to the swollen bag of sadness that lived in her chest. She had an impulse to do what she'd done as a child: to go to her room and have a good cry. She said, "It has been hard," and her voice cracked.

"Shirtless is next on my list. He's practicing his speech," June said, diverting the attention away from Cat's emotion.

Cat considered telling June about the fraudulent data, telling her to mention it to Shirtless. She decided against it; there was already too much reality to handle. Besides, this was her problem, not Shirtless's or the staff's. She would shoulder it if she had to, and although this noble thought came through loud and clear, it also came with another clang of her anxiety gong. By God, she wished she felt as positive as the staff did that the night would be a success, because right about now she was starting to get nauseated.

"How's it going?"

The green girl playing a witch transformed into a shiny-eyed woman in love. "He's so amazing. He's going to be great. I keep telling him to speak from the heart, and he won't run out of words. This place means so much to us. The people, the trees, it's like being in an inclusive space where no one is anything but kind." She shot Cat an embarrassed look. "I don't need to tell you. You grew up here."

"No. I like to hear what others think about it," Cat said.

June dug in the bottom of her hat and pulled out a round compact and a sponge. "Could you touch up my neck, maybe under my ear? I think I wiped some off swatting a bug."

The round plastic case flipped open with a click. June offered her throat, and Cat dabbed the makeup sponge into the green foundation. There was nothing to fix on the girl's jaw, but Cat made a show of gently dabbing a smudge of green at the base of her ear.

"I'll read our character cards," June said, reaching into her hat again. "Here's mine. 'Elphaba. An intelligent and strong-willed girl who tries to always do what's suitable for others. Even if no one can see that.'"

Cat dabbed a film of foundation on the pink ridge of June's ear.

"Here's yours. 'Dorothy Gale, a sweet, innocent young lady with a streak of boldness, outspoken and headstrong.'"

"I think they got our costumes wrong. You should be Dorothy. I'm much more problematic."

"Everyone is so grateful that you're here," June said. "That you dropped everything and pitched in. You're one of us."

"Thank you, that's kind of you, but not everyone feels that way, nor should they." Cat closed the compact, noting a tiny tremor in her hand. "All done. You look great."

"Awesome," June said.

"Totally awesome." And moments before June walked out, Cat added, "By the way. Your secret power is wicked goodness."

June lifted her green hand and waved.

CHAPTER THIRTY-FOUR

NO MORE DRUGS

"Hey, June. You look fantastic," Norm said, stopping the screen door from slamming with his tennis shoe, the only part of him that didn't look clownish. There he was, a full-size Mayor of Munchkin City, in short pants, a plaid vest, and a bow tie. Cat bit her lip but couldn't hide what she thought of his outfit. The silliness layered on top of the specter of calamity was almost too much for her.

"Laugh it up, Dorothy. Meet Toto."

Connie, the therapy chicken, sat serenely in a round-handled basket filled with straw. Someone had tied a miniature piece of faux fur around her head to simulate dog ears. There was a little bow under her knobby chicken neck.

"Where's my actual dog?"

"Shirtless needs him for moral canine support. Lefty steadies him. He said you wouldn't mind."

Cat took the basket. Connie had one eye closed, the other eyeing her with sleepy suspicion. Cat clicked her heels together. "We really, really want to go home," she said. "Are those lederhosen?"

"No. They're supposed to be long pants, but they were made for a kid. A tubby kid, but one with short legs. Every time I take a step, they creep right up my ass."

Then they giggled while Connie jerked her head around like the chicken she was.

"Apparently, as long as she's in her special straw, she stays put. Penelope says you don't have to carry her around all night. Pretty sure Brittany will keep a close eye on you." Norm adjusted his bow tie, pulling it away from his throat and scratching the skin beneath it. They looked each other up and down.

"Maybe everyone will be swept away by the creative magic of the place. Look at Burning Man," Cat said. "The art makes the news, but people go for the unhinged spectacle of it all. Right?"

"I was so into this when I was high. How am I going to go out there and face those people? I've worked with some of them."

"I think it's too late for doubts. You must get right out there and be the mayor, my friend."

"And if they ask for Bob?"

"We'll say he's got a terrible case of poison ivy. Don't leave the paths. He sends his best."

"It's good at least one levelheaded adult will be out there," Norm said.

"Ha," Cat said. "Hey, how'd you start working for Steve?"

He shrugged. "How does anyone get mixed up with asshats? You don't know how bad they are at first, and then once you figure it out, you have to give up what they're offering. In my case it was money."

"You don't need money anymore?" Cat said, checking the straps of her pinafore, trying to hide how much she needed a bit of financial wisdom to calm her fears for her future.

"Money is a renewable resource. Family, truly caring people, are not," Norm said.

Connie opened her eyes as if to say, *Listen up, Kitty. The mayor is dropping some wisdom.*

Gary popped his head in, dressed as the Tin Man. "Wynn?"

"She hasn't turned up?" Cat said, trying not to show her shock at Gary's getup.

Gary closed his silver eyes in frustration and, stiff-limbed, turned and lurched out of the lodge. It was as if Penelope had hung a sign around his neck: BEWARE THE MAN WITH NO HEART, AS HE WILL BREAK YOURS EVERY TIME. The door swung wide again, and Gary poked his head back into the room. "Come on." As usual, he looked peeved. "She listens to you," he added.

"Norm. Give Connie to my sister." She slipped off the ruby slippers and snugged them into the basket with Toto, jammed her trusty Keds on for the search. "Once we find Wynn, I'll go to the office and announce for all the staff to join at the entrance. Then you'll know we found her."

Outside, she hustled to catch up with Gary, the clouds keeping the grounds cooler than usual, but it could change in a second. Wisconsin weather was as unpredictable as Henry VIII: one moment sunny about the future, the next denying promises of any sort with a single blow.

Gary moved easily in his silver spray-painted painter's pants, and Cat hustled to keep up. The camp was quiet save for Camille practicing her scales somewhere out of view. They were on the west side of camp, a place she hadn't visited since she was a child.

Gary put his finger to his lips and pointed into the woods. Approximately three yards below, in a dense thicket of leaves and stems, Wynn struggled to free her dress from a branch as she swiped at the underbrush with her wand.

"Wynn," Gary said. "Hang on. I'm coming." Whispering to Cat, he said, "You stay put."

"No. Gary. I don't need your help. I'm getting Bob," Wynn said with a voice filled with tears and frustration.

"Almost there," Gary said above the sound of twigs and brush giving away. "I've got you," he said as he arrived at Wynn's side.

Cat dislodged a stick poking her thigh and thought, *It would be nice to be loved by him.*

"Bob!" Wynn yelled. "I know you're in there."

"Okay. Let me get your dress free," Gary said.

Wynn turned, and with wide eyes and her tilted tiara hung up on a curl, she said, "Hi, Gar."

"What's up, Wynn?" Gary said, as if she were in her kitchen making breakfast and not squatting in the dark looking like a gumdrop that Hansel and Gretel might have lost.

She sniffed and said, "I'm stuck."

"Cat is here too."

"Oh, hey," she said, and she waved at Cat with her wand.

"Let's get you out of here. Okay?" Gary said.

Wynn resisted at first and shook her head, and the crown tumbled to Gary's feet. He picked it up and inelegantly plopped it on Glinda's head.

"I think Bob's in the old Nature Center," Wynn said, and with help from Gary, she took a step toward Cat.

"Gary will go look," Cat said. "Let's get ready for the party."

Gary gathered Wynn into his tin can arms and carried her up the hill. When they passed Cat, she heard Wynn say, "Gar, you'd make such a good dad."

Cat stepped out of the way of the Tin Man as he carried Glinda the Good Witch out of the woods, a cardboard hatchet dangling from his tool belt.

———

In the Trading Post, Cat watched Penelope stitch pink thread through a small tear in Glinda's skirt.

"Oh, honey. This is a nasty scratch on your forehead," said Cat. "That must have hurt."

Penelope helped Wynn don a pair of gossamer wings. "It's good you weren't wearing these, or they'd be in ribbons. What were you doing in the woods?"

"Looking for Bob. I got to thinking. He'd never leave without seeing his party, without standing in front of the group. I think he's hiding out. Down where nobody goes—in the old Nature Center."

Penelope glanced at Cat as she lifted Wynn's glittery crown and pulled a twig from it.

"Bob, not a bad person. He's . . ." Wynn hesitated. "He's unsure. Elaine rules him, you know? But he loves this place so much. Believed in it, even if he didn't get it right."

Wynn waited for Cat to look at her before saying this next thing: "He loves Ginger."

Cat would need a lot of filling in the blanks for her to believe and understand that illogical leap. His behavior did not look like love to Cat. Sleeping with her sister while married to someone else, evacuating the premises at the first sign of trouble, telling Ginger nothing, and leaving her empty-handed to sort the camp out after he left.

Wynn brushed a curl away from her eyebrow with her wand and said, "I know. I know. Adultery, ethics, or whatever, but I heard them together. They didn't judge each other for their weaknesses. Maybe that's what love is, right? Like, two people who can handle each other's failings without taking it personally."

"Maybe so," Cat said, gently poking her finger into one of Wynn's curls, hoping the pink witch knew how wise she was.

"Your cakes are going to be a hit," Penelope said.

"Really?" Wynn nodded. "Good. You were right, Kitty. No more drugs. Not for me either. All night, it felt like my hair was going to crawl off my head and run off with my crown. I'm super thirsty." Cat handed the girl a water bottle. "Gary will sort everything out, Cat. He knows you don't like him, but he'll get the job done anyway."

"I think you've got that the wrong way around, Glinda. The Tin Man can't stand Dorothy."

"Don't be dumb. That's just Gary's face."

"That's his face when he's looking at me, that's for sure," Cat said, taking Connie the chicken in her basket from Penelope's outstretched hand. Connie tilted her head, fixed her eyeball on Cat, and hopped and bobbed as far away from Cat's roller-coaster energy as she could get and still be in the basket.

"It's showtime, guys," said Penelope. "Cat, aren't you going to make the call over the PA?"

There could be no more distracting herself with to-do lists, irritation with her sister, Gary, or the bizarreness of the night to come. Cat knew nothing of her financial skin in this game, but she was well aware there were legal ramifications associated with fraud and drug running, not to mention concealing a pregnancy from a father. She wasn't certain if this last one was illegal, but it could be added to the ethical concerns of running a fake wellness camp.

Like an animal too tired and unfit to fight or flee, Cat froze in place until Penelope said, "Cat!"

And Dorothy took off toward the Administration Building for what felt the thousandth time in a matter of days.

CHAPTER THIRTY-FIVE

A SHOWER SCRUBBY

Cat trembled as her fingers hovered over the button of the intercom, nervous that once the Littles' everyday lives were exposed, the visitors would sneer at them.

Being a part of a group has its own ecosystem that outsiders can't possibly understand. Math Bowl kids practice multiplication tables, while gamers fight imaginary wars with spaceships, neither understanding the allure of the other. Open the doors on any closed group, and suddenly what is accepted, even celebrated, becomes a point of shame.

Cat's protective bells and whistles were ringing as she retrieved a crumpled yellow notebook page with Shirtless's handwriting on it. He must have worked on his speech at the scratched desk, tossing rejected efforts into the garbage bin. *Welcome to Oz. Welcome to "The Cure to What Ails Us." Welcome to our humble camp.* Under these beginnings, Shirtless had written, *You can do this. You are brave. June needs this. Mom . . .* And this was where his messages stopped. The wait must have been killing him.

Cat hit the intercom. Connie flapped a wing.

"Hello. Hi. Okay. Here we go. Everyone not at a food station, come to the camp entrance." She heard the echo of her announcement and felt the adrenaline ratchet her heart rate into her throat. She tried to think of what a coach would say before a big game. *Winning isn't everything.* It's what? She should have thought of something before she hit the button. She needed a force field of words to shelter them. What would Bob the scoundrel have said?

Cat touched the mic, and it scattered static through the camp. She cleared her throat and spoke the first few lines of "We're Off to See the Wizard" with as much gravitas as she could. Then she swallowed. Another zap of electricity filled the space, and Cat thought, *Winning isn't everything,* which she revised it with her father in mind. "Winning isn't everything. But, you know, we'll give it a try."

Ginger poked her head into the office dressed as the Scarecrow, looking appropriately ragged and sipping tea. She'd smudged brown greasepaint on her nose and wore a pointed canvas hat tied with a rope at her throat. A stuffed black bird leaned and wobbled on her shoulder, and straw poked out of every joint. Before Cat could laugh at the resemblance, the silly, spot-on costume, she remembered what the Scarecrow was missing.

Cat took Ginger's shoulders: "You've always had a brain."

Ginger shook her head, and it killed Cat to see her wearing her fragility like a scarlet letter for all to see.

"Your brain isn't filled with the black-and-white nonsense of math, of stupid calendar dates and addresses. Yours is Technicolor. It's people like you who are going to save the oceans. You creatives will dream it up, and engineers will be put to the task. There are no tasks without dreamers."

Ginger held her hand up to get Cat to stop. "Can you not?" she croaked, and she unfolded a piece of paper and read from it. "'The Scarecrow is cheerful, easygoing, loyal to Dorothy, and helps her while working toward his own goal of getting a brain.'"

Cat had spent so many years angry at Ginger that she didn't know how to handle this new, matter-of-fact, annoyed, and defeated version of her sister.

"Is that ginger tea you're sipping, Ginger?" Cat said to lighten her mood.

Ginger mouthed the word *meta* without a smile.

"As soon as people start to come . . . ," Cat started. She was going to add, *I'm going to sneak off. I'll be watching from the Secret Garden, cheering everyone on*, but she couldn't say another self-serving, predictable sentence. She noticed a faint odor coming from the direction of the Auditorium and said, "I hope the wind picks up," and she looked to the heavens for a helping hand.

Penelope was the first to emerge from the Trading Post, dressed in an orange plaid shirt, a white collar buttoned to her neck, and brown shorts. "I'm one of the Lollipop Guild. There're three of us: Matt is the green one, but he's got his hands full with Camille, so I doubt we'll ever be seen together." She saluted with a thick cardboard cutout of a red-and-white all-day sucker. "I think I did a pretty good job of matching people to costumes." She smiled like a costume designer who'd won an Oscar for her creative eye.

One by one, like a scene in a zombie movie, bodies appeared from the darkness. As they passed under the yellow-and-white lights strung across the paths, Cat recognized a couple of staff wearing too-small monkey suits, their tails bobbing with internal wires that held them aloft. Two palace guards held spears that were obviously crafted from old wrapping paper tubes, tinfoil tips fitted into their tops. When they reached Cat, she could see that the hats appeared to be made from the same fake fur that Connie had affixed to her head.

"Carry on," Cat said, appreciating their all-out commitment, but as each minute passed, she found her legs had a loose and liquid feel to them. Like her nervous heart couldn't move enough blood for her body to stay upright. Cat kicked her legs, bent her knees, and inhaled slowly.

After she'd left the camp, she'd forgotten the intimacy of the singular focus that a stage production required. How time, judgment, and criticism fell away in favor of inclusion, which was something theater kids and football teams had in common. The other thing they had in common was the way they shared the burden of anxiety, everyone united, everyone shouldering one another's responsibilities. Though she felt undeserving, she tried to believe what Elphaba had said was true, that Cat was one of them.

When Brittany came out of the shadows, Cat saw the true depth of support everyone would need. The girl who made animals her life wore a purple fleece hoodie with a long mane of variegated yarn in blues and greens. She wore forest-green yoga pants and mismatched red-and-yellow mittens on her hands and feet. When she got to Cat, she whinnied and said, "I'm a Horse of a Different Color."

"Good thing it's dark," said Cat, and Brittany stomped her feet in protest and whinnied again.

From the direction of Cat's family's cabin, Matt walked, dressed in a blue shirt, too-short gray shorts, and white-and-gray-striped tights. Nothing fit right; the shorts gripped him wrongly, the tights bagged at the knees, and there was no way the spiritual yogi could downward dawg tonight.

"You don't like Matt much, do you?" Cat said to Penelope.

"Nope. I don't. He acts like he can't stand Camille, but he is obsessed with her. I'm not down for that."

Matt turned and presented Camille, dressed in a bushy pink costume that showed her legs from midthigh down. It was as if all the tulle from every fairy costume ever had been gathered into a ball, and Camille had been stuffed inside it. Flat-footed, she plodded out with her white flip-flops.

"What the . . . ?"

Penelope leaned into Cat's ear and said, "She thinks she's Glinda, but Wynn is the only person that should ever be Glinda."

"Who is she, then?"

"She's not a character. She's a loofah."

"Like a shower scrubby?" said Cat, trying not to be delighted.

Penelope swung her lollipop in a circle. "Yup. She's got no idea. Watch this. Give us a twirl, Camille."

Tickled pink and probably still high, Camille held her arms out like a helicopter and twirled.

Swinging behind her was a loopy white rope that dangled from her midback.

"She's a human exfoliator," Brittany said.

"A fun sponge," Penelope added.

Forgetting what was ahead of her for a glorious second, Cat hugged Penelope and kissed her forehead. Ginger tapped Cat on the shoulder and pointed at June in her green gown and regal posture. Shirtless joined her, wearing brown, adult-size footed pajamas with two dyed mops on his head. He had holes in his mittens, and his bare hands gripped the pages of his script. Lefty leaned against Shirtless, who was somehow tolerating a stringy lion's mane around his head.

Her beloved nephew, Shirtless, fully shirted up in what had to be a skin-suffocating number. The painted whiskers on his face wriggled, and Cat wondered what self-talk he was using to remain dressed.

A slow clap broke out as Norm performed a side jig, straightening his bow tie.

"Everyone, you look fantastic," Cat said. They appeared on the verge of a fever dream, but she wanted to be supportive. And with that thought, a cloud rolled over the setting sun, and the lights twinkled more brightly against the darker backdrop. "Let's give Ginger's vision and Penelope's execution a big hand. Together they knocked it out of the park in such a short time and with so little." While the crowd clapped, Cat waved Norm over to her and said, "People will be here any minute. Where's Gary?"

Before Norm could reply, Penelope said, "He's doing something for Wynn. Don't worry. He'll be here." She said to the others, "Let's get the bar carts up toward the entrance. We'll hand everyone a drink and move them through the food and then over to the patio for Shirtless's speech."

"You're going to have to give him the signal to go ahead," Cat said.

"Where will you be?" said Norm.

Cat didn't say, *I'm going to hide under my bed until the night is over.* Instead of answering him, she said, "Should we say something rousing? Sing a camp song for solidarity?"

"I can sing the camper crowd favorite 'Grey Squirrel, shake your bushy tail.'" He looked at his watch and then past the camp entrance to the highway. "I don't see any headlights."

He was right. It was time for the visitors to arrive, and in Wisconsin, people came early to things. It was the Midwest way. Yet it was after seven.

The group quieted, and Norm said, looking at his watch, "They're late."

What if they don't come? Ginger signed. *What if Elaine canceled the gala?*

As much as she'd dreaded Steve, the press, and guests arriving, Cat hadn't considered the loss of hope, the letdown if no one showed—never for one moment considered it—but now she saw she'd been fighting against it while holding out hope for this strange hero of a gala.

"They'll be here," she said, having no idea if that was true. Cat took a deep breath and held it.

The smell of the multiple small campfires filled the air. Frogs began their cheerful calls; there was no moon, but the stage was set.

Shirtless scanned the parking lot and beyond.

"Don't hold your breath, Cat," Ginger rasped. It was an anxiety thing Cat did when nervous, or in trouble. Once, she'd held her breath so long she'd passed out. It scared the crap out of everyone.

"Cat. Let go of your breath," Ginger said. "Breathe."

Cat exhaled, Ginger's fingers found Cat's hand and squeezed, and once again they were two little girls in the woods, working to make sure everyone else had fun.

CHAPTER THIRTY-SIX

DON'T HIT THE RICH PEOPLE

"They'll come," Ginger said.

"Maybe Bob and Elaine canceled the party the day they drove off?" Cat said, and she watched while expectation and anticipation turned to worry on the faces of the Horse of a Different Color and all three members of the Lollipop Guild.

"He didn't," said Ginger.

It was a strange place to be, not knowing what to hope for: *Embarrassing last-ditch-effort gala*, or *Camp buckles under the weight of mismanagement and does what has to be done, whatever that may be*. Or the least likely of all scenarios, *The camp's okay, she goes home, resumes life*. She pictured herself driving home in her MINI, Jackson Browne's solo voice tired but welcoming her back.

"Remember when Mom used to say, 'It's a relief to not have all the answers'?" Cat said.

"I don't remember her saying that."

"You probably didn't need to hear it like I did. I should have listened to her more," Cat said. She scanned the thin line of black asphalt at the edge of the camp, her hand damp with her sister's perspiration, the other flat against the baby with her own ticking clock.

She'd chosen Steve for his inability to attach because that was how Cat had wanted it. No attachments, requests, delivery failures, guilt, or big feelings. God forbid big feelings.

Cat tapped her belly and realized that while she'd planned to stay hidden during the entire gala, she'd also been looking forward to seeing Steve, even from afar. She'd wanted to see if he was as devious as she thought. Would he see this eager group and still make an offer, order the bulldozers?

The bigger she got, the more she thought about the personality of her child, Steve's DNA mingling with hers, needing her yum to throttle his yuck. Or was Cat just like him, and this child didn't have a chance? She wondered what the staff was thinking, except for Camille, who twirled while Matt tried to get her to stop. They were all dressed up with no one to show off for.

Ginger leaned close to Cat's ear. "They'll be here," she whispered, a little air brushing against her vocal cords.

For her sister's sake, Cat hoped so. She lifted her chin and sent a deal out to the universe. If they came, she wouldn't stay in hiding. She'd stand up to Steve, look into his eyes, and say, "Yup, I'm pregnant. What of it?" It was folly to think she could hide it from him forever.

And that's when someone from the back of the group said, "Wait. Look." Behind the tall trees that lined the Summer Camp property was a chain of white lights, like pearls on a necklace, moving slowly in an orderly line toward the entrance. No one breathed until the first car sharply turned onto the property. Cat closed her eyes, took a deep breath, and said, "Okay, everybody scatter. June, you stay here with Ginger and me."

Ginger let go of Cat's hand and signed, *Go. Now!*

"I changed my mind. Connie, get your cluck on. We've got a job to do."

Camille started to sing, and Matt's voice came over the speaker: "Not yet." It sounded like he'd put his hand over her mouth while she tried to sing through his fingers. He must have succeeded in wrestling her away from the microphone. Matt placed the needle on the record. It scratched once, and then the soundtrack of *The Wizard of Oz* musical, the karaoke version, drifted through the camp. Cat didn't want to know how he would keep her quiet until after dinner for her solo.

June smoothed her green gown, and Ginger straightened her shabby hat while they waited for the BMWs, Range Rovers, and Teslas to park and the people to cross under Summer Camp's arbor.

"Do you think Bob is somewhere here?" said June out of the corner of her mouth. Cat felt Ginger stiffen.

"Do you want to check on Wynn in the kitchen? Rest your voice?" Cat said. Ginger nodded and gave her sister's hand a grateful squeeze. If people were going to ask for Bob, Ginger shouldn't have to rasp her way through excuses all night.

When her sister was out of earshot, Cat said, "At this point, Bob can suck it," and she beamed at the first person who entered the grounds.

———

For the next forty minutes, Cat and June welcomed, pointed to the golf slash bar carts, and directed guests to Penelope. Two of the Lollipop Guild members collected phones for an immersive experience, assuring everyone they could retrieve them from the mounted basket at the gate. One of the palace guards paired the visitors with a staff member who guided them to follow the Yellow Brick Road past the food stations.

"Welcome to Oz," June said to a couple with disparate ideas about the dress code for a night in the woods. The man, who must have heard *camp* as the operative word for the evening, wore a putty-colored safari leisure suit with a large flask dangling at his hip. On the other hand, the woman had heard the word *gala* and swished past in a shimmery gown with stilettos and a bottle of champagne under her arm.

"Oh boy, she's going to have some trouble on the grounds," said June. They watched her wobble behind the geezer, who paid her no heed. The woman stepped, and her stiletto heel pierced the ground and sank. She pulled herself free and took another step, repeating the pierce-sink routine to the stone ledge, where she parked herself.

"After she leaves, the whole camp lawn will be aerated," said Cat, making jokes to mask her unease, her sharp eye trained on the parking lot so she could see Steve before he saw her.

At first, she'd hoped the rich wouldn't ridicule them. She'd done it herself. Now Cat stood taller with a touch of her father's pride of place.

June smiled and welcomed a nondescript couple dressed casually and appropriately for dinner at a camp. After they'd been escorted by a flying monkey, she said, "They looked normal. Maybe they're from the press."

The staff had been given buzzwords to drop into conversations: *tax-free*, *deductible*, *serenity*, *tranquility*, and *happiness* were the top-tier words. Shirtless had wanted everyone to say that Summer Camp would soon disrupt the tech space, and people everywhere would shut their phones off and partake in forest bathing.

June had whispered, "Baby steps. We don't want to attack how they make their money."

An extremely short man chewing on a twig walked through the arbor and leered at June, his eyes taking her in from top to bottom. "Did you know instead of a toothbrush, you can use a twig to clean your teeth?" He offered a branch broken from their own arbor to Cat.

"Maybe later," Cat said, and she handed him off to a Munchkin.

"Later it is," he said, walking backward, keeping an eye on them.

"Stay away from Tiny Little Nature Man tonight if you don't want to be groped behind the Emerald City," said Cat.

June wrinkled her nose. "Ugh."

A tall white-haired man with ironed khaki pants and a crisp white button-down shirt offered his hand to June. He did not remove his mirrored aviator sunglasses as he moved past them, bemused.

"Is it weird that no one has said anything about our costumes?" June said.

"Maybe? I honestly don't know."

"Do you think that guy thought he should be in costume? Can he see with those glasses on?"

"If I were to guess, that guy wants everyone to know he is a pilot. I bet he'll tell you he flew Black Hawk helicopters in his day. Or maybe he just wanted to."

A strikingly handsome couple ducked through the arbor, each in Martha's Vineyard–style linens, looking as if their car had ironed them as they drove.

"That's Digby and Poppy Houndstooth. Old money. The kids are named Peyton," Cat said, trying to relax, nauseous with anticipation.

"Really?"

"Not really. I'm joking."

Cat would have said more, but Steve entered her sight line. He sat in his car, the interior light falling on his spotty head of hair. A frisson of angst snapped through her. She clenched and released her fists. *You are the mother,* she told herself, thinking of that song by Queen, "We Are the Champions."

"Do you know any of these people?"

"Only one," said Cat.

She felt June look at her as she watched Steve get out of his car and move his hand over his hair, a characteristic vanity gesture connected to his fear of balding. Cat handed Connie in her basket to June and said, "I'll take this one." She ran her hand down her blue apron skirt, and when he walked through the arbor, she said, "While I live and breathe, Steve Jameson."

He wasn't surprised to see her. That was clear. There was no big manufactured grin on his thin lips. "I wondered where you'd gotten to." As if Cat had ghosted him, which she kind of had.

Like the confident human being he role-played, he put his hands on his hips and eyed her figure. "Did you gain weight, or are you just happy to see me?"

The effect of this non sequitur greeting, this rude commentary on her pregnancy, gave Cat pause. She could deny weight gain, explain her biology, or highlight that *happy* was not their adjective. She wasn't about to chitchat about her body or define their emotional relationship, so she didn't respond.

"What's all this?"

"It's our fundraising gala," Cat said. "But you know that." *You are the mother.*

Steve licked his lips and looked at June. "And you are . . ."

"Ju . . . Elpha . . . ," June said. "I'm the camp nurse."

"I'm Steve Jameson, Cat's man." He cupped June's hand in his. "I used to be, that is. Not sure how Dorothy got in this condition, though, so stay tuned," he said with a quick wink.

Since Cat's decision to come out of hiding had been so last minute, she hadn't visualized their meeting, run scenarios, written a script, or practiced anything regarding how to talk to Steve. But, of the schemes she might have imagined, Steve professing that he was her man and then hinting that Cat slept around had her making two tight fists.

"I don't want to keep you. I'm sure you have friends here." June slipped her hand free. "Go get some of our homemade camp fare. Follow the path to the lake. The presentation will start soon in the outdoor space to the right of the Admin Building." Only Cat saw June wipe her hand on her long skirt.

"I know my way around. I've been here many times." Steve turned his attention to the guests under the white lights.

"Be sure to save room for cake," June said.

Hand in his pocket, a whiskey bottle under his arm, he slapped Cat on the butt with a chuckle and walked away.

Cat pulled her fist back like a hammer, and June grabbed her wrist before she could let it fly.

"Don't hit the rich people," June said and handed Connie back to Cat. "How could Uncle Bob have invited him?"

"Steve wants this camp," Cat said, seething. "Wants to put up a stinking water park. He's the father of this baby, but as far as I can tell, he doesn't realize this yet."

Showing no surprise or judgment, like the sensitive nurse she would become, June said, "He's not going to hear it from me" and twisted an invisible key at her lips.

Cat polished her fist like a fighter and said, "It's good you stopped me."

"Violence is beneath you," said June.

"Is it?" Cat asked, knowing that wasn't true.

CHAPTER THIRTY-SEVEN

TOUCH THE TREES

"I'm going to see how everything is going. Stay here, you're doing great," Cat said and then stepped away from June, shaken from the interaction with Steve, unsettled by his statement *I've been here many times*. A gust of air rattled the string lights. She squinted at the sky, looking for her childhood constellations, Orion, the Big Dipper. Cat couldn't make them out tonight. Not even the anchor star she couldn't remember the name of.

Approximately every other guest had a staff member guiding them, chatting, and making woodsy puns while they walked from station to station. Cat strolled on and off the path, trying to get a feel for the guests' impressions. Her toe brushed against a crumpled Frito package, and she collected the trash, insulted for the grounds.

A man beside the stone wall, the echo chamber that carried voices, said, "They've got to be kidding," and the woman with him said, "I don't know. I think it's cute." But she said it in the condescending way people often remarked on ugly babies or a kindergartner's egg crate art.

Next to the couple, a tight-skinned woman with chiseled arms said, "They have a lot of work to do before anyone donates anything to this place."

"Now, CeCe, let's wait until after the program to decide. We promised."

"I'm just saying what everyone else is thinking. You know me. Brutal honesty."

"'The cure for what ails us.' It'll take a lot more than a nature walk to fix what ails the US," said the man.

CeCe slapped a mosquito on her neck. "Steve was right, though. Perfect place for a water park."

"That's something I can get behind," said the man as he emptied the bag of Bear Poop into his mouth and crunched.

"I can't wait to see this Bob. I hear he's something else," said a man strolling by, his hand on a woman's bare back.

"And not a good something else," said the woman none too quietly.

Cat scanned the grounds. There were clusters of people, heads together, standing like adolescents at a middle school dance. It was as if they didn't know what to do with themselves outside without a golf course or swimming pool. Gary's guys were handing out drinks and snacks; others transported people in evening shoes to the lake. Still, the guests oozed impatience and a *so what* energy.

This wasn't working. *It's over,* Cat thought. The camp was going to go under and drag her life with it.

The wide-open space of the camp dwarfed the guests. Fifty people for dinner at a restaurant was a lot of people. Here, clumped on the path and picking bark out of melted marshmallows, they were no different from the little kids who'd attended the camp in its theater days. Awkward, bored, trying to fit in.

A man and woman moved up the path, their heels tapping the paved asphalt. "That bathroom wasn't fit for man nor beast," the woman said.

"You're going to have to check me for ticks when we get home." The man shivered dramatically, and they stalked straight to the parking lot.

Leaving? Were they leaving? She wanted to stop them, insist that they stay.

A thick, humid breeze blew up from the lake and stroked Cat's cheek, riffling the top of her hair. *Balmy* is how an author would describe it. She closed her eyes and imagined what the trees had to say to the guests. *Look up, we're here! The sky's the limit.* The frog chorus, reptilian ventriloquists, sang to their prospective mates, throwing their voices to confound predators. If the guests would listen, the forest would share everything with them. But no, they were deaf to the charms of the woods. More hearing impaired than any child Cat had ever worked with.

The guests had come for the spectacle. To case the joint, to watch failure firsthand like bullies do. Cat moved out of the shadows, wanting to say something. *Listen. Can't you hear it? Touch the trees. They're trying to tell you something.* Before she could say anything, a woman with a jawline that could gut a fish said, "Oh, aren't you just adorable. Dorothy! So much body positivity in this generation."

What is wrong with you people? was on the tip of Cat's tongue, ready to be spat out, when another woman clapped and said, "Glinda!" Just as Cat felt a hand on her elbow.

"'There is no place like home,'" Glinda trilled while guiding Cat away and moving her toward the Canteen.

"You got that right," the man said, taking a swig of his drink.

Cat had an overwhelming desire to swing Connie in her basket and hit each one of them with a poultry roundhouse.

"These people," Cat sputtered.

"Well, yeah," Wynn said with her hands on Cat's back. "We don't need to like them," she added.

Inside the cedar building stood Penelope, gazing at Brittany in her horse costume, and Gary with his head down, hands on his hips. He looked seriously angry despite the silver makeup on his face. Seated on a chair in front of him was Bob.

Cat handed Connie to Wynn with hold-my-beer energy and tried to grab Bob by his collar. If Gary hadn't caught the ties on the back of Cat's dress and gently pulled her out of reach, she would have shaken the teeth out of his mouth.

With an unruffled, delighted look on his face, he said, "Cat. Awesome to see you. You guys pulled it off. And I hear Shirtless is giving the speech."

"He was in the old Nature Center. I was right," Wynn said.

"Where are the loan papers, you little weasel? Where's Elaine?"

"Oh, she left. No vision. Traditional schooling for that one," he said conversationally, as if he wasn't a blue gingham apron tie away from death. "Kills the creative mind," he said, pointing to his brain. "You get it."

Cat clenched her fists, her nails biting into her palms.

Gary was making a move to get between the two of them when Bob said, "I knew I picked the right people for this camp. You guys are wonderful." He moved to look out the window, but Gary stopped him with a stiff arm on his shoulder. "The old place looks stunning." As if he hadn't seen the camp for a decade.

"Ginger said you would come. I thought you wouldn't dare return after lying and cheating the people who trusted you." Cat swept her hand toward the goings-on outside the Canteen's walls. "What are you doing here, anyway? You think there's going to be money? Is that it? That you deserve it? My sister believed in you. My sister," Cat said with such force that even Gary took a step back.

"And she was right to. Here I am! Ready to lead." Bob pushed back in the chair and held his hands up as if being arrested. "I knew you'd step up if I got out of the way. This was the ultimate empowerment exercise."

Cat sputtered, unable to form words strong enough to carry her anger. "Do you have any idea how miserable this week has been?"

She narrowed her eyes, calculating the crappiest possible punishment for him. Maybe it was to trot him out into the fray of scornful guests. The green Wizard of Oz costume that Penelope had set aside for him hung on a hook on the back of the closed door. The girl had been sure he'd show up. Trusting that the lessons they'd learned at Summer Camp weren't as fragile as the presence of one man. And that man would surely return.

Suddenly Cat reached for the costume, and Bob flinched. "Here. Put this on."

He squinted at the costume. "Yes, I can see it now. The theme. Perfect."

It was an outlandish costume with a monstrous green cape, furry hat, and oversize matching sleeves. Cat expected him to protest, to resist being represented in such an overt parody of a leader. But no. Bob didn't understand irony. Like a bullfighter about to enter the ring, he swung the cape around his shoulders and attached the hook at the neck.

"Hand me the sleeves," he said to no one, a maestro asking for his baton. Gary held the faux fur sleeves above Bob's head, and when the man reached for them, he let them drop to the floor.

"That was childish, Gary. I expect better from you."

Expressionless, Gary held out the hat that matched the sleeves. Just before Bob's finger made contact, Gary let the hat go, and it hit the cedar floor.

"Honestly," Bob said.

The strains of music that Cat had barely registered stopped, and the PA screeched. She recognized Norm's voice. "Hello again, and welcome to Summer Camp. Our own over-the-rainbow haven in the middle of the north woods. Please join us at the outside theater, where we will listen to our own Bard McCarthy, the grandson of the camp's founder, speak about this camp's tradition of excellence." When no one had apparently moved, he said, "There will be lots of time to enjoy the grounds after our presentation." Still, when no one seemed to have moved, he added, "The bar carts will be at each entrance for refills."

Steve's laughter, that's what Cat could hear. She spotted him patting the backs of his golf buddies, glad-handing and throwing his head back as if this were his party. He would leave with the camp signed, sealed, and delivered in his pocket. The confidence of the marginal male lover on display—someone with a slightly better-than-average bank balance and a golf handicap in the double digits.

Cat had to think fast. The plan for the night could not be disturbed because Bob had shown up. She wouldn't give him the satisfaction, and really, no one on staff was as mean as Cat was. Besides maybe Gary, but who could ever tell what he was thinking. Cat was the only person truly outraged at Bob's presence, the only one who would be able to keep him in check. It was time to step up.

"Okay, here's how it's going to go down," Cat said. "I mean, if it's okay with all of you." She checked faces, waited a beat. "Wynn, I want you to help the people get seated for the presentation. Radiate your Glinda glitter, talk about dessert."

"Great. Then I'll head to the kitchen to make sure there's cake for everyone."

"Penelope and the Lollipop Guild have to be in the front, making sure Shirtless is ready, everyone has eyes forward, and the rest of the crew is front and center," Cat said.

"We need all the major characters available," said Wynn, joining in.

"Gary, the Tin Man is every woman's favorite character. Get in there with your strong forearms and silent sex appeal and charm the chicks. Open that trapdoor and show them what's missing, wink at them, and make them think that only they could help you find your heart."

Brittany laughed and Gary scoffed loudly, and Bob looked like he was going to protest. If anyone would be a heartthrob, he wanted it to be him.

"Gary, I don't care what you think of me. Get in there and use your sex appeal for something other than making me crazy. And you can shut right up, Bob. You abdicated your charming rights when you sent out false data and abandoned this place without so much as a 'Peace out.' This group has put their hearts and hopes into this night, and you aren't going to screw it up. You stay silent unless we need you. Got it?"

Bob nodded, and Gary apparently wasn't sure whether to protest against being objectified or get over it and capitalize on it.

"This coat is too small," Bob said, yanking on the sleeves of the velvet green jacket.

"June is counting on her uncle Bob," said Glinda, and poof, the girl was out the door and heading toward the half-lit outside seating area.

CHAPTER THIRTY-EIGHT

BEYOND THE RAINBOW

"Penelope, off you go. I will deal with Bob." The girl looked hesitant to leave. As if Cat might commit murder in the Canteen and mess up the merch. "Don't worry. We'll respect the space, I promise," Cat said.

"I'll watch her," said Gary, and with a slow turn, Penelope stepped into the fracas of trying to salvage the night.

"No, Gary. I've got this. I need to do this part," Cat said, trying for a confident hands-on-her-hips posture, but her back hurt, and she stretched instead.

"Torture? I want to stay and watch."

"Such kidders, you two," Bob said with a nervous giggle, his eyes pinging from Cat to Gary to the door and back.

"He's all yours, Dorothy," Gary said, and he left.

Cat paced in the tight space, trying to prioritize her next moves. The night was a bust. No one would donate money to save this place, not with Steve making deals. Deals he possibly didn't need because, in the end, the owner was in financial trouble and carrying his kid.

Her gaze fell on Connie, a stunning black-and-white chicken who had more dignity despite her cluck and bob than most people. Possibly feeling Cat's stare, Connie's left eye slid sideways as if to say, *We don't have all day.*

"Okay," Cat said. "Let's get a few things straight—"

"Cat. Cat. Cat," Bob said, interrupting her. "You don't want this camp. You never did like it. You with your *Seventeen* magazine cutouts and dreams for a bigger life. Let me speak to these people. I'll make the best case for its future. You can leave here knowing you did your best. Get on with your life. If they donate, amazing. If we sell, it's fine. There will be money for you, Ginger, Shirtless. People are resilient."

"What are you playing at?" Cat said, eyeing Bob. This speech sounded nothing like him, and there was no time to figure out the goodness or evilness of Bob. "You know what makes you dangerous, Bob?" Cat said. "You make a convincing argument, but it's made of nothing, fluff, straw, words. My dad used to say, 'I started with nothing, and I still have most of it.' He was joking. That was never him, but it sure is you."

Bob straightened his coat, brushed unseen lint from his shoulder, and looked at Cat as her father might have, with satisfaction . . . and a tinge of pride?

She thought of railing against him. Blaming him for the state of the camp's finances, this train wreck of a night, but she knew he wasn't totally at fault. She'd had a hand in this as well. Cat's fingers gently traced the arc of her stomach. She'd been marching around as if she were carrying a bushel of apples instead of her future inside her.

"You're hard on yourself," Bob said. "You have that in common with your wonderful sister." His voice had switched from performer to personal, sincere even, and the shift threw her off. Cat visualized Ginger, her eyes tired, dressed as a dopey scarecrow, ready and willing.

"The world is so enamored with people who risk it all to reach the summit. It's a lot of pressure for the leaders who are no more or less than part of a team."

"Don't you dare," Cat said. "You are not a misunderstood hero here."

"No, Cat. You are."

Was he playing with her? Using kindness to soften her up, unnerve her?

He cleared his throat. "I know what you think of me. I have much explaining to do. Until we have more time, I am at your service and will not vanish again."

"I hate you." Because what else was there to say to this man who lived in his own world and appeared as if always delivering lines from a stage? Who played and dreamed and beguiled as if life was all fun and games? A great adventure and not a full-time job.

"I love your sister," he said.

The man stood before her, his face open, wearing the costume of a mysterious ruler, but in reality he was just a regular guy with bank account numbers and a crush.

"Why wouldn't you be. She's amazing."

"Now that all of that is settled, let's go out there and watch Shirtless be amazing." Bob bowed to Cat. "If I can be of service, I will step in."

"That's exactly what we're doing," Cat said. "But because I don't want to miss it and you are glued to my side, not because you're calling the shots." She grabbed the door handle and said, "Get going, Bob. And don't get any ideas."

They crouch-jogged to the outside meeting area but didn't walk under the bedazzled plasterboard rainbow entrance. Instead, they stepped unnoticed behind the woodpile. You'd think the two of them would be a hard-to-miss spectacle, but the night had dropped its darkest cloak over the moon and stars. The guests who hadn't defected—because there was no ignoring it; initial numbers were down—sat in folding chairs. Their skin was jaundiced, lit by the galvanized yellow lighting that hung over their heads.

"I believe you already know of this hidey-hole," Bob said.

Cat knew he'd seen her that first day she'd watched him. She felt she should assert her dominance and show him who was in charge. But her nerves were on edge as she worried for her nephew.

She hadn't noticed music playing overhead until the zipper sound of the needle skating across a record shot through the speakers. Someone in the crowd said, "Ugh, stop."

The stack of wood smelled of pine and her childhood, when she and Ginger had collected the sap to make a love potion for two of the teenage counselors. Shirtless stood, thin as a rail in his brown one-piece pajamas, looking like a lion who'd given up meat for political reasons. Lefty leaned next to him, his regal head pulling the attention from his one missing leg. Shirtless pushed his headdress back, cleared his vision of mop tendrils, and stepped up to the microphone. "Welcome," he said.

Cat spotted Ginger, poised to sprint to her son's side if necessary. The group quieted and lifted their gaze. Bob whispered so only Cat could hear: "It's okay, buddy. Take your time."

If you knew Shirtless, the early signs of a collapse could be predicted. There was a slight nasal flaring. His left eyelid fluttered almost imperceptibly. Cat held her breath.

"Welcome," he said again, and a woman on the end of a row crossed and recrossed her legs. Shirtless moved his lips to form the letter for the next word, and Cat, without thinking, stood. Shirtless caught the movement, as did Lefty. Bob gently tugged on Connie's basket.

"He's fine," Bob whispered, and Cat decided not to fight him and returned to her hunched position. Lefty touched his nose to Shirtless's leg.

"Welcome to Summer Camp," he said.

"Where's Bob?" said a voice. Steve's.

Someday, Cat promised herself, she would kill Steve for those two words.

"Bob who?" Shirtless said.

"Attaboy," Bob said.

Shirtless dropped his hand, and Lefty, with an archer's accuracy, licked his favorite person's thumb.

"This is Lefty," Shirtless said. "He's with me because I'm shy. I don't like to speak in public." He swallowed hard, and the microphone picked up a throat gurgle.

"Maybe go get Bob. He's who we came for," said Steve. And Bob grabbed Cat's wrist, which was good because she was about to sprint off and find an electrical cord to throttle her baby's father with.

There was a chorus of shh's from the chairs, and at least one man told Steve to shut up.

"And I'm nervous." Shirtless ignored Steve. He smiled bashfully, and Cat wondered how every man, woman, and squirrel didn't fall in love with him in that instant. "We know you're used to fancier digs," he said. "It's what we've got. And we think it's enough." He stopped, looked down at his hands, and clasped them. "We also know how this looks." He glanced at his mother, and she danced a little scarecrow soft shoe. His eyes moved to find Gary, who had an oilcan in his hand, and he pretended to oil the place where his heart should be.

Brittany, in her Horse of a Different Color costume, whinnied and pawed the air.

"We'd like you to think about being in a place that you feel so strongly about, so comfortable at, that you would dress in an Oz costume in front of people who could decide its fate to save it."

Cat watched through the woody peephole, barely able to contain her pride. Shirtless, his voice so clear, his chin held high. If she had birthed the boy, she wouldn't have felt even one scrap more love for him.

"You don't have any history here, but this place was here long before any of us discovered it. Patiently waiting, hoping a bunch of outsiders might come and revel in its mysteries. Play among the trees and understand that the value of the property is in the joy it brings to the many, not the cash it brings to the few."

Cat gasped at the perfect wording for the place of her childhood, a home she didn't understand half as well as this young man. She'd been so blind and so sure she was right about everything. That the camp was a liability, that it couldn't, maybe even shouldn't, be saved. And if someone was going to save it, it had to be her, on her own, with no help whatsoever. She'd always said that if you're the help, you don't get help, but after this week, that theory had been disproved time and time again.

Lefty wagged his tail, and Shirtless bowed. "Thank you."

"Bring on the drinks," Steve said, and Bob handed Cat his sleeve so she could wipe her nose with it.

On cue, Camille took the microphone and walked as regally as possible when dressed as a shower scrubby. Offstage, Matt placed the needle on a record, and the first notes of "Somewhere Over the Rainbow" filled the camp, carrying Camille's voice with it.

Even through the wood fragments, seeing only the backs of heads and shoulders, Cat saw the effect of the music on the crowd. And with some kind of wood sprite magic, the highlighted path and the Emerald City backdrop and rainbow exit glowed as Camille's pitch-perfect voice gathered the crowd like a bouquet.

Every living thing seemed to be listening, the peepers respectively quiet as the words lifted into the air. Cat listened, her eyes drifting to find Gary. Could he feel what was happening? Did he realize something had changed? She found him, his eyes searching for hers, possibly thinking of dreams he dared to dream.

They broke eye contact, interrupted by Steve with a lit-up phone. Of course he hadn't relinquished his connection to the world. He clipped Gary, trying to get to the exit. Gary didn't budge, and Steve said something in Gary's tinny ear. The two men, one she wished she hadn't slept with and the other, beyond reason, she wished she had. A bat swooped over their heads. Steve ducked, and Cat followed the creature with her eyes as it returned to the darkness.

Ginger and Shirtless were hugging offstage. The guests looked like props, immobile, mesmerized.

Camille's voice cracked with emotion when she hit the part about lemon drops, and swelled again when she asked why—oh why—she couldn't just fly away with the bluebirds.

Cat felt her throat fill, not with panic or anxiety but with what she could only label as *everything*.

The last strains of the music wrapped around the camp and threaded through the canopy above. Through pricking eyes, Cat watched the branches bend and cover the tiny, try-hard creatures on the ground, all unaware of the abundance and power overhead, as emergency sirens filled the air.

CHAPTER THIRTY-NINE

CONNIE LAID AN EGG

The trumpetlike sound crescendoed into a solid earsplitting whine throughout the camp's mounted speakers. At first Cat thought Matt had switched records to screw with Camille, because that seemed so like him. That's when the reason-finding part of her brain stopped and her *Danger! Where's my sister?* brain took over.

Bob and Cat stood directly under one of the speakers, so she couldn't hear and didn't care what Bob said before he dashed off. She lurched away from the woodpile and shouted, "Ginger! Bard!" but the emergency siren overwhelmed her call.

The reaction of the guests to the blasting noise was varied. A woman with a large amber-beaded necklace had an *I want to speak to the manager* expression on her face, while her husband tried to get her up and moving. Cat saw an angry man mouth the words, *Shut that damn thing off.*

"Get up!" Cat shouted again. The wind, rain, siren, it all said *tornado*, and she chose to cradle her belly instead of cover her ears. She had to get to the microphone. Get people moving. "Ginger!"

Another man downed his drink in one swallow and signaled to one of the flying monkeys for a refill. It was as if the visitors didn't have emergencies that couldn't be solved with haughty irritation and a drink.

Shirtless, Lefty's leash in hand, hurled himself at the microphone and said, "Stay calm."

"Good. I'll be right there," Cat screamed, but a blast of hot wind swept her words into the next county and shoved her body sideways.

The guests finally reacted appropriately and either trembled and froze or had the wild eyes of bolting greyhounds and were on the move. Cat watched Camille throw her fluffy self off the stage and into Matt's awaiting arms. Hand in hand, they began to organize the guests, starting with those on their feet.

Even before Cat had made sense of it, the Littles who didn't know a salad fork from a hole in the ground were experts in crowd control, whether it be for a potato sack race or a tornado warning.

The monkeys moved seamlessly from bartenders to securing the perimeter, while the Munchkins created a human chain to lead people to safety. The Lollipop Guild, minus Matt and the palace guards, created a bucket brigade, moving guests across the lawn and into the Mess Hall, the only safety building large enough to hold the group. Shirtless and Lefty took up the rear, appearing entirely in control.

The sky was oddly bright; Cat searched for Ginger. Rain blew sideways, and Cat hung on to the rainbow and clutched Connie in her basket, her fear freezing her in place as she shouted encouragement while scanning the crowd for Ginger, her brown hat losing straw in the wind. "You're doing great!" she shouted over the sirens. "Hold hands and stick together."

A man tried to break free from the monkey chain, and his wife said, "Get your ass over here," and he did.

"Take off your shoes," Cat called to the woman with the spike heels, and she complied, tossing the shoes into the grass.

"Preposterous," said the man dressed for a safari but angry at the ineffectiveness of his pith helmet, not the weather.

As people entered the building, Gary's team battened down the storm shutters. Shirtless grabbed Elphaba, her first aid kit in hand, and took the rear with Lefty at their side. Almost everyone was on the lawn or inside the Mess Hall, and Ginger was nowhere in sight.

"Ginger!" Cat called, feeling white-hot panic for the first time. The wind picked up, whipping her hair around her neck like a scarf. She had to get inside. Her baby!

When they were kids, Ginger would go to the Boathouse and listen to the rain above and the water below. Her father chastised her, "Nature can turn on you; it doesn't mean to, but it does."

No, Cat told herself; she was artistic, not stupid. She'd be . . . Cat was at a loss, panic obscuring her thoughts. She didn't know her sister anymore. Not really, and a sob escaped her lips.

The sound of a freight train filled the air, and the top of the rainbow broke off and flopped toward the lake. A rush of air threw Connie from her basket, and, like a football spiraling from a quarterback, she was pitched toward the ground.

"Connie!" Cat shouted in terror.

Cat protected her belly with one hand, holding the basket with the other, and watched as the bedraggled bird hit the ground in front of the Craft Lodge. Pushed from behind by the disorganized wind, Cat stumbled to collect Toto from the grass.

"Help. Me," Cat screamed, the words a duo of caged birds, finally given freedom.

Gary appeared, scooped up Connie, tore the basket from Cat's grasp, and let the wind take it. He lifted Cat into his arms and shouted, "Hang on." In three strides, they were on the stoop of the Craft Lodge and in the building. "Get in the tub," Gary said.

"Ginger! Bard!" Cat said, protesting.

"They're safe."

Disbelieving, Cat wriggled to get free to find Ginger, but Gary held her fast. "Look at me. Your family is safe."

In a final spurt of effort before fear for herself took over, Cat grabbed Connie's slippery, ribbed chicken leg and dragged her into the bathroom. The lodge went dark, and Cat heard Gary outside latching shutters. Cat flipped the light switch. No power.

She tucked Connie into the small space between her legs, trying to get comfortable in the ceramic tub. She massaged the chicken and her own belly, murmuring, "It's fine. It's all fine. It's good. We're good," trying to talk herself into believing she and her child would be safe.

When she tried to reposition Connie to remove one of her talons from her shinbone, she felt something slide onto her leg. In the middle of a ruckus, Connie had laid an egg, and Cat began to shiver.

"Why didn't you shut the door?" Gary said much louder than necessary in the six-by-five-foot bathroom.

"You weren't here yet," Cat said amid chattering teeth and a flapping Connie, who tried to free herself from the wet, shaking human who held her. Her wing hit Cat in the chin when she semi-flew up and out of the tub and ducked under the toilet tank, a place that was perfectly fowl shaped.

The bathroom door slammed, and with one yank from Gary, the fabric shower curtain broke free of its plastic rings, and he wound it around Cat's shoulders. The roaring storm made Cat feel no bigger than a ladybug and her baby but a speck on her wing. How could she ever protect her speck; how did she think she could be in charge of anyone?

Oh, how the mighty they have fallen is what she would have said if she could speak through her chattering teeth.

Gary no longer wore his costume. Scratch that. He was missing the silver body barrel, the cardboard arms, and the dryer vent armpits. His tin hat held firm, planted at a jaunty angle on his head. Cat would have made a joke, *Funnel-ly meeting you here*, but her habit of making fun of everything seemed perilously cocky at the end of the world. As if Mother Nature would hear her and say, *You think you're funny? I'll give you funny.* Then her shivers turned to rigors.

With his grump face intact, he said, "Move over." The rain thrashed against the side of the cabin, the chugging train rushing down unseen tracks.

Cat tried for a coordinated repositioning but feared losing her grip on the perfectly smooth egg in her jittering hand. Like a long, muscular, foldable yardstick, Gary contracted his limbs and fit around the tub's edges. He lifted Cat onto his lap as if she were a child readying for a toboggan slide down a ski hill.

"Is everybody inside? Does anyone need help?" Cat said, and she flinched when she heard a loud thud overhead and a smattering of hail on the roof.

"Everyone is safe," murmured Gary, his body heat warming Cat's thin dress, then her skin, and bit by bit her core.

The way her body stuttered and slowed brought to mind her first car, an old Ford Granada. After a short drive, she'd remove the key, but the engine would sputter on until finally giving over to rest. When quiet came over Cat's muscles, she was able to say "Connie laid an egg" without stuttering and calmly pointing out the least important thing happening in that moment.

"What were you thinking out there?" Gary said, his ever-ready exasperation loud and clear, his stutter she'd been listening to forever since he'd written about it nowhere in sight.

"I couldn't leave them," Cat said, giving a final shudder before high winds throttled the roof above.

CHAPTER FORTY

AFTER YOU

Cat and Gary flinched in unison as massive windy fingers scrubbed the cabin's side. He pulled Cat into him, his entire body transformed into a clamshell, his mouth on her ear. "What is the matter with you? Are you selfish or not? You can't be both."

"Are we going to die?" Cat asked.

"What?"

"Are. We. Going. To. Die?" Cat shouted.

"No." His warm breath rushed exquisitely into her ear canal, and boy, howdy did she want to enjoy it, but she had a baby to consider, so she focused on staying small and hoped the eye of the storm wouldn't see her cowering in a tub with a man without a heart.

The din of a trash compactor's screech and crush entered the brawl between wind and the camp. Gary said, "Cars." The cringe-evoking sound repeated, with the added yawn and scrape of metal against metal.

"Another car," Gary said, and because nothing else seemed appropriate, she started to giggle uncontrollably.

"No crying," Gary said, his lips on the sensitive part of her outer ear, making her laugh harder. Until he kissed her earlobe, a small patch of her neck, then the tendon that always got sore when she slept wrong.

Cat moved her head in the opposite direction, like an actual feline helping its owner to reach the itch she wanted scratched.

Her thoughts bounced from *Wait, the rain, what's happening?* to *Gary, Hot Gary, is kissing my neck. Wow, that feels good.* As the wind turned to a downpour, it was Cat's body that became a tempest in a teapot.

Still holding the egg, she cradled Gary's head in what she hoped was an encouraging way. But his funnel hat poked her wrist, and she had to reposition. She slid her hand behind his neck, wanting to run her fingers through his wet hair, but the egg.

"Wait. I have to put something down"—and in a bump and tumble of knees, belly, and ungainly turning, she placed the egg on the floor and gave it a rolling push toward its mother, still crouching behind the toilet.

On her knees facing Gary, her belly on his chest, she held his head and guided his lips to hers. He lifted his chin with open eyes like a detail-oriented person wanting the best fit. When she felt his broad, strong hands on her belly, she rewarded him with her tongue. Then her concentration became laser-focused in a way she could have used during her psychology classes in college.

Cat would have kept going, but her nose was stuffy from the humidity, and she hadn't taken a deep enough breath to accommodate a prolonged lip-lock. She pulled away, took the kind of breath that a swimmer would need to take on the English Channel, and instead of diving in, said, "We're not going to die."

Gary shook his head, and his face, grumpy as always, said, "I want you," and Cat realized two things: *Oh, "crabby" is just his face*, and then, unable to give up winning even in this incredibly charged moment, she said, "I want you more."

Getting out of the tub without slipping and falling, as the rain continued outside, the camp's future uncertain, almost killed the vibe for Cat. Then there was the *After you, after you* that you never, ever saw on the big screen. Cat took the lead, grabbed his large, soft hands, and decided no matter how awkward this got, she would have these garden-ing paddles on her body.

"Oh God," she said, which seemed to fix their focus on politeness over pleasure. Cat hadn't had sex in seven months, and her body had been shaped entirely differently then, so there were a few *Oops, sorries* and sighs of earnest effort as they worked as a team to get the wet Dorothy costume up and out of the way, finally giving up and shoving the material north. When she tried to pull the silver funnel off his head in a fit of passion, his head went with it. "Gorilla Glue," he said.

Cat heard herself moan and didn't hear the storm again for a while.

———

Now that, ladies and gentlemen, is how it's done is what Cat wanted to announce. It hadn't been the usual point-and-shoot situation that can happen in a first-time sexual encounter.

Gary, surprise, surprise, was In. To. It.

He was the kind of lover like a foodie is an eater: wanting to expe-rience the feast, not just swallow it, and that kind of sex-having took some time. With the fear of survival having passed and a biblical rain-fall trapping them inside, Cat lost track of that time. *Thank you, Gary. Whew!*

After a mouthwatering release and the receding hormone tide, Cat opened her eyes. The bulk of her dress and apron were crumpled in her armpits, and the vista of her body was entirely exposed. With her abundant breasts lolling left and right, her linea nigra bisecting her tummy, Cat felt pride at her racehorse body. The sheer multitasking of creating a human, having sex, and surviving a storm during a hopeless fundraiser was what the Olympics should be about.

The rain slowed, and Gary lay prostrate, gasping for air.

"Whew. That was something," Cat said, not differentiating the events of the last who knew how long.

Cat rolled off the bed and tried to unroll her damp dress down, inch by inch, like a window awning. She found her underwear and pulled it on as quickly as she possibly could. While she knew how she felt about her body, she didn't know how she felt about what had just happened between them. Was she the kind of woman who slept with men who despised her? Is that what she was?

"Do you hate me?"

"What? Why would you say that?"

"Because you hate me," Cat said, "I suspect," adding the last bit because a therapist would say you can't tell another person how they feel.

"No, Cat."

"I think the rain has stopped. We'd better go," she said, because his sentence sounded like a *but* was on the way. Because there were dozens of people hunkered down and most likely terrified in the Mess Hall. Because there was no saving anything anymore, and she might as well face it.

"Cat. We need to talk."

And one more *because*. *We need to talk* was always a prelude to a breakup or a *This was a mistake* conversation, because obviously.

"I'm going to go get Connie. I think your pants are over by you." Cat rushed out of the bedroom.

Forsaking Connie for an escape out the door, she followed the eerie blue-green lighting that accompanied a tornado in Wisconsin. Although no one official had called it, Cat had lived through enough tornado watches, warnings, and tails to know what the aftermath looked like.

The sound of Gary rustling into action behind her spurred Cat to find her Birkenstocks and push her shoulder against the rarely closed, heavy outer door. At first glance, the camp appeared brighter, lusher, greener, and rejuvenated. The air had been scrubbed free of humidity, and a tinkle of rain dropped onto Cat's forehead. A tree-size branch that provided shade to entering guests had been cleaved from its glorious oak and rested precariously on the WELCOME TO SUMMER CAMP entry arch. As if awaiting human acknowledgment, the branch slid off its support and landed with a wallop, blocking the exit and pointing to the parking lot.

The violence of it, the epic nature of nature, made Cat pause in reverence. In the gravel lot, a white Honda and an orange Subaru were on top of each other, much like she and Gary had been. The Accord was unbothered by the Crosstrek. Gary joined her on the porch, and he chuckled, then stopped.

A flat-topped Range Rover lay upside down and on top of a Tesla. As if a child had been stacking Hot Wheels and been called to supper with no intention of sorting it all out. The parking lot had become a zigzagged maze that nobody was getting out of anytime soon.

Tornados and their tails were oddly specific in their devastation. During the Stoughton, Wisconsin, tornado touchdown, Cat had read that a house had been ransacked by gale-force winds, the owners expecting annihilation. Once they were cleared to enter, they found a pair of pearl earrings unbothered on a bedside table amid the rubble of the rest of the house.

"I wonder if we have tornado insurance," Cat said, expecting a riot of demands in the Mess Hall. She'd watched reality shows where the rich, floating on yachts, threw fits at their below-temperature cappuccinos. The tantrums, the off-with-your-head reactions during weddings when the greenery in a bouquet wasn't green enough.

"Cat," Gary said.

Cat stopped walking, part of her brain curling like a kitten around the sound of her name, the other part alert and protective. "There's probably an uprising in the Mess Hall. Maybe we could return to our old ways of minimal words between us. I'd like to keep our survival booty call as a lovely memory for a few more minutes."

"Booty call?" Gary said.

CHAPTER FORTY-ONE

BUMMER CAMP

Cat pushed on the door of the Mess Hall, listening for angry voices, demands, or worse, the moaning of terrified, injured people. In the vestibule, her nose pressed against the screen that separated them from the inside, she saw what looked like a party.

Shirtless was sitting on a picnic table and leading a sing-along of "If I Were King of the Forest," pulling his Adam's apple for a vibrato. Clusters of guests sat on benches and tables with flashlights spotlighting the Cowardly Lion. A woman wore his headpiece while stroking Lefty's head in her lap.

June hugged the first aid kit, her green makeup intact, her hat hanging by an elastic string down her back. Camille and Matt led a game of charades by candlelight in the opposite corner. All of the therapy animals were on laps, watched over by Penelope and Brittany. Two guests sat cross-legged and barefoot stroking Alistair and Raj by the light of a camping lantern.

How was it possible that no one appeared injured, angry, or the least bit worried? By all accounts, people were having a good ol' campy time. She scanned the crowd for her sister, wanting to clap eyes on her, see her safe.

Cat felt Gary close by watching the happenings inside. The scene tamped her adrenaline down, her worst-case scenario in hand. She might let herself feel relief if she caught sight of an open checkbook.

Ginger appeared with Bob, holding a black plastic trash bag. Her sister's expression flashed from a fake mask of *Isn't this fun?* to a look of real worry. Bob spoke into her ear with a soft, consoling expression. Ginger shrugged him off, then crumpled a tissue paper flower and shoved it into the trash. The guests paid no attention to Bob, the man who'd lured them to the camp under false pretenses. Had they realized what Ginger's expression suggested, that the man behind the curtain was nothing more than a man?

Seeing Ginger without her childlike cheer and optimism invited a new pit in Cat's stomach. Cat had demanded her sister to *get with the program*, and she had. And this program seemed to have squeezed her sister's essence right out of her.

Ginger's painted nose lay smudged and smeared across her cheek. She looked like their mother after a hard, complicated day. Cat pushed into the room, and the warm smell of bodies, wet floor, and dirt filled her nostrils.

One look at Cat, and Ginger dropped the garbage and skipped over legs and around bodies. "I was so worried," Ginger said, her voice free from laryngitis.

"Your voice is back!" Cat said through a mouthful of Ginger's hair.

"Gary said he'd take care of you." Ginger grabbed Gary's forearm. "You said you would, and you did. You always do what you say." Cat was envious of the intimacy of their history. "You guys! It's Cat!" Ginger announced.

Activity in the room stopped, and everyone, literally everyone, cheered in one way or another.

"Thank goodness!"

"Dorothy's here!"

"Who?"

Shirtless long-limbed it across the room. Instead of his head bonk, he clasped Cat to him. "Aunt Kitty."

"Oh, honey," Cat said, deeply affected by the lack of caution in his embrace.

Brittany and Penelope held hands and said, "We looked for you."

An extraordinarily tall and empathetic woman dropped her head to look Cat directly in the eye. "We knew someone who helped produce this event would be fine." Then she took Cat's hands and said, "We just knew it."

"We were less sure, so we prayed," Camille said, nodding at Matt.

"Because bad things do happen to good people," Matt said, as if sure he'd come up with that phrase all on his own.

"We did pray," Norm said. "All of us."

"Wow. I'm sorry to worry you all. I had no idea . . ." Cat stopped before saying *that anyone cared.* It was too woe-is-me, achingly pathetic, but also true. She'd been bossing everyone around, collapsing in front of them, and then falling into a slumber; what was there to like about her enough to pray for?

Holding a cake high like a sparkly pink waitress in a diner, Wynn called out, "I told you guys she was with Gary. He'd never let anything hurt our Cat."

The words *our Cat* hummed a love song into Cat's ear.

"So where have you two been?" Wynn said, yanking the back of Cat's dress free from a pair of underwear that would embarrass a dead person. "I told you he liked you," Wynn whispered. In a louder voice she said, "Gary likes everyone. Don't you, Gar?"

"In fact, I don't," Gary said.

"This is one of our last frosted cakes. I just sliced it. Want some?" Glinda lowered the sheet cake for Cat to see. It was the one Cat had decorated, writing with a shaky hand, *Welcome to Summer Camp.* When Glinda slid the knife through the frosted letter *S* in *Summer Camp*, it transformed into a *B*. The cake now read *Welcome to Bummer Camp.*

Even the cake knew.

As delighted as everyone was about survival, Cat's joy was ungratefully blunted. The camp's financial troubles, fraudulent data, unpaid mortgage, and bad actors were still afoot. This camp for anxious and depressed adults run by anxious and depressed adults was finished. Bummer Camp indeed. Cat considered dipping her finger into the frosting but couldn't manage sugar having her in a choke hold too.

Brittany moved to Cat's side with a penlight and a clipboard. "We sold all the art and stories. We have a grand total of one hundred and sixteen dollars, but nobody wants to take it home. We can use them for our next fundraiser. I gave everyone my Cash App. I'll transfer it all to you when I get my phone back."

Cat took the penlight, shined it in Brittany's glassy eyes. "Britt. Are you high?"

"Oh yeah. Everyone is, except Wynn, Ginger, and a few others." She glanced around. "June isn't. A nurse can't be high when she's on duty. I don't think. After we prayed, those metal sounds scared the crap out of everyone. Wynn handed out a lot of brownies."

"She drugged everyone?"

"Nah. She got everyone to sign a waiver before handing them out." Brittany flipped over the auction page. Cat read the words *I want weed*, followed by an uneven row of signatures down to the bottom of the page.

"Well, they can't drive home now," Cat said.

"Nobody wants to go anywhere. They're having the time of their lives," Brittany said. She'd tied the top part of her one-piece horse costume around her waist and wore a green Summer Camp T-shirt underneath.

The man petting Lefty said, "Let's go swimming," and as if it had been a command from the Almighty herself, the group filed past Cat into the summer night. Shirtless shot up and shouted, "Swim with a buddy. Swim with a buddy," jogging after the high and happy group.

"That's not safe," Cat said with little conviction.

"No worries. My uncle was in the coast guard," Brittany said as she galloped after the crowd.

Gary's walkie-talkie sputtered at his belt.

"Tiny Dancer. Come in, Tiny Dancer. Do you read me?"

"Norm," Gary said in his *Cut the crap* voice.

"Come to family cabin. The eagle has landed."

Cat grabbed the walkie-talkie. "Norm. What is happening?"

"Over and out," he said.

Put a walkie-talkie in a man's hand, and he instantly becomes a secret operative wary of enemy ears.

CHAPTER FORTY-TWO

SUM CAMP

Gary, Ginger, Bob, and Cat hustled past the Admin Building, across the highway, and toward Cat and Ginger's childhood cabin. "What now?" Ginger said, her voice clear, tired.

"I'm sorry I worried you," Cat said.

"It's not your fault. I'm ready for this night to end."

Ginger sounded more like the grumpy Cat than her animated, eternally optimistic self.

"Well, I think this night is a success!" Bob said, apropos of nothing, negative data to the contrary.

Ginger closed her eyes, and the irritated tilt of Gary's silver headpiece spoke volumes: Bob should stay out of swinging range if he knew what was good for him.

Through the outer door, Cat heard Steve's voice.

"I'll pay you double, man. Get me out of here."

"Keep begging. I love it," said Norm.

Cat pushed past Gary, brushing his hip, clocking his energy, unable to get a read on him.

Norm, the man, the Munchkin mayor, stood in the living room smiling at a pile of cushions and rubble on the floor. On closer examination, Cat saw Steve, face down, trapped under her father's recliner, with half the stone fireplace and chimney on top of it. His head rested on an old-fashioned suitcase, and he clutched the handle as if it were a lifesaver.

"Ta-da!" Norm said with a showbiz flourish. "Look who showed up as predicted."

Cat hadn't had one thought about Steve's whereabouts during the storm, so it wasn't she who had predicted the scene in front of her. He was like the smell in the Auditorium, a stink that drifted into every low part of the day.

"The roof is gone!" Ginger gasped.

"Well, look at that. It sure is," said Bob.

Where the chimney had been was now a jagged hole in the ceiling. It was as if someone had plucked out the shingles, reached inside, and flicked the old chimney over. The night sky above was unreasonably clear, and the boughs of an old oak peeked in at the destruction.

"Cat. Help me. My ankle. I'm injured," Steve said, neither ankle looking the least bit stressed.

"What are you doing on the floor?" Cat said, as if Steve were an unruly child and she'd had enough of him.

"I wanted the money in here for us."

"That's Daddy's suitcase. I haven't seen it in years," Ginger said.

The luggage had been a prop in theater productions. In between stage appearances, Cat and Ginger had used it for picnics or collecting pine cones to paint in the Craft Lodge. Steve snugged the suitcase closer to him.

"What are you talking about?" Cat said. "What money?"

"For the grounds. The mortgage, the baby's future," Steve said, listing two things that were none of his business.

"The baby," Cat said. She wanted to deliver a top-notch comeback but could only summon Alicia Silverstone's character Cher in the 1995 movie *Clueless*. "As if, Steve. As if."

"It's true. Elaine wanted a water park, but I said, 'No, Cat would never go for that,'" Steve said.

Cat wanted to disavow everything to do with Steve. No one knew the details of her and Steve's nonrelationship, her accidental pregnancy. She'd been lonely, that was all. And years of gaslighting herself had led Cat to making a baby with the shallow mess at her feet. Which is not how a girl dreams of creating a life.

"What's in here is for us," Steve said, his face having zero idea how to look romantic.

"Cut the crap, Steve. There is no *us*."

"Somebody explain to me what is going on here," Ginger said.

Norm pointed to a cupboard over their heads next to the fireplace. One of the doors hung open, and Cat saw her mother's Scrabble game and an old cribbage board stacked on the inner shelves.

"I think he stood on that chair to get to the cupboard next to the fireplace, and it all went badly from there."

"My dad used that suitcase for scavenger hunt treasures, prizes for the team that found it," said Ginger.

Bob nodded like an excited kid, allowed to stay up past his bedtime with the adults.

"Is Elaine here?" Ginger said warily, steeling herself for a jump scare.

"I knew she'd find her way back here. There was too much money at stake," Bob said.

"She took off. Left me," Steve said with a *Can you believe it?* look on his face.

"Oh yeah." Bob smiled. "She's a runner. Loves a getaway vehicle. A real lead foot."

"One look at Cat today and I figured I was going to be a baby daddy. I told Elaine and poof," Steve said, trying for an exploited look; his lower lip almost managed a pout.

There was a collective recoil at the appropriated slang term for fatherhood, and everyone looked at Cat. "Oh, for Pete's sake," Cat said. "Yes, everyone, Steve is the father, and no one is more grossed out by this fact than I am."

"Hey," Steve said.

"Let's talk about that suitcase, shall we, Steve?" Cat said.

Steve tightened his grip on the old leather handle and said, "Cat, can we speak privately?"

"Don't be ridiculous," said Cat.

Steve tried to aim his lips in her direction, for a private conversation. "Your dad's treasure map led me to this."

"My dad's treasure map," Cat said. She added, "Which one, Steve? He made dozens of them."

Confused, Steve said, "*The* map?" then wrenched his neck to look at Bob. "You said . . ." He wriggled, tried to stand. "Bob told Elaine that your dad hid money on the grounds. Cash. The deed. Stocks. Bob knows. Gave the map to Elaine. Told her to meet him here. They'd find it. Leave together, after the gala."

"I did say that." Bob looked thrilled. "This is the surprise I was telling you about, Ginger."

"I don't follow," Ginger said, uncharmed.

"My dear, soon you will see that I am a better man than wizard, though I did attempt a bit of magic in these enchanted woods."

"Please just tell us what went on," Ginger said. "It's late."

"You're a lawyer, Cat. You can make this all work, right? Some for them. Some for us," said Steve.

Cat realized Elaine must have believed Ginger's lie that Cat was a lawyer and transferred the information to Steve. And what did Steve know? Nothing, and yet here he was using his lack of information to finagle something for himself. *Oh, to be a man. On your back, no idea what is going on, and still believing you can negotiate.*

"You were right, Bobby," Norm said. "You said he'd hightail it in here, and he sure did. Did you order the tornado too?" Norm strolled over to Bob and clapped him on the back. "A bit over the top, my man, but a nice touch."

"Oh no, no, no," Bob said modestly. "That storm was just ol' Mother Nature getting in on the fun."

Steve slowly tried to reach his phone, which lay inches out of reach. Cat recalled Steve at the assembly, his screen lit up, his hasty exit past Gary.

"You saw the tornado watch, didn't you? It came through on your phone. Instead of warning us, you ran off to find this suitcase? What, were you hoping we'd all be killed, and you and Elaine would get whatever's in there, plus the camp?"

"No," he gasped, but he'd hesitated.

With a blaze of unnecessary heroics, Norm kicked the phone out of Steve's reach, unlocked the phone with Steve's face, yanked his shorts out of his butt, and said, "Dialing 911 now."

"Good," Bob said with a nod. "Nicely done."

"We're at Summer Camp. County Road A," Norm said. "Tornado damage. No injuries. One burglary suspect apprehended."

"Burglary? No. I found this," Steve said, as if to invoke the well-known legal tenet of finders keepers.

"Keep an eye out for a car thief, one Elaine Durand," said Norm.

"Not Durand. Lewis. Elaine Lewis. We're not married. Not even common law," Bob said, clarifying something no one had even considered.

"Lewis. Elaine Lewis," Norm continued. "The woman in question is in a white commuter van, license plate SUM CAMP." Bob silently lip-synched along, as if playing crime karaoke.

"You're not married?" Cat said.

Ginger rubbed her eyes, and Cat couldn't tell if she'd known this or not.

"Enough," Gary said as he wrenched the suitcase out of Steve's grasp. It was the size of a TV tray, about eight inches deep. He spun the case toward Cat and hit the spring-loaded clasps, and the lid popped open, blocking Steve's view of the contents. Cat smiled and Ginger's face went soft. The suitcase was filled with leather bracelets like the one Cat had found that first day, which Norm had worn on his wrist.

"Dad was always so encouraging, wanting us to know that if we made mistakes, we weren't a failure and that we could try again," Ginger said as if their father had filled their heads with fairy tales and she had aged out of believing them.

For Cat, this message had had the opposite effect on her. She'd believed that avoiding failure was of primary importance. That the *begin again* part was for Cat to coach Ginger, to help her focus, finish her jobs. As an adult, Cat understood what her father had been trying to teach her, that failure was but a step in a journey. But the little girl Cat whispered, *Failure is bad. Don't let people down.*

Cat ran her thumb over the words. What was it about those early lessons in life? Debunk each one with logic, data, and therapy, but the shadow lesson endures.

Steve craned his neck to see what everyone had their eyes on. Cat nudged the case with her foot, turning it one hundred and eighty degrees to show him the treasure trove of inspiration.

"What the . . . ?" Steve said.

"We need to get that covered, Gary," Norm said.

Everyone looked at the wet hole in the roof, except Cat, who watched Steve dig through the bracelets looking for his due. At the bottom of the suitcase, against the satin and stained insides, he found a bulky craft envelope and peered inside. Trying for a magician's sleight of hand, he tucked the envelope into his coat.

Bob met Cat's eye, put his finger to his lips, and shook his head.

Ginger saw the exchange. "Okay, everyone out," she said. "Let's let Gary and the police do their jobs."

Cat resisted; she needed to talk to Gary. It made her sick to think that he might think that she and Steve had been in cahoots. Or worse, a couple.

"Norm, please ask the police to arrive without a siren. We don't want to alarm our guests," said Ginger.

Norm gave Ginger a two-fingered salute and hustled out to meet the uniformed cops.

"Cat," Steve said, his cajoling tone gone, "if I'm the father, you will be hearing from my lawyers."

Cat ignored the *if* and said, "Good idea. Child support is important."

Steve hadn't considered that a *crib lizard* costs money and looked like a bigmouth bass who'd swallowed too large a fly.

"A word of advice, Steve," Bob said, lifting a finger. "Women are better and brighter than their male compadres. To work with women, you have to think like one." He tapped his head. "I'm not a woman, but I am an INFJ. Introvert, intuitive, feeling, and judging." Bob let that sink in. "I see your surprise, Steve. Very astute. You thought I'd be an extrovert. But no, I enjoy small groups with focused projects, like keeping this camp safe from predators. I'm like Raj. I like my local carrots and the love of one good woman who would have me."

Bob had no idea that he had been the problem, not the solution, and Cat saw that Ginger had seen the same thing.

"Good grief," Ginger said as she pushed Bob toward the door.

Ginger's spiritless expression remained as they walked out into the night. The reality that Cat had been insisting on had landed flat on top of her sister's previously lighthearted ways. Ginger finally had taken on what Cat wanted, a real-world attitude, and it looked like hopeless heartbreak.

CHAPTER FORTY-THREE

BLUE-SKY PLANS

The police arrived and lit up the parking lot. The red-and-blue strobes highlighted the precise nature of the tornado's damage. Cars were scattered, toppled, but Summer Camp's arbor and fence were intact. Cat had no faith that the police would arrest Steve for stealing motivational bracelets and charge Elaine with grand theft auto for borrowing the camp van. Still, she would have liked to watch Gary wrestle Steve outside, a display of good over evil.

Cat fingered her chin, remembering that Gary's cheek had brushed the spot just before his lips touched her jaw. She wanted to dine out on the feeling, preserve it with repetition, as she suspected it would take another natural disaster to happen again.

Cat eyed her sister's bowed head. The night wasn't over, and Cat needed her sister's can-do positive Ginger energy to return.

A loud whooping came from the lake, accompanied by splashing that sounded like rowdy kids having a great time among the water bugs and fish. There was no evidence of the wealthy adults accustomed to chlorinated swimming pools or tropical beaches.

"I think we should go down to the lakefront. Make sure everyone stays put until the police leave," Ginger said. "I know the camp can't be saved, but at least we can keep the guests safe from drug-use questions."

"Oh, the camp doesn't need saving," Bob said.

"Don't start, Bob," said Cat.

"It doesn't. If you'll let me explain, Ginger. I'd like to show you that your instincts were right. About me."

Ginger washed her hands over her face, their father's mannerism when he was exhausted and frustrated.

"I'll go to the lake," Cat said.

"No, don't. I'm going to hear him out. You might as well stay. I won't have the energy to repeat it."

Cat hated that this Ginger was the one she'd always hoped for. One as jaded and annoyed as she.

"Let's talk in the Canteen for privacy," Bob said, ushering the sisters into the cedar shed.

"I'm not paying for this," Cat said, grabbing a Slim Jim and taking a bite.

"Nor should you," said Bob. He'd ditched his green overcoat and stood before them wearing a too-small emerald-colored vest.

"Start talking. The shortest version you can come up with," said Cat, offering Ginger a bite of her salty snack.

"Of course." He nodded. "After I met Ginger, I knew she was my forever home," Bob said.

Ginger snatched the Slim Jim and shoved the whole thing in her mouth.

"Bold start," Cat said, opening another beef stick. "You've got until the Slim Jims are gone."

"The camp did well this summer. The adults came sad and left happy. But that wasn't enough for Elaine. 'Level up, Bob,' she kept saying, and not in a nice way." He glanced between the two sisters. "Have you ever tried to break up with someone who just won't leave?"

Um, yeah, Bob, Cat wanted to say. *This camp!*

"It gets ugly." Bob eyed the Slim Jims. "Way back after my book went big, I offered Elaine royalties if she left me alone, and you know what she said? 'You're nothing without me,' and I knew I'd made the gravest of errors. The day before my interview with Oprah's bestie aired, she launched a smear campaign on all the conservative social threads, and pretty soon Alistair and Raj were labeled all kinds of things. Liberal, pro-choice, socialist, culturally appropriated, gay, and antiproductivity. They were bunnies," Bob said. "Bunnies with differences who respected each other." He shook his head. "The trolls went wild, and as the kids say, we were doxed. She took both of us down, just to show me she could. And still wouldn't leave. Elaine is made of spite and persistence." Bob rubbed his eyes with the memory. "Elaine cut off her foot to save her nose."

There was something engaging about Bob's childlike belief in fairness, his unearned optimism. Especially given his missteps in life.

"When Steve showed up out of the blue, talking water parks, I knew something had to be done. Elaine kept saying, 'This is it, Bobby, a water park is the big break we've been waiting for,' as if I didn't know she was using me for my charisma."

Cat saw Ginger's expression. *Oh, Bob.*

Elaine had been using him, all right, but for access to the camp, bank statements, and as a future scapegoat.

"Steve was her big break, and if I put all the pieces in place, I could do what I promised Ginger: I could protect and serve the camp."

Cat shifted her weight. Her feet were wet, and while her dress had dried, the fabric pinched her armpits, and she longed for one of her stretchy onesies. She wondered how quickly everyone would have to exit the grounds once the bank took over, and the thought made her want to eat a whole cake and go to bed without brushing her teeth.

"I need some fresh air," Ginger said and then let herself out of the Canteen. Cat grabbed a bag of chips and a bottle of water and followed.

Bob caught up to them, raised his voice. "I needed Elaine and Steve to commit a crime. Not the kind of thing that would wreck their lives forever, but enough that nobody would want to do business with them."

The sister who wholeheartedly believed in UFOs was shaking her head in disbelief. She leaned against the totem pole. "Can you wrap this up, please," she said, like Cat had heard her mother speak to their father, as though she was at her limit.

"I told Elaine and Steve that the camp was broke, and we needed a gala for potential investors. I sent out the invitations, made the insert about the health benefits of camp, told Elaine it was a ruse to get people here and then pitch them the water park. I had faith in the richness of nature to convince guests it should remain what it is: a place to get away from everything a water park represents." He took another breath. "Ginger told me everything I needed to know about you, Cat, and I knew the two of you would terrify Elaine. She's afraid of powerful women. She looks for shortcuts and people she can fool and bully." He looked at his feet and said, "Like me."

There was truth and hurt in those last two words, and Cat took pity on him. "Go on."

"I learned that the theft of two thousand five hundred dollars is enough for you to press charges, to hurt his reputation. I gave the map to Elaine in the car when we went to the bank. Told her to get the van ready when the gala was in gear. I knew she'd tell Steve, take the money, and run." He paused. "I know I make things harder than they should be. I get carried away."

"Where did you get the money from?" Ginger asked. "Are you saying the camp isn't bankrupt?"

"Right, it's not." In a slower voice he said, "There's the same amount of money as there's always been. Elaine never did the math or looked at the books." Bob shrugged one shoulder. "She trusted me."

Normally, Cat would have launched herself at Bob, demanded more information, gotten angry. But there was no need for her outrage because her sister had that covered.

"You have got to be kidding me," Ginger said as she snatched the bag of chips from Cat's hand and yanked it open. "How am I supposed to feel about this? It's outlandish!"

"Innovations start with outlandish needs and tall tales. The iPhone, satellites, the ThighMaster. People needed problems solved, and they told a wild story to get people on board. What is life but blue-sky plans stitched together with high hopes and the right people?" Bob said wistfully, like the Wizard himself. "We're the right people," Bob said, gesturing to the three of them. "And, Cat, none of this would have worked if not for you."

"Is that right?" she said, crunching on a chip.

"I asked Ginger to call you. She didn't want to, but I encouraged her. I told her we needed your support. Your presence proved to Elaine that something serious was happening here at Summer Camp."

"Bob . . . ," Ginger started, and Cat could see her sister wondering how she'd lost control, missed so much. She had to be thinking Cat was judging her. "I can't do this."

"May I ask you a question, Cat?" Bob asked. "Why did you come?"

"My name was on the mortgage. The camp was in trouble," Cat said, tired of repeating herself, afraid it would hurt her sister.

"Respectfully, you could have done any number of things," said Bob. "Gone to the bank, called your mortgage lender, but you didn't. You hopped into the car and drove here."

"I had to see for myself what was going on. Shirtless texted me," Cat said, watching her sister's face.

"And when you came and saw your nephew was fine—better than fine, in love and surrounded by friends—you stayed on. Why?"

Cat brushed the salt of the potato chips onto her dress. Crumpled the empty bag. "I tried to go. Things kept getting worse. Wynnie was drugging people. The smell in the Auditorium, the gala. I couldn't leave."

Bob's eye caught something over Cat's head, and he smiled before Cat felt a damp arm hug her around the top of her belly. Glinda's voice singsonged in her ear about how she'd always had the power to get back home. Cat didn't pull away; in fact she squeezed Wynn's arm twice.

Under the now-clear starry sky, Cat counted the times she'd been touched, held, kissed, patted, carried, caressed, and cared for in the last few days. She'd easily made it to the *Forbes* recommended number of twelve to thrive, and there was no doubt that her child had felt the silent nurturing zing of each touch. Wynn slipped her arm away and moved off, the warmth of her embrace lingering.

"I wanted to stay." Cat took a long drink from the water bottle and met her sister's eyes. "No matter what happened, I wanted to be here."

"Hey, Wynn, what's happening down there? Are people getting ready to leave?" Bob said.

"No! We're getting them all in cabins. Brittany is tucking them in. Shirtless is telling stories in Hodag. Nobody wants to go anywhere. I'm going to raid the Canteen for snacks." And off she twirled. "Come on down, you guys, it's so fun!"

"In a minute," Ginger said.

"Bobby," Ginger said slowly. "So financially, the camp is fine. Is Cat on the mortgage?"

"No. Oh jeez. Sorry. Didn't I say that?"

"No. You didn't say that," Ginger said.

"Is that true?" Cat gasped.

Bob nodded repeatedly.

Cat felt the top of her head go hot. "I've been running around all week, sure this place was about to crumble underneath us. I questioned my father's motives, blamed my mother and Ginger, and all this time, you knew we were fine?" Cat heard herself sputter. "I thought I was going to lose my home."

Bob tilted his head and said, "No offense, Cat, but from what I understand, you lost your home long ago. All I did was show you what it would be like if it was really gone, and then made sure it was in good shape if you came back."

Cat dropped the chips and reached for Bob's throat, only to be hauled to a stop by something tugging on her dress. "I'm going to kill you," Cat said, and she whipped around to see what was slowing the homicide down. Gary had ahold of her and she said, "Did you hear that? The camp is fine!"

She wriggled around. "Ginger!" she said. "Fine!"

"It's fine," Ginger said.

"Norm is helping the police. They're taking 'em," Gary said to Bob as if they were having a quiet conversation, just the two of them alone under the stars.

"Did you know about this?" Cat said.

"Not all of it," Gary said in his usual obtuse way.

"I've been in an escape room, and you've all had the key?" Cat said.

Ginger shook her head. "We were both in that room. Fine," she said dreamily, then let out a breath and swung on Bob, punching his shoulder, hard. Bob nodded like he deserved it. Ginger used to win the breath-holding and swimming competition when they were kids. She'd wait for everyone to surface, then burst through with her arms overhead, yelling, "Winner, winner, Kitty's a sinner."

"That's not a saying!" Cat would yell.

Rubbing his arm, Bob said, "Elaine was right to be scared of you two."

"I'm not on the mortgage?" Cat said.

"It's funny you missed that. And you a lawyer, Cat," Bob teased.

"I'm not a lawyer," Cat said.

"You're not?" said Ginger with a wink.

Gary let her dress go, and Cat turned, grabbed his arms hanging straight at his sides, and pushed her head into his chest. Right or wrong, he was a comfort and smelled like grass, theater paint, and wintergreen.

She tried to recall her life, only a week ago. When she was independent, financially secure, and awaiting the arrival of her child. "I'm not on the mortgage," she repeated, and she found that the message of financial freedom carried with it the sensation of a drifting balloon.

The string floating out of reach over the treetops, light but without direction. Her nose pricked and tears came on too fast. She could go home free and clear, and the thought made her want to be alone so she could figure her tears out.

Gary touched her back, and the warmth of his hand made her cry harder.

"Oh, honey, come here." Ginger poked her sister in the cheek with a stiff piece of straw, repositioned, and gave Cat a rough burlap hug. "It's okay."

There had been many a time that the two girls had howled with laughter, unable to stop until one of them had wet their pants or gagged. This cry felt unstoppable, like that.

"I've been gone so long," Cat said.

"We needed some space," Ginger said.

She heard Gary move away, and Ginger motioned for Bob to take off. When they were alone, Cat said, "By God, you were right about Bob after all."

"Well, my faith was wavering."

"I actually hated that for you," Cat said. "I like it better when you're blindly hopeful and unreasonably optimistic."

"It was good for me to get a taste of your life. 'It's the hard nut life for you,'" Ginger said with a sideways grin, referring to the lyric they loved.

"'It's the hard nut life,'" Cat said.

"You've got a booger," Ginger said, pointing to Cat's cheek.

"Yuck." She tried to wipe it on Ginger as her sister dodged away. "I miss Mom and Dad."

"Me too," Ginger said.

The sound of one of the golf carts thrummed down the path in front of the Administration Building. Several palace guards dragged an enormous tarp behind Gary, leading the way.

"So you and Gary, huh? Not so heartless after all."

"I think he's in love with Norm," Cat said.

"And what would you think about that?"

"Lucky Norm."

With that, the camp came alive. Norm strode across the parking lot in his knickers, shouting directions. Wynn emerged from the Canteen with two filled grocery bags, and when she passed Cat, she grabbed the skirt of her dress and said, "You've got to see this."

Cat hesitated; there was so much to be done. The hole in her parents' cabin, the sticky garbage in the Mess Hall.

"Go," Ginger said. "You might have a good time. I've got some things to check on."

"You faked your voice, didn't you? So Shirtless would have to be brave."

Ginger signed, *Nobody can step up if the top step is occupied.*

"I was always on that top step, wasn't I?" Cat said.

"Not tonight. Go have some fun."

Maybe Monday Cat might have refused, begrudgingly taken the lead in cleaning, checked her car, or figured out how to make pizza from nothing for the guests. Tonight, Cat was going to do something different and hang out with a Horse of a Different Color in the guest cabins, just for fun.

CHAPTER FORTY-FOUR

BONER CAMP

The Good Witch skipped her way down the path, with Cat following a few yards behind her. At the door of the largest cabin near the lake, she heard Wynn shout, "I raided the Canteen, besties!" The screen door slapped shut as the people inside cheered.

Cat stepped over a fallen branch, collected a wet paper plate that had taken flight during the storm, and decided that she would believe Bob. She'd trust that the camp wasn't on the edge of financial disaster and that Bob would produce accurate documents, putting all their minds at ease. Maybe after some time, they'd have a shaky, nervous laugh about the whole thing. If more surprises came to light, she'd talk to Ginger. Cat wouldn't roll her eyes, tsk, or demand anything, like a disappointed dictator. No, they'd speak like two sisters emerging from roles neither one was happy with.

At the door of the cabin, Cat watched their guests, the rusty screen pixelating her view. Someone had ferried lanterns from other cabins and placed them on windowsills and corners. The effect gave the cabin a storybook ambiance and helped hide any failures in housekeeping.

The golden light pulled Cat in, and she joined the crew, cozy in cots and on camping pads, giggling like kids on their first sleepover with friends.

Even with soaking-wet hair, wearing T-shirts from the lost and found, the "kids" looked moneyed. Maybe it was their bone structure or their innate certainty that this night was but a brief foray into rugged living; whatever it was, it didn't impress the staff one way or the other. They did their jobs so well that the guests appeared to forget the larger world and focus only on the story being told about a time when trouble melts like lemon drops.

Brittany had a timer and allowed five-minute cuddles with Alistair and Raj for interested guests. And June handed out pillows and clean towels to anyone who waved her down.

It was easy for Cat to pick out the press. While they, too, appeared to be enjoying themselves, they did so as observers, slightly removed, taking mental notes. Possibly as surprised as Cat to see the masters of the universe singing the words "Father Abraham had seven sons." Camille and Matt, of all people, handed out the junk food: the last of Wynn's cookies and Bear Poop snacks.

Remembering her years of leading sing-alongs, Cat relaxed and casually eavesdropped on the two men chatting to her right.

"A week here and you could sort yourself out, you know what I mean?"

"Right? No need for a chiropractor with that tire swing. My back never felt so good."

"A person needs to get away."

"Have someone to talk to."

It was as if the two men had discovered a brand-new concept, forgetting that vacations, therapy, and rehabilitation had been things for a long time.

A woman to Cat's right, with an eyebrow arch to die for, said to the woman next to her, "There's something about the great outdoors."

"And these kids. They're so"—her new friend searched for the right word—"so smart. No. Wise." While unconsciously fiddling with the fat diamond in her ring, she added, "I'm going to invest in this business."

"Oh, for sure." The woman raised her beautiful brows. "No question."

Carefully, Cat said, "Did you see the research study? In the invitation?"

The woman said, "Sure, but I don't need numbers to tell me what I already know. I can see for myself this place is amazing."

"Awesome," the other woman agreed.

While that sounded like a certainty, Cat knew the statement could be impulsive, born of post-storm, survival adrenaline. Cat enjoyed seeing the camp through these women's storybook gazes. The great outdoors were indeed great, but she'd wait until the sobering light of day to see if the magic of one night at sleepaway camp did the same thing for adults as it did for kids. That despite a difficult start, the guests would wax nostalgic minutes after leaving and make plans to preserve their memories and set a date to return.

No matter if the place was flush or not, a hideaway for adults or a camp for theater kids, Summer Camp would need positive press, gossip, curiosity, and yes, some funds. They'd need a proper marketing plan, a skilled accountant, a couple of people with degrees. As if dipping her toe into cold water before diving under, she thought, *They who? Me?* For once, she didn't shudder in disgust; instead she did what her therapist had suggested: let thoughts enter her mind with observation, not judgment.

"I heard this used to be a theater camp," a third man she couldn't make out in the dim light said. "Wouldn't it be great if they brought that back, but for adults?"

The other man nodded and crunched and sighed his way through a bag of chips, as if nothing had ever tasted so good.

After a scary tale about a locked cabin and a hitchhiker, the group collectively trembled and then groaned when Shirtless said, "Lights out, folks. Don't touch each other," and everybody laughed.

Cat stayed until the diamond-wearing ladies and gentlemen had cuddled beneath the rough sheets of Summer Camp and drifted off. She opened the door, leaving Lefty with Shirtless, and marveled at the competent and anxious Littles who'd showcased Summer Camp better than any expensive fundraiser could have ever done. Better than she herself imagined.

As a kid, she'd thought she had to do everything. Now, she saw that if you trusted people, even oddballs, you could sleep while you made a baby. It was that thought that turned her inner spotlight off, and she knew tonight she wouldn't have an insomniac visit to the lake.

Cat nearly sleepwalked out of the Hodag Cabin, across the grounds, and into the Craft Lodge. Instead of returning to the room where she and Gary had, what . . . hooked up? Made love? Cat crawled into one of the twin beds in her sister's room. The storm already had a long-ago feeling about it. What if her memories of Gary in the tub, Gary in the bed, were a pregnant lady's fever dream? He'd been so aloof after finding everyone in the Mess Hall and Steve in the rubble. Had his arm on her back during her crying jag been care or an awkward moment between awkward people?

If the sex had been but a figment, Cat could go home with one less hard conversation to have and pick up where she'd left off. But if the covers were tossed aside and the sheets were damp with rainwater, Cat would have to deal with something that would feel less like hooking up and more like making love.

Instead of wearing herself out with uncertain thoughts, she closed her eyes and felt her breathing slow. When Cat had arrived at camp that first day, she'd been like a computer functioning on an old operating system. Ginger had grown, the camp had changed, but Cat was the rainbow wheel turning and turning with old information, trying to make it all fit a new model she couldn't see. She'd been blind, and it had taken odd little Bob and an epic storm to teach her how to be part of something, not a reluctant commander in chief.

———

Cat woke to chirping birds and the scent of pancakes wafting from the Mess Hall. The sun streamed in the window, and Cat pushed herself up in bed, which woke her bladder up. Connie had created a nest of shredded toilet paper and a hand towel behind the toilet bowl. "You're a good mom," Cat said.

Under the hot stream of water from the shower, Cat ran her hands over her curves. Between the missing curtain and the scuffs of stubborn face paint in not-so-surprising places, Cat had all the evidence she needed that their tumble had been real. They'd need to talk today. Gary could fill her in on anything she'd missed, and she could say whatever she needed to say. *I'm sorry. Thank you. I like you.*

Before that, she'd mop the bathroom floor, survey the tornado damage, and maybe check in on the guests. Would they wake with sore backs, covered in mosquito bites, with new opinions of roughing it camp-style, and go home grumbling? Someone should document an hourly account of the night and check on the camp's insurance.

Instead, Cat lay down on the bed and counted the weeks before her due date. She considered what she'd tell her child about how Summer Camp had been saved. *Once upon a time, there were two sisters, a wicked witch, and a wizard with a map. When a storm came to wipe out their home, everyone chipped in and . . .* Cat yawned; she had time to finish that story, and she returned to counting the weeks before her biggest dream would come true. Tapping the number on her belly, Cat hoped her child understood her Morse code promise. *I'll do my best. I'll ask for help. Over and out.*

The lodge door creaked, and footsteps headed her way. She pulled the sheet to her shoulders and considered playing possum. When Gary walked past her doorway to the room across the hall, her room, she said, "Gary?"

The Tin Man had been replaced by an all-business groundskeeper in pants and his camp shirt, and holding a cup of coffee in his hand.

"What are you in here frowning about?" she said.

"Decaf," he said.

"Tell me about it. Decaf sucks."

"It's for you," he said, extending the mug for her to take.

Had he brought her a gift to soften the hard talk they were about to have? How the emergency had pushed them together, but now in the light of day, blah, blah, blah? She tried engineering herself into a sitting position without exposing naked parts but decided that was moot modesty.

She swung her bare legs out from under the covers and sat on the side of the bed, then tucked a corner of the covers into her armpit. "Thank you. Wait, did Ginger put you up to this? Never mind. I don't care. Thank you." Cat took a sip and peered at him over the rim. "You missed a spot of makeup."

He rolled his eyes and pointed to the remnants of the funnel attached to his head.

"Here. Sit. I'll take a look." He folded his legs into easy angles and sat on the floor, the back of his head touching her belly. A plastic ring of the funnel clung to the fine hairs on the crown of Gary's head. She tugged, and it came off in her hand, but she didn't let on. Instead, she said, "Yeah, it's on tight." And pretended to keep working. "I'm sorry for teasing you about . . ." She hesitated. How to put this more sensitively than she had all week? "The economics of your words."

He shrugged.

Cat put down her coffee and touched his shoulder. "I'm really sorry. I thought I was justified because you hated me."

"Thought you were selfish the way you left," he said, slower than the Wisconsin rapid-fire cadence typical for the Midwest. "If I thought you were wrong to leave, then I was right to stay."

"My leaving and you staying could both be right," she said, wondering why this truth had eluded her for so long.

"I like to be right," he said.

"You don't say." Cat smiled, enjoying the moment instead of examining every second for the burden it might become in the future. "How much did you know about Bob's plan?"

"Not much at first. I put two and two together, eventually."

"I missed all of it," Cat said. "You have bits of glue in your hair." She plucked at nothing to keep him seated as she worked up her courage to say something real.

Cat had filled the space next to herself with herself for so long that she didn't know what would fit in the gap if she moved aside. How big would that gap be? What was she asking for, exactly? His friendship? A relationship?

Years ago, her father had made the case for doing several scenes from Shakespeare's histories. He tried to choose his favorites and created an ambitious schedule for kids who'd rather be swimming than on a stage from nine to five. Her mom had been hemming a cape and, without looking up, said, "I love chocolate pudding, but I don't want to eat a bathtub of it."

Her father stared at her, grabbed a large pink eraser, and said, "How 'bout we start with one." Her mom, while a weirdo, had always been damn good at boundaries.

Cat would try in earnest to call them in the next two days, invite them to return, tell them she loved them. Find out as much as she could about her father's memory.

"What's going on out there?" Cat finally said. She let her fingers rest on his shoulder, her hand touching his neck.

"What isn't? Bob's doing his thing with the fancy people. Collecting donations. Some bigwig wants mushrooms and microdosing retreats in the winter. Keep it bespoke."

When he said *bespoke*, there was a slight hesitation on the *b*. He let Cat hear it. Didn't cover it up or get up and leave.

"We're nothing if we're not bespoke," Cat said. "Does he feel bad that neither Ira Glass nor Terry Gross showed?"

"Nah. Not sure he noticed. They're talking about doing theater again."

"Do you think Bob engineered this whole thing? You know, thought it through?"

"I do not know."

"Maybe it doesn't matter." Cat shrugged.

"Norm's still in his mayor costume. Wants a job. Head of security and safety. June is going to finish nursing school. Shirtless is talking about enrolling in biology classes. Lefty is glued to him. Wynn, well, who knows what she's going to do. She got an offer to be a personal chef but looked bored by the idea."

The old Cat from a day ago would have pointed out this long-flowing sentence. Tease him for using so many words. New Cat would consider it a gift from a man who must have accepted her apology. Might trust that she was also a human, with hitches and hesitations.

"Wynn could do anything she wants," Cat said.

"Camille is signing autographs, and Matt is holding extra pens."

"I'm leaving Lefty here when I head out. That way I won't have to find a sitter for him when the baby comes." She hadn't meant to bring up an exit; she didn't want to break the spell of peace between them. Or even tangentially refer to Steve.

His jaw tensed, then relaxed. "When are you heading out?"

"I'm not sure," she said truthfully.

The silence stretched. Snippets of conversation reached the room, an occasional car horn. The steady beeping of tow trucks backing up.

"One of the women hooked up with some fighter pilot in Thunderbird Two," said Gary.

"I wonder if they knew that was the cabin's name," Cat said. "Did they pick it on purpose?"

"They're calling this place 'Boner Camp.'"

Cat laughed and thought she'd better say something, *now or never.* "If they only knew." She scrunched her eyes shut behind him, waited. Would he ignore this obvious reference to their night?

"So you think I'm hot?" Gary said.

"You know I do," she said.

"How hot?" he said, turning.

"I'll say this: Tiny Dancer should not be your walkie-talkie nickname."

And she barely got these words out before his lips said "Cat" against her mouth.

CHAPTER FORTY-FIVE

SUMMER CAMP

Two months, two days, and fifteen hours later, Cat delivered in the Birthing Center at the Stevens Point hospital. Holding her hand, her mother spouted lines from *The Importance of Being Earnest* between contractions—"'You have filled my tea with lumps of sugar, and though I asked most distinctly for bread and butter, you have given me cake'"—until the nurses sent her to the cafeteria for a sandwich.

"Your mom is something else."

In reply, Cat said, "She's earnest, and that's important." Before another contraction hit, she had a moment to wish her mother had heard her retort. She would have loved it.

By the time her mom returned with tuna fish on her breath, Cat was ready to push. Her mom stood at Cat's shoulder, averting her gaze from the "soupy action," as she called it, and pressed her lips to Cat's temple. "Oh, strong girl; oh, good mother," as if quoting a speech from a great playwright. But, Cat knew, it was an original, from one woman who knew what it took to bring a child into the world to another.

Afterward, her mom instructed Cat on swaddling and cooed at the pink hairless thing in her lap. Cat had seen her mother emotional and doting one other time, and it had been when Bard was born. Their complicated and distant parent may not have been the kind of person who dabbled in love notes in lunches, but boy, when a kid had a baby, she did not disappoint. She was who she was.

If there was one thing Cat had learned, it was that once you found your people, the square pegs didn't have to morph into round holes. No matter the shape, all would be welcome. Blissed out by her daughter's dimpled chin, Cat had the thought. Maybe while she Kegeled her way to a strong pelvic floor, she'd make a meme for Instagram. *If you're a square peg, find the people who celebrate quadrilaterals.* It was a geometry lesson and a life lesson. She'd add an exclamation point. Make mugs and sell them if the camp ever got an Etsy store.

"You look like you're on another planet," her mother said, her hand on Cat's shoulder.

"I'm on Planet Baby, and everything feels possible in Baby Land."

Her mother nodded. Brushed a strand of Cat's hair off her forehead. "Your father will be thrilled to meet this tiny thing. It did him good to get away. Get evaluated at Mayo. It's better that he's back." Her mother tutted with the corner of the soft fabric around the baby's face and said, "Strokes, they think. Little ones add up, I hear."

Cat had welcomed her father back to camp, after Gary had built a ramp in case he needed a wheelchair in the future. After Shirtless had helped repaint the ceiling where the tree had come through. After Norm had investigated and ordered ham radios, satellite phones, and CB radios so they would never be incommunicado with the outside world again.

She'd hugged her father tight and told him that he'd soon be a grandfather, and he'd said, "That happened long ago," easily remembering Bard. When she'd left that day, her bed at home the only place she could get a good night's rest, he said, "Don't forget that Ginger needs to clean up her crafts."

"Evenings are harder," her mother said, leading him to a chair with a view of the campgrounds.

After the nurses put away all the labor and delivery paraphernalia and the hospital room became cozier, the lights dimmed, a bassinet rolled next to the bed, her mother said, "Bob is staying on, of course. Has good ideas. Needs a strong hand."

"That's the understatement of the year."

"Not bad at raising money after all. And of course he's devoted to Ginger," her mother said. She lifted the baby from Cat's arms and said, "I've always thought that there is the loved and the beloved in a relationship." When the dinner tray came, her mother continued: "I'm the beloved. I think you might be too." Then she side-eyed her daughter, maybe fishing for her plans.

When Cat woke the next morning, her child lay sleeping in the bassinet, and Ginger had taken their mother's place. "They're discharging you after you get organized and try to nurse again."

"Nursing hurts way more than anyone tells you," Cat said, supporting the seven-pound bundle so latching could happen. "You'd think they'd have something more scientific and less sexist to call this position than the 'football hold.'"

"It gets better," Ginger said as she helped fan the baby's lips over Cat's nipple.

"Can you feed me that roast beef sandwich Mom left? I'm starving."

Ginger peeled back the cellophane on the triangle package and let Cat take a bite of the dry and delicious vending machine meal.

"God, that's good." Cat sighed, swallowing a large lump without tasting it.

"You're baby drunk," Ginger said.

Cat nodded, smiled, and opened her mouth for another bite.

As Cat dressed to leave, she watched Ginger tenderly, expertly, wrap a multicolored blanket she'd crocheted around the infant.

"If we were in high school and I was signing your yearbook, I'd write, 'Dear Ginger. Never change.'"

"I tried to change," Ginger said, then whispered into the baby's ear, "The world can only handle one of your mother."

"And everything is better with a little Ginger," Cat said.

Once they got to Cat's house and changed the baby, she nursed again and stacked diapers on any surface that might do as a changing table. Ginger said, "Time for me to go. You going to be all right until next week?"

"Oh yes, I've been training my whole life for this," Cat said.

"You certainly have been."

When Cat heard the camp van pull out of her driveway, she dialed.

"Hi, Gary. You still okay to come and help me?" she said, and when he agreed she said, "Thank you," and she realized this was how other people did things. Phone calls, requests, offers, and thank-yous. Guilt and worry need not be a part of these conversations, and asking for help was a perfectly acceptable thing to do.

———

After a week together, Gary in the guest room, Cat letting him know it wasn't forever, they'd found their rhythm. She'd learned to listen to what he wasn't saying, and Gary helped when needed and stood back and watched with curiosity when he wasn't. They'd been learning the truths about each other. How he'd come to mistrust her, how Cat had mistrusted herself. They'd eaten dinners and talked until the baby fussed or Cat needed a sitz bath or a shower.

"I'm thinking of renting this place out to visiting nurses," Cat said.

"Or keep it, for when you need a break. You don't have to live there," Gary said, referring to her still-unmade decision about taking the job as the camp's process person.

"You'll be there, though."

He shrugged. "I have a car."

"My dad."

"Lots of help these days."

When transporting Cat and the baby to camp, Gary's solid and certain moves became unsure and tender. He helped her out of the car in the gravel parking lot near where the two cars had mounted each other after the tornado.

"Have you heard any more from Steve?" Gary asked.

"The lawyers are chatting."

"Are you worried?"

"Maybe it's nursing, the oxytocin, or having made a whole human, but I feel uncharacteristically calm. I'll always be this child's mom, and the rest will follow from there. Whatever will be will be."

They picked their way across the parking lot and over the grounds.

"That would be a good bracelet saying," he said.

"'Little leather lessons,' we can call them. I thought of another one. 'Bad with boundaries' for the people who come with terrible boundaries. Then they can graduate to a bracelet that says, simply, 'No.'"

"You can tell Penelope, our marketing intern," Gary said before blocking Lefty, bounding on all threes to their side. "We got that hefty donation from that pilot." As they entered the grassy lawn, Cat spotted Ginger.

When her sister squealed, arms outstretched, Gary put his hands over the baby's ears and gave Ginger a very Gary look, and she dropped her voice an octave.

"June and Wynn are off-site but said they'd stop by later. Wynn has a cake," said Ginger. "We're making plans for the winter alumni gathering of the gala visitors. They're helping, so they will work part-time in programming. Bob is here. Of course he is. He wouldn't miss this for anything."

Cat stepped carefully over the fairy circle, past the stone wall and woodpile. She wanted to remember the details of baby's first day at camp. She spotted the familiar tilt of her father's head, as if he were listening to the fire telling the story of the big bang. Fall in Wisconsin was the quiet superstar of the Midwest. The sun shone through the leaves, creating gold out of cellulose, later lining the paths with yellow. Shirtless and Norm wore shorts, unwilling to acknowledge the changing season. Her parents appeared smaller than she remembered but also rooted in place.

Shirtless, with his new showman skills, said, "I give to you the new member of the Council of McCarthys!"

Her father turned, his brown eyes the same as Cat's and Ginger's.

"Hey, Dad," Cat said.

He looked as if he knew she was someone he loved but couldn't quite place her. Their mother said it took a minute sometimes. Depending on the day, it could change. She'd said the time they were gone was a year of hard realizations and the swapping of caregiver roles. His good days were like old times, but his bad days harkened to a future that they couldn't control or ignore.

"Here you go," Cat said as she placed her sleeping child into the cradle he'd made with his arms. Her father adjusted his body, tucking his grandchild into his chest.

"Can you imagine what it's like to be held like this?" he said, and Ginger backed into Bob as he wrapped his arms around her.

"Hi, Kitty. Hello there," her father said.

"Oh!" Cat said, hearing her name. She glanced at her mother for direction.

"No, Fred, this is Summer's daughter. Her name is Marigold. Mari for short."

Her father blinked. "Of course. Marigold."

Gary and Bob exchanged a glance. "Summer?"

"My dad always called us his kittens," said Ginger. "When we were really little. Didn't you, Dad? It got shortened to Kitty, and whenever Kitty got bossy, I would call her Cat. Just to bug her. We fought so much that pretty soon, it was Cat this, Cat that, every day."

"Unless Ginger wants something." Cat smiled.

"Summer is your real name?" Gary said.

"Son of a gun," Bob said. "This place was named after you?"

"Well, I don't brag about it. It was named after my failure onstage."

"When Cat was six, she tried out for a part in the high school play *The Little Mermaid*," her mother said, her voice sounding older tonight, something Cat wanted to put the brakes to. But she wasn't in charge of time. She wasn't responsible for aging. "They needed a bunch of first graders to play bit parts—the fish, clams, a fork, that kind of thing. Nonspeaking roles, of course."

"I really wanted to be a lobster," Cat said, hearing the catch in her voice.

"In her tryout, she didn't know her left from right," said Ginger.

"I guess I got confused and knocked into the person playing Ursula. I got cut. I don't even remember it."

"You threw a fit," her father said, his eyes on Marigold.

Bob, delighted, exchanged a glance with Shirtless, who'd been recording their reunion with a phone.

"Mom made her big red felt claws so she could wear them around," said Ginger.

"I was furious. First mistake, you're out?" their mother said, still incensed at the intolerance for the would-be thespian. "Theater is for everyone."

"It was my mom who found this place," said Ginger. "She said kids should always get picked for things they want to do."

"So they named the place Summer Camp for the girl who didn't get picked." Cat laughed.

"It was a lot of pressure," her mother said. "We didn't mean it that way, did we, Fred?"

"No, we sure didn't," he said, brushing some fluff off Marigold's cheek.

"I was terrible at theater. I didn't like the spotlight. Dad gave me other jobs."

"I was good at it," said Ginger. "Obviously." She took a bow. "I acted like a diva and left all my chores for Cat."

Bob nudged her.

". . . and that wasn't right. Not right at all," Ginger added dutifully.

Gary moved closer to Cat, mimicking the way her father held Marigold. With his warm breath in her ear, he whispered, "Hello, Summer." And the goose bumps she'd begun to get used to appeared along her arms.

"Glad you're home, Kitty," her father said.

She tried to answer him. To apologize, to tell him how grateful she was for her magical, hardworking childhood. His trust that she was capable had translated into Cat knowing she could raise a child. And for helping her see that she was the Summer in this little patch of green, and her daughter would be the annual flower that would be planted in her footsteps and grow. Cat cleared her throat, wanting so badly to say something now that she was home.

"He knows," Gary said, and he pulled a blue bandanna from his back pocket to wipe a tear that had appeared at the edge of Cat's lashes. "He knows you."

Acknowledgments

After attending a birthday party or playdate, my mother always told me, upon leaving, to smile and say to the host, "Thank you for inviting me. I had a nice time." I've used those two sentences often in my life, sometimes appropriately, say, after speaking at a conference. Other times, when at a loss, I've defaulted and used them at the dentist's office or after a mammogram. It's weird for everyone in those cases, but I believe gratitude is never wasted.

While the wonderful readers who have taken time out of their lives to read my books didn't invite me to write, it's the readers who have allowed me to continue to write. If not for readers, my friends, family, and dogs would have a tough go of it. I can be relentless when I have an idea for a book, and I'm sure all my loved ones are relieved that I have an outlet for my pretend stories about pretend people.

There aren't enough *thank you for inviting me*s in the world for my agents at Folio Literary Management, Margaret Sutherland Brown and Claudia Cross. Their endless support is breathtaking in this challenging industry. They've never once rolled their eyes in front of me, and that feels like real devotion.

I feel the same way about Melissa Valentine, my editor at Lake Union. Her name says it all. Experts say you must find someone who *gets you* in romance and publishing. Okay, experts do not say this, I'm saying this, and Melissa is the hearts and flowers in publishing for me. What Carissa Bluestone has done to get this book to market goes above and beyond. I wasn't on her dance card for this year, but she budged me in line, and I won't soon forget it.

An enormous thank-you to my developmental editor, Tiffany Yates Martin, who does the hardest thing when working with me. She sees the future glitter that is my book and guides me toward the light.

Now, for the friends I call at 2:00 p.m. when what I really need is a glass of water and a nap. These are the people on call during every phase of book production from idea to cover to party. You know who you are, but the rest of the world should as well: Carolyn Bach, Stephanie Burns, Margie Gilmore, Samantha Hoffman, Karen Karbo, Annie McCormick, Jackie Mitchard, Lisa Roe, Tammy Scerpella, Carol Schfro, Cheryl Tessier, and Linda Wick. I wish I could give every person in this alphabetized list a little personal-joke shout-out, but I need a nap and a glass of water, and they need a break from reading my words.

Finally, I want to thank the Tall Poppy Writers for being the sunshine that lights up my author's life. The generosity, grit, and encouragement you effortlessly provide make up the model all collaborative groups should follow. Thank you for joining me. I'm having the best time.

Discussion Questions

1. The author's dedication reads: "To all the weirdos of the world, and when I say weirdos, I mean all of us." Why do you think the author calls out all people as weirdos? What point is she trying to make that might help readers understand humanity in general and the characters in the book specifically?

2. The book opens with Cat trying to ignore calls for help from her sister. Is there anyone you are close to in your life that you try to avoid, and does that avoidance give you a lot of mixed feelings? Have you ever tried to distance yourself from a stressful relationship and not been entirely successful doing it?

3. Cat is pregnant at the start of this book and is worried about being judged by her sister, Gary, and others. There are a lot of reasons why a woman might feel judged for a pregnancy. Why do you think Cat, specifically, is worried about that? What is it about Cat's personality that fosters her fear of judgment?

4. The author writes: "Being a part of a group has its own ecosystem that outsiders can't possibly understand. Math Bowl kids practice multiplication tables, while gamers fight imaginary wars with spaceships, neither understanding the allure of the other. Open the doors on any closed group, and suddenly what is accepted, even celebrated, becomes a point of shame." Or embarrassment or filled with inside jokes. Why do you think the author makes this point? Have you ever been in a group like this where you might have acted in a way that friends and family may not understand? And when

you've tried to describe it, you fall short of explaining its significance to you?

5. How do Cat's and Ginger's childhood selves affect—or even misinform—their illusions of their adult selves? Are we all still versions of the creative one, the overachiever, or the wallflower?

6. The theme of human differences is ever present in the book, manifesting through a deep exploration of characters who manage life and stress in sometimes curious ways. Do you remember a time in your life when you felt different from your friends and wished you had a place to belong even with all your perceived failings?

7. Why do you think the author used *The Wizard of Oz* to underscore the themes of friendship between strangers, of journey and home, and of humans flourishing against the odds?

8. Cat and Ginger's mother said, "I love chocolate pudding, but I don't want to eat a bathtub of it." What is the significance of their mother's statement that might be emblematic of life at camp, life alone, or any kind of life we choose for ourselves? What is she trying to say?

9. After reading the book, do you think the characters represented are more unusual than most people you know? Do you know anyone that would fit right in at Summer Camp and want to return year after year?

10. Cat's real name is Summer, but she is reluctant to admit it, let alone be called by it. How is her resistance to this name reflected in her character and her attitude toward her childhood responsibilities and embracing a new and different future?

About the Author

Ann Garvin, PhD, is the *USA Today* bestselling author of *There's No Coming Back from This, I Thought You Said This Would Work, I Like You Just Fine When You're Not Around,* and other funny and sad novels about people who do too much, in a world that asks too much from them. Ann teaches in the low-residency master of fine arts program at Drexel University and lives in Wisconsin with her anxious and overly protective dog, Peanut. She is the founder of the Tall Poppy Writers and is dedicated to helping authors find readers and vice versa. For more information, visit www.anngarvin.com.